Wel̶ ̶ ̶ ̶ ̶ ̶ ̶ ̶n

Imagine a night of seductive passion
under a starlit sky…

The eternal rhythm of the desert
awakens your senses…

The sensual fragrance of the oasis
heightens your pleasure…

The handsome, all-powerful sheikh
cannot be denied!

**Two fabulous bestselling novels
from the international bestselling author**

PENNY JORDAN

MILLS & BOON
100
YEARS
of pure reading pleasure

100 Reasons to Celebrate

We invite you to join us in celebrating Mills & Boon's centenary. Gerald Mills and Charles Boon founded Mills & Boon Limited in 1908 and opened offices in London's Covent Garden. Since then, Mills & Boon has become a hallmark for romantic fiction, recognised around the world.

We're proud of our 100 years of publishing excellence, which wouldn't have been achieved without the loyalty and enthusiasm of our authors and readers.

Thank you!

Each month throughout the year there will be something new and exciting to mark the centenary, so watch for your favourite authors, captivating new stories, special limited edition collections...and more!

THE DESERT

Sheikh's

V I R G I N

PENNY JORDAN

*M&B™ and M&B™ with the Rose Device
are trademarks of the publisher.
Harlequin Mills & Boon Limited, Eton House,
18-24 Paradise Road, Richmond, Surrey TW9 1SR*

THE DESERT SHEIKH'S VIRGIN
© by Harlequin Books SA 2008

Possessed by the Sheikh © Penny Jordan 2005
Prince of the Desert © Penny Jordan 2006

Possessed by the Sheikh and *Prince of the Desert* were first
published in Great Britain by Harlequin Mills & Boon Limited
in separate, single volumes.

ISBN: 978 0 263 86680 3

10-0808

*Printed and bound in Spain
by Litografía Rosés S.A., Barcelona*

Possessed by the Sheikh

PENNY JORDAN

The Desert Sheikhs
COLLECTION

August 2008
THE DESERT SHEIKH'S VIRGIN
Penny Jordan

September 2008
THE DESERT SHEIKH'S PASSION
Sharon Kendrick & Susan Mallery

October 2008
THE DESERT SHEIKH'S BRIDE
Lucy Monroe & Alexandra Sellers

November 2008
THE DESERT SHEIKH'S MARRIAGE
Jane Porter & Sarah Morgan

Penny Jordan has been writing for more than twenty years and has an outstanding record: over one hundred and sixty-five novels published, including the phenomenally successful *A Perfect Family, To Love, Honour & Betray, The Perfect Sinner* and *Power Play,* which hit *The Sunday Times* and *New York Times* bestseller lists. Penny Jordan was born in Preston, Lancashire, and now lives in rural Cheshire.

Penny Jordan has a new novel,
Virgin for the Billionaire's Taking,
published in October 2008 in Mills & Boon®
Modern™. Don't miss it!

CHAPTER ONE

KATRINA was standing in the middle of the souk when she saw him. She had been about to start bargaining with the stallholder for a length of embroidered silk she had picked up, when something made her turn her head. He was standing on the other side of the narrow alleyway dressed in a traditional white *disha-dasha*, the sunlight filtering striking shards of light against the honey-coloured warmth of his skin, and glittering on the cruelly sharp-looking knife that was thrust into his belt.

Sensing that he had lost her attention, the stallholder looked past her, following the direction of her helplessly enmeshed gaze.

'He is from the Ayghar Tuareg Tribe,' he said.

Katrina made no response. She knew from the research she had done before coming out to Zuran that the Ayghar Tuaregs had been a fierce tribe of warriors who, in previous centuries, had been paid to escort the trading caravans across the desert, and the tribe still preferred their traditional nomadic way of life.

Unlike other robed men she had seen, he was clean-shaven. His eyes, glittering over her with a haughty lack of interest, were heart-stoppingly dark amber, set with flecks of pure gold between the thickness of his black lashes.

They, like him, reminded her of the magnificence of a dangerous predator; something, someone who could never be tamed or constrained in the cage of

5

modern urban civilisation. This was a man of the desert, a man who made and then lived by a moral code of his own devising. There was an arrogance about his features and his stance that both appalled her and yet at the same time compelled her to keep looking at him.

And he had a dangerously passionate mouth!

An unwanted sensual shiver skittered along her spine as she was caught off guard by the unexpected detour of her own thoughts.

She was not here in the desert kingdom of Zuran to think about men with dangerously passionate mouths. She was here as part of a visiting team of dedicated scientists working to protect the area's natural flora and fauna, she reminded herself firmly. But still she couldn't stop watching him.

Seemingly oblivious of her, he glanced up and down the alleyway of the busy bazaar. It truly was a scene from an Arabian fantasy come to life, at least so far as Katrina was concerned, although she knew that her boss, Richard Walker, would have derided her contemptuously if she were ever to say so in his presence. But she didn't want to think about Richard. Despite the fact that she had made it plain to him that she wasn't interested in him, and in addition to the fact that he was a married man, Richard had been subjecting her to a toxic mix of unpleasant sexual interest combined with outright nastiness when she rejected his advances.

Just thinking about Richard and his unwanted pursuit of her was enough to make her shrink back into the shadows of the stall. Immediately the amber gaze found and trapped her, pillaging the shadows for her, and making her shrink instinctively even further into them without seeking to analyse why she should feel the need to do such a thing.

But even though the shadows were surely concealing her, she could see that he had focused on exactly where she was. Her heart drummed a warning tattoo, and she could feel an anxious beading of perspiration break out on her skin.

A group of black-robed and veiled women walking down the alleyway came between them, cutting off her view of him and, she hoped, his view of her. By the time they had gone and she could see him again it was obvious that he had lost interest in her because he was turning away, pulling the loose end of the indigo-dyed cloth wrapped around his head over his face as he did so, so that only his eyes could be seen, in the traditional manner of men of the Tuareg tribe. Then, with his back to her, he turned to enter the doorway behind him, his height forcing him to duck his head.

Katrina noticed that the hand he had placed on the door frame was lean and brown, long-fingered, his nails well cared for. A small frown pleated her forehead. She knew a great deal about the nomad tribes of the Arabian desert and their history and it struck her sharply how much of an anomaly it was, both that a supposed Tuareg tribesman should go against centuries of tradition and reveal his face for the world to see, and additionally that a member of a tribe so well known for their indigo-dyed clothes that they were often referred to as 'blue men' should have such manicured hands that would not disgrace a millionaire businessman.

Her stomach muscles tensed and her heart lurched against her ribs. She was no foolish, impressionable girl ready to believe that every man in a *disha-dasha* was a powerful leader of men, and nor was she hiding some secret fantasy desire for sex in the sand with such a man! She was a qualified scientist of twenty-four! And yet…

As he finally disappeared through the doorway she let out her pent-up breath in a leaky sigh of relief.

'You want this? It's very fine silk… Very fine. And a very good price.'

Obediently she gave her attention to the silk. It was gossamer-fine and just the right shade of ice-blue for her own strawberry-blonde colouring. Because she was out in public on her own, she had taken the precaution of scraping her hair back off her face and tucking it up into the deep brimmed hat she was wearing.

But in such a fabric her body could be tantalisingly semi-revealed by its gauzy layers, and she could let her hair down in a silken cloud as a man with golden lion eyes looked upon her…

Katrina let the silk drop from her fingers as though it had burned her. As the stallholder picked it up a group of uniformed men came striding into the alley, causing people to scatter as they pushed past them, thrusting open doors and pulling coverings from stalls, quite plainly looking for someone and equally plainly not caring what damage they might cause to either people or belongings as they did so.

For some reason she could not understand, Katrina's gaze went to the door through which the tribesman had disappeared.

The uniformed men were on a level with her now.

Behind her the door opened and a man stepped into the street. Tall and dark-haired, he was wearing

European clothes—chinos and a linen shirt—but Katrina recognised him immediately, her eyes widening in surprise.

The tribesman had become a European. He turned and started to walk down the alleyway. He had just drawn level with the stall where Katrina was standing when one of the uniformed men saw him and pushed past Katrina, calling out to him in English and Zuranese.

'You! Stop!'

Katrina saw the way the tribesman's golden gaze hardened, checking, searching…and then stopping as it alighted on her.

'Darling! There you are—I warned you not to go wandering off without me.'

The lean fingers she had noticed only minutes ago were now manacling her wrist, sliding down over her hand and entwining with her own, in a parody of a lover's intimacy, holding her hand fast in a locked grip she couldn't break. A smile that was merely a calculated curling of his mouth briefly broke up the hard arrogance of his face. He took a step towards her.

'I am not your darling,' Katrina told him breathlessly.

'Start walking…' he told her quietly, the intimidating, hard gaze imprisoning her under its magnetic spell.

Hostility darkened the normal gentleness of her own speedwell-blue eyes, but it was a hostility that was spiked with something much more primitive and dangerous, she admitted numbly as she did as he was instructing her. He moved closer to her and through the hot, sun-baked scent of spices and perfumes she was sharply aware of, first, the discreet expensive lemony scent of his cologne, and then far more disturbingly as he moved closer to her the intimate, faintly musky scent of his body itself.

The alleyway was full of armed men now, pushing open the doors to the small houses and overturning the stalls as they searched impatiently beneath them, plainly intent on finding something or someone!

The earlier atmosphere of relaxed happiness had gone and instead the alleyway and the people in it had become a place of sharply raised voices and almost palpable fear.

A large four-wheel-drive vehicle with blacked out windows came tearing down the alleyway, sending people scattering, and then screeching to a halt. The uniformed man who got out was heavily guarded and Katrina drew in a small gasp of breath as she recognised Zuran's Minister of Internal Affairs, the cousin of Zuran's ruler himself.

Apprehensively she looked at her captor, torn between conflicting emotions. She had seen him enter the building across the alleyway dressed as a Tuareg tribesman, and his behaviour was hardly that of a man with nothing to hide. By rights she should at the very least draw the attention of the fearsome heavily armed men swarming the alleyway to his presence and her own suspicions, but… But what? But he possessed a dangerous fascination that was seducing her into… Into what? Determinedly she started to pull away from him. He checked her small movement immediately, not merely tightening his hold on her, but actually dragging her further back into a narrow space in the shadows of the alley, which was so confined that she was pressed right up against his body.

'Look, I don't know what's going on, but—' she began bravely.

'Quiet.' The icy, emotionless command was whispered against her ear. She told herself that the reason her own body was trembling so violently was because she was shocked and afraid; nothing to do with the fact that she was sharply aware of the male hardness of the muscular thigh pressing into her. And the heavy thump of the male heart was beating so strongly that it seemed to pound, not just through his body, but through her own as well, overriding the shallow beat of her own heart, overwhelming her with its life force, making her feel as though his heart were providing the life force for both of them.

The sudden echo of an old, sharp pain speared her. Her parents' love for one another had been like that: total and all-encompassing, and for ever.

She made a small sound, an incoherent murmur of private emotional angst, but his reaction was swift and punitive.

His hand gripped her throat, his head blotted out the street, and his mouth silenced any protest she could have made even before she had thought to take the breath to make it.

He tasted of heat and the desert, and a thousand and one things that had been imprinted on him, and which were alien to her. Alien and somehow dangerously and erotically exciting, she recognised in self-disgust as against her will an uncheckable surge of primitive female reaction seized her body.

Her lips softened and parted. She felt his missed heartbeat and then the sledgehammer blow of recognition that followed it as he seized like a predator the advantage she had given him. The hard pressure of his mouth on hers increased and fire jolted through her as his tongue thrust fiercely against her own, demanding her compliance.

Her body shook with reaction. Never, ever had she envisaged that she would kiss a man with such intimate sensuality in public and in full daylight, and certainly not a man who was a complete stranger to her.

She was vaguely aware of the sound of the four-wheel drive moving off, but his mouth was still covering hers.

Then, so abruptly that she almost stumbled, he released her. One hand steadied her with a merciless lack of emotion and then he was gone, disappearing into the crowd, leaving her feeling overwhelmed and, more shockingly, as though she had been abandoned.

'Your Highness…' Low, respectful bows followed his swift progress through his older half-brother's royal palace as he made his way to his presence.

The armed guards on duty outside the heavy gold-leaf-covered double doors that led to the Ruler's formal audience room threw both doors open and then bowed and left.

Xander was now in his half-brother's presence, and so he bowed deeply as the doors closed behind him. They might share the same father, his elder brother might have a well-known fondness for him, but the man in front of him was Zuran's ruler, and in public at least respect had to be paid to that fact.

Immediately the Ruler stood up and then commanded Xander to rise and come forward to embrace him.

'It is good to have you back. I have heard excellent

things about you from other world leaders, little brother, and from our embassies in America and Europe.'

'You are too kind, Your Highness. All such credit must go to you in deigning to honour me with the task of ensuring that our embassies have the personnel they need in order to promote your plans for greater democracy.'

Without any command needing to be given a door opened and a servant appeared, followed by two more bringing fragrantly fresh coffee.

Both men waited until the small ceremony had been completed.

As soon as they were alone the Ruler walked over to Xander.

'Come, let us walk in the garden.' He told him, 'We can talk more easily there.'

Beyond the audience room and screened from it by a heavy curtain lay a lushly planted private courtyard garden, alive with the sound of water from its many fountains.

Not a single speck of dust marred the perfection of the mosaic-tiled pathways as the two men walked side by side in their pristine white robes.

'It is as we suspected,' Xander announced quietly as they came to a halt in front of one of the many fishponds, and then he bent down to take a handful of food from the nearby bowl and drop it into the water.

'Nazir is plotting against you.'

'You have clear evidence of that?' the Ruler demanded sharply.

Xander shook his head. 'Not as yet. As you know,

I have managed to infiltrate and join the band of thieves and renegades led by El Khalid.'

'That traitorous wretch. I should have had him imprisoned for life instead of being so lenient with him.' The Ruler snorted.

'El Khalid has never forgiven you for depriving him of his lands and assets when you discovered his fraudulent activities. I suspect that Nazir has promised him that if he succeeds in overthrowing you he will reinstate him. I also suspect that Nazir is intending that it is El Khalid who will be seen as the one to strike against you. Of course, he himself cannot afford to be seen to be connected in any way to your assassination.' He frowned. 'You must be on your guard—'

'I am well protected, never fear, and as you say, for all that he hates me and always has done ever since we were boys, Nazir will not dare to strike openly against me.'

'It is a great pity that you cannot have him deported and banished.'

The Ruler laughed. 'No, we cannot do anything without concrete evidence, my brother. We are a democracy now, thanks in part to your own mother, but we must do everything according to the law of this land.'

His half-brother's reference to his own mother made Xander frown slightly. His mother had originally been employed as the Ruler's own governess. A passionate liberal thinker, she had taught her young pupil, and at the same time she had fallen in love with his father—a love that he had returned.

Xander himself was the result of that love, but he had never known his mother. She had died of a fever a month after his birth, having first made his father promise that he would respect her own cultural heritage in bringing up their son.

As a result of that deathbed promise, Xander had been educated in Europe and America, before being appointed as a roving Ambassador for Zuran.

'It is you who faces the greater danger, Xander,' the Ruler said warningly now. 'And, as both your brother and your ruler, I am not happy that you should be taking such a risk.'

Xander gave a small, dismissive shrug. 'We have already agreed there is no one else who we can trust implicitly and, besides, the danger is not that great. El Khalid has already accepted me in my role as a disaffected Tuareg tribesman, ostracised by his tribe for criminal activities. Indeed I have already proved my worth to him. We stopped a caravan of merchants last week and relieved them of their merchandise—'

The Ruler frowned. 'Who were they? I must see that they are recompensed, although no one has made any complaint to me of such an attack.'

'Nor will they do, I fancy,' Xander told him dryly. 'For one thing the attack took place in the empty quarter beyond Zuran's border, which is where El Khalid has his base and, for another, the merchandise we relieved them of was counterfeit currency.'

'Ah. No wonder they haven't lodged a complaint!'

'Although there have been hints and boasts from El Khalid of his involvement with some very important person, I have not as yet seen Nazir or any of his men making contact with him.

'However, if, as I suspect, Nazir plans to have you assassinated during one of your public appearances on our National Day, he will have to meet up with El

Khalid soon. Coincidentally, El Khalid has let it be known that he intends to hold an important meeting which we are all to attend, but as yet he has not said either when or where this is to be.'

'And you think that Nazir will be at this meeting?'

'Probably. I suspect his hand will be the one that guides its agenda, yes. He will want to ensure that the men chosen to accompany Khalid on an assassination mission can be relied on. Nazir won't want to risk using any of his own men, of course, so, yes, I believe he will be there. And so shall I.'

The Ruler frowned. 'You aren't concerned that Nazir may recognise you?'

'Disguised as a Tuareg?' Xander shook his head. 'I doubt it. It is after all their custom to cover their faces.'

The Ruler was still looking concerned.

'So, Highness, you are pleased then, with the progress of the new hotel complex development? I heard much praise of our country's existing tourism facilities whilst I was visiting our embassies,' Xander announced smoothly, looking warningly at his half-brother as he caught the soft sound of someone walking quietly towards them.

The greenery parted to reveal the small but powerfully stocky figure of the man they had just been discussing coming towards them, his fingers covered in heavy jewel-encrusted rings, his venomous glance resting resentfully first on Xander and then on the Ruler himself. Ignoring Xander completely, he bowed stiffly to the Ruler.

'Nazir.' The Ruler greeted him coolly. 'What brings you here? It's not often you can spare the time from your duties as our Minister of Internal Affairs to visit us socially.'

'I am extremely busy, it is true!' Nazir responded self-importantly.

'I hear there was some trouble earlier in the souk,' Xander murmured.

Immediately Nazir shot him a suspicious look. 'It was nothing... A petty thief was causing some disruption, that is all.'

'A petty thief? But you were there yourself!'

'I happened to be in the area. Besides, what business is it of yours how I conduct my duties?'

'None, other than that of a concerned citizen,' Xander answered him blandly.

His mouth compressing, Nazir turned away from him, deliberately keeping his back to him as he addressed the Sheikh. 'I understand, Your Highness, that you have ignored my advice and that you are choosing not to have the armed escort of my personal guard to ensure your safety during the National Day celebrations.'

'I am most grateful to you for your concern, cousin, but we must remember at all times our duty to the people. Our guests from other nations—especially those we hope will support our growing tourist industry—will not be reassured as to the stability of our country if they think that its ruler cannot go amongst his own people on such a joyful occasion without a phalanx of armed guards.'

'And then, of course,' Xander drawled *sotto voce* into the tension-filled silence that followed the Ruler's gentle words, 'one must always wonder *who guards the guards...*?'

A murderous look of hatred crossed Nazir's face. 'If you are suggesting—' he began savagely.

'I am suggesting nothing.' Xander stopped him coldly. 'I am merely stating fact.'

'Fact?'

'It is already proven that the presence of heavily armed personnel can lead to relatively small incidents getting completely out of hand.

'I'm sure that none of us wants to have to explain to the ambassador from another nation that one of their nationals has been shot to death by an over-enthusiastic and under-trained guard.'

'We will talk of this again, cousin, in private,' Nazir informed the Ruler grimly, pointedly ignoring Xander as he bowed briefly and left.

The Sheikh frowned as he exchanged looks with his younger half-brother.

'Our cousin forgets what is due to you, Xander,' he said angrily.

Xander gave a dismissive shrug. 'He has never hidden the fact that he has no liking for me, or my mother.'

'And your father? Our father was the greatest ruler this country has ever had! Nazir would do well to remember that! Nazir was unkind to you when you were a small child, I know, Xander, and neither I nor my father knew of his cruelty towards you then.'

'I learned to deal with it and with him.'

'Both he and his father hated your mother. They resented the influence she had over my father. And then when he made her his wife…'

'He might dislike me, but it is you he wishes to overthrow,' Xander pointed out dryly before adding, 'I have to return to the desert before my absence causes any comment. I was concerned earlier that Nazir might have become suspicious of me after he had his men turn the souk upside down looking for me, but I have learned since that it was another Tuareg they were looking for!'

'The official story is that you have only returned to Zuran briefly and are leaving the country again tonight to enjoy a well deserved rest. It is a pity you do not have time, though, to look over our new joint ventures. Your mares have produced a handsome crop of new foals, and the first phase of the marina development is approaching completion.'

Xander smiled a flash of strong white teeth against the golden honey of his skin.

The Ruler was famous throughout the world for his involvement in the world of horse racing.

As they turned to walk back to the palace the Ruler turned towards him. 'I am not sure that I should be allowing you to do this, you know,' he told him seriously. 'You are very dear to me, my little brother. Even dearer than you know. Your mother was the closest I had to a mother myself. She opened my mind to a wealth of knowledge. It was her influence on our father that led to him thinking about the long-term future of our country and when she died I believe he himself lost the will to live. I have lost both of them, little brother. I do not wish to lose you.'

'Nor I you,' Xander answered him steadily as they embraced one another.

'Hello there, beautiful! How about coming out with me tonight? I hear that His Highness is holding a very grand reception to celebrate the start of the racing season, and then afterwards we could go on to a club.'

The light-hearted invitation she was being given by the group's bachelor photographer made Katrina smile. Tom Hudson was an unashamed and incorrigible flirt, but one could not help but like him.

She started to shake her head, sunlight bouncing off the soft waves of her shoulder-length hair, but before she could say anything Richard broke in sharply.

'We are all here to work, and not to socialise, and you would do well to remember that, Hudson. Besides, we've got an early start in the morning,' he reminded them.

In the uncomfortable silence that followed the expedition leader's outburst, Tom pulled a wry face at Richard behind his back.

For all that he was very highly qualified, Richard was not popular with any of them, although it was Katrina who suffered most from his presence.

'He's gruesome,' Beverley Thomas, the only other female member of the group, commented later, giving a small shudder as she sat on the edge of Katrina's bed.

The luxurious private villa that had been put at the team's disposal was built on traditional lines, with the women's quarters apart from those of the men, and additional staff accommodation.

At first it had bemused Katrina to discover that she and Bev were to be locked into their quarters at night, but now in view of unwanted advances from Richard she was heartily glad of the fact that they were expected to adopt the country's customs.

'I can't help feeling sorry for his wife,' Katrina admitted.

'Mmm, me too! Not that he likes us mentioning

her. You do realise that he's well on the way to developing an obsession with you, don't you?'

When she saw the apprehensive look Katrina was giving her she relented a little and added, 'Well, perhaps calling it an obsession is going a bit too far, but he's certainly determined to get you into his bed.'

'He might want to but he's not going to,' Katrina assured her determinedly. 'I could cope with his unwanted advances, Bev, but it's when he starts using his position as expedition leader to punish me for rejecting him that I start to worry. This is my first job and I'm only on probation.'

'Try not to let him get to you,' Beverley advised her, stifling a yawn. 'I'm off to bed. It's been a long day and, as dear old Richard reminded us, we've got a pre-dawn start in the morning.'

Katrina smiled. Personally she was looking forward to their expedition into the desert to examine one of the area's desert ridges known as wadis.

She should be sleeping. It was over an hour since she had come to bed but every time she closed her eyes she was confronted with a disturbing mental image of the man with the golden eyes, as she had privately nicknamed him.

And it wasn't just the colour of his eyes that was imprinted on her memory. Her body quivered as fiercely and delicately as though strong fingers had plucked a single chord on a lyre.

This was ridiculous, she told herself stoutly. A woman of twenty-four with a doctorate in biochemistry could not submit herself to some foolish, primitive sexual response to a complete stranger. And not just a stranger, but very probably a criminal as well!

But her fingertips were already investigating the smooth curve of her mouth, restlessly seeking the imprint of his on hers. Her memory was faultlessly replaying to her everything that she had felt beneath the hard domination of his kiss.

Angrily she tried to deny what she was feeling. Her parents had been a pair of highly qualified scientists totally devoted to one another; they had lived for one another and died with one another when they'd been killed after the site they had been excavating had collapsed on them.

She had been seventeen at the time. Not a child any more, but not an adult either. Her parents, both only children, had had no other family, and their deaths had not only orphaned her but left her both with an aching need for someone to love her, someone to complete her, and with a deep-rooted fear of those feelings and the vulnerability they created within her.

Because of that she had buried them very deep inside herself, too immature and too frightened to cope with them. Instead she had concentrated on her studies, cautiously allowing herself to make friends, but not allowing anyone to get too close.

At twenty-four she had considered herself to be reasonably well adjusted and emotionally mature, but now... It was most definitely neither well adjusted nor emotionally mature to feel the way she did about a stranger.

Let's analyse this, she told herself determinedly.

You are in a different country with different customs; a country, moreover, that has always fascinated you, which is why you were so keen to come here, why you learned Zuranese in the first place.

Additionally you were on an adrenalin high brought on by an automatic fight or flight response to an unfamiliar situation. Of course such a highly charged situation was bound to affect you.

To the extent that she responded physically to a man she didn't know? A man she obviously should have been on her guard against?

Everyone was entitled to one little mistake, she tried to comfort herself. And, after all, it was extremely unlikely that she would ever see him again. She didn't want to accept how much that knowledge depressed her.

CHAPTER TWO

THE sun was just starting to rise over the horizon as they drove out of the villa in a convoy of sturdy, well-equipped four-wheel-drive vehicles heading for the desert. To Katrina's dismay, Richard had insisted that she was to travel on her own with him in the vehicle that he was driving.

'You'll be much more comfortable here with me in the lead vehicle,' he told her, laughing as he added unkindly, 'The others will all be choking on our dust.'

It was true that the speed at which he was driving was throwing up a heavy cloud of fine sand, but Katrina would still far rather have been with someone else.

'Why don't you relax and close your eyes?' Richard suggested oilily. 'Catch up on your sleep. It's going to be a long drive. But drink some water first. You know the rules about making sure we don't get dehydrated.'

Obediently she took the open bottle of water he was handing her and drank from it.

Perhaps it would be a good idea to try to sleep, Katrina acknowledged fifteen minutes or so later as she stifled a yawn and then gave in to a sudden over-whelming temptation to close her eyes. If only so that she could avoid having to make conversation with Richard. And she did feel extraordinarily sleepy. Probably because she had spent far too much of the night thinking about the man with the golden eyes. As she drifted off to sleep she felt the vehicle start to pick up speed.

It was the late afternoon sun that finally woke her as it shone in through the windscreen. The realisation of how long she had been asleep made her sit bolt upright in her seat and turn to Richard in consternation.

'You should have woken me,' she told him. 'How much longer will it be before we reach the wadi?'

It was several seconds before Richard answered her, the look in his eyes as he turned his head towards her making her feel sharply apprehensive. 'We aren't going to the wadi,' he replied smugly. 'We are going somewhere much more secluded and romantic... Somewhere where I can have you all to myself. Somewhere where I can show you...teach you...'

Katrina stared at him in dismay, hoping that she had misunderstood him, but it was obvious from the look on his face that she had not.

'Richard, you simply can't behave like this! We have to go to the wadi. The others will be expecting us...'

'They think that we've had to turn back,' he announced calmly. 'I told them that you weren't feeling very well. It was a good idea, I think, to get you to drink that water, which had some sleeping tablets in it.'

Katrina stared at him in horror.

'Richard, this is ridiculous. I'm going to telephone the others right now and—'

'You can't do that, I'm afraid.' He gave her a self-satisfied smile. 'I've got your mobile. I took it out of your bag when I stopped to tell the others we were turning back.'

Katrina couldn't believe what she was hearing.

'This is crazy! Let's just go and join the others and forget—'

'No!' He silenced her passionately. 'We are going to the oasis. I've been planning how to get you to myself for days, and this is the perfect opportunity and the oasis is the perfect place. It is in the empty quarter of the desert, a veritable no man's land, and this should appeal to you, Katrina, with your love of this region's history. It was once used as a stopping-off place by the camel trains.'

Katrina stared at him. Her throat had gone dry and her heart was thudding uncomfortably hard with apprehension. It wasn't that she was frightened of Richard exactly, but there was no denying that his behaviour pointed uncomfortably towards, if not an obsession with her, then certainly an unpleasant and unwanted preoccupation with her, just as Bev had shrewdly suspected.

'Look, there's the oasis,' Richard declared unnecessarily as the dusty track wound between a rocky outcrop revealing a clutch of palm trees and other vegetation, beyond which lay the blue shimmer of water.

As Richard stopped the vehicle Katrina acknowledged that in different circumstances—very different circumstances—she would have been entranced and fascinated by her surroundings.

The vegetation surrounding the oasis was unexpectedly lush and thick, especially on its far bank. At one time surely a river must have run here, for what else could have carved a path through the steep rocky escarpment on the other side of the oasis? Perhaps even a waterfall had plunged down the smooth, sheer rock face.

Certainly there must be an underground spring filling the oasis itself, or perhaps an underground river. But, undeniably beautiful though the oasis and its surroundings were, Katrina had no wish to remain there on her own with Richard.

Somehow she doubted that he would be responsive to any attempt from her to persuade him to abandon his plans, which meant that if she was to escape she would have to find a way to distract him long enough to allow her to get her hands on the vehicle's keys and drive off in it before Richard could stop her.

'I've brought a tent with me and everything else we will need.'

'Oh, how clever of you!' Katrina told him, trying to sound impressed. 'I'll stay here, shall I, whilst you unpack everything?'

Richard shook his head at her.

'No, I'm afraid you can't do that, my dear! I haven't gone to all this trouble to have you do something silly like trying to run away from me!'

He couldn't *make* her move, Katrina comforted herself, but a few seconds later, after she had told him quietly that she was not prepared to get out of the vehicle, she realised she had under-estimated the lengths he was prepared to go to.

'Well, in that case, my dear, I'm afraid you leave me no option but to use these.' He reached into his pockets and produced a pair of handcuffs. 'I really wish it wasn't necessary to do this, but if you refuse to do as I ask then I am going to have to handcuff you to the door of the vehicle.'

She had been wrong not to feel afraid of him,

Katrina acknowledged as a cold sweat broke out on her skin. He had already locked the doors of the vehicle and if she allowed him to handcuff her inside it then she'd be trapped.

'It would be nice to have some fresh air,' she conceded, trying to keep her voice steady. 'Perhaps I could sit by the oasis whilst you unpack everything?'

'Of course you can, my dear,' Richard agreed, smiling at her. 'Let's go and find somewhere comfortable for you, shall we?'

She mustn't give up hope, Katrina told herself stoutly five minutes later. Richard was escorting her to the oasis, his behaviour more that of a jailer than a would-be lover.

'This will do,' he announced, indicating one of the palm trees, but as Katrina walked towards it he held back. When she caught the warning chink of metal on metal she knew immediately that it was the handcuffs he had shown her earlier. Without stopping to think, she started to run, her flight from him as panic-stricken as that of a delicately boned gazelle. Fear drove her forward, towards the narrow pass between the steep rocks, oblivious to the sound of vehicles being driven fast over the bumpy terrain and the cries of warrior horsemen. Too late to realise what those sounds were, she burst through the pass and into full view of the group of fugitives.

They were led by El Khalid, but it was one of his young lieutenants who saw her first. He swerved the battered Land Rover he was driving round so hard that he almost overturned it.

Behind Katrina, at the pass between the rocks, Richard fell back in terror, and then turned and ran towards his own vehicle, ignoring Katrina's plight. He leapt into it and started the engine, driving back in the direction he had come as fast as he could.

Katrina, though, was oblivious to his desertion of her.

The air around her was thick with choking dust, the last dying rays of the sun striking blindingly against the metal of the vehicle racing alongside her. The driver was leaning out of the window, one hand on the steering wheel, the other reaching for her, a lascivious grin slicing his face.

Immediately she turned to run back the way she had come. Unwanted though Richard's attentions were, she could deal far more easily with him than she could with what she was now facing, but to her horror she recognised that her escape route was already being blocked off by the horse and rider bearing down on her even as she still tried to run from him.

The sound of his horse's hooves mingled with the fierce cries of the men surrounding her. He was so close to her that she could feel the heat of the horse's breath on her skin. Her heart felt as though it were about to burst. She saw him draw level with her and bend low in his saddle, his hand coming out, and then unbelievably she was being lifted off the ground and swept up onto the horse's back in front of him, as his prisoner.

Sobbing for breath, her heart pounding sickly, her face pressed against the coarsely woven cloth of the tunic he was wearing, she could do nothing other than lie there, forced to breathe in the smell of the fabric, with its faint lemony scent. Katrina stiffened. She now realised the lemony cologne, like the scent of the man himself, were both immediately familiar to her.

The drumming of horse's hooves became the drumming of her own heart as she struggled to twist her body so that she could look up into his face.

As she had expected all she could see of it were his eyes—gold-flecked, reminding her of a tiger's eye. Her heart leapt and banged against her chest wall as she looked into them and saw them flash gold sparks of molten anger back at her.

Quickly she turned her head, too shocked to withstand the contempt in his eyes. In the distance she could see the four-wheel drive disappearing as Richard drove himself to safety, having left her to her fate. Tears welled in her eyes and one rolled down her face to land on the golden warmth of the male hand holding the horse's reins.

His mouth hardening, he shook it away. He murmured to the horse as he wheeled round and started to head back to the group of men watching them.

As he did so out of nowhere, or so it seemed to Katrina, a vehicle appeared, driven at frightening speed right at them. In the driver's seat was the man who had first pursued her, his face contorted with savagery as he shook his fist at her captor and mouthed some words in a dialect she could not understand before driving off again, reaching the waiting onlookers ahead of them.

There were a hundred, no, a thousand questions she wanted to ask, Katrina acknowledged, but before she could do so he was reining in his mount in front of a powerfully built man of medium height, who was gesturing to him to dismount.

Katrina shivered to see the powerful-looking rifle he was wearing slung over one shoulder, an ammu-

nition belt around his waist, into which was thrust a
wicked-looking traditionally curved dagger.

At his side was the man who had pursued her, ges-
ticulating angrily as he pointed towards her and burst
into a rapid speech, of which she could only catch
the odd word.

A brief inclination of his head from the man at her
side told Katrina that the man with the gun must be
the leader of the men. But whilst he obviously commanded the obedience of everyone else, she was
aware that her captor's body language was subtly em-
phasising his own independence.

'Why did you let the man get away?' Katrina heard
the leader demand angrily in Zuranese.

There was a brief pause before her captor answered
him coolly, 'El Khalid, you're asking me a question
you should surely be asking another! A man on horse-
back, even when that animal is as fast as any mount
in the Ruler's fabled stable, cannot hope to outrun a
four-wheel drive. Sulimen could have caught up with
him had he not decided to pursue an easier prey.'

'He has taken my prize and now he seeks to dis-
credit me. The girl is mine, El Khalid,' the driver of
the Land Rover protested hotly.

'You hear what Sulimen says, Tuareg! What do
you answer him?'

Katrina had to bite down hard on her lip to stop
herself from turning to her captor and begging him
not to let Sulimen take her. The leader had called him
'Tuareg', using only his tribal name, whereas he had
used the more intimate Sulimen for the other man.
Did that mean he would favour the other's claim?
Katrina felt sick at the thought.

Why didn't her captor say something...? She could

feel him looking at her, but she could not bring herself to lift her head and look back at him. She was too afraid of what she might see in his eyes.

'I answer him that I have the girl and he does not. She will earn me a fat purse when I take her back to Zuran City and ransom her back to her people.'

'No one is to leave this camp until I say so,' came the harsh response. 'I have gathered you all here in this place for a special mission. Our success in it will make us all very rich men.

'Since both of you lay claim to the girl, then you might fight one another for her.' He gave a small jerk of his head, and before Katrina could protest she was being led forcibly away by two fierce-looking armed men.

Anxiously she turned round just in time to see El Khalid removing the glitteringly sharp-edged hooked dagger from his belt and throwing it towards her captor.

The breath left her lungs in a rush as he caught it and he and Sulimen began to circle one another. Sulimen already had a similar dagger in his hand and almost immediately he jabbed savagely at his opponent with it. The other men had begun to form a circle around them.

Standing behind them between her jailers, Katrina could only catch maddeningly brief glimpses of the two men as they fought.

Not that she liked watching men fight—far from it—but on this occasion she had a very strong reason for wanting to know which one was going to be the victor. Whilst the men had dragged her away, the two opponents, whilst retaining their headgear, had removed their cloaks and tunics and were fighting bare-chested as they circled one another barefoot.

It was now dark and lanterns had been lit to illuminate the scene that to Katrina looked like something from another world.

The light from one of the lanterns glittered on the daggers as they were raised in clenched hands, and the sickening sounds of human combat echoed the thuds of bare feet on sand.

She heard a low grunt of pain and heard the watching men roar in approval; above their heads she could see the hand holding a dagger aloft, the light catching the tiny droplets of blood that fell from it. Her stomach heaved. Was the man with the golden eyes badly wounded? Ridiculously, given all she already knew about him and all that she didn't, her anxiety and concern were not for her own plight and safety, but for his, and she knew that had she been able to do so she would have rushed to his side.

She heard another groan and another roar of approval, but this time it was the name 'Tuareg' the watching men were calling out in praise.

The fight seemed to go on for ever, and Katrina was becoming increasingly sickened by the thought of such violence and cruelty. She was simply not programmed to find anything about physical violence acceptable, Katrina acknowledged. Her initial anxious need to see what was happening had been overlaid by relief that she was spared witnessing such a loathsome spectacle.

But at last it was apparently over, the watching men cheering loudly as she was pulled through their ranks to where the two antagonists stood in front of El Khalid.

Only one of the three men commanded her attention, though, and her stomach churned with a mixture of nausea and guilty relief as she heard the crowd chanting 'Tuareg' and saw that in his hands he was holding aloft both of the daggers, whilst his opponent slumped despondently beside him.

But then he turned round and Katrina sucked in a shocked breath as she saw the blood-beaded wounds on his flesh. One had slit the taut skin of his face along his cheekbone and dangerously close to his eye, another was carved just above his heart, and blood was dripping from a third on his upper arm.

A feeling of sick dizziness began to threaten her, but she ignored it, dragging her gaze away from the sweat-gilded expanse of taut male chest in front of her. Sulimen, in contrast, did not appear to have any wounds at all, which puzzled Katrina a little since 'Tuareg' was obviously the victor.

'Here is your prize,' she heard El Khalid telling him. 'Take her.'

Was it her imagination or was the slight bow her captor made in El Khalid's direction more cynical than respectful? If so, no one else seemed to have thought so.

He still hadn't so much as acknowledged her presence, turning to toss El Khalid's dagger back to him, and then turning back to lean forward and scoop up his discarded tunic.

Out of the corner of her eye Katrina saw Sulimen go to sheathe his own dagger, but then terrifyingly, instead of doing so, he lunged violently towards her captor's unprotected back, the dagger clenched in his raised hand.

Katrina heard her own sharp sound of shocked

warning, but it seemed something else must have
alerted 'Tuareg' to the danger because he had already
whirled round, and in a movement so fast that
Katrina's eyes could not follow it he had kicked out
at Sulimen's raised hand, dislodging the knife.

Immediately three men seized Sulimen and dragged
him away. As though nothing at all out of the ordi-
nary had happened, her captor picked up his tunic and
pulled it on before indicating with a brusque inclination of his head that she was to join him.

'Come,' he said peremptorily. He took such long
strides that she had difficulty in keeping up with him,
but the moment she reached his side he stopped walking and turned to look down at her.

'You will not walk at my side, but behind me,' he
told her coldly.

Katrina could hardly believe her ears. And as for
walking behind him! The traumas she had endured
were forgotten, in the full fury of her outraged female
pride.

'I will do no such thing,' she refused hotly. 'I am
not your...your chattel... And besides, in Zuran men
walk alongside their partners.'

'This is not Zuran, it is the desert, and you are mine
to do with as I choose, when and how I choose.'

Without giving her the opportunity to answer him,
he turned away and continued to walk swiftly towards
the pitched tents, which were cleverly concealed from
view in a protective natural enclosure of steep-sided
rocky outcrops.

Several fires had been started in a clearing in front
of some of the tents and dark-robed women were stirring the contents of cooking pots. The rich smell of
cooking food made Katrina realise just how long it

was since she herself had eaten, and her stomach growled hungrily.

Predictably, she felt, the tent her captor had led her to was set apart from the others.

A battered-looking utility-type vehicle was parked alongside it and behind that his horse was tethered, happily munching on some food, watched over by a young boy. But Katrina wasn't given any time to study her surroundings; a hard hand in the middle of her back was already pushing her into the tent.

She had of course seen similar tents set up for display and educational purposes on a cultural education site in Zuran City, but she had never imagined she might occupy one of them! Several lamps cast a soft glow over the tent's main living area, with its richly patterned carpets and traditional divan. There were several cushions on the floor and a low wooden table with a coffee pot on it.

All at once the events of the day caught up with her and reaction swamped her, causing exhausted tears to fill her eyes.

'What are you crying for? Your lover? I doubt he is wasting any tears on you, to judge by the speed with which he abandoned you.'

Katrina stared at him. 'Richard is not my lover! He's a married man…'

'But of course. Otherwise, why would he bring you to such a remote place?' A cynical smile hardened the narrowed eyes.

'I did not allow him. He…he forced me…'

'Of course he did!' he agreed mockingly.

Katrina lifted her head and looked challengingly at him.

'Why are you pretending to be a Tuareg when it is obvious that you are not—?'

'Silence!' he commanded her angrily.

'No. I will not be silent. I remember you from the alleyway in Zuran City, even if you don't.'

She gave a small breathless gasp as his hand closed hard over her mouth, a menacing look glittering in his eyes as he bent towards her and said softly, 'You will be silent.'

Katrina had had enough! She had been kidnapped, bullied, threatened, and now this! Angrily she bit sharply into the hand covering her mouth, more shocked by the salt taste of his blood than by the savagery of the oath he uttered as he wrenched away from her.

'Woman, you are a hell-cat!' he stormed as he frowned down at the tiny pinpricks of blood on the soft pad of flesh just below his thumb. 'But no way will I allow you to poison me with your venom! Clean it.'

Katrina stared at him in disbelief, her face starting to burn. What she had done had shocked her. Outraged female fury stiffened her whole body. And yet shockingly there, deep down inside her, was a vagrant acknowledgement of intoxicatingly dangerous awareness of the sensuality of her own thoughts. Thoughts that mirrored her own actual desires? Desires she secretly wanted to turn into actions?

Absolutely not! She could feel his breath against her ear, and she took the cloth he was handing her, dipped it in the bowl of water next to her and dabbed the wound.

Abruptly he released her and stepped back from her, his voice both harsh and somehow distorted as he demanded thickly, 'No! Why should I give you the opportunity to inflict even more damage?'

'Why are you behaving like this?' Katrina demanded tremulously. 'Who are you? In the souk, you looked European.'

'You will not say such things. You know nothing about me!'

She could hear the savage rejection and hostility in his voice. 'I know that you are not a Tuareg,' she persisted.

'And you would know, of course,' he taunted her, his anger replaced by mockery.

'Yes, I would,' Katrina confirmed bravely. 'I have studied Zuranese history and culture and no true Tuareg male would ever uncover his face in public the way you did the other day in the alleyway…'

There was a small telling silence before he said quietly but oh, so menacingly, 'If I were you, I would forget all about Zuran City and its alleyways.'

Katrina took a deep breath and then exhaled it raggedly. 'So, are you going to tell me who you are?'

For a few seconds she thought he wasn't going to reply. And then he gave a small dismissive shrug. 'Who I am does not matter. But what I am does. Those of us who have given our allegiance to El Khalid have strong reasons for doing so. We live outside the law as you know it and you would do well to remember that.'

'You're a criminal?' she guessed. 'A fugitive?'

'You ask too many questions and, I can assure you, you would not want to know who and what I really am.'

It was hard not to allow herself to shiver in reaction to those menacing words, and to demand instead,

'Well, at least give me a name that I may call you. You cannot really want to be called Tuareg. I would certainly not want to be called English!'

To her astonishment he laughed.

'Very well, then. You may call me...' Xander paused. To give her his real name of Allessandro was impossible. It was far too easily recognisable. Here in the rebel camp, where a man's lawful identity was respected as his own private business, he was known by everyone only as 'Tuareg' and had given himself the very common family name of bin Sadeen. But 'Tuareg' wasn't the name he wanted to hear falling from this woman's lips, although just why he should feel like that he wasn't prepared to analyse.

'You may call me Xander,' he heard himself telling her. Xander was the shortened version of his name used only by those who were closest to him, his half-brother and sister-in-law, and so would not be recognised by anyone else.

'Xander?' A small frown etched Katrina's smooth forehead. 'That is very unusual. I do not believe I have heard it before.'

'It was my mother's choice,' he told her curtly. 'And what am I to call you?'

'My name is Katrina Blake,' she informed him, hesitating before finding the courage to burst out anxiously, 'How long will it be before...before I can go back to Zuran City?'

'I cannot say. El Khalid has given orders that no one is to leave the oasis until he permits it.'

For a moment Katrina was tempted to ask him what had brought them to the oasis, and indeed the question was already on the tip of her tongue, but cautiously she decided not to ask it.

'Very wise,' he told her coolly, as though he had guessed what she was thinking.

'Stay here,' he ordered her. 'Do not leave the tent.'

'Where are you going?' Katrina demanded wildly as he started to walk away from her.

Turning round, he told her smoothly. 'To my sleeping quarters to remove my soiled clothes.'

Oh! Katrina felt herself begin to blush.

'Oh, your cuts,' she remembered with guilt. 'Shouldn't you have them attended to?'

He shrugged carelessly. 'They are mere scratches, that is all, and will heal quickly enough.'

Katrina suddenly remembered something. 'Why was it Sulimen who lost the fight when you were the one who was injured?' she asked him curiously.

'The aim is not to carve slices from one's opponent, but to disarm him,' he told her dispassionately.

As he turned away again she looked towards the exit.

'There are two hundred miles of empty desert between here and Zuran City.'

The clinically detached words sent a tingle of apprehensive hostility and despair zinging over her skin. The desert was its own kind of prison—a guard designed by nature to prevent her from escaping him, and he of course knew that. Did he also know how afraid she had been when Sulimen had claimed her as his trophy? How relieved she had been when he had stepped in? How complex and disquieting the tangled mass of her own emotions was? Her mouth compressed. She sincerely hoped not! He was already making her feel far more emotionally vulnerable than she knew was wise.

Determinedly she turned round to confront him.

'You won't get away with this, you know. Richard will alert the authorities and—'

'We are in the empty quarter—beyond the reach of both your lover and the authorities,' he replied chillingly.

'Richard is my boss, not my lover.' Katrina's face burned as she saw the way he was looking at her.

'So why else would you be at the oasis, together and alone? Though I'm not surprised that you should deny your relationship with him after the way he has abandoned you.'

'He obviously thought it made good sense for him to go for help rather than for both of us to be taken hostage,' Katrina returned shortly.

'"Good sense"? Oh, of course, you are European!' he taunted her. 'Here in the desert it is not "good sense". We are driven by our interactions with your sex, especially when we are bound to a woman, emotionally committed to them. But then, of course, your culture does not consider such things important, does it? I would rather cut out my own heart than abandon the woman who held it to any kind of discomfort or danger.'

Something in his voice was raising goose-bumps on Katrina's skin and a dangerous burning sensation at the backs of her eyes. The intimate and intense images his words were conjuring for her were intruding on dreams she held so private and secret that just the sound of his voice was enough to bring them to the front of her mind. Hadn't she always longed for such a man and such a love and hadn't she told herself that she was hungering for something that did not exist? Hadn't she strived to make herself put aside such foolishness and to concentrate instead on the realities of life?

Swallowing hard against the ball of emotion blocking her throat, she turned away from him.

'Go if you wish,' she heard him say carelessly from behind her. 'If Sulimen does not take you, then the desert most surely will.'

Katrina made no response. How could she when she knew that he was speaking the truth?

Although she had her back to him, disconcertingly she knew immediately when he had left the living area of the pavilion and gone through to his sleeping quarters.

The rush of adrenalin that had given her the courage to speak so challengingly to him had gone and she felt weak and shaky. The pavilion and its owner were her prison and her guard, but they were also her place of safety and her protection, she acknowledged.

But she must not allow herself to forget just what he was! She could remember reading somewhere of the intense and dangerous emotional dependence a captive could end up having on his or her captor. She must not let that happen to her.

Because he had kissed her? Just because he had used her? Her head had begun to ache and she was beginning to feel slightly sick on the heavy mixture of adrenalin and anxiety unleavened by anything else.

She paced the soft carpet of the pavilion, checking and tensing at every alien sound, but she was still caught off guard when she turned round and saw that Xander had padded soft-footed into the room and was standing watching her.

He was wearing a clean soft white tunic that he was still fastening, his feet and head bare. In the lamplight she could see the golden gleam of his chest through the soft mesh of fine dark hair.

A feeling she couldn't control exploded deep down inside her body, releasing an ache so shocking and intimate that it made her catch her breath on a betraying indrawn rattle.

His hair was damp and as he walked across the carpet towards her he brought with him the smell of clean skin and the subtle cologne she was already associating with him. Her heart did a neat double somersault inside her body and then just in case she had not got the message, it took a high dive on a trapeze that left her feeling as though it had somehow become lodged in her throat.

He was making her feel uncomfortable and very aware of the difference between his clean, fresh appearance and her own tired stickiness. But even without that he was making her feel uncomfortable, full stop, Katrina acknowledged mutely. She was trying desperately to drag her traitorous gaze away from the dark hand casually fastening the robe buttons and concealing from her the matt satin gold of his bare flesh.

In an attempt to cover what she was feeling she demanded sharply, 'Just how long do you plan to keep me here?'

He shot her a look of cold arrogance. 'For as long as I have to!'

She was finding it difficult to swallow. 'What... what will you do?' Could he hear the nervousness in her voice?

He gave her a look of narrow-eyed scrutiny and then questioned mockingly, 'Do?'

'Yes. I mean—' She had to stop speaking to swallow again. 'I mean, how will you let the expedition know that—?'

'You ask far too many questions! There is a saying, isn't there, in your country about curiosity?'

'About curiosity killing the cat, you mean?' Katrina managed to croak.

'In your shoes I should concern myself more with questioning how willing your friends are to buy your freedom and at what price than how I intend to go about informing them of your whereabouts.'

Katrina could feel the panic biting into her, but she refused to give in to it. Her parents' death had forced her into self-reliance at a young age and the habit of depending on herself and facing up to sometimes very unpleasant truths and realities was one she had forced herself to adopt.

And right now there was a very unpleasant question she had to have an answer to. Moistening her over-dry lips, she pressed him huskily, 'And if my…if the company cannot pay the ransom demand?'

There was a small pause and a flash of something she couldn't interpret in his eyes before he said softly, 'Then in that case I shall have to take my goods to a wider market.' When she looked blankly at him he derided her, 'Who else will pay handsomely for a young attractive woman?'

Katrina's eyes widened as she stared at him in appalled anxiety. He couldn't mean what he was saying. Could he?

Without another word he pulled on his Tuareg headdress, slid his feet into a pair of sandals and, pulling back the heavy curtain, stepped out of the tent.

She was alone! He had gone! She could simply walk out if she wished. But walk out to what? She was pretty sure that a group of men such as these, bound together by their illegal activities, would post guards on their camp. If she tried to leave she would suffer the ignominy of being forcibly brought back, and even if she should succeed in escaping, she knew she could not possibly walk back to Zuran City. No, she had no option other than to wait tamely here, for him and whatever fate he chose to impose on her. And of course he knew that!

Whatever fate?

Supposing he himself should decide that he found her desirable? Her heart thumped heavily against her ribs, and a frisson of sensation that shamingly had nothing whatsoever to do with either fear or outrage stroked feather touches of liquid and dangerous excitement over her.

His dishonesty must obviously pay him well, she decided cynically, at least if the interior of the pavilion and its furnishings were anything to go by.

The carpets covering the floor and 'walls' were exquisitely worked and far superior to anything she had seen in the shops she had visited. She touched one of them tentatively, stroking her fingertip along one of the branches and then down the thick trunk of its richly hued tree of life. The silky threads felt as warm as though they were a living, breathing entity. If she closed her eyes she could almost imagine...

Her face was on fire as she snatched her hand back from the carpet as though she had been burned. The carved and gilded raised divan was draped with something dark and soft, jewel-coloured velvet cushions piled on top of it. The flickering oil lamps cast mysterious shadows, which echoed the sensual richness of the fabrics. A discarded lute-like instrument lay on the floor to one side of the divan, and behind them she could see a pile of leather-bound books.

Automatically she went over to them and picked one of them up. Its title was picked out in gold leaf, *The Rubaiyat of Omar Khayyam*... A book of poetry. It seemed out of character somehow. She put the book back and sat down on one of the cushions. Her head was still aching and she felt both physically and emotionally exhausted. Tiredly she closed her eyes.

Pensively Xander picked his way through the tents towards his own, pausing to check on the mare he had been riding earlier. When she saw him she tossed her head and pushed her nose into his arm, begging for the tidbit he always gave her. The boy whom he paid to keep an eye on her sprang up from where he had been lying several feet away from her and then settled down again as he recognised him.

Katrina's challenge to him about his European inheritance had rubbed against a raw place in his emotional make-up. His mother had been loved and respected by all of his Zurani family, with the exception of Nazir and Nazir's late father. And, according to his half-brother, his mother had happily embraced the way of life of her husband. She had loved the desert and its people, as he did himself, but she had not been totally and completely desert blood, bone and sinew, just as he wasn't himself. His father had chosen to have him educated in Europe, wanting him to experience his European cultural inheritance, and to keep the promise he had made to his dying wife, but Xander had never forgotten overhearing a conversation between his father and the British government official who had undertaken to escort him to his new school in England.

'The thing is that the boy is neither fish nor fowl, really...' the diplomat had announced critically, or so it had seemed to Xander's ears at that time.

And the diplomat had spoken the truth, Xander acknowledged bleakly now. Whilst the greatest part of him would always belong here in the desert, there was another part of him that felt most fulfilled when he was involved in the cut and thrust of diplomacy in Washington and London and Paris, and the work he did promoting Zuran. He had grown up surrounded by the love of his Zurani relatives, yes, but at the same time he had been aware that he was different from them. He was not European, but neither was he totally Zurani either!

And because of that, coupled no doubt with the loss of his mother, he carried with him the secret, guarded burden of his own inner sense of isolation.

But somehow Katrina had breached his defences and touched the darkness buried deep within his own soul. And because of that more than anything else he wanted her out of his life!

After all, whilst as a child he had seen his mixed heritage as a source of confusion and anxiety, as an adult he had learned to view it in a much more positive light and to use it for the benefit of others. But, even so, he was still very much aware that in some people's eyes his mixed heritage made him an object of their contempt.

With his elder half-brother's blessing he had worked tirelessly to promote better relations between his country and the rest of the world, and indeed he had been honoured for the work he had done by the

Ruling Council by being appointed as a Special Envoy. It was a scheme he had personally advocated and set up involving a student exchange between Middle Eastern and European students so that each might better understand the other, and had been so highly acclaimed that there was talk of his name being put forward for the Nobel Peace Prize.

But right now his emotions were turbulent rather than peaceful! And all because of Katrina Blake! Of all the complications and problems he could have envisaged that might jeopardise his carefully made plans, the unexpected and unwanted presence of Katrina Blake was surely the last one he could have logically expected. It was certainly the last one he wanted, he acknowledged savagely. And definitely the last one he had been prepared for! She was a danger, both to him and to herself! By rights, surely the situation she was in should have caused her to be struck dumb with fear, not bombarding him with questions. And certainly not making her observations and information about him common knowledge. Potentially she could ruin everything! She was a liability he could not afford to have, here where she could threaten and unwittingly sabotage his own secret mission. But El Khalid had given the edict that no one was to leave the camp. Otherwise he could have driven her safely out of the way, radioed ahead and got a car and a driver to pick her up and take her back to her friends—and her laggardly cowardly lover—and then been left unencumbered to return here to do what he had come here to do.

Instead of which…

He should have left her to fate and to Sulimen, he decided bitterly. Reluctantly he found himself acknowledging that she had spirit and courage. And she had a mouth that smelled of scented damask roses and tasted of honey-drenched almonds. Her body was as slender as a young gazelle's and her eyes...

He wrenched his thoughts back under control. His half-brother's wife had introduced any number of suitable young women to him as potential brides but none of them had interested him. They had been too sweet, too docile, too lacking in spirit. Soft, tame doves, who would flutter to any man's hand, where something in him craved a little of the proud independence, the desert wildness of the she falcon, who would only allow herself to be tamed by one man— and even then only on her own terms.

A woman who would melt into his arms in a sweetly wild passion, which would meet and match his own fiercely strong male hunger for her. A woman who would give herself to him body and soul and who would demand from him in return all that there was of him. A woman who would race him neck and neck across the desert sands and who would place her head upon his lap whilst he played music for her and read her the sweetest and most tender of love poems. A woman who was all that he had been told his own mother had been and yet who at the same time was individually and uniquely herself.

He had long ago decided that such a woman could not and did not exist, outside his own imagination, and he still thought that, he told himself fiercely. Katrina Blake certainly wasn't such a woman. How could she be?

And more importantly by far: how could he be wasting time thinking about her when his thoughts and his energies should be focused on much more important matters? He was as sure as he could be that the important personage El Khalid had spoken of had to be Nazir.

Even though he had tried discreetly to persuade El Khalid to be more specific about when he was expecting the important person to arrive, the rebel leader had insisted that a definite time had not yet been arranged, and Xander had been reluctant to push El Khalid too hard for information in case he began to suspect his motives.

Nazir could not afford to delay too long. The celebration of the country's National Day was only five days away, after all. And Nazir certainly would not welcome Katrina's presence within the camp—a woman who, if she chanced to see him, could potentially betray him if she was returned to her own people. Indeed, from Nazir's point of view it would be far simpler and safer if she did not return!

The smell of cooking food reminded him that he had not had anything to eat. Going over to the communal fire, he helped himself to a plate of lamb stew from the pot and then picked up some of the flat unleavened bread.

CHAPTER THREE

THE first thing Xander saw when he swept aside the heavy curtain and walked into the pavilion was Katrina, lying fast asleep on one of the cushions, her face pale with exhaustion and her lashes lying in delicately curled twin black semi-circles against her skin.

He started to frown. Her hair, which had been caught back, had started to escape and several tendrils clung to the exposed curve of her throat. Such a pretty colour couldn't possibly be natural, Xander decided contemptuously, and would no doubt be as false as everything else about her, right down to the lie she had told him about being forced to come to the oasis.

His frown deepened. If she continued to sleep lying the way she was she would end up with cramped muscles and a stiff neck. He put the food he was carrying down on the table and went over to her, hunkering down beside her.

His mother had been very pale skinned and fair-haired, which was no doubt why his own skin was warmly golden rather than teak brown. His mother had loved his father passionately and he her, at least according to his half-brother, and he had no reason to doubt him.

The angle of Katrina's sleeping body revealed the softly rounded curves of her breasts beneath the short-sleeved round-necked shirt she was wearing. He could see where the fabric of her shirt pulled slightly to reveal the soft thrust of her nipples. His stomach muscles contracted sharply, the pressure of his fierce attempt to quell his body's fierce surging reaction to her causing the air to squeeze out of his lungs.

He had seen plenty of nubile young women dressed far more revealingly and provocatively—and not just on the streets of the European cities he had visited—without ever feeling even the slightest twinge of sexual reaction, and it both disturbed and infuriated him that he should be so immediately and intensely aroused now and by a woman he had no business allowing himself to feel such a physical reaction to.

He was not, after all, some sexually deprived teenager! And far from inexperienced! If he wanted a woman there were any number who would be all too eager to share his bed. Any number maybe, but what about this particular one? She was another man's lover. A married man's lover, he reminded himself.

Broodingly he looked down at Katrina, his intellect rejecting the message his body was giving him, and the urge to simply pick her up and carry her into the inner privacy of his sleeping quarters.

She moved her head and a thick lock of her hair fell across her face, making her frown in her sleep. Automatically he reached out to brush it away for her.

Abruptly Katrina opened her eyes, her heart hammering frantically fast inside her chest as she looked up into the molten gold of Xander's fiercely predatory gaze. Helplessly she lay motionless and vulnerable beneath it, pinioned by it, her lips parting as she took short gulps of air.

His fingertips were touching her cheek, four cool, hard pressure points, each one sending shock waves of pleasure that were making her tremble. She could see the dark shadow along his jaw, her eyes widening in betraying female acknowledgement of its message of maleness.

Immediately he lifted his hand from her face, something dark and dangerous glittering in his eyes before he veiled his expression from her.

'I have brought you some food,' he told her curtly.

Katrina could smell it, and her stomach rumbled hungrily, but she compressed her mouth and shook her head, telling him untruthfully, 'I'm not hungry.'

He was frowning as he looked at her.

'Liar,' he said to her flatly, before demanding coldly, 'What is it? Is our food not good enough for you?'

'No, it isn't that!'

'No? Then what exactly is it?' he challenged her sardonically.

'I...Richard—'

'Richard? Your lover, you mean?'

'He is not my lover. He wanted to be, but I... He tricked me and...and drugged me...'

'Drugged you? And you think I might do the same?'

She had angered him; she could tell that!

'Why should I want to do that?'

Stubbornly Katrina refused to answer him.

'Are you really suggesting that I would drug you in order to have sex with you?'

Katrina's face burned.

Put like that it did sound far-fetched, especially when one look at him would tell any fully functioning woman that making love with him would be all pleasure and no penance!

'Even so! Isn't it normally the custom for desert tribesmen to eat first, before their women?'

'Their women? But you are not my woman, are you?' he pointed out softly. 'And we also have a custom that a guest is invited to eat first.'

'But I am not your guest.' Katrina couldn't help answering him sharply. 'I am your prisoner!'

Picking up the stew, he sat down cross-legged on the divan and began to dip a piece of bread into it, scooping up chunks of delicious-smelling lamb.

Katrina's mouth watered. She felt faint with hunger. Pausing between mouthfuls, he demanded brusquely, 'Tell me more about this lover of yours. This Richard…'

'He is not my lover!' Katrina denied angrily. 'I have told you that already.'

'But you agreed to accompany him into the desert…alone…'

'No! It was an expedition—several of us… We are cataloguing the flora and fauna of the area. Richard tricked me into getting into his vehicle, and then…'

Against her will she could feel her own emotions threatening to overwhelm her.

'By the time I realised what he was planning it was too late. When he stopped at the oasis I hoped that I might be able to distract him and escape.'

'Distract him? In what manner? No, I can guess. There is after all only one reliable method by which a woman can distract a man.'

Katrina had had enough!

'You're as bad as Richard! You just don't understand! Believe what you like, I don't care.'

'And neither do I. At least not so far as your sexual history is concerned. What I do care about, however, is your financial value to me.' He stood up and started to walk determinedly towards her.

A sharp thrill of fear seized her. Apprehensively Katrina looked towards the door, but he was standing between her and it.

'Here.' He told her curtly, handing her the bowl of stew. 'It is not drugged. Now sit down and eat!'

Relief filled her. For a moment she had feared... She knew not what she had feared, only that she had been afraid! But it seemed that after all there was a kinder, more compassionate side to her captor!

The stew was every bit as good as it had looked, and she was even hungrier than she had known.

When she had finished Xander told her coolly, 'I have some business I need to discuss with El Khalid, and my horse to see to, but first I will show you where you will sleep.'

She was so tired she could hardly keep her eyes open, never mind follow Xander as he swung back the heavy fabric hanging that separated the outer compartment of the tent from the inner one, and she stumbled exhaustedly after him.

It took her eyes several seconds to adjust to the shadowy darkness of the inner chamber, and its low, wide bed heaped with cushions.

'Through here you will find a shower and—'

'A shower!' Her voice betrayed both her surprise and her relief. The thought of water on her dusty skin was a wonderful prospect, but it was not enough to completely distract her from the sight of the large bed. Quite obviously it was her captor's bed!

But he was already turning away from her and before she could say anything he had gone, leaving her alone in the shadowy darkness of the dimly lit chamber. Warily she started to investigate her surroundings. The bed was easily large enough for two people, and the discovery of the portable shower and loo, which lay in their own tented area beyond it and which, whilst very simple, were immaculately clean, made her exhale a gusty sigh of relief.

Since she was not sure how long Xander would be gone and, therefore, how much privacy she would have, she showered quickly, hesitating a little before wrapping her wet body in one of the obviously luxurious and expensive thick towels she had found neatly stacked on a hanging shelf. Were they someone else's property? Property which had been acquired by theft? It was hard for her to ignore her moral disquiet about using them, but she had no alternative other than to do so, she told herself grimly before fastidiously rinsing out her underwear and tee shirt.

By the time she had done all that it was all she could do to find the energy to crawl onto the bed still wrapped in her towel.

Virtually all the members of the band of renegades who had associated themselves with El Khalid were already waiting for him to begin his evening council when Xander joined them and found a space to sit down cross-legged amongst them.

'You are late, Tuareg,' one of them commented.

'He was probably too busy enjoying his prize,' another joined in coarsely, before adding in warning, 'You had best be on your guard, Tuareg. Sulimen is making no secret of the fact that he believes that the girl is rightfully his and that he wants her back.'

Xander gave a dismissive shrug.

'Sulimen may make as many empty threats as he wishes, the girl stays with me. Has El Khalid spoken yet of this mysterious personage of importance who is to make us all wealthy?' he demanded.

The other men shook their heads, and then fell silent as El Khalid himself appeared from within his large pavilion, flanked by his lieutenants.

Two hours later although many questions had been asked El Khalid had still not informed them of the identity of the man they had come to the oasis to meet, and Xander suspected that he did not as yet know Nazir's true identity himself.

It was gone midnight when the meeting broke up, and Xander made his way slowly back to his own tent, pausing only to check up on his horse and the sleeping boy who looked after her.

The boy was an orphan who had attached himself to El Khalid's camp. When all this was over he would ask his half-brother to find him a bed, an education and a job in his stables, Xander decided.

Once inside the pavilion, he removed his mobile phone from his pocket and switched it on. He had deliberately cleared it of any information that might betray him, and he dialled his half-brother's private number quickly, whilst he faced the entrance to the tent, just in case anyone should decide to enter.

'Little brother!'

He could hear the pleasure in his half-brother's voice, and quickly filled him in with what had been happening, using the special code they had arranged.

'You may have been informed of the kidnap of a certain young British woman, a member of an explorative scientific expedition,' he added carefully.

'I have heard of such an incident,' the Ruler agreed equally carefully. 'The head of the expedition has informed us that it took place in the desert some thirty or so miles to the east of our city, and a search is to be made in that area.'

Xander frowned. The oasis was over two hundred miles north of the city, which meant that Richard had lied about where he and Katrina had been when she had been 'kidnapped'.

'The girl is safe—no thanks to the one who placed her in danger. And I shall ensure that she remains so,' Xander informed his half-brother, before they ended the call. Richard might have desired Katrina, but he certainly could not have had any genuine love for her, Xander decided with angry contempt. His hostility towards the other man had grown with every damning word his half-brother had spoken. Not that he believed for one minute the wild fiction Katrina had invented about Richard tricking her into accompanying him. She was no sheltered, inexperienced girl after all, but a travelled and independent young woman who had no doubt long ago lost count of the number of men who had shared her bed.

But that did not make her deserving of the fate that would have been hers if Sulimen had been allowed to claim her.

He hadn't really needed the information relayed to him earlier by his fellows that Sulimen had a weakness for young women and he had a reputation too for treating them very badly. Sulimen didn't just want Katrina for the purpose of ransoming her, that he was sure about...

Xander's mouth compressed. She might be an unwanted complication that he could well do without, but there was no way he could abandon her to

Sulimen. As she was a stranger in his country and a woman, he had a moral duty to protect her.

His half-brother had informed him during their telephone conversation that Nazir had let it be known that he was about to leave the country for several weeks. They had both agreed that this was merely an alibi he had created, which would not only enable him to meet and plot with El Khalid, but also to mastermind his planned coup without attracting suspicion to himself.

With the Ruler's sons being under age and too young to step into their father's shoes once Nazir had disposed of him, Nazir was no doubt planning to lay claim to the throne by means of suggesting himself as Regent. Therefore, he would not want the Ruling Council to suspect what he had done.

Nazir would leave it as long as he dared before putting his plan to El Khalid in order to lessen the risk of someone betraying it and him, but he would have to make his move soon.

As he walked into the sleeping area of the pavilion, Xander started to remove his Tuareg headdress, smoothly unwinding the yards of indigo-dyed fabric that comprised it and provided him with his disguise.

Katrina had been both right and wrong in accusing him of not being Tuareg—his father did have some Tuareg blood.

Katrina. Her name had a special melody to it, a musical harmony that fell sweetly on the ear. A poet…a lover might be tempted to use it to write of his love for her. A poet? A lover? Long ago as a callow youth, he might have believed himself to have the soul of a poet, but he was most certainly not the latter. And did not want to be?

Casting aside the indigo fabric, he strode towards the bed and then stopped as he saw Katrina lying where she had fallen asleep on top of it. Her head lay on one of its silk-covered cushions; her body was wrapped in a towel that revealed more of her than it concealed, fully exposing the slender length of her legs with their creamy thighs and delicately boned ankles, so fine he suspected he could have circled one with one hand. An equally delicately boned arm was flung out to one side of her, the other tucked beneath her. She looked more child than woman, at least until one moved closer as he had just done and saw what he had not observed before, which was the upper curve of her breasts, revealed right down to the areolae surrounding her nipples and beyond them to the rosy peaked flare of the nipples themselves.

A sensation he tried savagely to repudiate exploded inside him and with it a need and a hunger that turned his eyes the colour of molten gold slashed with amber. Desire, hot, urgent and compelling, surged through him, threatening to breach his self-control.

If he touched her now he would be no better than Sulimen, he warned himself as he forced himself to walk past her and into the simple shower area, where he stripped off his clothes with swift angry movements before standing beneath the shower's lukewarm spray.

It took longer than he wanted to acknowledge for the uncomfortably hard, swollen evidence of his arousal to subside; he was still aware of it and Katrina herself when he walked past her without looking at her.

*   *   *

In the darkness of the desert night a horse whinnied shrilly, disturbed by a prowling predator. The sound woke Katrina up.

At first her unfamiliar surroundings confused her, but all too quickly she remembered where she was and why.

Desert nights were bitingly cold, especially in winter, and Katrina shivered as she pulled the still-damp towel around herself before glancing fearfully across the bed.

The empty bed! A small frown puckered her forehead. She looked at her watch. It was three o'clock in the morning and the silken bed cover was smoothly undisturbed. She was alone on the bed, and alone too it seemed in the pavilion's sleeping area.

Surely that wasn't disappointment that she was feeling? Not after all those dreams she had cherished for so long, of the man, her man; her soul mate…the one and only man to whom she would give the whole of herself, with whom she would share the whole of herself. Her first and last lover.

This man, Xander, was not that man! How could he possibly be?

The man she had dreamed of was noble, in spirit and in deed, honourable, good and kind. Xander was none of those things. She could not respect him, nor trust him, and she certainly could not love him, surely?

Maybe not, but she could and did want him! Katrina had to swallow hard against her own feelings. Shock fought with need. Anger with hunger. Caution with urgency, and pride with a wild, fierce passion.

This could not be. She could not…*must* not feel like this.

She slid off the bed, careless of both her nakedness

and the cool air as her mind and her body fought with one another.

What would she really do if he were to come in here now and lay claim to her, to her body? For it was impossible that he would want anything else of her! How would she feel if he were to reach out and touch her, his lean, hard hands shaping her, exploring her, knowing her, cupping her breasts, and then moving lower, over her belly and lower still? A shudder of twisted, dangerous, sensual pleasure ripped through her.

How could she allow herself to think like this? What warped inner part of herself was doing this to her? She had always believed that she would love first and desire second, that it would be a meeting and matching of minds and moral values that would be her prelude to emotional and physical arousal.

There was nothing about Xander or the manner in which he lived his life that remotely equated in any kind of way to her own beliefs or values. He was a liar and maybe a criminal, a man who put his own needs first. How could she possibly want him? The kind of people she admired put others first, and the greater good of mankind.

She needed to breathe fresh air to clear her head. Picking up the towel, she wrapped it firmly around herself and made her way hesitantly through to the outer area of the tent.

Xander had woken up the minute he had heard Katrina move, and when he saw her edging her way to the exit of the tent he pushed back the covers of the impromptu bed that he had made for himself and went after her.

Her hand was on the heavy exit curtain ready to

push it back when Katrina felt Xander's fasten over her bare arm.

'Going somewhere?' he asked her softly.

Immediately she panicked, pulling back from him and demanding passionately, 'Let go of me.'

Her reaction to him ignited the still-smouldering embers of Xander's earlier arousal.

Instead of releasing her he tightened his grip on her, and closed the space between their bodies.

The downward swoop of his head had all the predatory intent of a desert falcon, swift and merciless, his mouth possessing hers before she could even cry out in denial.

But it was her own need that was defeating and betraying her, Katrina acknowledged dizzily as her mouth clung to his, her lips parting with wanton speed and eagerness as they offered his probing tongue the sweet spoils of victory. Longing burned hotly inside her, melting whatever resistance she might have summoned to her aid as their tongues twined and battled for the sweetest intimacies of their shared hunger. Tipping back her head, she let him plunder her mouth, as she in turn wanted to plunder his. She felt her towel slipping away from her body, not with a sense of anxiety, but instead with a wild thrill of female pleasure, for she had already seen—and felt—that the robe he was wearing hung open over his own nakedness.

If their tongues had meshed savagely together in mutual eager hunger, that pleasure was just a tame shadow of how it felt to have him press her the full length of his body. Her skin, her flesh, her innermost self was so intensely aroused just by the feel of him that she pressed herself even closer, moving against him, craving him as so many centuries ago men had craved the hashish to which they had become so addicted that it had destroyed them. As the unbearable craving she felt now for Xander would ultimately destroy her?

With a sharp cry of self-disgust she pulled herself away from him and, picking up her towel, fled back to the privacy of the inner chamber.

Would he come after her, and if he did would she be able to be strong enough to deny her body what it was craving? She took a deep breath and held it, nervously fixing her gaze on the curtained doorway, and waited…

But Xander did not appear.

When the breath started to leak painfully from her lungs she told herself that she was glad that he had not come after her.

On the other side of the curtain Xander told himself that Katrina had only pre-empted his own rejection of her by a mere heartbeat. But for the second time in less than twelve hours he had to wait longer than he wanted to admit for the desire for her to slowly and painfully subside to a bearable level.

CHAPTER FOUR

KATRINA frowned in concentration as she sketched the plant she was studying.

She had decided that since she was stuck here at the oasis with no means of escape she might as well put the time to good use, and although he had frowned initially over her request for paper and drawing and writing implements, Xander had produced what she had asked for plus a small stool for her to sit on whilst she worked.

It was three days since she had been kidnapped and nearly three nights since... Quickly she tried to refocus on the plant, but, fascinating though it was, it simply did not have the power to compel her thoughts in the same way that Xander did.

A movement caught her eye and she looked up to see Sulimen standing watching her. A small quiver of apprehension raced down her spine, but determinedly she refused either to acknowledge his presence or to let him see how nervous he was making her feel.

This wasn't the first time she had noticed him watching her, and his presence made her feel on edge and vulnerable.

She tried to continue sketching as though she were completely unfazed by his presence directly in her line of vision, but it was impossible. And impossible too for her not to be aware of the brooding concentration of his gaze as he stared openly and boldly at her.

The way he was looking at her made her wish that she had the protection of the traditional black garments and veils, like those worn by the women she had seen within the camp, to take refuge behind, instead of just her tee shirt and jeans.

But with every second that passed she became more and more on edge and in the end she was forced to concede that her attempts to ignore him were not working, and that the fact that he was continuing to stand boldly staring at her made her feel too uncomfortable to remain.

Turning her back on him, she started to gather up her things, as quickly as she could, telling herself that she would have had to stop working anyway, as the sun was dropping quickly towards the horizon and it would soon be dark.

Seconds later, though, when she headed back towards Xander's tent, Sulimen slipped away into the shadows. Walking through the pitched tents, she was sharply aware of the growing tension that was gripping the whole camp—a combination of a sense of expectancy mingled with something darker and far more dangerous. She gave a small shiver. These were criminals she was living amongst, she reminded herself; men who were outcasts from society because of what they had done. And Xander was one of them, and she had better remember that.

She gave a frightened gasp as she felt a hand on her shoulder, and realised too late that whilst she had been engrossed in her own thoughts Sulimen had emerged from the shadows to catch up with her, and was now subjecting her to a hot-eyed look of sexual greed.

Immediately she pulled away from him, and started

to walk as fast as she could towards Xander's tent, and then broke into a run as her fear overwhelmed her.

'Katrina!'

She came to an abrupt halt as she saw Xander standing in front of her, frowning darkly at her. He wasn't on his own; El Khalid and several other men were with him.

'Tuareg. The woman. How much do you want for her?' she heard Sulimen demanding.

Shock and fear poured through her veins in an icy surge. Sulimen was offering to buy her from Xander? This couldn't be happening. Please, please let it not be happening, she began to panic. But it was.

Wildly she looked into Xander's closed dark face, her mute gaze fixed on him as she prayed that he would not sell her to the other man.

Xander didn't seem disposed to be in any hurry to respond. Was he weighing up how much he could get for her? Or perhaps whether it would be more profitable for him to sell her now to Sulimen rather than to keep her and ransom her once they could return to Zuran City?

She could feel him looking at her. Her pleading, anxious gaze met his; the knowledge that she had to beg him to keep her rubbed her pride raw.

'She is not for sale.'

The terse words made her eyes burn with relieved tears. Without waiting for him to say anything else she almost ran to his side in relief.

But as she quickly discovered, her relief had been premature.

'I will have her,' Sulimen declared angrily. 'I will

give you twice what you can ransom her for, Tuareg. Is that not a fair offer, El Khalid?'

Katrina could see the way El Khalid was looking from Sulimen to Xander.

'The offer is indeed a fair one, Tuareg. I do not wish to have dissent amongst my brothers. It is my wish that you let Sulimen have her.'

Katrina thought she was going to be physically sick, she felt so distraught and afraid.

Sulimen was walking towards them, and she shrank back against Xander's side, making a small sound of acute distress as she did so.

Her vulnerability combined with her fear and his own very real awareness of exactly what kind of man Sulimen was had Xander acknowledging inwardly that he could not in all conscience allow Katrina to be handed over to Sulimen and that he had to do something to protect her. Even without that tell-tale little movement she had made towards him, his own sense of honour and decency would have made it imperative that he did everything he could to prevent such a fate befalling her. But he could think of only one course of action that would save her.

'A thousand apologies, El Khalid, but I cannot do as you ask,' he protested quickly.

'What?'

Katrina could see how infuriated El Khalid looked. His two henchmen were already reaching for the daggers that were stuck into their belts, which, ornate as they were, and as Katrina already had good cause to know, were not in any way merely pretty ornaments.

She couldn't bring herself to look at Xander. She knew that he would have to give her up.

'What is this?' El Khalid was challenging Xander, whilst Sulimen moved closer.

'I have decided to take the woman as my wife,' Xander announced calmly.

There was a small silence during which Katrina discovered that she was trembling violently. She knew that Xander didn't mean it, of course. He was just claiming that he wanted her as his wife in order to protect her. As she knew from her study of the area's history and customs, as a man's intended wife she immediately became totally off limits to any other man. Even so...

'He is lying,' Sulimen shouted angrily. 'Do not listen to him!'

Katrina saw El Khalid look from Sulimen's angry, contorted face to Xander's coolly implacable one.

'I want an end to this matter. We shall soon have important business to do, and I will not have dissent amongst my followers. Tuareg, you have said you want to take the woman as your wife, and so you shall. You and the woman will both present yourselves to me before my divan tonight. And you, Sulimen, I do not need to tell you of the penalty for approaching the wife of another man.'

As he turned to leave El Khalid looked at Xander and told him, 'You have two hours to prepare yourselves for your wedding.'

They were on their own in the shadows of the tents. Dusk had fallen but Katrina could see Xander's face quite plainly in the light of the stars. 'What... what...did El Khalid mean...about...about our wedding?' she began and then had to stop, as her emotions prevented her from continuing.

'He meant exactly what he said,' Xander informed her coldly. 'We have two hours to prepare ourselves for our marriage.'

'No!' Her denial was instant. Shock and sick disbelief filled her. This couldn't be happening.

'I thought it took weeks to prepare for a wedding in Zuran,' she heard herself protesting shakily. 'And the marriage itself...I thought it went on for several days and...'

'Normally it does, but there is a shorter version, created for circumstances such as these. It isn't so very long ago that different tribes warred with one another and sometimes to marry one's enemy's daughter or sister was a good way of resolving the issue. It has only two requirements, the first being that we present ourselves before El Khalid and declare that we wish to be married. The—'

'But how can we be married?' Katrina demanded numbly.

'Quite easily. By tradition, as the leader of his men El Khalid has the authority to perform such a ceremony. Of course if you would prefer me to hand you over to Sulimen—'

'No,' Katrina stopped him frantically. 'You can't want to marry me.'

'I don't,' he agreed grimly. 'But there is some honour even here amongst thieves and I have heard things of Sulimen that would not allow me to sleep easily with my own conscience were I to let him buy you from me.'

'Buy me! I am a human being and not a...a possession!' she protested wildly.

Immediately Xander took hold of her arm, giving

her a small warning shake as he did so. 'Fine words, but they mean nothing out here.'

'That is barbaric. *You* are barbaric,' she told him, hurling the words at him as her shocked emotions burst through the frail barriers of her self-control.

'This isn't Europe…and it isn't Zuran either,' he answered her. 'The desert is a harsh master and those who inhabit it live by its harsh law—or die.'

There was something about the words he had chosen, the way he was looking at her that sent a curl of icy fear chasing over her nerve endings. Suddenly all the fears and the suspicions she had tried to ignore overwhelmed her.

'What are you all doing out here? What is going on?' she demanded, beginning to panic. 'You are planning something, I know, and I know too that it must be something truly dreadful.' The words were pouring from her in a feverish stream as she finally succumbed to the trauma of everything she had undergone.

'Silence!'

The savage command, accompanied by an even more savage shake, made her tremble from head to foot—with anger and not fear, Katrina decided as she glared furiously at him.

'If you value your life you will not repeat those words!' Xander warned her grimly.

Katrina caught her bottom lip between her teeth as she fought to stop her mouth from trembling. 'If I agree to go through with this…this marriage, I shall want your assurance that it will not be a real marriage!'

'What do you mean by a ''real'' marriage? In the eyes of El Khalid and his followers it will most certainly be real. Or are you asking me if I intend to take you to my bed as tradition says every bridegroom has a right to do with his bride? Even if I did, I wouldn't be able to provide evidence that you came to me with your virtue intact by producing a bloodstained sheet for the tribe's inspection, would I?'

'That was not what I meant!' Katrina could feel her face burning and she was glad of the darkness to conceal her reaction from him.

'I…what I meant… What I wanted was to be assured that the marriage will not be truly legal.'

There was the briefest of pauses before he answered her, but in her anxiety Katrina was unaware of it. 'It will certainly not be legal under European law, or international law,' he told her.

It was the answer she had been hoping for, and she exhaled shakily. She might not want to be forced into this marriage; her pride might rebel in outrage and disgust at Xander's cynical observations and references to her as a possession to be bought and sold, but logically she knew being with him was infinitely preferable to being handed over to Sulimen. But how did she feel emotionally about the situation she was in? That was a question she just did not want to answer. From the first moment she had seen him, her reaction to Xander had been illogical and far too immediate and intense for her to be comfortable with. The harsh flames of reality and everything she had learned about him and his way of life since then should have burnt those foolish tendrils of female longing and desire to ash—she knew that. So why hadn't they? Why couldn't she look at him and see, not a dangerously sensual man whose powerful physical presence affected her like no other man ever had, but a liar and a thief, a man totally devoid of anything in his make-up that could command her respect? Or her love!

A fierce thrill of pain shocked through her. She did not love him! But you want him, an inner voice insisted sharply. You desire him…you ache for him, and if he…

No! No, she was not going to think about this. She was not going to acknowledge it, nor admit to it, and she certainly wasn't going to think about it. She certainly wasn't going to think about the intimacies of marriage to Xander, of being his wife. Of the dark, velvet silence of the desert night and the feel of his hands on her eager body as he reached for her. She wasn't going to think either about the satin heat of his naked body, or the pleasure it would give her to touch his skin, to breathe in its scent, to place her lips against the solid strength of his chest and to… She gave a small violent shudder of rejection and self-disgust. She wasn't going to think about those things because none of them were going to happen!

She could not…would not allow herself to feel this way about a man like Xander. How could she respect herself if she did? How could there be true love without respect? There couldn't!

Grimly Xander stood in the open entrance to his tent and stared unseeingly into the darkness that lay beyond it. He was waiting for Katrina to join him so that they could present themselves before El Khalid and declare their desire to be married to one another. He might have allowed Katrina to believe that their marriage would not be legally binding, but he was well aware that within Zuran such a traditional form

of marriage was normally perfectly acceptable and ir-
revocable. In their case, though, the marriage would
have to be formally and legally set aside once his
business here was finished. As a member of the ruling
family, he needed his half-brother's approval before
marrying, and he was confident that his half-brother
would be willing to expedite a swift ending of their
union. His half-brother would understand that he'd
had no option other than to give Katrina the protection of making her his wife. No matter what her lifestyle had been, he could not allow her to be subjected
to the fate Sulimen had in store for her. It was no
secret around the campfires that amongst his other
crimes Sulimen had been accused of both raping and
beating at least two women, and that he possessed a
streak of sexual carnality and sadism.

None of this, though, was information he could
give Katrina.

Earlier in the day he had managed to have a brief
secret meeting with the three special agents appointed
by the Zuranese Ruling Council who had also infil-
trated El Khalid's forces. Like him, they had heard of
the important personage with whom El Khalid was
expecting to do business, but also like him they had
not been able to discover when he would be arriving.

Xander suspected that they were not as fully convinced of the danger to Zuran's ruler as he was himself. He had also heard from his half-brother that
Nazir had left Zuran supposedly to deal with his business affairs in Europe.

He heard a small sound behind him and turned
round. Katrina was standing hesitantly in the shadows
of the tent's living area, her eyes huge and dark with

apprehension. His mouth hardened. She was a complication he just did not need!

'A word of warning,' he said grimly as he stepped back inside the tent. 'Once we are married, you cannot do anything that might attract the attentions of other men.'

Katrina glared angrily at him. She had spent the last half an hour wondering how on earth she was going to go through with what lay ahead of her, and trying to fight back her feelings of despair and loneliness. This was not the way she had envisaged herself being married! She ached for the lost protection and love of her patents, for someone of her own she could turn to. But of course there was no one. She was completely alone. Alone and a prisoner, forced into a degrading sham of a marriage for reasons that had nothing whatsoever to do with love.

'How dare you say that to me?' she protested emotionally. 'It's not my fault that Sulimen—'

'No?' The slanting look he was giving her was not a kind one.

'If I had wanted him I would not be here, would I?' she challenged him fiercely.

'I did not say that you wanted him. But maybe you did encourage him? Maybe you were missing the attentions of your lover? Or maybe—'

Katrina curled her fingers into the palms of her hands, her nails digging into her own tender flesh as she seethed with fury. 'I did not encourage him, and Richard was not my lover!'

'That's an easy denial to make, and of course one that cannot be proved!' That was where he was wrong, but Katrina was not going to tell him as much.

As yet no man had been her lover—but of course she was not going to do any such thing!

When she committed herself to a man, and to her love for him and his for her, that commitment would be for ever, and it would involve far more than mere physical intimacy. She had her dreams, even if by some other people's standards they were too idealistic.

'It's time for us to go.'

Xander was holding the curtain aside for her, the tawny gaze fixed on her like a falcon's on its prey.

He was wearing his Tuareg headdress, but instinctively she knew that his mouth would be curved into a hard scimitar-sharp line of disdain and irritation. For all that she had tried to deny it, she was sharply aware that he carried with him a very powerful aura of command and authority. And never more so than tonight.

She had no idea where the richly embroidered overcloak he was wearing had come from—to judge from its richness it must have once been the property of some very wealthy man. A part of her tried to insist that he should look ridiculous dressed in such theatrical clothes, but another, stronger part of her couldn't help responding to what she could see.

Though she knew he was not, he looked like a man of nobility and power and tradition, a man as forbidding and compelling as the desert itself; a man apart, whose mere presence sent the same shiver of intense reaction whispering over her skin as the awe-inspiring might of this land, which was named so eloquently. He was a man other men would instinctively respect, and whom other women would immediately desire.

As she did?

So much so that she was afraid even to admit to

herself that she was aware of it, never mind accepting the strength of her feelings for him!

Proudly she stood as tall as she could, and looked back at him. 'If you're expecting me to walk mutely several paces behind you—' she began.

'I thought you said you'd studied the history of the desert tribes?' he stopped her immediately.

'I have,' Katrina agreed.

'Well, in that case you should know that Tuareg society is a matriarchal society.'

'But you aren't really Tuareg, are you?' was all she could manage to say as she walked reluctantly to his side.

As they walked a young boy suddenly ran up to Xander's side, and to Katrina's astonishment Xander immediately smiled down at him, putting his hand on the boy's head in a gesture that was almost tender, before saying something to him in a dialect Katrina could not understand.

'He's an orphan,' he explained to her as the boy darted away again. 'I pay him to keep an eye on my horse. The animal is used to company and the boy needs a warm bed.'

Emotions Katrina did not want to feel clogged her throat. For all the harshness he displayed, there was obviously a compassionate, caring side to him.

There was already a distinct chill to the evening air, although whether it was that or her own nervousness that was causing a rash of goose-bumps to break out on her flesh, Katrina didn't want to investigate too thoroughly.

The smell of roasting lamb from the campfires wafted towards them, making her feel slightly sick, her stomach rebelling at the thought of food. By the time they had reached the clearing where El Khalid held his nightly meetings, there was a small crowd waiting to watch the wedding. She could hear music playing, and women singing.

When she turned apprehensively to look over her shoulder towards them, Xander told her quietly, 'They will have heard about our marriage and will have come as is customary to witness it. The music is a traditional wedding song. There is no need for you to be afraid.'

He was offering her reassurance? Once again she had to swallow against an unwanted lump of emotion.

El Khalid was already seated on his makeshift divan, his henchmen surrounding him, the women of his family grouped behind him along with the musicians.

Katrina froze. She couldn't do it. She couldn't go through with it. Panic seized her, and she made a small, inarticulate noise of despair, her gaze darting frantically around the circle of onlookers surrounding them as she looked for a way to escape. She was quivering from head to foot with fear.

'Remember it isn't a real marriage! It doesn't mean anything!'

The cool, calming words fell against her raw nerve endings like a soothing balm on burning flesh.

Xander's hand clasped hers, holding it gently, almost as though he was trying to comfort and reassure her. Wide-eyed, she looked up at him.

The music had stopped. El Khalid was beckoning them forward. Xander's fingers entwined with her own. Shakily she started to move forward with him, not following behind him, but walking at his side.

They had reached the rebel leader. Xander released

her hand and immediately she ached to have him holding it again and for the comfort of that physical contact with him.

Everything that had happened to her was so alien to her, and somehow he had become the only thing that made the brutal nightmare bearable. Without him... Without him she would have been subjected to Sulimen's unchecked demands, without him...

Instinctively she moved closer to him, somehow comforted just by being within the warmth given off by his body, as though it were some kind of magic circle that enfolded and protected her. Just as love was a magic circle that protected and enfolded those who shared it?

Frantically she dragged her thoughts away from such a dangerous road, concentrating instead on El Khalid.

'Give me your hand,' he instructed Katrina.

Reluctantly she did so. Unlike Xander's, his nails were dirty and unkempt, the cuticles bitten and ragged.

'And yours,' he told Xander.

Katrina quivered as Xander placed his lean brown hand over her own and it was clasped and held there by El Khalid.

'Is it the wish of both of you that you should be married?'

Katrina knew the ceremony meant nothing and that it was simply a means to an end, but somehow she discovered that she was affected by it—which was ridiculous. El Khalid was not a man of religion; he was a thief and heaven alone knew what else, and this was just a charade. Nothing more.

'Yes. That is our wish,' she heard Xander saying.

El Khalid was looking at her. Bowing her head, Katrina whispered shakily, 'Yes.'

'Very well, then! As is our custom, it is my right to give this woman to you in marriage, Tuareg.'

Katrina's eyes widened a little with apprehension. El Khalid sounded so solemn.

'Take the woman's hand, Tuareg,' the rebel leader commanded.

Her throat had gone dry and her heart was thudding heavily against her chest wall. Xander was reaching out for her hand, sliding cool, hard fingers between her own, locking her hand to his.

The intimacy of their entwined fingers made her catch her breath, aware of the emotional and sexual significance of their interlocked flesh. Some things needed no words. Palm to palm, flesh to flesh, naked body to naked body, his fingers lying between hers, possessing hers. No wonder an old-fashioned word for marriage was 'hand-fast'.

Her body shuddered and her head seethed with turbulent and frightening thoughts.

El Khalid uttered a sharp command, and a woman, heavily veiled with only her bright dark eyes visible, stepped forward holding a length of silk fabric, so fine that it fluttered in the soft breeze.

Taking it from her, El Khalid started to bind it around both their wrists, muttering some words in Zuranese as he did so. Nervously Katrina risked looking up into Xander's face and then wished she had not done so as she witnessed the grimness of his closed, severe expression.

Her heart was beating slowly and heavily. It felt as though the life force of Xander's blood pulsing through his veins was actually driving her blood through her body as her own pulse matched and echoed the fierce beat of his. The intimate, intense symbolism of what was happening was way, way too much for her to cope with, Katrina recognised emotionally as she felt tears sting the backs of her eyes and her heart lurch against her ribs.

Xander had said that their 'marriage' meant nothing, and maybe it didn't to him, but for her the symbolism of what was happening was a very big 'something' indeed!

Whilst she was still grappling with her feelings, El Khalid spoke some more words over the binding, and then El Khalid turned to Xander and told him, 'You have taken this woman to you as your wife, Tuareg. From now on where you go, she goes. May you be blessed with a long and happy marriage and many children!'

The woman was removing the scarf. Slowly Xander released her hand. Katrina could feel the unsteady, frantic thud of the blood in her veins. The musicians had started to play again. Helplessly she looked into the glinting gold of Xander's eyes. Far from being meaningless, as she had expected, the ceremony had made her feel that they were now joined together in a way that was primitive and eternal. That knowledge filled her with something akin to shocked awe. No matter how many miles might lie between them in the future, nothing ever could or ever would erase what had just happened. How could Xander be so calm about something that to her felt so irreversible?

Logically Katrina knew that other people might think she was overreacting—after all, there was no legal tie between them—but she couldn't help the way she felt about the ceremony they had just undergone. Her hand, her flesh, her very self would bear the imprint of him and their marriage for ever! Shockingly, she felt as though they had shared an intimacy as great as though he had possessed her physically!

The crowd had parted to make a pathway for them. Numbly Katrina let Xander lead her down it whilst the watching men sang and cheered. 'If you're going to faint, at least wait until we get back to the tent,' she heard him say warningly.

CHAPTER FIVE

'WHY didn't you tell me...warn me about...what was going to happen?' Katrina demanded huskily as soon as she knew they could not be overheard.

At her side she felt Xander shrug. 'The binding of our wrists? For the simple reason that I didn't realise that it was going to happen,' he answered her dismissively. 'It's a very old custom, and seldom used any more.'

'Why did they do it that way, then?' she persisted.

'El Khalid's word is law here, not mine,' he pointed out dryly as he started to unwind his headdress. 'Besides. It was hardly important...'

Xander kept his back to her as he spoke, not wanting her to guess that he too had been strongly affected by the ceremony. By being bound together as they had been, they were now tied to one another in a way that had its roots deep in the tradition of his tribe. He started to frown, not wanting to dwell on the surge of primitive male possessiveness that had filled him.

He could not afford to dwell on such feelings and he certainly could not afford to allow them—or Katrina herself—to become important to him. Immediately he frowned. 'It is a Berber custom, that is all. Don't make too much of it.'

He could see how shocked and distressed she was, and the truth was that he felt equally affected by what had happened himself, but of course he could not afford to let her see that.

'There is no need for us to discuss the subject any further,' he told her, feigning a dismissiveness he was far from feeling, before looking thoughtfully towards the exit. It could well be that Nazir might decide to visit El Khalid tonight, and if he did, then Xander needed to be aware of it.

'I suggest that you retire to the sleeping quarters,' he told Katrina, peremptorily.

Her eyes widened as she listened to him. They hadn't been married more than a handful of minutes and already he was behaving as though she were his to order about as he wished. As though... A hotly dangerous trickle of sensual awareness spread through her. This was her wedding night and if Xander chose...to lay claim to his rights as her husband physically, she would not be able to stop him. The only weapon she had was words.

'This is not a real marriage,' she reminded him. 'You can't tell me what to do.'

'Not as a husband,' he agreed grimly. 'But you appear to be forgetting that I am your captor as well as your husband; you are in my power and you are my possession—to do with as I choose! You will go to the sleeping quarters and you will remain there!'

For what purpose, Katrina wondered feverishly as he stood, arms folded, in front of her, silently waiting for her to obey him.

To be used as though she were a concubine? Her imagination was proving to be her worst enemy, she acknowledged as he turned away from her. But Katrina wasn't ready for their conversation to end.

It was in her nature to want to think the best of everyone, she tried to reassure herself. And that was the reason she wanted Xander to prove to her that he had some redeeming qualities. For his sake or for her own? Because of her inability to deny the attraction she felt towards him, the desire she felt for him? She must not allow such thoughts to take root, she warned herself. And besides, any attraction she might think she felt for Xander now would soon disappear once she was free and living her normal life. Even so, somehow she could not prevent herself from asking him.

'Why did you marry me? Was it because of the ransom money you hope to get for me or was it really because you wanted to protect me? To save me from Sulimen?'

She saw the liquid flash of his darkly intent gaze as he turned his head to look at her. She felt as though it were burning into her, seeking out all those things she most wanted to keep secret. For a man who earned his living in such a shameful manner he possessed a proud arrogance that should have been risible, but which instead suited him perfectly, she acknowledged unwillingly.

It was very, very rare for anything or anyone to catch him off guard, but Katrina had done exactly that, Xander admitted grimly. It was almost as though she was actually looking for a reason to think better of him, he recognised incredulously.

An austere look darkened his face. Had she somehow seen through his camouflage and the subterfuge he had been forced to adopt, to the person he really was? Could she sense his vulnerability where she was concerned? Could she feel it in the tense air between them? The hard heat of his desire for her, and the struggle he was having in fighting against it? The fierce longing he felt to take her in his arms and make the vows they had just exchanged a reality?

He had actually taken steps towards her before he managed to remind himself of the real situation. She was a modern young woman who was no doubt used to using her sexuality to get what she wanted, if she chose to do so.

'What are you hoping I will say? That I married you to save you? Are you hoping that I might be vulnerable to you myself and that you could use that against me in some way? Perhaps seduce me into giving you your freedom?' he taunted her silkily, whilst Katrina's face burned a dark, hot red.

'I might have known you would think something like that!' she retorted bitterly. 'That Machiavellian mind of yours wouldn't allow you to think anything else, would it?'

'What else is there to think?' Xander retaliated grimly.

'For your information, I was hoping that I might have found something in you that I could respect!' Katrina told him shakily. 'Some saving grace that would mean—'

'That you could manipulate me at will,' Xander stopped her curtly.

She was touching a place in his emotions he didn't want to have touched by anyone, but least of all by her. Her words came far too close to his own private thoughts on the subject of love and marriage. According to his half-brother, his mother and father had loved one another very deeply. Certainly enough for them both to step outside the familiar boundaries of their own cultures in order to be together. Such a love cast a very long shadow and he knew that he wanted a union as strong as that. But his pride was fiercely strong. He could never, ever love a woman he did not respect. And growing up in his father's culture had ensured that he could not respect a woman who was sexually or indeed emotionally promiscuous.

For any woman, but even more a woman such as Katrina, to dare to accuse him of not being worthy of her respect irked and infuriated him. For such an insult she would have to be punished!

'I'm not your foolish, weak, easy-to-seduce English lover,' he said contemptuously. 'He might be easily bedazzled by the fake glitter of the tawdry goods you have on sale and unable to see that they and you have no true worth, but I am not so easily pleased or deceived.'

Katrina's mouth had gone very dry. Her whole body was feeling the impact of the insult he had just delivered and its thinly veiled implications regarding her sexual morals.

'You have no right to say such things to me,' was all she could manage to say as she somehow managed to choke out the words above the brittle fragility of her emotional defences.

He knew how to hurt, and how to wound and maim. Katrina couldn't imagine that any woman would want to be forced to listen to a man speaking about her in such a way.

'And in case you've forgotten, Richard was not my lover!' she told him fiercely.

Xander gave a dismissive shrug. 'I have no interest in who has or has not shared your bed and your favours.'

He was lying and he knew it, but what else could

he do? He had to finish this conversation and find out if Nazir had arrived, for his half-brother's sake.

'I have to go out,' he announced tersely. 'And don't wait for me so that you can try and persuade me again. My advice to you is not to bother wasting your time.'

He gave her a look that stripped her pride to the bone and left it and her mercilessly exposed.

There were so many angry words she wanted to hurl at him, but it was already too late. His hand was already lifting the heavy curtain, and he was stepping through it, leaving her alone to confront the unpalatable reality behind her angry reaction to their conversation.

No matter how hard she fought to ignore it, the word 'seduce' hung dangerously in her thoughts. He might have been wrong about there being any intention on her part to seduce him, but that word on his lips had caused her stomach to clench and her heart to flip over whilst her legs had turned weak and the slow ache of longing pulsing deep inside her had flared into a hungry, driving beat.

No, she did not want to seduce him, but shamingly she acknowledged that she could not say the same in reverse. What on earth was the matter with her? He was a criminal, callous, arrogant and dishonest. There was not one single redeeming thing about him. And she was a fool for trying to find something in him she could respect, some excuse for him she could use to justify her feelings for him.

It was not even as though he had done or said anything to make her think he shared her confusing and disturbing feelings in any kind of way—quite the opposite. Her whole body burned with indignation as she remembered the contemptuous way in which he had spoken to her. He was not just unprincipled and untrustworthy, he was bigoted as well! It would have given her a great deal of pleasure to have thrown his words back at him and told him that she had not in fact had any lovers, never mind the scores he had chosen to imply, but of course that was something she could and would not do. Her virginity was a lifestyle choice she had made because of her own profound and private beliefs and not so that she could demean herself by claiming it in front of someone like Xander.

He simply wasn't worthy of the foolish feelings she was silly enough to have for him, and for her own sake she had to root them out of her heart immediately. If only it were that easy. She gave a small shiver. There was something dark and dangerous about him, something raw and untamed that the female core of her responded to wantonly and rebelliously, and there was nothing she could do about it, she admitted despairingly.

As he made his way silently through the camp, his movements as fluid and as soft-footed as a mountain lion, Xander derided himself grimly for the fierce surge of male hunger Katrina had made him feel. His mind might question how he could possibly want such a woman, but his body was questioning even more fiercely how he could resist her.

She affected him as no other woman had ever done, in a thousand and one different ways, every single one of which was unwelcome. There was no place in his life for this kind of situation and no place in his pride for the kind of need she aroused in him.

As he neared El Khalid's tent he forced himself to put Katrina out of his mind and to focus instead on his half-cousin Nazir, and the reason he himself was here. He'd been wondering whether he'd made a dangerous error of judgement. The special agents were doubtful about Nazir's involvement. But Nazir was planning to strike against the Ruler, Xander was convinced of that. It was just a question of how and when.

He had reached El Khalid's tent, and he kept himself concealed in the shadows. A small frown creased his forehead beneath his disguise as he heard the sound of a moving vehicle. A smart four-wheel-drive vehicle swept in from the desert, creating its own personal sandstorm, the vehicle skidding to a sharp halt within a short walk from the rebel leader's group of tents. Xander could hardly believe his own luck as he watched the doors open and two heavily armed guards get out, quickly followed by his half-cousin.

Before they could reach El Khalid's tent the rebel leader himself emerged from it, coming forward to greet Nazir, bowing low in front of him before inviting him into the tent.

So he'd been right after all! This was something the special agents needed to know about, Xander acknowledged, and now! Quietly he began to make his way to their tent.

CHAPTER SIX

KATRINA woke abruptly from the wantonly erotic and symbolic dream she'd been having, in which she had been carried in the folds of a richly hued carpet into the tent of a powerful warrior who'd borne a heart-shaking resemblance to Xander—in the same way that Cleopatra had offered herself to Anthony.

Her face burned as she tried to ignore the sensuality of her dream and the manner in which she had presented herself to Xander, her body clad in diaphanous rainbow-coloured veils so sheer that her body had been openly visible through them. Her nipples had been painted with a soft gold paste, her sex lightly covered in a sheath of the transparent silk that had done far more to enhance its mystery than modestly protect it.

As she had advanced towards Xander her kohl-painted eyes had seen how he had tried not to show any interest in her, and her pink-stained mouth had parted on a small female breath of wanton knowingness when her gaze had slid from his face to his manhood, which had been openly straining against the cloth that had constrained it as his body had given her female power that his facial expression would not.

Her tongue had pressed against her parted lips whilst she had boldly moved closer to him, her whole body heavy with sweet, hot desire for him, and ready for the promise held by the swollen flesh of his manhood.

Not one single word had he spoken to her as she'd reached the raised dais on which he'd been seated, but she had witnessed his swiftly indrawn breath as she'd mounted it without asking his permission. She'd walked proudly towards him instead of humbly awaiting his permission to draw closer to him.

Only once she had reached him had she dropped gracefully to her knees in front of him, the high, taut thrust of her gilded breasts swelling eagerly beneath his hooded gaze as they'd flaunted their eager desire for his touch.

Slowly and deliberately she had reached out towards him, placing her fingertips on his thigh, only a breath away from the thick outline of his penis. When she had exhaled in heady excitement and arousal, she had felt the outer lips of her own sex swell and the small secret place of pleasure within them throb eagerly.

She had lifted her hand to close it over his hardness, but before she had been able to do so he had reached for her, dragging her onto his lap, and holding her there whilst his mouth had fastened fiercely on one gilt-tipped nipple, his tongue tip playing with its quivering hardness whilst his hand had opened her thighs, and pushed away the shimmering veils of silk, so that the eager wetness of her sex had been fully open to his touch.

Her small cry of wanton pleasure had elicited from him an immediate response of triumphant reaction.

Long, deft fingers had parted the enclosing folds of flesh, and when her body had jerked against his touch in mute, hot, sensual delight, his mouth had tugged fiercely on her sensitised nipple so that she had been burning with aching need for him.

His fingers had moved more intimately on her, first one and then another erotically rubbing against the wetness and then probing the innermost heart of her. When she had cried out to him in sweet, hot, eager need, he had spread her thighs wider and taken her mouth in a savagely passionate kiss that had stolen her breath, and with it her reason. The stroking caress of his fingertip against the small, secret nub of flesh that had swelled for his touch had caused her whole body to tighten on the edge of shockingly intense pleasure. She had felt the waves of it radiating out and she had lifted her body against it, wanting more of it, and of him!

She didn't want to remember any more, especially not the very real sensation of being poised on the edge of her own orgasm. Shamefully she still ached with the physical arousal her dream had caused, Katrina recognised, mortified that she should have had such a dream at all, never mind about Xander. She was grateful for her solitude and for the darkness that hid the hot burn of her face. And the hot burn of her body?

She lay rigidly still in the darkness almost afraid to let herself go back to sleep.

In another three hours or so it would be dawn. Xander stood completely still in the silence of the tent. The special agents had agreed that as soon as El Khalid had announced the purpose of Nazir's visit to the men he had gathered around him, they would leave the camp and report their findings to the Ruling Council.

Xander's mouth compressed. He had urged them not to delay, but they had remained adamant. They were not prepared to recommend a move against

Nazir until they had unassailable proof that he meant to harm Zuran's Ruler.

From inside the sleeping area of the tent he could hear the soft little sound Katrina made in her sleep. Katrina... His wife... But another man's woman? Probably more than just one other man's woman! A primitive, all-male feeling of mingled anger and jealousy ripped through him. He took a step towards the sleeping area, and then froze. What he was feeling was merely a shimmering mirage, he told himself fiercely. It had no reality to it, and if he ignored it and refused to acknowledge it or give it room in his heart or head then it would disappear. And so too would the urgent, hungry stirring of his body.

Katrina woke up briefly and muzzily at the sound of the morning calls to prayer, but the events of the previous day had taken their toll, and sleep was claiming her again before she could stop it.

Xander on the other hand was already awake, tension coiling his body like a tightly wound spring. As soon as the call to morning prayers had died away, news swept through the camp, like dust carried on the desert wind, that El Khalid had had an important visitor. An immediate meeting had been called to discuss his visit with his men.

Like the other men, Xander made his way to the open area in front of El Khalid's tent, taking care to position himself close to the three disguised special agents, but not directly with them. He was pretty sure that at least two of the men now stationed outside El Khalid's tent were in reality Nazir's personal guards and he suspected they would have been instructed to report back to their master if they saw anything they considered suspicious or not in Nazir's best interests.

El Khalid's speech to them was brief and to the point. He and his men were being hired to infiltrate the National Day celebrations in Zuran and cause civil unrest.

'No mention was made of any attempt to harm your brother,' one of the agents pointed out sharply to Xander when the meeting was over.

'Nazir will not entrust anyone else to assassinate my brother. He will kill him himself under cover of the rioting El Khalid will cause. Officially he will be out of the country, we already know this. There is no doubt in my mind that this is what he plans to do,' Xander told the agents grimly. 'My guess is that he will disguise himself as one of El Khalid's men, and strike when my brother makes his traditional walk amongst his people.'

'We have no proof that this is what he plans to do,' one of the agents objected.

'Are you prepared to take the risk that I am wrong?' Xander challenged him. 'The life of the Ruler is more important.'

There was a small silence and then another member of the trio said firmly, 'We are leaving now to make our report. As soon as we are out of radio range from the camp we shall phone for a helicopter to pick us up. Our report will be delivered to the Ruling Council within a matter of hours. We shall recommend that an armed force be dispatched here to this camp immediately to surround it and take everyone here into custody. If you are correct then that will surely include Nazir.'

Xander knew that this was as much as he could

hope for, and that it was as pointless chivvying the agents as it was to beg his half-brother to think of his own safety and to cancel his traditional public walk-about on Zuran's National Day.

The sun was warming the desert as he strode back through the camp, the smell of cooking food filling the air.

It was the scent of freshly brewing coffee that woke Katrina from her heavy sleep. For a few precious seconds between waking and remembering she basked lazily in the comfort of her bed and the delicious coffee smell, and then abruptly reality returned with menacing darkness.

She was not just a prisoner; she was also now married to her captor! She looked down at her wrist. She was bound now to Xander. She sat up in the bed, feeling slightly sick and dizzy.

As always she listened edgily for any sounds that would indicate where Xander was before sliding out of the bed and hurrying into the small bathroom. Once there she showered quickly, her face suddenly suffused with hot colour as she felt the unfamiliar sensitivity of her breasts when she soaped her skin. Last night might only have been a dream but it had still left as much of an actual physical memory with her body as if Xander had really made love to her.

It was a relief to dry herself and pull on her clothes so that she no longer had to see the openly eager, swollen thrust of her own nipples.

Two minutes later she was standing beside the curtain that separated the areas of the tent from one another. Taking a deep breath, she exhaled slowly whilst reminding herself of just what Xander was. He was not the man her vulnerable heart longed for him to be. Far from it. That man was simply a creation of her own foolish emotions.

Determinedly she pulled back the curtain and stepped into the outer area. Xander was standing several feet away watching her. A bloom of delicate pink colour washed tellingly over her face as she battled to meet his gaze and failed.

This man was her husband; she was joined to him now and that joining was surely in its own way just as intimate as if he had taken her in his arms last night and to his bed. A tremor like that of a young gazelle shivered through her.

Watching her, Xander acknowledged grimly that the blush staining her skin and her modestly downcast look were everything that an old-fashioned husband might expect from a new bride on the first morning of her marriage. And no doubt had they been such a couple, having witnessed her self-conscious modesty he would have gone immediately to her and swept her into his arms, taking her back to the bed they had so recently shared to show her fresh delights and pleasures.

But of course they were no such thing.

Whilst he removed the long scarf of indigo-coloured cloth that acted both as his means of disguise and proclaimed him as Tuareg, a bitter, almost cruel smile hardened his mouth. Katrina was as far removed from an innocent shy bride as it was possible to get. How many other lovers had there been before the cowardly fool who had abandoned her in order to save himself? He could feel his ancestry and upbringing battling against the European blood of his mother.

How could he ever hope to find a woman who

could both accept and understand both opposing sides of him, and at the same time appeal to both of them in a way that made him feel he needed and loved her so much that he could not bear to live without her?

How indeed! He already knew that he could not. And right now he was more than happy to live his life without a woman. After all he had far more important things to worry about.

'There was a lot of noise and excitement a little while ago,' Katrina announced, bravely trying to act as though everything was normal, and not in any way as though she was acutely conscious of the fact that last night they had been married and she was now in the eyes of those who had witnessed that marriage Xander's wife, but also his possession!

'No more than normal,' Xander lied coolly, before adding tauntingly, 'What were you hoping? That your lover had come to rescue you?'

Angry colour flamed up under her skin. 'I was simply trying to make conversation,' she informed him sharply.

'I've brought you this,' Xander said, ignoring both her comment and her anger as he produced one of the all-enveloping black garments worn by women in public.

'In future you will not leave the tent unless you are wearing it.'

Katrina's eyes rounded both with shock and disbelief.

'I will do no such thing!' she refused immediately.

'You will not leave this tent unless you are wearing the robes,' Xander repeated before adding ominously, 'And if you do not agree to do so, then you will leave me with no choice other than to take steps to ensure your compliance.'

'By doing what?' Katrina challenged him fiercely. 'By dressing me in it yourself?'

'No,' he answered her evenly. 'If you do not agree, then I shall simply make sure that you are not able to leave the tent. If necessary by tethering you inside it in the same way that a goat herder might fetter his goats.'

Katrina could hardly believe her ears as she recoiled from the primitiveness of his threat.

She couldn't trust herself to speak, so instead she let her body language voice her outrage and fury to him as she looked coldly past him.

'It is time for us to eat. Pick it up and put it on,' Xander ordered her calmly.

'I will not wear it,' she told him stubbornly. 'It smells of another woman's perfume,' she added angrily.

Xander made no response. He'd had to haggle hard and pay way over what it was worth in order to persuade one of El Khalid's women to part with the garment. His own keen nose acknowledged that the heaviness of the other woman's perfume did cling to the fabric, but he had to make sure that Katrina took his threat seriously—for her own sake as much as anything else. If Nazir was going to return to the camp as Xander suspected he would, then he did not want his half-cousin to see Katrina and wonder suspiciously what a European woman was doing here. If he thought that Katrina posed the slightest degree of risk to him, Nazir would kill her, without any qualms whatsoever. Xander had no doubt about that, and so for her own sake she had to be protected. As the wife of a Tuareg tribesman wearing the robes she would not arouse Nazir's suspicions in the way a European woman would.

'You must wear it for your own safety,' he told her quietly.

The unexpectedness of something that could almost have been genuine concern for her in his voice caught and held Katrina's attention. Was there a warmer, caring side to his nature after all?

'Because of Sulimen?' she guessed, unable to hide her fear.

Immediately Xander took a step towards her, as though he wanted to reassure her. 'Have no fear, he shall not harm you. I shall see to that, but it will be expected by the women that you will dress as they do and by the men that you dress as my wife. Truly it is for your own protection that you must dress traditionally.'

Instinctively she knew that he was speaking the truth. Yet again, she could feel herself reacting to his compassion. And to him! More to give herself something to do than for any other reason, she picked up the black garment and pulled it on, grimacing a little as she did so, unable to stop herself from wrinkling her nose against its strong scent.

Quickly Xander shielded his eyes from her, not wanting her to read in his expression how relieved he was not to be tormented by the subtle natural scent of her own body and the far too powerful and dangerous effect it had on him whenever he was close enough to her to breathe it in.

It took Katrina several minutes to settle the all-encompassing folds of the robes—made quite obviously for someone much larger than she was herself—

comfortably around her own slender person. During which time, Xander strode past her and into the bedroom, emerging almost immediately carrying a sheet.

Uncomprehendingly Katrina watched as he unfolded it, and then deliberately squeezed it in his powerful hands to crumple it a little before unsheathing his dagger, pushing up the sleeve of his robe and making a small cut on the inside of his arm, which immediately began to bleed.

Balling up the centre of the sheet, he held it against the cut.

'What are you doing?' she asked him in bewilderment.

'As El Khalid's mother reminded me when I bartered with her cousin for the robe, it is a tribal custom amongst the nomad population that a blood-stained sheet is produced on the morning after a young woman is married as proof of her virginity. Your failure to be declared a virgin bride will dishonour both you as my wife and me as your husband.'

Katrina was outraged beyond words and could only stare at him in white-faced revulsion.

After what Xander had just told her, the last thing she felt able to do was to show herself in public!

'What is it?' Xander demanded as she stepped back from him and started to remove her enfolding black robes.

'I've decided that I'm not hungry,' she told him woodenly.

The look he was giving her smashed through her fragile self-control and before she could stop herself she was demanding emotionally, 'Do you really think I am going to let you parade me along with that sheet to satisfy other people's prurient curiosity?'

She could hear the threat of tears in her own voice and tried to fight them away, gulping in air as she did so. She would not, could not cry in front of him. How could she have thought him compassionate?

'You must not judge us as though we were Europeans. We are not. There is nothing prurient in this traditional act. Far from it. And it is designed to protect your sex, not to humiliate it.'

'How do you work that one out?' Katrina challenged him bitterly.

'Easily,' Xander told her coolly. 'For instance, the nomad tribes lived dangerous lives. Men fought and were often killed. If a man died, his family could refuse to accept his wife's child unless they had proof that she'd been a virgin when they'd married. Proof of a bride's virginity protects her honour, and the honour of her family. A Tuareg girl in your position would accompany her husband proudly to this showing of the proof of her virgin state.'

'Maybe, but I am not a Tuareg woman,' Katrina told him fiercely.

'You are not a virgin either,' Xander said coldly.

'Yes, I—' Katrina began heatedly.

She was silenced as Xander cut across her with a sharply curt, 'I am hungry even if you are not.' He started to rewind the covering Tuareg cloth around his head and lower face. He looked austere and compelling and her stupid heart was turning over as though it actually enjoyed the aura of subtle magnificence and danger he gave off. Pausing only to gather up the sheet, he cast her a brief hard look and headed for the exit.

She could not follow him. She just could not, Katrina admitted as she watched him leave.

CHAPTER SEVEN

HALF an hour later Katrina's stomach was growling hungrily, but she ignored the noise it was making.

'I've brought you some coffee and some food.'

Katrina whirled round and stared as Xander stepped back into the tent carrying a pot of coffee and a small dish piled high with fruit and small cakes. He had brought her some food? Confusion darkened her eyes. She had mentally labelled him as cruel and sadistic, but right now he was behaving with a thoughtfulness and concern that was proving her wrong. And not for the first time! These glimpses of another side of him both tormented and delighted her. It was as though somewhere deep inside her a small spring of happiness had welled up and was bubbling over.

'Luckily for you El Khalid's mother has decided that your refusal to show yourself this morning is a sign of your modesty.'

But he did not think she was modest! Her joyful happiness was extinguished by angry pain.

Xander was placing the coffee pot and the dish down on a low table and, despite the intensity of her feelings, Katrina realised how hungry she was.

'I have to go out—remember you are not to leave this tent unless you are properly robed and veiled.'

Katrina waited until he had gone before pouncing on the food. The coffee smelled heavenly and tasted even better, the fruit sharp and juicy on her taste buds, whilst the small, sweet almond pastries melted on her tongue.

As he busied himself checking on his horse Xander's mind was in reality far from totally focusing on the patient animal that was nuzzling his shoulder so affectionately.

Why had he allowed the thought of Katrina with another man to affect him so intensely? Why had he allowed himself to be so aroused by the sight of her that he had had to leave the tent in order to put a safe distance between them? Surely he was not fool enough to be affected by a centuries-old marriage ritual, was he? It had after all been nothing more than a necessity, the only way he'd had of protecting Katrina from Sulimen, and he had already made up his mind to ask his half-brother to have the marriage set aside.

Xander rubbed gently behind the mare's ears. She was pure Arab bloodstock and bred from one of his half-brother's prized stallions. Her wise dark eyes reflected her breeding and her purity.

Why had he allowed himself to be so affected by the dark smudges beneath Katrina's eyes this morning? Why had he wanted to go to her and kiss the soft tremble from her mouth? Such thoughts, such feelings were virtually akin to insanity. There was no place for them in his life.

Having checked on the mare, he walked as casually as he could in the direction of the oasis, sauntering easily as though merely passing the time. Whilst El Khalid might have cautioned his most trustworthy men to keep a watch on the rest of them, Nazir most undoubtedly would have left his own loyal spies behind to ensure his own safety.

Xander was tempted to telephone his half-brother. His mobile was in his pocket, but he was concerned that Nazir might be intercepting the Ruler's telephone calls, even though officially he was supposed to be out of the country.

Xander frowned as a small sound caught his attention. Shading his eyes, he stared towards the horizon, watching the small dot that was a low-flying helicopter grow larger.

Nazir! It had to be! And what better means of re-entering Zuran and then leaving the city quickly once he had achieved his goal and murdered the Ruler? Had Nazir told El Khalid what he intended to do? Somehow Xander doubted it. Not that the rebel leader would shrink from the violence of murder. No, he would not do that but he would certainly demand a great deal of money to be involved in it!

And besides Nazir was far too wily to give anyone the kind of information that could ever be used against him. No. The Ruler's death would publicly be attributed to the rebels, Xander acknowledged.

The helicopter, camouflage painted and without any identifying markings, was coming closer. Xander turned his back on it and pretended to be studying the oasis. There was no sense in drawing attention to himself by appearing to be too curious.

He wanted to be there, though, when the helicopter landed, so he started to make his way back to the camp.

As was only to be expected, the arrival of the helicopter was causing a flurry of curiosity and speculation, and Xander attached himself to the group of men standing closest to it.

A man was climbing out of the stationary aircraft

and, although he had disguised himself by growing a beard, and wearing traditional robes instead of the Western-style Italian suits he normally favoured, Xander had no trouble whatsoever in recognising his half-cousin simply from the way he moved.

So he had been right! Good as it felt to have his suspicions of Nazir confirmed, Xander's overriding emotion was one of anger against Nazir. He had received nothing but love and generosity from the Ruler, but his greed and lust for power were such that he was ready to murder him in order to step into his shoes. No way was Xander going to allow that to happen! He did feel happier now, though, knowing that he would be able to keep Nazir under closer observation.

El Khalid had come out of his tent to greet the new arrival, bowing low before him as he made him welcome. As casually as he could, Xander moved closer, trying to overhear what the two men were saying to one another.

It was over an hour since Xander had left, and Katrina had grown bored with sitting cooped up in the tent.

Defiantly she got up and walked determinedly towards the exit. There was no reason why she should allow him to tell her what to do. She wasn't really his wife, after all.

The thought of Xander, treating her as an equal, respecting her, loving her, was causing a surge of complex emotions within her that she knew she was not currently strong enough emotionally to handle.

And whilst she might not really be Xander's wife, she was his prisoner, she reminded herself.

How much was he planning to demand for her return? The government department for whom she worked was a small one, with very limited funds. Or was he thinking that she would have family who would be prepared to pay him for her release? One heard of such things, hostages being taken and then ransomed, but she had never envisaged such a fate befalling her!

She wished that she could be brave enough to try to escape, but the camp was heavily guarded. Even if she could evade those guards, she knew what would happen to her if she succeeded in getting away from the oasis. She would die in the desert.

Of course she could try to steal a vehicle, but it would have to be one with a modern satellite navigation system installed in it, she admitted wryly, plus a full tank of petrol.

It made much more sense to remain where she was.

Sense? That was what was motivating her, was it? Was she really sure about that? Was she totally sure that she was not being influenced by those dangerous emotions she knew she felt for Xander, and that she was not secretly longing for...? For what? she challenged herself angrily. Her face had grown hot. She could feel the now familiar and distinctive intimate ache seizing her body.

This was the twenty-first century; women no longer needed to hide the fact that they could experience physical desire as a need in itself and by itself. They no longer had to tell themselves that physical desire could only be born out of love. They had every right if they wished to do so to engage in physical intimacy without any emotional commitment, for the simple reason that it pleased them to do so. To be blunt about it, if they so desired, they could have sex with a man and then walk away from him. Could she do that? Did she really want to?

As she paced the carpeted floor of the tent, her mind on her own deep thoughts and not on what was underfoot, she stubbed her toe on the edge of a wooden box just protruding from beneath the low divan.

Frowning, she bent to rub her toe, and then kneeled down intending to push the box out of the way, but instead she discovered that she was actually tugging it out of its place of semi-concealment, panting a little as she did so because of its weight.

What was inside it? She had no right to look, she told herself, but despite that she still lifted the lid.

Inside the chest were several books. No wonder it had been heavy. Carefully she lifted the top one out, her breath catching on a small gasp as she did so. These weren't just books, they were works of art, books fit for the library of a connoisseur—a very wealthy connoisseur, leather-bound, and tooled, with thick gold lettering on the spine, the pages gold-edged. When it had been new, such a book would have been very expensive. Reverently Katrina opened it. A first edition. A collector's item, and probably extremely rare. It was a book of poetry, including amongst others Robert Browning's poems for Elizabeth Barrett. Inscribed inside it in elegant handwriting were the words:

'For my own beloved Elizabeth.'

Hot, emotional tears misted her eyes. Such simple words, but to her they were of more value than a thousand first editions. This book had been a gift of love; it had been given with love. Very gently she closed it, and put it down before removing another from the box.

This one was French—the belles-lettres of an author whose name she did not recognise, but like its fellow it was dedicated to 'Elizabeth'. And the strong male signature on it was set above the familiar crest of the Ruler of Zuran.

Her heart skipped a beat. That must surely mean that the books had come originally from the royal palace. And that Elizabeth, whoever she was, had been deeply loved by a royal prince.

She picked out another one—this time a book written in Arabic.

She didn't need to be an expert to guess that these books were worth a fortune and irreplaceable, Katrina acknowledged, but of far more value and importance in her eyes was not their material worth but the sentimental value demonstrated by the inscriptions. Those books had been a gift of love, to a woman very deeply loved.

Everything about them said that they had been cherished and treasured, but now they were in Xander's possession, and she was in no doubt as to how they had got there. They had been stolen from their rightful owner, Katrina acknowledged bleakly.

Although she wasn't cold, she shivered. Why was she feeling so shocked? She had already known what Xander was, hadn't she?

That incident in the alleyway, his cold-hearted avowal to ransom her; discovering that he possessed stolen goods should not be causing her the sick misery that it was. Slowly, her heart aching, she started to replace them in the box, pausing with the last one.

'What do you think you are doing?'

She hadn't heard Xander come in, and she jumped in shock, almost dropping the book as she heard the savage fury in his voice. She wasn't going to give into it, though—nor to him. Scrambling to her feet, she turned to confront him, but he was ignoring her, kneeling instead to examine the contents of the chest, before closing the lid and removing a small key from his belt, which he used to lock it.

'How dare you pry amongst my possessions?' he said savagely.

'Your possessions!' Katrina challenged him bravely. 'Those books do not belong to you. I saw the inscription. You stole them from someone!'

Xander could hardly believe what he was hearing. Katrina had been rifling through his personal possessions—the treasured mementoes he had of his parents—and she had the gall to accuse him of stealing them! In the intensity of his fury, Xander forgot all the reasons Katrina believed she had to question his honesty, and remembered only how protectively he had always cherished the books that had been his father's love gift to his mother before their marriage.

That feeling had meant so much to him as a small child, unable to articulate his feelings properly, only knowing that holding the books somehow made him feel as though he was clinging to a part of the mother he had never known. They had become his talisman and he never went anywhere without them. Were any of El Khalid's rebels to find them he would of course have to pretend he had stolen them, but it was an unwritten law amongst the rebels that they respected one another's privacy and possessions.

A law that was not observed by Katrina, though! And now here she was, the woman who had already caused him more sleepless nights and disturbed thoughts than she had any right to do, daring to claim that he had no right to his mother's possessions.

'The books are mine,' he told her fiercely, obvious anger darkening his eyes.

Katrina was in no mood to believe him, though. She gave him a look of contemptuous disbelief. 'That's impossible. They are worth a fortune—museum pieces, first editions,' she pointed out sharply.

Xander was standing up now, and far too close to her, towering over her, filling the air around her with his hostility. Too late she recognised exactly what effect her words were having on him and how furiously and dangerously angry he was. A small pulse was beating heavily in the hollow of his throat, and fury blazed from his eyes. Apprehensively she tried to move away, and started to step back from him, but her action simply brought her up against the hard edge of the divan.

'Do you actually dare to accuse me of being a liar?' he demanded with soft savagery as he stepped closer to her—so soft that the cold words were little more than the icy chill of breath against her skin.

Katrina was not going to allow herself to give in to him! Why should she?

'You are a liar!' she threw back at him recklessly. 'A liar and a thief!'

The fierily passionate words, the contempt he could hear in her voice and see in her eyes burnt Xander's pride as though it had been acid.

Katrina winced as he took hold of her upper arms, gripping them so tightly that it hurt.

'You will not say such things to me, do you hear me?' he thundered furiously.

'Why not? I am only speaking the truth!' Katrina retaliated, her own fury as great as his.

'Those books were a gift to me from my mother.' Xander couldn't hold back the words any longer. They felt as though they had been torn physically from his heart, and had left behind a place that burned with bitter pain.

Katrina stared at him, unable to credit what she was hearing. Did he really expect her to believe him?

She could almost taste the intensity of their emotions in the air surrounding them, bitter as aloes and sharp on her tongue.

She could feel the heat coming off Xander's body, and shockingly she could feel too her own immediate and undeniable female response to it—and to him. Panic twisted through her outrage. How could she feel like this? How could she be remotely aroused by a man she could not respect? She must not feel like this. She was having to fight to hold onto reality.

'That isn't possible.' She forced herself to make the denial, praying that he wouldn't see in her eyes how intensely she wished that it were and that he were not just telling her the truth, but also that he were finally admitting her into his confidence and allowing her to learn something about his true background.

But of course he was not! And knowing that was hurting her far, far more than she was able to cope with. She had to fight against the pain of her own emotions to make herself tell him quietly, 'The books bear the signature of the Ruler of Zuran.'

The words seemed to drop into the tense silence as heavily as stones in deep, still water. She couldn't bear to look at him. She couldn't bear to see in his eyes that he knew she could not be deceived. The tension in the room was such that it felt like an invisible pressure all around her, crushing her. She had to struggle to expand her lungs enough to draw in air.

'There's no point in continuing to lie to me, Xander,' she told him huskily. 'I can't believe you. You are a liar and a—'

The despairing resignation in her voice sliced into Xander's pride, and worse, he realised on a sharp, spearing pain of shock, her refusal to believe him was piercing him with searing emotional pain, like nothing he had previously experienced and which he just could not endure.

'Enough!' He groaned out the word as though he were dying, reaching for her, to silence both her and his own pain in the only way he could, with the hard pressure of his mouth on hers.

It was a kiss given in anger and in punishment, a deliberate branding of male domination, but the moment he felt her mouth beneath his something happened inside him that Xander knew he could neither resist nor control. Some alchemy over which he had no power transformed his anger into hunger, her punishment into his own as his senses ached with longing, overturning all the barriers he had so carefully erected against his own vulnerability towards her.

The softness of her mouth, the slight quiver of her body, the sweetness of her taste as his tongue drove possessively between her parted lips, sent desire leaping along his nerve endings, to every cell of his body.

He wanted her more than he had ever wanted anyone or anything… He wanted her…to taste her, hold her, possess her, lay his own mark upon her for the whole of eternity.

Thoughts, feelings...needs ran through him like quicksilver, and he was powerless to stop them, powerless to do anything other than respond to the driving need that possessed him. The driving need for him to possess her.

Katrina tried to stop what was happening, and to break free of the almost bruising pressure of his kiss and pull away from him, but her lips were clinging eagerly to his, parting hotly for the hard thrust of his tongue.

Sanity, logic, her normally alert sense of self-preservation had all somehow become subservient to the thrill of longing and excitement surging through her. Under her fingertips she could feel the crispness of his thick hair, the corded muscles of his neck and the warmth of his skin. He felt so male, and so dangerous. So why wasn't she pushing him away instead of burying her fingers in his hair and holding him closer whilst white-hot pleasure licked through her?

The bruising pressure of his kiss should have made her recoil from him but instead it was kicking up inside her hot flurries of urgent need.

As she twined her tongue against his she felt the immediate shudder that wrenched his body, and then he was pushing her backwards and down onto the soft nest of silk cushions that covered the divan. Her only and immediate response was to wind her arms possessively around him, holding him to her.

Fire licked along her veins, igniting the longing she had been fighting to resist. In her dreams she had known of a man like this, a man of fierce, raw passions, untameable and elemental, a man whose merest touch would arouse her senses in a thousand and one ways, just as Xander was arousing hers now. And in that one shockingly intimate dream she had felt the full power of her response to him. Just as she was doing now!

The hands that had gripped her arms had somehow slid beneath her as she fell onto the divan, supporting and protecting her.

He shouldn't be doing this, Xander knew that. But her refusal to believe him ignited emotions he could not control. Just how bitter pride and raging anger had fused together to produce the hot, male hunger he was feeling, he had no idea at all! But what he did know was that he was being driven by an elemental need to possess her as no other man had ever possessed her, to drive from her body's memory every image it possessed of any other man but him.

He lifted his free hand to cup her face, so that he could look down into her eyes and see there only his own image.

'Look at me!'

The harsh command compelled Katrina to look up into Xander's face. A quiver of totally female awareness of him ran sensually through her as he lifted lean fingers to brush her tumbled hair off her face.

If it had not been for the dark thread of anger she had heard running through his harsh words, she could almost have believed that there was something tender in the way he was touching her.

But the hard, demanding mouth claiming her own wasn't tender, yet her lips were responding to the sensation with a wanton eagerness. He parted their softness with the fierce drive of his tongue, whilst his weight pressed her deeper into the softness of the cushions.

The argument that had brought them to this place, and to this intimacy, had faded into insignificance. His actions were no longer dominated and driven by the fierce urgings of his pride and need to punish her, Xander recognised, but it was a brief fleeting recognition, swamped by the intensity of his body's need for her.

Katrina felt his hands on her body, removing the protective modesty of her clothes, but instead of trying to stop him she was twisting and turning eagerly, wanting to accommodate and assist his rapid despatch of the barriers to the touch of his hands on her flesh.

Only a thin mist of sunlight could penetrate the thick protective walls of the tent, but it was enough to gild her naked body, as though it had been brushed with gold dust. She saw Xander suddenly go very still as he stared down at her nakedness, and a small quiver of shyness and uncertainty ran through her. He was the first man who had ever seen her naked. The only man she had ever *wanted* to see her naked.

Uncertainly she looked up at him. There was a look in his eyes that sent a reaction jolting over her, which tightened her nipples and sent a fierce thrill of sensation coiling through the most intimate part of her. He hadn't even touched her and yet from the way her whole body was reacting he might just as well have run his fingertip around her jutting nipples and then moved lower to part the sensually swollen fleshy lips of her sex to find the eager, waiting need of her pulsing clitoris.

She wanted him, ached for him, hungered and longed for him, right now, right here… She made a soft, small sound of liquid arousal, and immediately dark colour ran up under the taut flesh of Xander's jaw. He pulled off his own clothes, scarcely giving her time for more than a blurred glimpse of honey-gold skin over powerful male muscles, and a dizzyingly tempting covering of silky dark hair that fanned out over his chest, arrowing downwards over his taut belly, before he reached for her.

The feel of Katrina in his arms was doing something to him he had never imagined *any* woman could do, much less this one, Xander acknowledged as he gave into the urgency of his need to fill his waiting senses with the scent, and feel, and taste of her.

The silk cushions heaped on the divan felt decadently sensuous against her naked skin, but more dangerously erotic and sensual by far was the feel of Xander's naked body against her own, Katrina recognised breathlessly. The feel of his skin against hers was surely the closest she was ever likely to get to heaven, she decided headily as she gave in to the pleasure of running her hands possessively over his shoulders, stroking his flesh as she did so, closing her eyes, in order to savour and relish the feel of him.

If she never touched him like this again she would remember for the rest of her life how he had felt, how she had touched him; she was creating a precious visual image of him on which she could imprint everything her senses were relating to her. His scent, his arousal overwhelming the cool cologne he always wore so that she was acutely aware of the raw, musky, pheromone-drenched maleness of him, and of how his skin felt hot and sleek, the powerful definition of his muscles beneath it giving her a small, sharp female thrill of recognition of his strength, and of his arousal. She hadn't touched him intimately yet, but she could feel the hot, swollen length of his penis pressing against her own flesh, and that thrilled her in some nameless female way that still had the power to shock her and to challenge her own beliefs about herself.

What bemused her even more was that she wanted desperately to touch him there, to explore and know him. To feel him grow even harder and more urgent beneath her touch, and that alone should have been enough to shock her, because she had certainly never experienced such a feeling before.

But analysing her thoughts and feelings was way beyond her now. Xander had taken possession of her mouth, his tongue thrusting hotly past her lips as he demanded entrance. His hands cupped her breasts, holding them as though he was savouring the feel of the rounded globes of flesh, but then his tongue drove deeper within her mouth and his fingers kneaded her breasts, plucking sensuously at the stiff peaks of her nipples.

Unable to help herself, Katrina writhed hotly against him, her skin suffused with the flush of her own desire.

Looking down at her as she arched into his hands, her eyes closed as she moaned her desire, Xander realised that the feeling taking possession of him was a fierce need to ensure that the only man her body would ever recognise or remember as its lover was him! He wanted, no, *needed* to put his own personal imprint on her in such a way that she would never, ever forget him.

He bent his head to her breast, flicking his tongue tip against her hard nipple. Immediately Katrina cried out to him. She was oblivious to the fact that her nails were digging into the smooth flesh of his shoulders, and that she was lifting her hips to press her lower body even closer to the hard length of his erection, frantically rubbing herself rhythmically against him as she sought an easing of the pulsing ache possessing her own body.

Her wantonness was destroying him, Xander recognised on a surge of mingled arousal and anger. Every sensual movement of her experienced, eager body was inciting a matching response within his own.

'Xander, I want you so badly.'

The choked words were whispered against his ear, the same ear that her hot, pointed tongue was hungrily exploring.

His self-control wasn't slipping away from him, it was exploding in a frenzy of white-hot lust.

'You're going to have me,' he answered her thickly. 'All of me. And I'm going to have you. I'm going to have you and fill you, and make you feel as no other man has ever done or will ever do... Is that what you want?'

'Yes. Oh, yes,' Katrina moaned. She who would have said anything, done anything he asked, she wanted him so much.

His hand was parting her thighs, stroking her soft, silky skin and making her quiver with the intensity of her longing.

He cupped her sex, parting her swollen outer lips, and rubbing one tormenting fingertip over her eager wetness. She heard the thick sound of satisfaction he made when he stroked the hard, erect flesh of her clitoris, his fingertip moving erotically over it, and arousing her to such a fever pitch of desire that she could hardly endure the intensity of her own pleasure.

Xander could hear the small quiet voice inside himself telling him what he was doing was wrong, but its warning was drowned out by the small excited sounds Katrina was making and his own intense desire.

He had never wanted a woman as he wanted this one, nor had he ever known he could feel such an overwhelming and passionate need. He could feel it driving, burning through him, possessing him as he ached to possess Katrina.

He positioned himself between her already open, welcoming thighs. Katrina shuddered. She could see Xander poised over her, and her heart hammered frantically against her ribs. This was it. The moment of intimacy she had wondered about, dreamed about with a virginal mixture of eager curiosity and slight trepidation.

She could feel Xander's muscles bunching. Almost pleadingly she lifted her hand to his face, whispering chokily, 'Kiss me...'

Swiftly Xander bent his head, his mouth taking hers in a long, slow kiss of scorching intimacy whilst he thrust fiercely past the swollen outer lips of her sex, and into the tight embrace of the most intimate part of her.

And she did feel tight, the close grip of her muscles almost unendurably erotic.

Foolishly, perhaps, she hadn't expected pain, Katrina acknowledged as her body clenched in shock, but her longing for him was stronger than both her shock and her pain. She clung to him, offering herself up to him, so that he thrust deeper and faster.

He felt the barrier of her virginity and heard her indrawn gasp of pain with a shock wave of stunned disbelief.

Katrina shuddered as his body stilled within hers; the pain had gone but the small, telling contractions pulsing deep inside her had not. They were intensifying, making her move rhythmically and urgently against Xander, compelling him to move with her.

She heard him groan, her own teeth nipping frantically at his shoulder as the urgency of her arousal seized her and she cried out to him in agonised pleasure. The deep, driving surge of his body within her own was all pleasure now and she gave herself up to it and to him, lost in what she was experiencing, the release of her orgasm making her tremble from head to foot. But it was the hot spill of Xander's completion within her that made her eyes burn with emotional tears.

On a small sigh of soft pleasure she turned her face into the curve of Xander's shoulder and curled up against him.

'How is it possible that you were a virgin?'

The harsh, angry words confused her.

'So far as I know there is only one way I could have been,' she responded flippantly.

What did it matter what she had been when right now she was gloriously, deliciously, totally fulfilled and by him?

'It isn't exactly unknown for women to buy themselves virginity via a skilled surgeon and a small operation,' Xander told her curtly.

'Maybe it isn't, but I certainly didn't,' Katrina told him.

Xander knew that she had done no such thing, but he was still fighting to overcome his own shock. Discovering that she had been a virgin and he her first and only lover changed everything. His upbringing meant that he felt a moral responsibility towards her. 'You should have told me.'

He sounded cold and angry, and to her own chagrin Katrina discovered that, instead of feeling blissfully happy, suddenly she felt totally miserable and dangerously close to tears.

'I did tell you that Richard wasn't my lover,' she reminded him.

'You could have asked me to stop.' He paused, an expression crossing his face that Katrina couldn't analyse. 'By the time I recognised that I needed to stop, it was far too late,' he added curtly.

He was criticising her for what had happened. Blaming her? Despite her immediate indignation and anger, Katrina knew that he had a valid point. She could have told him, but she had deliberately chosen not to do so! Why? Because she had intuitively known that he would not continue to make love to her? Because she had wanted him to do so, so desperately? Even so! Beneath the anger she was beginning to feel a very much deeper and more painful current of emotional misery that was slowly flooding her: a combination of rejection, despair, and the bleak realisation that her own emotional input into their sexual intimacy had not been reciprocated. A small shiver shook her still-naked body.

'Here, put this on.'

Katrina tensed as he wrapped his own discarded robe around her. He was frowning as she did so, his actions brisk and businesslike, and surely devoid of any kind of softening tenderness, even if his touch was surprisingly gentle.

'You realise, of course, that this changes everything

between us! Had I known of your virginity I would never—'

Katrina fought back the tears burning the backs of her eyes. 'Do you realise just how despicable you are?' she demanded hotly. 'You believed that…when you assumed that I had…that I was not…' She was so overwrought that she could hardly get the words out. Taking a deep breath, she started again. 'When you assumed I was Richard's lover, you obviously thought that it was perfectly acceptable for you to…to do what you did, but now that you've discovered that I was a virgin, things are different. Well, you may feel differently about me, but I do not feel differently about you!' she told him furiously. 'In fact, if anything I despise you now even more than I did before! The kind of man I could respect is a man who values me as a person, not just my virginity! You are despicable and loathsome!'

She could see the dark tide of angry colour seeping up under his skin, and the murderous flash of savage pride in his eyes, but she refused to be daunted. She had as much right to say what she thought as he did! She felt sick inside with shame and self-contempt at having been foolish enough to believe he was someone special. She had deluded herself, and now she had paid the price for that self-delusion—not with her virginity, but with her heart and her emotions.

At least now she would be able to destroy that burgeoning love by reminding herself of what had happened today and his cruelty towards her.

Her angry words caught Xander unprepared, just as his desire for her had done. They touched an exposed nerve and threw back to him an image of himself that hurt his pride.

He had lied to her when he had claimed that he had only made love to her because he had believed she was experienced. The truth was that he had made love to her because he had not been able to stop himself, but he had been too proud to admit that to her, and now it was too late to tell her that truth. It was also too late to admonish himself now for the fact that he had not taken any kind of precautions.

Healthwise he had no concerns. Despite what other people might choose to think about his sexual past, he was not littered with a stream of different partners, but there were other dangers, other risks, and he had not held himself back in any way at all!

He looked at Katrina. Her small heart-shaped face looked pale, her eyes huge.

Although the garment was wrapped around her, she was still shivering slightly.

Abruptly he stood up and then, grimly and without saying a word to her, he scooped Katrina up into his arms, fabric and all.

'What are you doing? Put me down!' Katrina commanded uselessly as he carried her through to the inner quarters of the tent.

Panic filled her. What was he going to do? But instead of turning into the sleeping area, he turned instead into the small bathroom. He pushed open the shower door with his shoulder and stepped into it, still holding her.

As he put her down he removed the cloth that was wrapped around her and dropped it on the floor outside the shower, firmly closing the door.

'What do you think you are doing?' Her question

was lost as he turned on the shower and she sputtered helplessly under the admittedly delicious warmth of the water.

'You're cold and possibly even slightly in shock,' he told her grimly. It was true that she did feel rather shaky, Katrina acknowledged, but she knew that that had more to do with Xander's angry comments to her than the intimacy they had shared.

She risked a small upward look at him. Xander might be soaping her wet skin with a look on his face that said there was nothing remotely sexual or pleasurable for him about what he was doing, but unfortunately her body was not capable of being so detached, Katrina recognised guiltily.

And of course it didn't help that he was as naked as she was herself. Unable to stop herself, she glanced down at his body, and then tensed as she saw that his penis was not small and flaccid as she had assumed naively it would be, but instead impressively thick and firm-looking.

A small perplexed frown creased her forehead.

'What's the matter?'

Her face burned with embarrassed colour. She hadn't realised that Xander was watching her so closely.

'Nothing. That is…I just thought…' she began in a suffocated voice, her face burning even more as he too looked at his own body.

'You thought what?' he challenged her coolly. 'That I might be planning to take you back to bed?'

'No!' Katrina denied immediately and truthfully, even though the distressing sudden tightening of her nipples told her how favourably her body was already viewing that possibility.

'No? Then what were you thinking?'

He was going to insist on her telling him the truth, Katrina recognised.

'I just thought that you...that after sex... You just looked much bigger than I'd imagined,' she finally blurted out uncomfortably.

'Imagined?'

The silky, challenging word caught her off guard, conjuring up the erotic thoughts and fantasies she had mentally created around him and rendering her tongue-tied and speechless.

Xander leaned forward, stroking the soapy sponge the length of her back, all the way down to the firm curve of her buttocks.

'So what exactly was it that you did imagine?' he asked her softly.

'Nothing,' Katrina denied quickly.

He dropped the sponge and looked at her, his intent, speculative gaze searching her face.

'Whilst men, like women, are all basically made the same, within the parameters of that sameness there are many different sizes, which is just one of the reasons why you should have told me that you were a virgin.'

He rinsed off the soap with the spray of the shower.

'I am surprised that your parents, your mother, and especially your father did not warn you about this kind of situation...'

'I do not have a mother or a father,' Katrina checked him quietly. 'They were killed in an accident when I was in my teens.'

'An accident?'

'They were scientists,' Katrina explained. 'They

were working on an ecological site in Turkey when a roof fell in on them.'

She heard the hiss of his indrawn breath.

'There is no need for you to feel sorry for me. I don't want anyone's pity. I am just glad that they died together, and I am so grateful for the love they gave me and the love they had for one another.'

She spoke with a quiet dignity that once again touched a raw, intimate place in Xander's own emotions. He had to fight against a sudden desire to put his arms around her and simply hold her.

'Stay here,' he said curtly instead, turning off the shower and stepping out, returning almost immediately with a huge soft towel that he wrapped firmly around her.

When she touched its softness with appreciative fingers he told her authoritatively, 'It's Egyptian cotton, and far superior to any other kind.'

'And far more expensive,' Katrina answered him ruefully before tensing and remembering just what he was.

But of course he had acquired the towels in the same way as he had acquired the books but, remembering the outcome of her accusations regarding them, she decided not to challenge him a second time.

Having wrapped her in one of the towels, he wrapped one around his waist and then started to rub her dry—more briskly than passionately, she had to admit. His self-imposed task completed, he wrapped her in a fresh dry towel and swung her into his arms.

'I can walk, you know,' she objected crossly, but she might just as well not have spoken for all the attention he paid to her.

In the close confines of the narrow corridor she

could smell the clean, soap-fresh scent of his skin. Her heart thumped heavily and then skidded against the bottom of her chest cavity. She badly wanted to press her lips against the smooth brown column of his throat and then to lick and nibble her way towards his mouth.

A now-familiar feeling of sensual tension was already starting to build again inside her. What had he done to her? Katrina wondered helplessly. How had he turned her from a naive virgin into a woman of wanton hungers and needs who was aching for him again already?

She told herself that it was relief she felt when he carried her into the sleeping area and placed her on the bed.

'Rest now,' he said.

'I don't need to rest,' Katrina objected immediately. 'Just because I was a virgin that does not mean I'm delicate.'

He had been about to turn away from her, but now he stopped and turned to look at her instead, sliding one long, lean-fingered hand against her throat so that she was forced to look back at him.

'You may have been a virgin but, admit it, you were eager and ready for me, weren't you?'

An expression she couldn't define, but which her body obviously understood, crossed his face, causing a small reactionary shiver of sensual excitement to grip her, but she still compressed her mouth and tried to look away from him.

'Answer me,' he insisted. The hard pad of his thumb was rubbing dangerously against her lips. She could feel them swelling sensitively against his touch and she ached to part them and taste the teasing thumb that was causing her so much torment.

'Answer me,' he repeated, removing his thumb.

'Very well. Yes, I was. You are obviously an experienced lover,' she told him colourlessly, determined not to let him see how she really felt.

'You will be in a far better position to know exactly how experienced by tomorrow's sunrise,' he told her mockingly. 'You have scarcely begun to know what sensual pleasure is, although I confess you are an extremely receptive pupil. Just now, in the shower, you looked at me as though you were as hungry for me as a woman of much greater experience. Have you any idea just how enticing and erotic it is for a woman to show a man how receptive she is to him?'

'I did no such thing!' Katrina objected, hot-faced.

'Liar!' he stopped her softly. 'Rest now, and tonight I will show you what pleasure really is.'

His arrogance was unbelievable, Katrina decided angrily, but underneath her anger she could feel the fierce, excited pulse of her own arousal. What she was allowing to happen was far too dangerous, she knew that, but somehow she just could not help herself.

She should hate and loathe him and not love him; she should…

Love him? She did not love him. She could not love him. What treachery had put that word into her head? She might want him. She might be excited by him, aroused and tantalised by him; she might be all those things and even a great deal more, but she did not love him!

CHAPTER EIGHT

MOROSELY Xander stared out across the oasis, beyond which the sun was dying fast towards the horizon.

By rights his sole concern, his every single thought, should have been for his half-brother, and the fact that tomorrow was Zuran's National Day, and the day Nazir had selected for his murder of the Ruler and his *coup d'état*.

But instead of focusing on that, his thoughts, and even worse his emotions, were rebelliously preoccupied with Katrina.

He had said and done things to her that were totally alien to his normal mode of behaviour, and that alone was enough to fill him with an explosive mix of anger and disbelief, without the additional discomfiting knowledge that he was now aching physically for her so intensely that he actually wanted to put into effect the ridiculous sexual boast he had made earlier. What on earth had prompted him to say such a thing? Surely he wasn't really so vain and shallow that just the wide-eyed, slightly awed and disbelieving way she had looked at his sex earlier had made him want to hear her make those little whimpers of pleasure all over again.

Where the hell were those agents? They should have returned by now with a formal warrant for Nazir's arrest and detainment. He was beginning to fear that they might not return in time. Which meant that he would have to find a way of stopping Nazir himself.

Xander's mouth compressed, a grim look darkening his eyes as Nazir strolled out from between the rows of tents, heading in the direction of the oasis.

Immediately Xander started to turn away from him, but, as though Nazir had somehow sensed his desire not to be noticed, Xander heard him call out sharply to him, 'You! Come here!'

Pretending not to have heard him, Xander started to walk away.

'Stop, or I shall shoot you.'

They were alone in the small palm grove, and Xander knew better than to delude himself that Nazir would not carry out his threat.

His own hand went automatically to the dagger in his belt. Like all the male members of the ruling family, he had undergone military training, but he had never killed anyone, nor imagined that he would have to. But now it seemed that fate was putting him in a position where he would have no option. If he ignored Nazir's demand Nazir would shoot him as he had threatened. And if he obeyed him then Nazir would no doubt quickly discover his real identity, and would guess that his plot had been discovered.

Taking hold of his dagger within the concealing folds of his clothes, Xander turned round to confront his half-cousin.

'You took too long, Tuareg.' Nazir was sneering. 'Perhaps I should kill you anyway.'

The gun was already in his hand and he was pointing it right at Xander's heart.

* * *

Katrina took a deep breath and stepped out of the tent. She had to find Xander and make him agree to release her. She had spent virtually the whole of the afternoon going over and over what had happened between them and she was acutely aware of how vulnerable to him she was.

That frightening word 'love', which had crept into her thoughts earlier, had lodged painfully in her heart, making her sickeningly aware of her own danger. She hated the thought of lowering her pride and pleading with him, but she had no other option. She had made up her mind that she was going to ask him how much ransom he intended to demand for her and somehow she would find a way to raise the money herself. She had the small house in England her parents had left her. Surely she could raise some money on that?

She had waited as patiently as she could for him to return, but now her patience had run out, and so she had decided to go and look for him. Soon it would be dark, and once she was alone with him in the intimacy of the tent with the sensual weight of the words he had said earlier still hanging on the air she was afraid that she might weaken.

It had been more instinct than anything else that had drawn her down to the oasis. And now she stood frozen in shocked fear as she witnessed what was happening.

The man pointing the gun at Xander had an obvious air of authority about him, and it crossed her mind that he might have come to the oasis in search of her, alerted to her plight by Richard.

Xander was standing still several yards away from the other man.

'Come closer,' Katrina heard the other man order sharply.

Her heart was thudding frantically against her ribs and a feeling of pain and anxiety was wrenching at her insides. Xander was a thief, and a kidnapper, she reminded herself. She owed him no loyalty whatsoever.

Xander still hadn't moved.

'You dare to disobey me, Tuareg? Very well, then.' There was a malevolent pleasure in the man's voice as he pulled back the trigger.

He was going to shoot Xander... Kill him!

Franatically Katrina rushed forward protesting emotionally, 'No...'

Both men turned towards her, Xander's harsh, 'Katrina!' leaving his lips at the same time as he flung himself towards her, but it was already too late. As fast as he was, he could not match the speed of a bullet.

Katrina felt it hit her with a sense of disbelief and bewilderment, which immediately became an intense, obliterating pain.

She could see Xander looking at her, his lips moving as he spoke to her, but the pain would not let her answer. It was clawing and tearing at her, dragging her away to its dark, cold lair. But at least Xander was safe and the man had not killed him.

Her last thought as she lost consciousness was one of confused awareness that Xander was holding her. But not even the warmth of his arms was enough to stop the icy cold that was filling her veins and stealing her away from him.

CHAPTER NINE

'KATRINA?'

Reluctantly Katrina opened her eyes and looked up into the face of the uniformed nurse smiling down at her. Katrina's mouth was dry and she felt heavy-headed, unable to think properly or clearly. Confusing images filled her slow-moving thoughts.

She was lying in what was obviously a hospital bed, but the room she was in was like no hospital room she had ever seen or imagined seeing. It looked more like a super-luxurious hotel bedroom: a sparkling clean, luxurious hotel bedroom, she acknowledged as she tried to sit up.

Immediately the nurse shook her head and showed Katrina a small but very complicated-looking remote-control device.

'You can alter the position of your bed with this,' she instructed Katrina, before adding, 'The doctor will be in to see you soon. Are you in any pain? You were given an intravenous painkiller after the operation last night to remove the bullet from your arm.'

The bullet! Agitation filled her as everything came rushing back to her. Xander. The desert. The man with the gun. Xander...Xander...Xander...

'Where am I? Where is...?'

'You are in the special private royal ward of the Zuran Hospital,' the nurse answered her importantly, plainly impressed with the status that Katrina had been accorded. 'The Ruler himself has told the chief surgeon that he wishes to be informed of your progress hourly, and the Sheikha, Her Highness, the Ruler's wife herself will be visiting you this morning. We've received a gift of some clothes for you to wear when Her Highness comes to see you. You cannot receive Her Highness in what you were wearing when you were brought in to us. It would be a disgrace!'

The royal ward of Zuran Hospital? What was she doing here? How had she got here? She had no memory of anything after the explosion of pain she had experienced when she had been shot.

'Let me pour you some water,' the nurse offered. 'You must drink as much as you can to wash the anaesthetic from your system and to prevent you from becoming dehydrated.'

Katrina's eyes widened as she saw that the bottle of water she removed from the discreetly hidden fridge bore a royal crest, and her eyes widened even more when the nurse produced a heavily cut crystal tumbler for her to drink from.

But even as she gulped eagerly at the crystal-clear cool water it wasn't her own situation that was on her mind so much as Xander's. Where was he?

'The man,' she began hesitantly, but the nurse stopped her immediately, a look of contempt and anger darkening her eyes.

'He has been taken into custody by the special agents from the Ruling Council. By good fortune they had arrived at the desert camp of the renegade El Khalid in time to witness everything. Indeed it is thanks to them that you were brought immediately here to Zuran. The Council will decide on the ultimate fate of this unspeakable villain, but there is no doubt that he will receive his just deserts. Such a man truly deserves to be punished for what he has done!'

Katrina's heart sank lower with every word the other girl uttered. 'Where is he now?' Katrina asked her chokily. Her drug-fogged brain was already planning recklessly to plead Xander's case, and to beg for mercy to be extended to him. Wildly Katrina wondered how much money she could borrow against her small home and if it would be sufficient to buy Xander his freedom.

She was halfway to working out the details of such a plan when she realised abruptly what her frantic thoughts meant.

She had told herself that she did not love Xander, but why else would she be feeling the way she was? Surely a much more appropriate emotion ought to be more of relief at having finally escaped from him. She should feel determined to put everything that had happened to her and Xander right out of her mind for ever. But instead she was making desperate plans to help him!

'The special agents from the Ruling Council have taken custody of him in prison and he will be held there until his trial. His Highness made an announcement to the nation this morning to alert us to what has been happening, and of the bravery of his half-brother Sheikh Allessandro, who was the one who discovered the plot against the Ruler. Sheikh Allessandro is to join His Highness in his walkabout today during our National Day celebrations. I will put the television on for you and you will be able to watch the celebrations,' the nurse told her enthusiastically, beaming with delight.

Katrina felt too sick with despair to respond. She

tried to remind herself that she had known all along what Xander was, and how much his moral outlook on life differed from her own. She had warned herself of the emotional danger she'd been in and how foolish it would be for her to allow herself to weave dreams and fantasies around him, but she might as well not have bothered! Stupidly she had done exactly what she had told herself she must not do!

Where was Xander now? Was he already incarcerated in some cramped prison cell? She tried to imagine the proud features contorted with fear, but she could not do so. The image of him that was burned for ever in her memory was that of him standing tall and magnificent before her.

'What…what will they charge him with?' she asked the nurse huskily.

'Treason—he dared to threaten the life of our beloved Ruler,' the other girl responded darkly.

Katrina made a small sound of anguished protest, but the nurse didn't hear it, she was too busy putting the television on, her back turned towards Katrina.

As soon as the nurse had gone, the consultant himself arrived. Katrina lay stiffly in the bed, consumed with despair and anxiety for Xander, whilst the consultant inspected the wound to her arm.

'You are a very fortunate young woman,' he told Katrina benignly. 'Another few centimetres and the bullet would have penetrated your heart. Mind you, you are not alone in your good fortune, for I would not have cared to have to inform His Highness that you were seriously injured. He was beside himself with anxiety for you.'

He was trying to be amiable, Katrina realised, forcing herself to try to smile in response to his jocular comments.

'Excellent,' he pronounced when he'd finished examining her wound. 'I do not think we need have any concerns about your ultimate full recovery. You have had a lucky escape!'

She might have had a lucky escape, but Xander had not escaped, had he?

Every particle of her ached with anxiety for him. She wanted to go to him, to be with him, to tell him that she would do everything she could to help him.

Every second she spent here in hospital was a second wasted, a second she could have spent helping Xander.

'When will I be able to leave?' she asked the consultant impatiently.

He pursed his lips consideringly before answering her, frowning slightly as he looked at her. 'Certainly not for at least another twenty-four hours. If there is some problem and you feel we have not taken proper care of you, then please do say so. I would not want His Highness to think you were not totally happy with the care you have received here.'

He looked so concerned that Katrina immediately felt a small twinge of guilt.

'It is not that,' she tried to reassure him. 'It is just…' She stopped and bit her lip. How could she explain to him why she was so anxious to leave?

His pager started to bleep, and he turned away from Katrina to answer it.

'Her Highness is on her way to see you,' he told Katrina. 'I shall send a nurse in immediately in order to help you to prepare for her visit.'

He had gone before Katrina could say anything.

His departure was followed almost immediately by the arrival of a young nurse, carrying several glossy carrier bags.

'We must be quick. We only have half an hour before Her Highness will arrive. I will run a bath for you, and we must of course keep the dressing on your arm dry.'

It was like being caught up in a small whirlwind, Katrina decided as she was gently but firmly escorted from her bed to an *en suite* bathroom of such luxury that she could only stare open-mouthed at it.

She tried to insist that she could manage by herself, but her self-appointed guardian took no notice, albeit discreetly turning her back when Katrina slipped out of her hospital gown and into her bath.

Ten minutes later she was engulfed in a thick snowy-white towel, her eyes blurred with anguished tears as she remembered another bathroom and another towel and Xander saying coolly to her that the finest towels were made from Egyptian cotton. Xander! She could hardly bear to think of the conditions under which he was probably being held, never mind contrast them to the luxury with which she was surrounded.

It seemed that for the Sheikha's visit protocol demanded that she must be fully dressed.

But she soon discovered that it was not her own clothes she was to wear, but instead she had to choose from the contents of the carrier bags that the nurse had spread out on the bed for her consideration.

'But these are expensive designer clothes,' Katrina protested. 'I cannot afford any of these.'

'They are a gift from Her Highness,' the nurse informed her, and then added anxiously as she saw

Katrina hesitate and frown, 'It would be an insult to Her Highness if you were to refuse her gift.'

Reluctantly Katrina picked up one of the outfits— a pair of cream trousers in a mixture of linen and silk, with a soft blouson-style long-sleeved matching top. It disturbed her a little to be handed a set of brand-new, obviously expensive, delicately embroidered cream silk underwear, knowing just how much it was likely to have cost and that ultimately she would want to insist on paying for it herself.

Even so the delicate fabric felt wonderful against her skin, whilst both the demi-cup bra and the minute low-waisted, short-cut briefs that clung seductively to her skin were a perfect fit, although they were a rather more sensual design than she would have chosen for herself. As she caught sight of her own reflection in the mirror the rounded shape of her breasts was enhanced by the bra, whilst the briefs emphasised the slender length of her legs and the curve of her bottom. She couldn't help thinking that she might have chosen them to wear for Xander.

'Quick, we must hurry. Her Highness will be here soon,' the nurse was urging her, and dutifully Katrina reached for the cream trousers.

She might be dressed, but obviously she was still not deemed to be ready, she recognised as the nurse guided her to the dressing table and asked her to sit.

'I will dry your hair for you,' she announced, producing a hair-dryer from the dressing-table cupboard and proceeding to dry Katrina's newly washed hair.

Katrina wanted to protest that she could dry her hair herself, but she was conscious of her injured and bandaged arm.

Ten minutes later, with her hair dry and sleekly

brushed, the nurse just had time to whisk away the brush and dryer before there was a knock on the door and another nurse hurried in to say that the Sheikha had arrived.

'She will receive you in the state waiting room,' Katrina was informed. 'We will escort you there.'

A hospital with a state waiting room! Just how cool was that? Katrina wondered ruefully as she was hurried from her own room, down a long, carpeted corridor to a door outside which the consultant was standing.

'Her Highness will receive you now,' he told Katrina, opening the door for her and then standing back.

Katrina's first thought was one of surprise that the Ruler's wife was so tiny. She was seated on a raised dais, and when she saw Katrina she beckoned her to enter the room.

Although she had not planned to do so, Katrina found herself automatically and instinctively bowing her head as she remembered the protocol she had learned before coming to Zuran. In the East, after all, the act of prostration was one of respect rather than one of subservience. But to her surprise as the door was closed, leaving them alone in the room, the Sheikha got up off her seat and indicated that Katrina was to rise.

Coming over to Katrina, she unclipped her veil and took hold of Katrina's hands in her own, leaning forward to kiss Katrina on first one cheek and then the other.

'We are so much in your debt,' she exclaimed so emotionally that Katrina felt slightly overwhelmed.

'I have done nothing, Your Highness. I—'

'Your modesty is very becoming, but unnecessary since I have already heard all that we owe you. Your arm is not troubling you too much, I hope? The surgeon says that you will make a full recovery and that there will not be any scar. His Highness instructed me to express to you his devout hope that you will forgive him for being the cause of your suffering. I cannot bear to think of what would have happened if that unspeakable wretch had been allowed to carry out his murderous plan!'

Katrina took a deep breath. It might be a breach of protocol, but she had to seize the chance to do what she could for Xander.

'Highness, if I might speak?' Without waiting for the Ruler's wife to respond, she plunged on. 'I know what Xander planned to do was a terrible thing, a truly dreadful thing, and I…I can well understand why…why he should be about to face trial, but if I could beg for him to be shown some clemency…? Truthfully I do not believe him to be an evil man, even though…' Katrina knew the risk she was taking and the extent to which she was breaking the unwritten rules governing protocol, but she had to try to help Xander. Fearful tears were burning the backs of her eyes. The Ruler's wife was frowning so much that Katrina dared not continue. Her mouth had gone dry with nervous tension and her heart was thudding against her chest wall.

'Xander?' the Sheikha demanded, an expression Katrina could not define crossing her face.

'So! You wish to plead for mercy for this… this… Xander?'

Numbly, Katrina nodded, not trusting herself to speak.

'I understand that you were kidnapped by El Khalid's men, and that you suffered a great deal of indignity at their hands. Surely instead of pleading for mercy for…one of them, you should be urging my husband to punish him most severely.'

Katrina bit her lip. 'I'm not saying he shouldn't be punished—just that the way he protected me should be taken into account at the trial.'

'I shall speak with my husband,' the Ruler's wife announced evenly, stepping back from Katrina to return to her seat.

'It seems you are compassionate as well as modest. These are excellent virtues in a wife…and a mother,' she informed Katrina, causing her to do a small double take as she heard the amusement in the Ruler's wife's voice and then saw as she secured her veil that she was smiling broadly as though something had amused her.

'I hope that this…this Xander is aware of what a passionate champion he has in you!' she murmured dryly. 'Indeed one might almost suppose that you had fallen in love with him!'

Ten minutes later, her audience over, Katrina was back in her own room, her stomach still churning with nervous tension. The television was still on, and she paused to glance at it. On the screen in front of her she could see the packed streets of Zuran City as people waited to cheer the Ruler as he walked amongst them.

Katrina knew that Zuran's Ruler was held in very high regard, not just by his people, but also by the international community and its leaders. He was considered to be a forward-thinking, modern-minded man who had done a great deal to improve the lives of his people. Thanks to his foresight and vision Zuran had become a major luxury holiday destination; his racing stable and the Zuran Cup race were world famous, as was the golf tournament he had instigated, and now there was talk of the country being added to the international formula one racing circuit.

How on earth had Xander become involved in a plot to depose such a highly thought-of man and, in doing so, to destabilise Zuran's political and economic situation?

She knew the answer to that question, she acknowledged bleakly. Xander would do anything for money. He had even gone through a fake marriage ceremony with her for it!

Why couldn't she despise him as she knew she ought to do, instead of despising herself for feeling the way she did about him?

She looked absently at the television screen. As well as the Ruler himself, several other obviously high-ranking men were accompanying him on his walkabout, and the television announcer was explaining who they were for the benefit of his viewers.

'His Highness is accompanied by several members of his family, the most important of whom of course is his half-brother and saviour, Sheikh Allessandro Bin Ahmeed Sayed. Sheikh Allessandro's mother, as many of our viewers will know, was originally His Highness's English governess before his esteemed father married her. It has always been known that a tremendous closeness exists between His Highness and his younger half-brother. But now this bond has been intensified a thousand thousand times with the

Sheikh's bold action in personally seeking out His Highness's would-be assassin.

'And there is Sheikh Allessandro now, standing on the right of our esteemed Ruler.'

Bitterly Katrina reached for the remote. She did not want to see the man who had put Xander in prison, but it was too late. The camera had zoomed in on the face of the man standing beside the Ruler of Zuran.

And it was a face as familiar to her now as her own!

Rigid with shock and disbelief, Katrina stared fixedly at the screen, 'Xander!' she whispered numbly in shocked denial. It couldn't be! But it was!

The man standing beside the Ruler, the man the commentator was describing in such glowing, admiring terms...the man he had named Sheikh Allessandro, and half-brother to the Ruler, was Xander!

She blinked and refocused on the screen, half convinced she must have been hallucinating, but, no, she wasn't. Xander was not imprisoned in some horrid jail, but instead walking freely through the streets of Zuran, being heaped with praise and admiration. Xander was not a penniless Tuareg nomad, he was an extremely wealthy man. But he was a liar and a thief. He had lied to her deliberately and knowingly, and he had stolen from her too. He had stolen her heart.

No wonder the Ruler's wife had laughed when Katrina had pleaded for leniency for him.

Her whole body burned with painful self-contempt and bitterness. No doubt Xander would be richly amused when he learned of her concern for him!

Angrily she stabbed at the remote and switched off the television.

Well, Xander could laugh as much as he liked; she would be on the other side of the world and too far away to hear him! She was going home to where she belonged and she was going right now! She pressed the bell to summon a nurse. She had left her handbag in Richard's car and her passport and credit cards had been in it so she would have to call at the small office he rented to collect them, and then she would go straight from there to the airport and she would stay there until she got a seat on a plane to take her back to England.

When the nurse arrived Katrina told her shakily, 'I would like my clothes, please. The ones I was wearing when I arrived? And I need to order a taxi, please.'

The nurse looked confused. 'A taxi? But you cannot leave the hospital until you have been discharged.'

Katrina lifted her chin. 'I am discharging myself. My clothes?' she reminded the other girl.

'I…I shall go and look for them for you,' the nurse said.

It might be as well to telephone Richard to warn him that she was on her way, Katrina acknowledged. That way he could have her personal papers ready for her. And perhaps she should ring the airport as well to find out when the next flight was.

It seemed a very long time before the nurse finally arrived back with her clothes.

'A car has been arranged for you,' she told Katrina. 'But the consultant should see you before you leave.'

'No! I do not need to see him. I am fine. Thank

you for bringing my clothes,' Katrina said to her gruffly.

She could see that the nurse wasn't entirely happy with the situation, but to Katrina's relief she did not try to argue with her or dissuade her.

Ten minutes later, Katrina was standing in the hospital's elegant reception area, feeling far weaker than she wanted to admit.

'I asked if a taxi could be ordered for me?' she said to the girl behind the reception desk.

'Oh!' For some reason the receptionist looked slightly flustered, glancing towards the smoked glass doors almost anxiously before telling Katrina, 'Yes. A limousine has been ordered and is waiting for you.'

A limousine! Ruefully Katrina acknowledged that it was unlikely that many of the hospital's patients had ever travelled in anything as mundane as a mere taxi. Thanking the girl, she made her way towards the exit. The doors swung open automatically, the brilliance of the sunlight dazzling her so much that she could hardly see.

Straight away, a highly polished black limousine with dark-tinted windows pulled up alongside her. The driver got out and bowed to her before opening the rear passenger door for her and then, after ensuring that she was comfortably settled, he resumed his own seat.

The car certainly was luxurious, Katrina reflected as she sank into its deep leather upholstery.

'I'm going to the airport,' she told the driver. 'I need to stop off somewhere first. L39 Bin Ahmed Street, please.'

A little to her surprise, the driver activated a glass

partition, which slid up to separate her from him, the faint clicking sound that followed it making her frown slightly as she recognised that the noise was the doors locking.

Perhaps he thought she looked like the kind of passenger who might try to get out without paying him, she decided ruefully as the car pulled out into the busy traffic.

Every taxi driver in Zuran City had to go through a rigorous training programme before he was given his licence, which included not only the ability to speak English, but also a thorough knowledge of the city's road system, and Katrina knew that her driver would know his way to the address she had given him.

There was a small nagging ache from the wound in her arm, and she realised that the painkillers she had been given every six hours in the hospital must be wearing off.

Despite the car's undeniable comfort and the coolness of the air-conditioning she began to feel slightly sick and shaky. A sign perhaps that physically she was not yet as fully recovered as she had believed?

She could visit her own doctor once she was home in England, she told herself stubbornly.

She had no idea how far the hospital was from the small office and accommodation the research team had been given to use, Katrina admitted, but it seemed to be taking a very long time for them to get there. They were travelling down an impressively straight dual carriageway. The central reservation and the verges either side were ornamented with an impressive formal display of plants, and the sea was on one side of the road while the desert was on the other.

Katrina began to frown. Had the driver mistaken her instructions and thought she wanted to go straight to the airport? She didn't remember the airport road looking like this, but it was obvious that a road so impressive had to lead somewhere important!

She leaned forward, tapping on the dark glass panel that separated her from the driver in an attempt to attract his attention, but to her frustration he did not respond.

Had he even heard her? The car started to slow down and she could see a huge wall rearing up in the desert ahead of them, stretching right across to the sea itself. Through the one-way dark glass she could see the sentries standing outside the ornate gold-coloured gates, ornamented with all manner of traditional designs picked out in dazzlingly vivid enamels.

It was like something out of an Arabian fairy tale, Katrina decided, bemused to see how the gates swung open as they approached, allowing them to sweep into the courtyard that lay beyond them.

More sentries guarded the imposing double doors, and the steps leading up to them by which the driver had brought the car to a halt.

Nervously Katrina stared out of the car at her unfamiliar surroundings. Where on earth was she, and more importantly what was she doing here? Katrina stiffened as the double doors opened and a man started to descend the steps. Xander!

One of the sentries leaped forward to open the car door before he could reach it, but it was his familiar hand that reached into the car and took hold of her arm as she automatically pressed herself back into the seat away from him.

'I'm not going anywhere with you,' she told him,

beginning to panic. 'So you can tell the driver to turn this car round and—'

'You have two choices, Katrina. Either you step out of the car willingly or…' He looked meaningfully at the impassive sentries standing several feet away.

Reluctantly Katrina got out of the car, casting a fulminatingly furious look at Xander as he ushered her towards and then up the flight of steps.

'You don't look well. It was extremely foolish of you to discharge yourself from the hospital. When the consultant telephoned me he was extremely concerned,' Xander announced as he guided her through the doors as they were flung open with faultless timing. They passed through them and into a cool, high-ceilinged room with an intricately carved staircase that led up to a gallery that ran the full length of the inner wall. Several doorways led off both the gallery and the ground floor, but Xander made no move towards any of them.

'The consultant had no right to discuss me with you,' Katrina told him.

'On the contrary, he had every right,' Xander corrected her. 'Since I am your husband!'

Katrina almost staggered with shock, as though she had been dealt a physical blow as well as an emotional one.

'That's not true,' she denied shakily.

'My brother chooses to think differently,' Xander informed her coolly. 'Especially now that his wife has spoken to him of a conversation she had with you during which you pleaded for me to be shown mercy and compassion—'

'That was before I realised that you weren't Xander, the thief, but Sheikh Allessandro, the liar,'

Katrina stopped him bitterly, still shocked that he'd heard about her conversation with the Sheikha.

'Come with me,' Xander said. 'The hallway of my brother's palace is not the place to discuss this!'

A palace! This place was a palace! She should perhaps have guessed, Katrina recognised, half dazed by the intensity of the conflicting emotions swamping her.

Xander had said he was her husband. But he wasn't. Not really. He couldn't be! Could he?

He had taken hold of her arm and she had no option other than to walk alongside him as he took her through one of the doors, and then along a long corridor, and then through a doorway, which opened out onto a small private garden.

As Katrina tried to focus on her surroundings through the blur of her angry tears she could hear Xander telling her grimly, 'This is my brother's private garden and he has allowed me the privilege of bringing you here so that we may talk in private.'

'We don't have anything private to talk about,' she shot back at him immediately.

'No? Why did you beg my sister-in-law to intervene on my behalf?'

'I'd have done the same for anyone I knew who I thought was going to face a harsh sentence. I thought you were a thief, but not a murderer. I didn't do it because of…of anything else! But of course you weren't facing treason charges, were you? Not that your sister-in-law told me that! No! I was left to find out when I saw you on television.'

She could feel and hear the bitterness and shock leaking from her heart into her voice.

'My sister-in-law pre-empted my own plans by visiting you before I could speak with you myself.' His voice was stiff—with regret or with lack of interest? It had to be lack of interest, Katrina decided.

'I couldn't say anything to you whilst we were in the desert,' he continued. 'I had to put my half-brother's safety first.'

'Your half-brother,' Katrina repeated bitterly. 'You even lied to me about that as well, didn't you?' When he remained silent she burst out, 'Do you really think I would really want to be married to someone like— a man who…who is everything I despise?'

She was shaking so badly she could hardly stand, but to her relief Xander had released her to turn away from her so that he couldn't see how agitated and distressed she was. 'Besides, you told me yourself that the ceremony we went through wasn't binding or legal. You are not my husband, Xander.'

'Unfortunately for us, it is not what you or I want that matters in Zuran. My brother is far from being a despot, but he does have certain beliefs, a certain stubbornness, if you wish to put it that way, that comes with being Ruler. He considers the traditions of our tribal ancestors to be a sacred trust, which he has a moral duty to respect. You and I were married according to one of those traditions and thus he feels…'

'How does he know that?' Katrina asked fiercely.

Caught up in her own feelings, Katrina was too agitated to notice Xander's small but telling hesitation before he answered her.

'El Khalid was held for questioning by Zuran's security forces.'

'And he told them? But such a ceremony can't possibly be legally binding!' Katrina protested.

'No, not in the eyes of the wider world, which is why my brother has arranged for us to go through a civil marriage ceremony discreetly and immediately.'

'No. No way, and what do you mean, "immediately"?' Katrina queried warily.

Xander inclined his head. 'I mean immediately,' he said evenly, ignoring the small sound of distress she made. 'The appropriate officials are waiting for us as we speak. My brother's wife has expressed her own disappointment that she cannot organise a more fitting ceremony for us—but my brother is adamant.'

'You can't do this! You had no right to bring me here! You can't make me marry you, Xander,' Katrina protested shakily. 'I am a British citizen and if I want to leave Zuran, which I do, I can right now...'

'According to Zuran law you are my wife, and as such a member of the Zurani royal family. No member of his family is allowed to leave the country without my brother's approval!'

Katrina stared at him. 'Why are you doing this?' she demanded in a shaken whisper. 'You must find the thought of a marriage between us as abhorrent as I do. You can't want to marry me any more than I want to marry you!'

'It is my duty to do as my brother commands me and, besides, since I took your virginity...' He gave her a look that made her stomach plunge nauseatingly.

'You're marrying me because of that! But that's... that's archaic...medieval...' Katrina protested in a distraught whisper.

'I will not have my child born without my name!'

Xander told her coldly. 'You are already my woman, now you must become my wife!'

Katrina's mouth had gone dry. 'What child?' she demanded recklessly. 'There isn't going to be any child,' she told him, looking deliberately at a point to one side of his shoulder instead of into his eyes. And then she held her breath, half expecting him to accuse her of lying, because the truth was that she could not say as yet whether or not she was carrying his child. To her relief, though, he didn't challenge her. Instead he simply told her curtly, 'Come…the officials are waiting.'

She didn't want to go. Apart from anything else, the pain in her arm had intensified to the point where she was having to grit her teeth against it. But the look on his face told her that he was all too likely to pick her up and carry her to her wedding bodily if she refused to walk there herself.

She was hardly dressed as a bride, Katrina admitted fifteen minutes later as she and Xander stood in front of the government official marrying them and legalising their desert ceremony. She certainly did not feel like one either. Neither did Xander look anything like a deliriously happy bridegroom.

He was reaching for her hand, as the official had instructed him to do, and to her chagrin it trembled frantically in his hold.

He had obviously come prepared because he produced a shiny new wedding ring to slide onto her ice-cold ring finger. Her fingers might be cold, but her arm was throbbing hotly and so was her head, Katrina acknowledged as she fought against the increasingly intense surges of pain washing over her.

'You may kiss the bride.'

Katrina felt herself shudder as she saw the downward movement of the dark head. She closed her eyes, not wanting to see Xander's face, not able to endure facing the reality of her own shattered dreams.

His lips barely touched her own. The kiss he was giving her was a parody of what a man's kiss for his new bride should have been. Pain, both emotional and physical, seized her, clawing and tearing at her as she tried to pull away.

'You are my wife, you will not recoil from me as though my touch is tainted,' she heard Xander hiss savagely against her ear.

Immediately she opened her eyes, bewildered both by his fury and his misinterpretation of her reaction. She snatched a brief glance at his face. It was set as hard as granite fused with marble—and just as cold and forbidding.

His hands were gripping her arms tightly and the pain in her injured one shot through her, making her cry out. But the sound was lost as Xander covered her mouth with his, taking it in a kiss of savage anger, his mouth burning her like a brand.

She could hear a buzzing in her ears, feel a dizziness in her head. Her body went weak and limp; only the grip of Xander's arms supported her as she slid into a dead faint.

CHAPTER TEN

KATRINA opened her eyes, and then moved her arm very cautiously. No pain!

'Good, you are awake. I will send someone to inform Xander. He is worrying himself sick and wearing out my new carpet by pacing the floor outside the women's quarters.'

Xander worrying himself sick about her! Katrina turned her head so that the Ruler's wife wouldn't see her expression.

'Our good chief consultant is very upset that you discharged yourself without his authority. He wanted to re-admit you to hospital but Xander wanted you to stay here.'

So that she couldn't escape from him, Katrina reflected dully.

'You should not be experiencing any pain now, because the consultant has seen to it that you have been given some medication, but if you are you must let me know and I shall tell Xander so that he can instruct the consultant to call and see you.'

'There isn't any pain,' Katrina told her woodenly. It wasn't true, of course. Her arm might not be hurting her, but the kind of pain she was now experiencing could not be cured by medical means, and would be with her for ever, she acknowledged.

'My husband is so pleased that Xander has finally met the right woman! A woman who loves him, and yet who understands the complexity of his mixed heritage,' the Sheikha announced.

Too late Katrina remembered the Sheikha's parting comment to her when she had visited her in hospital—about Katrina being a woman in love! Valiantly she tried to protect herself. 'I think there has been some mistake,' she began firmly, but immediately the Sheikha stopped her, saying gently, 'My husband, our beloved Ruler, does not make mistakes. He loves and knows what is best for all his family, but Xander has a special place in his heart. Not only is Xander his half-brother, but it was Xander's mother who taught my husband when he himself was young, when he was without a mother himself. It has long concerned him that Xander does not have a wife. But he knows he need not concern himself over Xander's marriage any longer!'

'That is all very well, but what about my feelings?' Katrina couldn't stop herself from protesting.

The Sheikha frowned slightly as she looked at her. 'But you love Xander,' she told Katrina. 'You pleaded with me to ask my husband to show him mercy!'

'That was before I knew who he was! He lied to me,' Katrina told her bitterly. 'He allowed me to think he was a…a thief and a…'

'He had no other option! It was his duty to put my husband's safety first,' the Sheikha continued. 'You should be proud of him for his loyalty to his brother and to Zuran. And besides, after hearing what happened at the oasis, my husband has decreed that your marriage must be legalised. As you are a young woman alone in our country my husband considers that you are under his protection, and naturally he is concerned to protect your reputation and act in your best interests. It would have been impossible for him to permit Xander to abandon you after what had happened. You have lived with him as his wife!'

'He told me that the ceremony meant nothing!' Katrina told her despairingly. But she could see that she was wasting her breath. In the Sheikha's eyes it was obviously unthinkable that she should not be legally married to Xander, and the woman was obviously relieved and grateful that she should be! But with her own eyes, all she could see was a future filled with pain and misery!

'Xander will be pleased that you are feeling better. He wishes to leave for the mountains tonight so that you can travel whilst it is cooler. I have instructed one of my maids to pack your things. I hope you like the clothes I had sent to the hospital for you. Xander will of course establish accounts for you with the designers of your choice once you return to Zuran. It is our custom that a newly married couple spend a month together on their own, getting to know one another, and I am sure you will love the villa in the mountains, which Xander's father left to him. He had it built for Xander's mother.'

Katrina wanted to protest that the only place she wanted to go was home to England, but she knew it would be no use.

Wearily she closed her eyes, wishing that there were a magic carpet on which she could fly away from the unwanted and unendurable life that lay ahead of her.

'You are quite sure you are well enough to travel?'

'The consultant has said so,' Katrina answered

Xander's curt question as they stood facing one another in the open courtyard where she had been taken to meet him by the Sheikha and her husband, Zuran's Ruler.

Katrina had been caught off guard by the Ruler's genuine display of warmth towards her, almost as though he was really pleased to welcome her into his family.

Now as he watched them he told Xander jovially, 'She is your wife now, Xander, and you may kiss her. In fact I would recommend that you do. The poor girl looks badly in need of some reassurance.'

'You are making her blush, my love,' the Sheikha joined in the conversation, linking her arm through his and smiling up at him as they dispensed with protocol and formality. 'Katrina is a very new bride and probably does not wish to share the tender intimacy of Xander's kiss with any onlookers.'

'Do you wish me to kiss you?' Xander asked Katrina promptly.

The Sheikha laughed. 'Oh, Xander. How very unromantic! Of course she does, but you must not expect her to tell you so!'

'Then she must wait for my kisses until she does,' Xander announced coolly. The Sheikha was still laughing, but Katrina felt more like crying. Her face was burning with a mixture of anger and humiliation and, although she hated admitting it even to herself, it would have been wonderfully comforting and reassuring to have Xander take her tenderly in his arms and hold her close. To have him whisper secretly to her that he loved and wanted her.

What foolishness was this? He was never, ever going to do that! And she suspected the only reason he had agreed to the convention of them spending a month together in private was so that he did not have to play the loving husband in public!

Xander might show her coldness and a lack of any kind of tenderness or loving emotion, but that was definitely not the way he behaved towards his family, Katrina noted. One by one, the Ruler's children presented themselves for a loving 'goodbye' hug from their uncle. And whilst he did not kiss the Sheikha, the warm, brotherly embrace he exchanged with her husband made Katrina feel very envious of their family closeness. No one watching them could dispute the strength of their love and respect for one another. But despite the love he had for Xander, the Ruler was still forcing his half-brother into a marriage he did not want, Katrina reminded herself.

'I pray your marriage will be a happy and a fruitful one,' the Sheikha told Katrina warmly as she embraced her. Her eyes burning with the pain of her unshed tears, Katrina tried to smile in response.

When the Sheikha released her Katrina saw that Xander was waiting. Wordlessly she walked with him across the courtyard. Two uniformed servants opened the gates for them, and Katrina caught her breath as she saw what was waiting for them in the much larger outer courtyard. There was not a car, as she'd expected, but a helicopter.

'We're travelling in that?' she asked Xander hesitantly.

'The villa is in the mountains and over twelve hours' drive away. You will be perfectly safe. I have held my pilot's licence for well over ten years and have never had an accident yet!'

'You will be flying the machine?' She couldn't control her surprise.

'I prefer to fly myself when I can.'

Silently Katrina digested his comments. There was so much about him that she did not know!

He was already striding towards the helicopter, obviously looking forward to flying it—no doubt far more than he was looking forward to his incarceration with her, Katrina reflected wryly as she hurried to catch up with him.

Katrina knew about the range of mountains inland and to the north of the city, but she had never imagined she would visit them, and certainly not under circumstances such as these.

Which reminded her... 'My colleagues—' she began.

'Their head office has been informed of your safety and our marriage.' His mouth hardened. 'Your colleagues returned to the UK within hours of your kidnap.'

'You forced them to return before the project was completed?' Katrina demanded angrily.

'I? I was in the desert with you, if you remember! The decision was made, I understand, following an urgent request from Richard claiming they wanted to return as he did not consider it safe for them to remain here following your kidnap.'

Katrina digested his information in silence. She had never liked Richard, but it still shocked her that he and the others had actually left the country without securing her own safety.

They had been travelling in darkness, the only illumination that of the stars against the inky dark sky and the thin sickle crescent of the new moon. Suddenly, up ahead of them, Katrina could see the illuminated sheer escarpment of what looked like a Moorish fortress, its turrets and fretted windows thrown into magical relief by the clever lighting.

'What's that?' she asked Xander, unable to contain her awe.

'That's our destination—the villa,' he answered calmly.

The villa? Unable to stop herself, she swung round to stare at him. 'That isn't a villa. It's...'

'It's the shell of a Saracen stronghold. My mother fell in love with the ruined building, apparently, and as a surprise for her my father had the villa built within the original outer walls. My parents spent as much time here as they could. It was their favourite home.'

They were starting to lose altitude as Xander skilfully brought the helicopter down over the escarpment, causing Katrina to hold her breath as they swept in over the high wall and then landed on the purpose-built helicopter pad within the ancient curtilage.

As soon as the blades had stopped rotating, servants seemed to appear from nowhere, hurrying to remove their luggage. But it was Xander himself who helped Katrina down from the helicopter, the cool strength of his hands on her skin making her ache inside with pain and longing and, even worse, remembered pleasure.

Quickly she pulled free of his grip, not wanting to be tortured by her body's memory of him any more than necessary.

Grimly Xander watched her, noting her averted profile and the way she recoiled from him.

He had tried to persuade his half-brother not to insist on this marriage, but he had been overruled. His sister-in-law had told him that she was convinced that Katrina loved him, and that, as much as anything else, had swayed his half-brother's decision. Xander's mouth compressed. Katrina did not love him. She loathed him. She had told him so herself. Pain seized him. When had he first started to love her? That first afternoon in the souk when he had kissed her? Certainly by the time Sulimen had tried to buy her from him he had known that there was no power on earth that would make him give her up. He had tried to pretend it was not love that possessed him, just as he had tried to tell himself that it was only his pride that was badly hurt by the fact that she did not return his feelings. Was he deluding himself in hoping that, out of the compassion she had shown in pleading for mercy towards him, love might grow?

Whether or not she grew to love him, as his brother had reminded him, he had certain responsibilities both towards her and towards his family.

As she walked with Xander from the outer courtyard into the villa courtyard proper, it was impossible for her not to feel awed and a little overwhelmed, Katrina acknowledged as she paused to take in her surroundings. Within the shell of the ancient edifice, a villa of such magical beauty had been created that she could only gaze at it with a lump in her throat.

There was a garden within the ancient walls. Discreet floodlighting revealed elegant waterways and fountains, walkways and arbours, whilst the scent of the flowers filled the night air.

'It's so beautiful,' she couldn't help whispering emotionally.

'My parents designed it together. My mother wanted it to be a perfect blending of east and west.'

His words were sharp and clipped, as though he resented having to speak to her, as though talking to her about his parents somehow contaminated them.

Did he really hate her so much?

Why should he not when he had been forced into a marriage with her that he did not want?

'The villa does not follow the traditional Zurani design,' Xander informed her as he put his hand on the small of her back to urge her forward. 'There are no separate women's and men's quarters.'

His touch caused a thrill of sensual pleasure and aching emotion to shoot through her. She wanted to turn round and beg him to take her fully in his arms, to hold her and kiss her and then to sweep her up and carry her to their bed. It must be the garden that was affecting her like this. She had no logical reason to want him and a hundred not to! But then love wasn't logical, was it? Love? She loved Xander? Really loved him? She trembled as violently as though she was experiencing a dreadful shock—or an unbearable truth!

'What is it? Is it your arm?' Xander demanded, frowning at her as he felt her trembling, but mercifully he had not realised that he himself was the cause of her reaction. 'Are you in pain?'

'No, I am just…tired, that's all.'

'I shall ask Miriam, the villa's housekeeper, to take you straight to your room. Dr Al Hajab has given me some painkillers for you.'

They were inside the villa now, standing in a

square hallway furnished with elegant simplicity in a pleasing mixture of Middle Eastern and western pieces of furniture set against pale blue colour-washed walls.

She could smell roses on the air, and everything about her surroundings breathed tranquillity and harmony, Katrina recognised. Inexplicably she felt as though someone had reached out and touched her with gentle lovingness, soothing her raw nerves and smoothing down her frayed emotional edges.

A sense of a weight being lifted from her shoulders stole softly through her.

'Ah, here is Miriam now!' Xander announced as a small and very rotund woman came hurrying excitedly towards them, and greeted Xander by flinging her arms around him. She was addressing him in terms of great affection in a flood of Zuranese spoken so fast Katrina struggled to understand what she was saying.

'Miriam, this is Katrina, my wife.'

Small, dark, shrewd eyes surveyed Katrina consideringly. 'Your mother would have liked her, I think.'

'Please take her to her room, Miriam. She is tired now, so you will have to wait until tomorrow to show her the rest of the villa.'

'A new bride and she is tired?' Miriam exclaimed forthrightly, making Katrina blush vividly.

'She has been injured,' Xander informed her evenly, before turning to Katrina and telling her, 'I shall leave you in Miriam's safe hands. I have some business to attend to, but if there is anything you want, then just tell Miriam and she will arrange it for you.'

Before she could say anything he was leaving, striding across the tiled floor and disappearing into a corridor.

'If you will follow me, please,' Miriam instructed Katrina, leading the way up the sweeping flight of marble stairs, and then across a wide landing to a pair of double doors, which she threw open almost theatrically, indicating that Katrina was to precede her into the room.

When she did, Katrina understood the reason for her small theatrical gesture, for the room she had walked into was unbelievably beautiful. Like the hallway, its walls were subtly colour-washed, this time in a shade somewhere between grey and a soft green that was infinitely relaxing to the senses. Priceless silk rugs warmed the cream marble of the floor, but it was the beautifully simple yet elegant Gustavian furniture that made Katrina gasp in delight. The wood was a slightly darker colour than the walls, the bed linen a cool off-white. The feeling of peace and harmony she had experienced earlier returned to her even more strongly and she had an overwhelming sense of a loving warmth that was not quite a presence and yet still very, very real for her.

'Was this Xander's mother's room?' she asked Miriam quietly.

The housekeeper nodded. 'The Sheikha chose everything for this villa herself. It was her special place, the only place where she could have the Ruler to herself. Do you sense her?'

'Yes,' Katrina acknowledged.

Miriam beamed. 'I knew it! I could tell the moment

you walked in that you were the right one for him. I was her maid,' she told Katrina quietly. 'I knew that she was carrying her child even before the Sheikh himself. She could not hide it from me! I was the one she wanted when she went into labour with him… She was so thrilled, so proud, to have given our Ruler a son. And she loved her baby so much! But then she became so very, very ill. She wanted so desperately to live, but it was not meant to be! Poor lady. She will be glad that you have married her son. You are of her own blood, and you love him, as she loved his father.'

It was a statement and not a question. Katrina didn't bother trying to argue.

'Your clothes have already been unpacked. I shall show you the dressing room and the bathroom and then I will leave you to sleep.'

Dutifully Katrina followed her into the dressing room, and then beyond it to a bathroom of such simple elegance that she sighed in mute pleasure. The room was fitted with plain white sanitary ware and the same Gustavian-style furniture as the bedroom and dressing room. There was a huge circular bath, half set into the floor, and beyond it floor-to-ceiling glass windows, which as Miriam demonstrated opened out onto a terrace. Beyond that, she explained, lay the small private garden that had been Xander's mother's personal retreat.

'I shall leave you now. Would you like me to send up something for you to eat…or drink?'

Tiredly Katrina shook her head. All she wanted was to shower the dust and grime of her journey off her skin and then to curl up in the bliss of her bed.

*   *   *

Xander opened the bedroom door and stood looking at the bed. The moonlight coming in through the patio windows revealed Katrina's sleeping form, her face turned towards him, her hair spread out over the pillow. Walking past her, he made his way silently through the dressing room to the bathroom, stripping off his clothes and turning on the shower.

He should not have allowed his half-brother to force him into this marriage to Katrina, he knew that. His sister-in-law might be firmly convinced that Katrina loved him, but he knew better. She did not love him, not as he wanted and needed her to do, with her heart and her soul as well as with her body. Physically she might have given herself to him, but that did not mean she loved him.

Even under the sting of the shower his body reacted immediately to the memory conjured up by his thoughts. Grimly he fought for self-control, turning the shower to cold and remaining under its icy lash until he was satisfied that he had subdued his physical yearning.

Stepping out of the shower, he reached for a towel and dried himself, and then padded naked back to the bedroom, pausing to look bleakly into Katrina's sleeping face. Her eyelashes made twin dark fans against her moon-pale skin, and she was so deeply asleep that even when he pulled back the bedcovers and got into the large bed, she didn't move.

Moonlight stroked the bare curve of her arm and the soft skin of her throat. He badly wanted to reach out and trace its silvered path, but he knew that if he gave in to that temptation he wouldn't be able to stop himself from taking her in his arms and kissing every delicious inch of her. Just as he had wanted to the first time he had seen her in the souk.

The stark reality of knowing that she did not love him as he did her cut into him with the slicing thrust of a dagger. Resolutely he turned away from her and put as much distance between them as he could.

CHAPTER ELEVEN

THE sound of crockery chinking and the rich smell of fresh coffee brought Katrina out of her sleep. Blinking a little against the dazzle of the morning sunlight, she looked in the direction where the discreet rattle of china was coming from. Beyond the now-open glass doors, which led onto the large terrace, she could see Miriam placing the crockery on a wrought-iron table.

On the point of throwing back the bed covers, she went completely still, her heart pounding heavily as she stared at the tell-tale indentation in the pillow next to her own, unable to drag her shocked glance away from it.

'So you are awake!' Miriam announced cheerfully, the sound of her voice finally breaking the horror of the realisation that she had not slept alone.

'I have instructed the staff to prepare for you the Sheikha's favourite breakfast! I hope you will like it!'

'I'm sure I shall, Miriam.' Katrina thanked her, trying not to feel uncomfortable as the housekeeper picked up her robe from the chair where she had left it.

Fortunately she had gone to bed wearing the newly washed nightdress that she had worn whilst in hospital instead of just sleeping in her skin as she preferred to do. The door to the dressing room suddenly opened and Katrina stiffened as Xander walked in. It was obvious that he had just had a shower. His hair was still damp and she could smell the clean, sharp scent of the soap he had used.

Still holding the robe, Miriam went over to him immediately, smiling broadly at him. Watching the affection with which he returned the older woman's hug, Katrina suffered a small pang of aloneness and exclusion.

'I thought you would like to have your breakfast on the terrace this morning. Katrina will enjoy seeing your mother's garden.' She handed Katrina's robe to Xander, and then, turning back to the bed, she said, 'When you are ready, Katrina, I shall show you the whole of the villa. I hope you will love it as we do, but if there are any changes you wish to make...'

'I am sure there won't be, Miriam,' Katrina reassured her immediately, and was rewarded with an approving smile before the housekeeper left.

As soon as she had gone Katrina ignored the fierce pounding of her heart and looked determinedly at Xander. He was leaning against the wall still holding her robe. 'You didn't tell me that we would be sharing a bedroom.'

Eyeing her thoughtfully, Xander prised his shoulders away from the wall, and her impressionable gaze was immediately attracted by the sensual ripple of male muscles beneath bronzed skin. Her heart was thudding now, her own muscles clenching as a result of the betraying quiver of sensation stirring within her. She couldn't be aroused by the mere sight of him! She must not be!

'I didn't think it was necessary, given the fact that we are a newly married couple. It is normal in marriage, after all, for a husband and wife to share a bedroom and a bed. To have told Miriam that we would be sleeping in separate rooms would have been bound to give rise to unpleasant speculation and gossip.'

'Maybe so, but our marriage is not normal,' Katrina couldn't stop herself from pointing out.

'Not normal?' Xander queried silkily. 'What exactly do you mean by that?'

'I mean that most people marry because…because they love one another and want to be together.'

There was a definite and disturbing pause, at least so far as Katrina and her thudding heartbeat were concerned, before he questioned even more silkily, 'Aren't you omitting one vital ingredient from that recipe? Wouldn't you agree that it is true that most people who marry desire one another physically?' he demanded softly. Katrina could feel her face starting to burn. There was something about the way he was looking at her…

'Physical desire does play a part in marriage,' she managed to agree, hot-faced.

'And you would agree that there has been physical desire between us?'

Why was he doing this to her—forcing her to humiliate herself like this? What was he trying to prove? And to whom? She already knew exactly how she felt about him! 'That…that was a mistake,' she told him. She might know how she felt, but no way did she want him to have access to that knowledge!

'A mistake?' He was walking towards the bed and she could feel herself starting to tremble as small, fiery darts of an emotion that was not the anger or rejection that she should have been feeling shot through her.

'Giving me your virginity was a mistake? When

you cried out beneath me you cried out with pleasure.'

'No!' Katrina's response came out as a small moan
of sound that was as much a denial of the intent she
could read in his gaze as it was of the claim he had
made.

'I say, "Yes", and I shall prove to you that I am
right,' Xander insisted softly.

'No! What happened that night was just…it meant
nothing to me.'

Just as she meant nothing to him, Katrina reminded
herself. She couldn't bear the pain of seeing in his
eyes that he knew of her foolish feelings, her yearning
and longing for him and for his love.

'You are lying and I intend to prove it.'

That speed and sinuous stealth was all desert warrior, Katrina acknowledged helplessly. He had
crossed the bedroom floor so quickly and was standing over her, his body blotting out the sunshine without her having the time to take any kind of evasive
action.

'Don't you dare touch me!' she told him bravely,
but she could see her words were not making any
impact on him.

A cruel, mocking smile curled his mouth as he
leaned down and whispered silkily, 'But I am going
to touch you, and you are going to want me to. You
are going to cry out to me to please you, to take you,
and to satisfy you.'

He was already manacling her wrists within a
steely hard grip, then lifting her flailing hands above
her head and keeping them there as he bent lower.
She did what she could to reject him, stiffening her

entire body and turning her head away from him, willing her lips to stay firmly clamped together.

But it wasn't her lips that received the shockingly slow, sweet, drifting caress of his mouth, but the inner curve of her exposed arm.

Ripples of pleasure quivered through her arm, building swiftly to a crescendo of sensation that leapt from nerve ending to nerve ending. She could feel the longing tightening her breasts, and causing her nipples to harden into defiant indications of their eagerness to share in the sensual delight he was giving the sensitised flesh of her arm.

She might be wearing a nightdress, but its fragile double layer of gauzy silk did nothing to conceal the effect he was having on her body as her nipples thrust tormentedly against it.

He was still kissing the soft flesh of her arm, but her pleasure had now become an increasingly agonising ache to feel his mouth against other, more needy parts of her body. The lips she had been compressing together so tightly had now parted, and if Xander had cared to look into them he could have seen quite plainly the aroused heat shimmering in her eyes.

She longed to take hold of his dark head and pull it down against her so that she could not just taste his mouth, but also lose herself in the pleasure of the passion. The intensity of her feelings should have shocked her—instead it incited her!

'Are you sure you don't want this?'

The taunting question jerked her back to reality.

'Quite sure,' she hissed at him fiercely. What kind of man was he that he could do something like this?

He was kissing her neck, pinioning her wrists in the firm grip of one of his hands whilst the other slid the straps of her nightgown down off her shoulders. His fingertips whispered against her skin. His lips feathered tormentingly light kisses along the line of her nightdress. A small shudder broke through her self-control, desire and need carrying her swiftly with their fierce current. Her body tensed, quivering like a tightly drawn bow. She heard Xander mutter something. A curse, or a prayer, she couldn't tell which. Then his mouth was on her breast, taking it through the layers of her nightdress as though he needed the feel of her too much to wait. A feverish burst of exultation shot through her, increasing a hundredfold as she felt him tug the fabric of her nightdress lower, exposing her other breast and allowing him to transfer the sensual attention of his lips and tongue to its silky flesh and tightly hot nipple.

She started to exhale and then stopped, gasping aloud in protest as he lifted his mouth from her breast.

'What is it you want?' His voice sounded thick and raw; the look in his eyes when his gaze roved her semi-nakedness matched the need she could feel burning through her. Mutely she shook her head.

'Tell me!' he insisted. 'Is it this?'

He had released her hands and he was kissing the valley between her breasts, his mouth moving downwards over the flesh he was exposing as he pushed her nightdress lower and then lower still.

'This—do you want this?'

'Yes!' she responded in desperation.

His tongue tip rimmed her navel, and whilst she fought to control the wet heat of the pleasure gripping her, in one fluid movement he removed her nightdress completely, leaving every inch of her open to his sight and touch.

The sight of his dark head bent over her naked body sent a raw, scalding heat pouring through her. He looked as though he was totally absorbed in her, totally committed to her pleasure.

His hand touched her thigh, his fingertips stroking lazily along the inside of it whilst she quivered helplessly beneath his erotic touch, gripped by seismic shudders that pulsated through her body.

Soon he would find her wetness and when he did… When he touched her there…

The erotic urgency of her own thoughts was only adding to her torment. Xander was kissing the top of her thigh, the inside of her thigh! His tongue was pushing its way demandingly between the swollen lips that should have been guarding her sex. She could feel her own eager wetness. His fingers were parting the lips of her sex, but it was his tongue and not his fingers that discovered her ready eagerness for him, tasting and savouring the intimacy of her as he caressed the engorged arousal of her clitoris.

It was impossible for her to sustain such an intensity of pleasure and even more impossible for her to withstand it.

Her body arched and convulsed, and without thinking about what she was doing she reached urgently for him, soliciting the hard, hot, silken thrust of him within her.

Xander gave in to the need driving him and thrust slowly and deeply into Katrina's waiting warmth.

Shudders of pleasure racked him as he felt her flesh close firmly around him, her muscles holding him caressing him, as he was gripped by a savage, visceral stab of white-hot reaction. He was supposed to be doing this for her pleasure and not his own, to show her...to give her something she would need so badly that she would never, ever want any other man but him. If he could not have her love, or her understanding or her respect, then he would have her sexual desire to hold her to him.

Only now the trap he had set for her had sprung back on him and he was caught helplessly within the moaning intensity of his need for her as he moved fiercely within her, drawn deeper by the determined female muscles, programmed to obey only Mother Nature.

Katrina sobbed with fierce, elemental pleasure against Xander's shoulder, shuddering intensely as her body clung to every thrust of him within her, and then contracted in a frenzy of convulsions that drew from him not just his orgasm, but the seed of life itself.

Releasing himself from her, Xander was bitterly aware of what he had done. He got up from the bed, leaving Katrina to battle against his rejection and her own tears.

'I know he's your son, but I don't know how much longer I can bear what he is doing to me.'

It was late in the afternoon and Katrina had come as she so often did to the cool, shadowed downstairs room that had been Xander's mother's library and private sitting room. Here in this room she felt able to voice her most private thoughts and feelings, out loud as though she were actually speaking them to a real person. A person who was not just Xander's mother, but also her own sympathetic and wise counsellor. Someone who understood how she felt.

She had discovered the room when Miriam had

taken her on a tour of the villa, and somehow she found a solace here she could not find anywhere else, especially not the elegant bedroom where, every night in the privacy of its large bed, Xander took her in his arms and took her to both heaven and hell.

'I know he believes he is humiliating me, but the truth is that he is humiliating both of us! He hates me for my "Englishness", I know that, but I know too that he is your son and that he cherishes the memory of you, and you too were English. He speaks to me as though he believes I do not respect his cultural heritage, and will not listen to me when I try to tell him that he is wrong. I love the person he is—everything and all that he is, the unique blend of cultures and characteristics that have made him.'

Her voice dropped. 'I cannot stay with him. I love him so much—too much!—but my love for him is destroying me!'

On the other side of the swivelling bookcase, which separated the study that had been his mother's from the more formal office that had been his father's, which they had had connected by means of a secret swivelling panel, Xander stood stock-still. His heart was beating in long, slow, reverberating thuds that seemed to echo ominously in his own ears.

It shocked him to hear Katrina appealing so passionately to his dead mother. He could hear in her voice her loneliness and despair, and a pain he had never expected to feel entered his heart. He had heard what Katrina was saying quite clearly, but how could he believe it? It was true that she had vociferously told him what she thought of him and how much she hated him.

* * *

Anguish seized Katrina, locking her throat muscles and making it impossible for her to speak. Blinking away the threatening tears, she focused on the library shelves, remembering Xander's fury when she had accused him of stealing the books she now knew had been his mother's.

What if there were to be a child from this bittersweet intimacy they were sharing? Those long, dark hours of kisses and caresses, which she promised herself each time she would not allow to be repeated and yet every night she found she longed for again.

Had she no pride, no sense of self-preservation? Was she really so weak that she was ready to accept sex when what she ached for was love?

She heard the door open. It would be Miriam coming to see if she wanted anything! Quickly she snatched a book from the shelves and opened it, hoping to conceal her distress from the housekeeper.

'What are you reading?'

She stared in shock. It wasn't Miriam; it was Xander.

'I...er...' Apprehensively she started to retreat back into the protective shadows, but Xander followed her, plucking the book from her nervous grasp.

'These are the poems my father wrote for my mother.'

His words were almost an accusation, as though he believed that just by touching the small leather-bound book she had defiled it, Katrina recognised painfully.

'I know that the writing of poetry is part of Middle Eastern culture and that poets are honoured and respected for their work,' was all she could think of to say.

'*Their* poems are written for public consumption;

the verses my father wrote for my mother were not. They were his private avowal of his love for her.'

'You mean that I am not allowed to read them?' Katrina challenged him. 'Well, then, in that case they should not be on the library shelves!'

Suddenly she had had enough. Before she could weaken she burst out, 'This can't go on, Xander, and it isn't going to. I want to go home to England. I *am* going home to England,' she corrected herself. 'And nothing you can say or do will stop me!'

Before he could respond she fled, almost running past him and through the open door.

CHAPTER TWELVE

'YOU say you want to go back to England, but a marriage is not so easily put aside!'

They were in the bedroom, Xander having followed her upstairs.

'I don't care about that,' Katrina told him fiercely.

'No? Then what do you care about?'

He had walked past her, propping himself up on the door whilst he folded his arms and watched her.

Her heart was skittering around inside her chest in nervous anxiety. She cared about him. Him! And she cared far too much!

Deliberately turning away from him so that she wouldn't have to look at him, she said quietly, 'I don't like the way we are living. It isn't…right.'

'What do you mean?' Xander challenged her. 'What isn't right?'

He was baiting her, Katrina was sure of it.

Swinging round, she told him hotly, 'You know what I mean. During the day I hardly ever see you and when I do you virtually ignore me, but at night…'

She stopped, unable to go on.

'At night what?' Xander pressed her.

Katrina shook her head. 'You know what I mean.'

'At night I take you in my arms and your body responds so hotly to my touch that I scarcely—'

'Stop it!' The pressure of her own emotions was bringing her perilously close to breaking-point. 'I

know how much you enjoy humiliating and tormenting me, Xander. You're a...sadist!'

'I can scarcely believe my good fortune in having
as my wife a woman who gives herself to me so completely and who touches places within me I never
imagined can be touched. No, I am not a sadist,
Katrina. But I can't allow you to leave me.'

'Because you think there might be a child?' Katrina
challenged him wildly. The words he had spoken had
shocked her, but she refused to believe they were anything more than a calculated ploy to undermine her
determination to leave.

'There isn't going to be a child, Xander!'

'No? You can be so sure?' he marvelled lightly.
'After all, it was only last night...'

'I knew this morning...' Katrina lied frantically,
well aware that, whilst she might have spoken out
loud when she'd been alone how much she loved
Xander, she had not voiced her other secret—her
growing suspicion that she might indeed have conceived Xander's child.

'Well, then, perhaps I had better make sure that
there is to be a child,' Xander murmured. 'For I assure you that if there is, there is no way I will allow
my child to go anywhere without me! Although you
of course may not feel the same love and devotion to
a child of our creating as I would...' His face hardened.

'Of course I would. I would love our child with all
my heart,' Katrina answered him.

'So why then do you want to leave me?'

Katrina blinked and then stammered. 'I... I... We
don't love one another, Xander.'

'You love me!'

She was probably gaping at him like a goldfish, Katrina decided dizzily as she went hot and then cold. How could he possibly know that? How did he know it to be able to state it so positively?

'I... What makes you think that?' she managed to ask him shakily.

There was a small pause, and then to her consternation he levered himself away from the door, and turned to lock it, placing the key in his pocket before he started to walk towards her.

'I heard you telling my mother.'

She had been sitting down on the bed, but now Katrina struggled to stand up, the better to confront her own nemesis.

'You couldn't have...' she whispered.

'But I did,' Xander assured her, slowly repeating for her her very own words, one by one as though he were tasting them first and finding them very much to his pleasure.

'I didn't mean it.'

To her disbelief he threw back his head and laughed. 'Liar,' he whispered back, but his whisper fell against her lips and his arms were already enfolding her and binding her to him.

The slow sweetness of his kiss was melting her mind and her inhibitions. It was impossible for her to resist him.

'You love me! Say it!' he demanded against her mouth.

'I do love you,' Katrina admitted woodenly as first one and then another tear spilled from her eyes and rolled down her face.

'Loving me makes you cry?' he questioned, catching the small drop of moisture with his fingertip.

'Love can hurt. My love for you caused me more pain than I thought I could bear.'

Katrina went completely still in his arms.

'Why are you saying that?' she demanded bitterly. 'You don't love me.'

'Of course I don't,' Xander agreed. 'And that of course is why I ignored everything I have always believed in to fight in the sand for you. Why I allowed El Khalid to force me into marrying you rather than lose you; why I took you to my bed even though I had promised myself I would not do so; why I hated myself with the deepest kind of loathing when I discovered that I had misjudged you and that you were a virgin. And that's why, too, it hurt me so badly when you refused to believe me when I told you those books had belonged to my mother; and why it hurt even more not to be able to tell you the truth about myself and who I was.'

'You never said anything,' Katrina told him in a small, agonised voice that betrayed her pain.

'Neither did you,' Xander pointed out gently. 'Marrying you a second time was a way of showing my strong feelings towards you.'

'I thought it was because the Ruler was insisting that you did. You said that it was…' she said, accusingly.

'After you had made it very clear that you found the idea of being married to me completely abhorrent!'

'I felt humiliated because I'd pleaded for you to be given mercy and then I discovered who you really were,' she said sadly. 'I imagined you laughing about it.'

'My sister-in-law told me that you loved me, but I refused to believe her.'

'I can't believe you love me,' Katrina murmured wonderingly.

'Would you like me to show you? I know you said you were... You said you knew today that you weren't pregnant...'

Katrina went pink.

'That wasn't exactly true... At the time I just wanted to get away from you.' She hesitated and bit her lip. Loving someone meant trusting them, didn't it?

'It is possible that I may be carrying our child, Xander, although it is far too soon to be properly sure at the moment,' she continued hurriedly.

Ignoring her, Xander reached out to cup her chin and tilt her face up so that he could gaze down into her eyes with a look of intensity and tenderness, and open and total commitment.

'There is only one thing I want more than for you to be the mother of my children, Katrina.'

'And what...what is that?' she asked him huskily.

'Your love,' he told her promptly.

'You have it, Xander.'

'And I shall cherish it and you for ever.' he promised her emotionally as he bent his head to hers and took sweet possession of her willing mouth.

EPILOGUE

'OH, XANDER, this is such a wonderful memorial to your mother and so very, very generous of your brother.'

'It is the perfect memorial to her,' Xander agreed as they stood side by side with other members of Xander's family whilst the Ruler officially opened the Women's University that had been built in Zuran in honour of Xander's mother and his governess.

'And it was you who suggested it.'

Katrina smiled lovingly at him as he hoisted their ten-month-old son a little higher in his arms.

'This isn't too much for you, is it?' he demanded anxiously, unable to stop himself looking betrayingly at the small bump of her new pregnancy.

'No, it isn't,' Katrina laughed.

'Pity,' Xander murmured wickedly. 'I was rather hoping we might have an early night tonight.'

Prince of the Desert

PENNY JORDAN

CHAPTER ONE

GWYNNETH exhaled with exhaustion as she paid off the taxi driver and stood looking up at the building in front of her—the building that contained her father's apartment. No, not her father's apartment any more, she reminded herself bleakly, but her own. Her father was dead, and in his will he had left all his assets to her.

And his responsibilities? He might not have willed those to her, but she nonetheless felt morally obliged to make them her own. Her slender shoulders bowed slightly. The last few weeks had taken their toll on her. Her father's fatal heart attack had been shockingly unexpected. It might be true that they had never shared a traditional father and daughter relationship. How could they have? But that didn't mean she hadn't cared about him. He was—*had been*—her father, after all.

Yes, it was true that after her parents' divorce her father had virtually abandoned her into the unloving care of her mother and stepfather. It was true that he had been absent from her life for most of the time she had been growing up, whilst he pursued his own hedonistic lifestyle and travelled the world. And it was also true that his absence had only been punctuated by sporadic visits to the small private boarding school where she had been left and virtually brought up by its kindly elderly headmistress. But of the two of them it was her mother who had hurt her the most. When a person had wealth and power, that person could break the rules and then remake them. And her stepfather was both very wealthy *and* very powerful.

Unlike her father, whose main assets had been his charismatic personality and his persuasive tongue. A rueful smile curved her lips as she remembered how he had boasted to her that it was via that latter asset that he had acquired this apartment in the Persian Gulf Kingdom of Zuran.

'The block it's in is right in the middle of a new marina development. I'm telling you, Gwynneth, I could have sold it ten times—no, a hundred times over, for double what I paid for it,' he had told her excitedly.

Gwynneth hadn't known very much about the desert kingdom of Zuran then—but she did now. Which was why she was here.

She shivered a little in the almost disturbingly sensual warmth of the Arabian Gulf night. It wrapped round her like silken gauze, teasing her skin with its subtle caress, cloaking the intimacy of its effect on her with its darkness, like a mystery lover whose face was hidden from her, his touch all the more erotic for being unknown. A deep shudder gripped her body as she tried to pull down the defensive inner blinds she always used to block out such sensual thoughts. She had fought all her adult female life to separate herself from the dangers of the deep, dark core of sexuality she had inherited from her father, which she tried so hard to deny and ignore.

So *why*, knowing that, had she reacted so emotionally to his recent claim that she was devoid of sexuality, and thus deprived of the pleasure of enjoying that sexuality? That was what she wanted, what she had chosen for herself, and so his words should have brought her pleasure instead of making her searingly conscious of what she was missing.

It was the stress of the last few weeks that was weakening those defences, somehow allowing an unfamiliar hunger and need to well up so forcefully inside her, she assured herself wearily. It was gone midnight here in Zuran, even though it was still only early evening at home.

She lifted her hand to push the slightly 'boho' tangle of long red-gold curls back off her face as she closed the sometimes too eloquent green eyes that, even at twenty-six, she could still not always control, and which could so easily betray what she was feeling. Like her dark eyelashes and her creamy skin, they were her heritage from her Irish mother, just as the delicacy of her bone structure and her supple, slender figure had come down from her paternal grandmother—at least according to her father. He had certainly once been a very handsome man. Once…

The familiar pain-cum-anger-cum-anguish knotted the muscles of her stomach. Her eyes opened, shadowed by hurtful memories. As a child she had often wondered what exactly she had done to deserve parents who did not love her. As an adult she had learned to tell herself that it was their inability to love one another that was responsible for their inability to love her, the child they had accidentally produced but never wanted.

Her mother had remarried within a year of the divorce, departing for Australia with her new husband to make a new life for herself. Her father, freed from a marriage he'd claimed he had never wanted, had roamed the world drinking, gambling, and on rare occasions turning up in England to see her—invariably when he was stoned, broke or drunk, and sometimes all three. A member of the hippy generation, her father had still in middle age embraced drugs and drink and the 'free love' culture. Had done. But no longer did—no longer could. Despite his lifestyle she had still been shocked by his death. A heart attack, the hospital had informed her, his daughter and next of kin.

His daughter, but not his only child. How could a man who had abandoned one child because he hadn't wanted her have so carelessly fathered a second?

She had had no idea of what was to happen when he'd telephoned out of the blue and told her that he was in London and staying at one of its most exclusive hotels. She had gone straight from the City bank where she worked as an analyst to the hotel where, to her surprise, she had discovered he was staying in not merely a room but a suite. Then had come the discovery that he had not come to London on his own, but had brought with him his Filipina girlfriend, Teresa, and their baby son.

'Teresa looks so young,' Gwynneth had protested, unable to conceal her distaste at the thought of such a young and pretty girl with a man as life-worn and jaded as her father.

'She's twenty-two,' he had told her carelessly.

Four years younger than she was herself. Her expression had obviously given her away, because he had shrugged his shoulders and told her unashamedly, 'You can look like that all you want. So I enjoy sex. So what's wrong with that? I never thought any kid of mine would turn out to be a sexless prude. Sex is a natural, normal, adult human appetite that should be a source of pleasure, not hang-ups. You don't know what you're missing. If I were you—'

'I don't want to know,' she had answered him sharply. 'And you aren't me.'

She had always known the danger of her inherited sensuality—just as she had always fought to repress it. But now, without her father here to remind her of why she was so determined to flatline her own sexuality, disturbing weaknesses had begun to appear in what she had believed to be the impregnable wall of her immunity to physical desire.

She looked up at the building in front of her again, and double-checked to make sure she had the right address before exhaling in relief. She had half expected to find her father had been exaggerating when he'd boasted to her about the luxury apartment he owned in what he had described as the most exclusive apartment block in Zuran.

Now, though, she could see that the development was every bit as exclusive as he had claimed. She could see the gleaming white hulls of luxury yachts bobbing gently on the protected waters of the marina in the moonlight. In the distance, at the end of a curved breakwater, she could see what looked like an all-glass restaurant, floodlit from beneath. Immaculate gardens surrounded the apartment block, which was one of several all linked together by glass walkways and gardens to an elegant hotel, and all set on the same spit of land, with the marina on one side of it and a private beach on the other. A true millionaire's paradise. But her father had not been a millionaire. He had been a wheeler-dealer, a chancer. Sometimes making money but more often than not losing it.

She had been dubious at first when she had taken the deeds of the apartment to have them checked out, but she had been assured by the Zurani Embassy in London that they were genuine.

Unfortunately, though, as they had explained politely, for legal reasons, in order to re-register the apartment in her name she would either have to go out to Zuran itself or appoint someone within Zuran to act for her.

Since she had not been happy with the idea of handing over the documentation relating to her father's ownership of the apartment to someone else, she had decided that she would have to come out to Zuran herself.

Removing her father's pass key from her handbag, Gwynneth walked determinedly towards the entrance, half expecting to be stopped or at least challenged, but to her relief the glass doors opened as swiftly and silently as though she had commanded *Open Sesame*. Of course the pass key was the modern equivalent to those magical words.

A lift—also activated by the pass key—took her up to the penthouse suite floor. She had no idea how much the apartment was worth, but surely it had to be a reasonably large sum? She wanted to get it sold as quickly as she could. The pressure on her bank account was increasing every day. She earned a reasonable salary, but she had her mortgage to cover, and other outgoings. Her father's bank accounts had been virtually empty, which meant that she had had to pay for his funeral as well as his hotel bill. At least with her here in Zuran there would be more room in her small flat for Teresa and baby Anthony, whom she had felt honour-bound to do all she could to help. Her stomach churned with nausea.

One thing at a time, she reminded herself firmly. One thing at a time. She slid the pass key into the lock, and exhaled slowly in relief as the light flashed green.

Double doors opened from the hallway into a corridor. Immediately facing her was another pair of double doors.

When she opened them she found that they led into a huge living room, elegantly furnished with a mix of modern and reproduction antique furniture, including a low divan heaped with cushions and covered with richly coloured silk and damask fabrics.

Her father had told her that he had not as yet stayed in the apartment himself. He had bought it off plan, fully furnished and ready to move into, right down to the bedlinen and towels, all chosen by a top-flight interior designer. This room certainly had an immaculate 'show house' air about it—right down to the subtle scent of sandalwood. This was a room designed to embrace each one of the five senses.

Off the living room she found an immaculate galley kitchen, complete with a fridge that dispensed iced water, and a terraced balcony with table and chairs. But right now it wasn't either food or drink she craved so much as sleep.

She found the bedroom at the other end of the corridor, and pushed open the door. She came to an abrupt halt. Its decor was so sensually opulent that just looking at it made her skin prickle with sensory overload. It was decorated in a blend of creams and beiges dramatically highlighted with black, and with the lavish use of rich fabrics and gilt-framed mirrors.

She went back to the corridor and opened the remaining door. Maybe originally the room had been intended to be used as a bedroom, but right now it was furnished as a home office.

She had left her case in the hallway and she went back to get it. She frowned a little to see that the main door did not have any kind of security chain, and then shrugged mentally as she reassured herself that it was impossible to get into the building without a pass key.

It was almost one o'clock, and she had an appointment with the government agency dealing with the ownership of Zurani property by foreign nationals in the morning, she reminded herself. And she undressed and stepped into the shower of the marble *en suite* bathroom.

Fifteen minutes later she was in bed and fast asleep.

'Tariq.'

A warm smile illuminated the face of Zuran's ruler as he greeted one of his favourite relatives. He embraced him as his equal, ruler to ruler, for although in Zuran *he* was the Ruler, and Tariq one of his subjects, Tariq's own small kingdom— a remote hidden valley where the desert met the mountains— meant that he was also a prince in his own right. 'I hear that you hope to begin work soon on the excavation of the ancient city of your ancestors?'

Tariq smiled back. 'Once the heat of the summer is over, work will start.'

'And you would rather be there, scratching around in the sand, than here at my court?' The Ruler laughed as he studied the younger man.

Although they were both wearing traditional Arab dress, Tariq was clean-shaven where the Ruler was bearded, grey-eyed where the Ruler's eyes were a more traditional dark brown, and his skin was more sun-browned than naturally olive, betraying his dual heritage. However, the two men shared the same arrogantly hawkish profile and the same scimitar-like mouths, the same pride of bearing and awareness of who and what they were.

The Ruler reached out and placed his hand on the younger man's arm whilst Tariq maintained a diplomatic silence. He had fondness and a great respect for the Ruler, both as a monarch and as a friend.

When his late mother's marriage had ended, after her British husband—his father—had walked out on them, she had accepted an invitation from the Ruler's late father to make her home beneath his roof rather than live alone with her young son. Tariq had virtually grown up here at the palace, although along with many other young men from Zuran he had received his schooling in England and America.

'So,' the Ruler invited him, 'what progress is there with your investigations into this matter of the double selling of those properties that were made available for purchase by non-Zurani nationals?

Tariq waved away the dish of sweetmeats he was being offered, the scimitar-shaped mouth softening into an amused smile as his somewhat plump relative bit into one. The Ruler was known for his sweet tooth.

'The leader of the gang—Chad—is a South African, and I have now been allowed to meet him. He has intimated to me that he is already receiving the help of someone high up within the Zurani Government, who has been providing them with the documents they need to claim ownership of the properties. They are then illegally selling them on, at an inflated price, and not just to one buyer but to two, doubling their profit. By the time their victims discover that they do not own the properties they believe they have bought it is too late—their money has gone.

'Unfortunately at the moment the gang leader obviously doesn't trust me enough to give me the name of the Zurani official who is assisting him. Chad is too clever to put himself at risk—so much so, in fact, that he controls his criminal operation from a sea-going yacht. As you know, I have represented myself to the gang as someone whose services can be bought—a disaffected and profoundly greedy junior member of the Zurani Royal Family—in the hope that the promise of my potential influence will cause them to reveal the identity of their contact. But Chad is a very cautious and suspicious man. It is obviously not enough for him that I have accepted the bribe he has already offered me, in the form of one of the apartments they have now acquired with my assistance.'

'This, of course, is the apartment in which you are now living?'

'It seemed a good way to reinforce his belief in my greed. I've also claimed that I'm short of ready cash because the inheritance from my mother is being kept from me and controlled by you. Although to cover myself I have let it be known that this is not public knowledge.' Tariq shrugged. 'After all, we must assume that whoever it is who is helping them will know who I am, and of my family's wealth, so they have to believe in my grudge-bearing and acquisitive nature.'

'I sense that you are not entirely happy with the role you have been called upon to play,' the Ruler remarked sympathetically. 'But you are one of the few people in whom I have absolute trust, Tariq, and this is a very sensitive matter.'

'Indeed! So far all the victims we know about have stated that they bought their property via a supposed "official agent". Unfortunately,' he added dryly, 'since this agent dressed in traditional Arab dress, had a beard and wore very large sunglasses, none of them felt able to recognise and identify him. We must assume that he either was or is connected with the Zurani official who is helping the gang. That being the case, if what is happening becomes public knowledge in the international arena it will damage Zuran's reputation very badly.'

'That must not be allowed to happen. This man must be found and unmasked,' said the Ruler sternly, his expression softening as he added, 'I know that I can trust you to do whatever is necessary.'

Having dismissed his car and driver a safe distance away from the apartment, Tariq paused to breathe in the warm late-night air. It was on nights like this that the desert called to him so strongly that his desire to leave the city behind and satisfy his need to return to it became a hunger in his soul.

He thought with contempt of the corrupt gang of men he was currently involved with. Only last night their leader had promised him the services of one of the skimpily dressed prostitutes who were also on board the yacht, as a further reward for Tariq's support.

Of course he'd had to pretend to be flattered by the offer, even though in reality he had been utterly revolted by the sleaziness of both the gang and their leader's offer. He had declined to accept, using the excuse that he was afraid that it might get to the ears of his cousin the Ruler, who would then be even less inclined to allow him control of his inheritance.

Despite the fact that he had been celibate for the last eighteen months—since the termination of a discreet relationship he had shared with an elegant divorced Frenchwoman who, like him, had had no desire to commit herself to marriage—the sight of the skimpily clad young women with their surgically enhanced breasts and vacant eyes had not aroused him at all. How many other members of the gang had enjoyed their favours? Some of them? All of them? And more? Other men as well?

His mouth curled in contemptuous disgust as he recalled how the gang leader had offered slyly, 'Why don't I arrange to have one of them sent up to your apartment so that you can enjoy her in private?'

'Thank you, but no,' Tariq had responded, feigning regret.

He reached the apartment block, and, reaching for his pass key, inserted it into the lock and waited for the doors to open.

Once inside the apartment Tariq strode through to the bedroom without bothering to switch on the light or glance towards the bed, stripping off before going into the wetroom attached to the *en suite* bathroom and then standing beneath the fierce lash of the shower.

Gwynneth woke up abruptly. Her face was on fire whilst her body ached with a different kind of heat. Why was this happening to her *now*, after all these years? Why had physical desire chosen *now* to voice its protest at her denial of it?

Her father had laughed at her and accused her of being unable to understand sexual desire. But she did understand it. She understood it all too well, she admitted. She understood her own vulnerability to it—which was why she had forced herself to learn to control it, to repress and restrain it, out of fear that it would lead her to become like him. But now, suddenly, she couldn't control it. It pulsed hotly and urgently within her body, clamouring for release, shocking and confusing her.

Abruptly she sat up in the bed—at the exact moment that Tariq opened the door from the *en suite* bathroom.

Gwynneth stared in mute disbelief at the man standing in the doorway, framed by the light from the bathroom behind him. Like her, he was completely naked. Well, no, he was not actually like her at all, she thought feverishly. His skin was warmly tanned where hers was pale, his shoulders broad, his chest softly furred with silky dark hair, his belly flat. He was, she acknowledged, the most sexily physically perfect man she could ever have imagined. Tall, dark and handsome. Plus he had that edgy, dangerous male air that produced a female frisson of erotic fear within her—the kind of fear that was not fear at all, but rather an excitement that was morally shocking. One brief glance. That was all she needed to tell her that everything about him pushed all the right buttons for her. How on earth had she conjured him up? She blinked determinedly. This couldn't really be happening. He was an illusion, a figment of her imagination.

Only he was still there, and no amount of blinking seemed to be banishing him. Which meant… Which meant that he had to be real! Hurriedly Gwynneth looked away from him, her face starting to burn.

It was that over-acted fake look of confusion with which she turned her head and then let it droop on the pale stem of her neck that was responsible for the savage increase in his anger, Tariq decided as he demanded bitingly, 'How did you get in here?'

As if he needed to ask. He knew perfectly well what she was and who was responsible for her presence here in his apartment—and in his bed.

Striding towards her, he said curtly, 'No, don't bother answering me. I already know the answer—just as I know exactly what you are!' He gave her a look of icy disdain. No way was she staying here. He wanted her out of the apartment—and speedily, even if that meant he had to dress her himself.

Her naked man wasn't an illusion at all, or a figment of her

imagination. He was very much real, and he had almost
reached the bed, Gwynneth realised in panic, her trapped
gaze skittering away from his chest.

She cried out in protest as his fingers tightened round her
upper arm, instinctively trying to pull away from him as he
virtually hauled her off the bed.

At least *these* breasts were real, Tariq couldn't help thinking, as he monitored the gentle bounce produced by her agitated movements and remembered the unmoving plastic look
of the surgically enhanced breasts of the girls he had seen on
the yacht and thought so repulsive. A woman's breasts surely
should be soft and malleable, just big enough to fill a man's
cupped hand, as this woman's breasts would surely do. He
could almost imagine how they would feel, her skin warm,
her nipples tightening against his touch, her breasts swelling
with arousal just as his own body—

The shock of what he was experiencing exploded into savage disbelief. He couldn't possibly be aroused by her.

'What are you doing? Let go of me!' She couldn't just give
in to him, Gwynneth told herself wildly as she pushed frantically against his chest with her free hand.

'Where are your clothes?'

Her clothes? His question bemused her, making her
frown slightly.

Tariq could feel the silky length of her hair brushing his
chest as she dipped her head and tried to raise her arms to conceal her naked breasts. Her skin looked milky pale against his
own, the movement of her arms bringing the fingers he had
wrapped around her arm into contact with the soft flesh of her
breast. Her eyes were a deep jade, her lips the soft pink of the
inside of a shell dredged up from the depths of the gulf. His

gaze dropped from her mouth to her breasts, creamy pale flesh mounted with warm brown nipples that were swelling and hardening beneath the heat of his gaze.

Gwynneth could hear the sound of her own breathing, feel the heavy sensual pound of her own blood. Her gaze, no longer under her control, dropped boldly down his body to where she had been so determined not to look, and a small sound that she would not allow to be a soft moan of pleasure leaked from her lungs.

Tariq could feel the savage surge of his own anger racing through him, overturning everything in its way. Anger against the woman he was holding, anger against the men who had sent her to him, anger against so many things—but most of all anger against himself. He was simply not prepared to admit to the unwanted piercing stab of desire that was currently arcing through him. It was impossible for him to be aroused by a woman such as this, impossible for him to want her, impossible for him to touch her. But, impossible or not, all three of those things were happening.

CHAPTER TWO

THIS couldn't possibly be happening, Gwynneth decided breathlessly. She could not be standing here naked, body-to-body with this man who was a stranger to her but whom her body was welcoming with such rejoicing.

And yet when he turned her towards him she reached out and touched his face with her fingertips, slowly exploring its structure. His flesh felt warm against the hard contours of his bones, and something about the sheer male arrogance and power of him set off a quivering sensation of wanton excitement inside her. She could feel the heat of his grey-eyed gaze burning into her own skin, her breath catching in her throat as she looked at the thick clumped black lashes shielding his eyes from her. His hands were resting on her waist, almost spanning it. They slid down to her bottom, kneading her flesh, pressing her into his own body and its hard erection. She made a soft sound of pleasure, rubbing herself against him, reaching up to pull his head down towards her so that she could offer up her mouth for him to plunder. The kneading had become a rhythm he was slowly forcing on her own body, using pleasure to make her flesh accept and reciprocate the sensual beat of physical arousal. Now she knew why the sound of softly beaten drums could be so erotic, Gwynneth thought feverishly, as his mouth took hers and his tongue reinforced the rhythm he had set her body.

Now she was her father's daughter. Now she was obeying the call of her own blood. Now she was exposed to that need within herself she had always tried to deny. Now she was not denying it, though. She was embracing it, welcoming it, abandoning herself to it, physically powerless to resist the relentless drive of her own need, and emotionally too flooded with what she was feeling even to want to do so.

There was a pagan drive within her, a stream of subconscious need from the dawn of womanhood, imprinting itself relentlessly over every protective pattern she had ever tried to teach her body.

She *wanted* to feel like this, she recognised dizzily. She needed to experience what she was now experiencing; she needed to take the sweet juicy flesh of sexual arousal and taste every bit of it, savouring its taste and its texture on her fingers, her lips, her tongue, in her mouth, her belly, her deepest self. She wanted to linger over every delicious mouthful, to breathe in its scent, absorb its reality; she wanted to take her own sexuality and relish every second of experiencing its coming of age.

These thoughts flashed hypnotically through her mind, glinting like tiny shoals of brilliantly coloured fish, dizzying in their speed and beauty.

Chad had certainly known what he was about in choosing to send this woman to him, Tariq recognised as his self-control gave up the fight to force his body not to respond to the dangerous shimmering sensuality she exuded. It was almost as though it surrounded her in a multi-layered invisible aura that weakened and then trapped his treacherous senses, until nothing mattered more than satisfying his desire for her.

The increasingly charged sound of their breathing echoed erotically on the sandalwood-scented air. Their lips met, their tongues entwining, and Gwynneth's soft moans were echoed by Tariq's harsher sound of raw male need. Gwynneth kissed his throat, sliding her open mouth over his newly sweat-dampened flesh, tasting the little beads of arousal glistening against the smooth tanned flesh, savouring the fresh, erotically musky scent with which his body was telling her its need. The feel of his hands spread over her bottom, pressing her closer to him, made her sigh with liquid pleasure. His hands stroked upwards to her waist, and up again, whilst the hard thrust of his thigh parted her own. His hands cupped her breasts. She moaned in eager delight, her teeth nipping at the strong column of his throat, her fingers digging into the muscles of his back as her body arched in a torment of longing.

Tariq swung her up into his arms. The moonlight shining in through his bedroom windows highlighted her slender delicacy, silvering the thrust of her hipbones and her desire-swollen mound, whilst shadows deepened the dark allure of her tightly erect nipples.

He had reached the bed, but, too impatient to wait until he had placed her on it, Tariq laid her back against his bent leg, one arm supporting her whilst he looked down at her. He could see the contraction of her ribcage as she breathed, could see too the tiny shudders of arousal quivering over her as she looked up at him, wantonly offering herself up to his visual and physical possession.

How could she be feeling this intensity of physical excitement in lying here, knowing that she was offering her body up to this stranger as a source of erotic pleasure they could both share and enjoy? How could she have come to disassociate herself from her flesh, as though she and this man were co-conspirators, both intent on the same goal of sharing the feast of sensuality they had prepared?

Tariq reached out and slowly stroked his fingertips from the base of her throat down between her breasts, watching as her heart jumped and her breathing deepened, moving lower across the concave dip of her belly to stroke up to the swollen flesh and soft hair covering her pubic bone.

He leaned forward, his tongue flicking against the hollow of her throat as his fingers carefully parted the folded outer lips of her sex.

The flick of his tongue-tip and the stroke of his fingers seemed to create a taut cord of intensity that coiled her pleasure higher and tighter with every touch.

When he lowered her to the bed, without ceasing to caress her, she reached up for him, telling him urgently how good his touch felt, then shuddering when he cupped her breast with his free hand, savouring the erotic texture of her nipple and its response to his sensual stimulation.

Mindlessly Gwynneth reached out for him, her eyes widening and her gaze focusing hotly on him as she tried to enclose him within her grip and realised his potency.

When she exhaled, it was with an instinctive and deep-rooted female recognition of sensual pleasure at his size and strength. Somehow, she realised, her body, her senses, had a knowledge that she herself had never allowed them.

Deep within her female muscles flexed and female flesh heated, whilst a sound that was almost a voluptuous purr of anticipated pleasure vibrated in her throat.

The male flesh she was touching felt hot and slick, the movement of the skin she was rhythmically caressing unexpectedly erotic to her own senses. She moved demandingly on the bed, opening her legs and arching her back as Tariq's fingers stroked over her, experiencing a pleasure that turned her body liquid with aching need.

Had there ever been another woman like this one? Surely she was unique in her erotic offering of herself, in her sensual abandonment to her own pleasure? It took from him the role of being pleasured and demanded instead that he should make himself the provider of her pleasure. She was surely a queen amongst houris, demanding his subservience to her desire, Tariq acknowledged, and the intensity of his own physical desire burned away both his pride and his contempt.

Her tight, erect nipples demanded the worship of his gaze, his touch and his tongue-tip. But to draw one fully into his mouth and to pleasure it rhythmically as he suckled on its swollen heat would, he knew, be a pleasure too far for his self-control. However, the slender fingers sliding into his hair and commanding that he did just that could not be denied.

Gwynneth moaned and trembled convulsively as pleasure leapt fiercely inside her, her fingers tightening around the hard, hot shaft of male flesh that was moving within her grasp in quick urgent strokes, whilst knowing male fingers stroked and tugged the swollen flesh of her clitoris until she cried out aloud in a frenzy of arousal that took her higher and higher, so high that she felt she couldn't bear any more. But even as she cried out against what she was feeling her orgasm was overwhelming her. She heard the man call out, but his words meant nothing. Her body shuddered into its own completion.

It was the way she had abandoned herself so utterly to her

own fulfilment that had thrust him past the barriers he had imposed on himself and overwhelmed his self-control, Tariq decided grimly as he moved away from her to deal with the resolution of his own release.

Five minutes later, when he returned from the bathroom, she was fast asleep.

Tariq frowned as he looked down at her. Why hadn't she dressed and left? That was certainly what he would have preferred her to have done—wasn't it? She opened her eyes and looked up at him and smiled. And then she closed them again. By the time he had exhaled, very, very slowly, she had fallen asleep again.

Still frowning, he pulled the covers over her. At least that way her body was concealed and could no longer be the source of any kind of temptation to him. He should feel nothing but disgust for himself. He *did* feel disgust for himself, Tariq decided grimly. How could he have wanted a woman who sold herself to any man who could afford to buy her? What hitherto unknown to him part of himself had she managed to reach in order to arouse a desire in him strong enough to overwhelm his self-control?

The blending of East and West that was his heritage had given him the advantage of not having any desire to experience the wanton sexuality so freely exhibited by so many Western women. He had never, as other Arab men he knew did, felt any urge to provide himself with the services of a Western mistress, a woman with whom he could have sex without censure and whom he could dismiss from his life when he chose.

Zuran's exclusive hotels did not permit the kind of behaviour indulged in by young Westerners in other foreign resorts.

Topless sunbathing, any kind of intimacy with a man in public—these things were banned by law. But there were men, rich men, who brought with them to Zuran women who were quite plainly not their wives. And, as he was discovering, Zuran had now become a target for the kind of sordid, seedy lifestyle he deplored, for drugs and prostitution racketeers. He was under no illusions; it was common knowledge that the two went hand in hand.

But, even knowing all of that, he had still been unable to stop himself from reacting to the skilled sensuality of a woman he simply shouldn't have wanted to touch.

How many of the other men in the gang had shared this woman's favours? One of them? All of them? Together?

First thing tomorrow morning he would find out who she was and arrange for her to be deported. He didn't want to find her waiting for him a second time, he told himself savagely. He wasn't going to risk another night like tonight. Nor did he want to have to share his bed with her. But, since she was already deeply asleep in it… He looked towards the bedroom door. He had converted the second bedroom into an office, and the furniture in the living room was not conducive to a decent night's sleep. Anyway, why the hell should he give up his right to sleep in his own comfortable king-sized bed because it already had an occupant?

He reached for the covers.

Sunlight pouring through the unshuttered windows slanted gold bars across Gwynneth's face, its heat drawing her reluctantly from sleep. Unfamiliar images and sensations curled like autumn smoke through her thoughts and her body, making her frown in rejection and try to ignore the way her heartbeat picked up.

Cautiously she opened her eyes, exhaling in relief when she found that she was lying in the same bed she had originally gone to sleep in last night—and, more importantly, she was lying there alone. But she had not slept there alone during the night, she recognised, her face starting to burn as she saw the telltale imprint of another head on the pillow next to hers. So last night had not just been a fevered dream or a trick of her imagination.

She pushed back the covers and swung her feet onto the floor, tensing as she did so. She certainly wasn't imagining the small bruises on her skin where hard hands had held her. She wasn't imagining either the heavy fullness of her breasts or the sensitivity of her nipples. There was an unfamiliar ache deep inside her. Of fulfillment? Or of longing for what she had not had? A longing for *more* of what she had had, for the satisfaction of being totally and completely sexually possessed?

She shook her head, trying to disperse the images that clung to her mind as betrayingly as the scent of him still clung to her skin.

She had no idea what had caused last night's aberration in her behaviour, the total deviation from the controlled pathway she normally imposed on it. She could come up with a variety of theories, though, ranging from mundane jet lag to some kind of delayed reaction to her father's death.

Since she did not know what had been responsible for the way she had acted, the best thing she could do now, she told herself sturdily, was to put the entire incident behind her and refuse to give in to the self-indulgence of spending time and energy focusing on it. Like anything else, once starved of energy it would quickly shrivel to nothing.

But the man who had shared the wild passion of the night

with her—who was he? How had he got into the apartment? Logic suggested that he must have a key, which further suggested that he must be employed to look after the apartments in some capacity. Was what had happened last night a regular occurrence? Something he considered to be a perk of the job? If so, she had had a very lucky escape. She shuddered to think now of the kind of health risks she had run in coming so close to unprotected sex with a stranger. Why hadn't she stopped him?

Inside her head she could hear her own voice, taunting her that she was after all her parents' daughter, and that all the years of struggling to deny the fact, to reject it and prove to herself she could never be caught in the trap of her father's sexuality, had been swept away by her physical desire for a stranger.

Her parents' marriage had been the result of her father's uncontrollable sexuality and her mother's equally out-of-control emotional neediness. In a word: lust. She had sworn she would never be like them.

So what had happened?

She didn't drink, and she most certainly didn't do drugs, so she couldn't blame either of them.

She walked into the bathroom and turned on the shower. As she had already told herself, she couldn't change what had happened, but she could refuse to dwell on it or endlessly analyse it. She could choose to ignore it, to seal it off and lock it away where she would never need to think about it again. And, thankfully, there was no reason why she would have to think about it again.

In three days' time she would be back in London, having arranged for ownership of the apartment to be put in her name and having put it up for sale.

She just hoped it would sell quickly. Her plan was that once the apartment had been sold she would have all the money put into a trust fund for Anthony and Teresa. They were both her late father's responsibility after all. Teresa was little more than a girl and Anthony was his son.

Gwynneth dried herself quickly, ignoring the small marks on her body that were evidence of last night's passion. A mental image of herself raking a tanned male shoulder with her teeth, clawing a male back in hunger, flashed through her mind. Defensively she dipped her head, hurrying to get herself some clean clothes. As she left the room, she hesitated. What if he was still here somewhere in the apartment, waiting….? Waiting for what? A repeat of last night? Her belly clenched fiercely around the distinctive and very betraying surge of hot excitement that stirred inside her. He wasn't here, she told herself. Instinctively she knew that. Taking a deep breath, she opened the bedroom door and stepped resolutely into the hallway.

Half an hour later, having been delighted to find some coffee in a kitchen that was otherwise bare of provisions, she was ready to leave for her appointment. Picking up her handbag, she frowned as she saw the thick wad of Zurani currency stuffed into her passport. How had that got there? Uneasily she removed the money from her handbag, her eyes widening as she saw the note that was with it. The words *To professional services for last night* were written firmly on the paper, and it was abundantly plain just what they meant.

Automatically she stiffened in angry rejection of both the meaning of the note and her own reaction to it. How could she possibly feel hurt because a man who was a complete stranger had made an error of judgement? Although even though he was a stranger, it was a very insulting error of judgement, she reminded herself shakily. After all, he was the one who had invaded her privacy and entered the apartment uninvited. Even so…

Hadn't she always believed that she had to be guardian of her own reputation and her own values? That she had to do everything she could to prevent herself being labelled as her father's daughter?

Maybe, but surely a woman could have sex with a man without being labelled a whore? By what right did a man who walked into an unknown woman's apartment and then had a sexual encounter with her assume she was selling the sex? By the right of being male? Did she really need to tell herself that? Wasn't it a given—something that all women instinctively understood? Outwardly things might have changed from the days when a woman's virtue and virginity were something to be prized, but inwardly they hadn't changed as much as people liked to think.

By leaving her money he was telling her brutally what he thought of her. She was a commodity he had bought and used. And having used her he was now discarding her.

Dry-eyed, but with her face burning and her heart hot with furious outrage, she left the apartment.

CHAPTER THREE

TARIQ frowned as he listened to the Ruler's Chief of Police deploring the fact that because they had not as yet discovered the identity of the Zurani who was working for the gang he could not give the order for the gang to be deported, after a warning of the very long prison sentence they would face if they were ever found in Zuran again.

Knowing that it was almost time for the Ruler to hold his regular monthly public *divan*—traditionally an opportunity for the Ruler's subjects to bring to him their problems and questions so that he might dispense with justice and answers—Tariq stood up and bowed formally to the Ruler, as did the Chief of Police.

On her way back to the apartment, following her appointment, Gwynneth had stopped off at a small supermarket to buy a few basic supplies. As she put these away in the empty cupboards and fridge freezer of the apartment it was what she had been told by the sympathetic young official she had met earlier that was occupying her thoughts.

It had never occurred to her that there might be a problem

registering her ownership of the apartment—especially since she had followed the advice she had been given by the Zurani Embassy in London and had brought with her documentation to prove her father's ownership of the apartment and to confirm her own identity. Fortunately, when her father had boasted to her about the apartment he had shown her the deeds and told her that he intended to deposit them with his London bank for safekeeping.

Now, though, it transpired that proving her father's ownership of the apartment was not going to be as straightforward as simply producing the deeds—as the charming official had explained to her, in an extremely grave tone of voice.

Her heart had sunk just about as low as she felt it could sink as she'd listened to him telling her about the double-selling scam that had resulted in two separate sets of buyers believing they had purchased the same property. And then had come the additional blow of hearing about the length of time it would take to make painstaking enquiries to establish who had been duped and who in fact did own a property.

'So what should I do now?' she had appealed.

'If you are able to do so, your best course of action would be to remain here in Zuran until we can establish whether or not your father owned the apartment.'

'I'm actually staying in the apartment,' Gwynneth had felt obliged to tell him, adding with concern, 'And I certainly can't afford to pay for a hotel. If there is another potential owner, then…'

'I shall make a note on the file to the effect that you are currently occupying the flat, but that you are aware of the issue of its ownership,' she had been told.

Now Gwynneth reached for her mobile and switched it on.

She would have to tell Teresa what had happened, but first she had another phone call to make.

As she pressed the speed dial for her boss's number she looked at her watch. It would be nine o'clock in the morning in the UK. Piers would have been at work for a while now. He was a workaholic who liked to be at his desk by eight.

He picked up the call within a couple of rings.

'Hi, Piers—it's Gwynneth,' she announced herself, smiling when she heard the warmth in his voice as he answered.

They had been working together for over a year, and Piers had made it plain that he wanted to put their relationship on a more personal footing. However, much as she liked him as a person, she had no desire for them to become a couple, and so had refused his offers to take her out as gently as she could.

Quickly she explained what was happening, exhaling in relief when he said immediately that she must stay in Zuran for as long as it took to get things sorted out.

'I know you aren't a clock-watcher, Gwynneth. You've put in a lot of extra hours these last few months, and I appreciate that. I'm going to miss you, though,' he told her softly. 'Pity I can't take some time off myself and fly out there to join you,' he added ruefully, before they ended their call.

Her duty to her employers dealt with, Gwynneth started to wonder if she ought to get in touch with the British Embassy in Zuran and get their opinion of the situation with regard to the apartment. But the young Zurani official had cautioned her not to discuss the matter with anyone, explaining that the Zurani authorities, whilst not responsible for the fraud in any way, were prepared to deal fairly and sympathetically with the victims providing they undertook not to fuel panic or potentially destructive rumours by talking publicly about what had happened.

Just how long would she have to stay here in Zuran before everything was sorted out? Long enough for last night's stranger to make a return visit? Immediately she stiffened in rejection of the feeling surging through her. She had told herself not to think about last night, or the man she had shared it with. It was over—gone—and for her own sake she should accept that.

But what if she didn't want to accept it? If she wanted…

What? A repeat performance? Was she totally crazy? She suddenly remembered that she still had the money he had left her in her handbag. Opening it, she removed the bundle of notes with trembling fingers. So much money. Even without counting it she could see that.

Money that Teresa and Anthony might need very badly if things went wrong and it turned out that the apartment wasn't her father's and the Zurani Government chose not to compensate her.

She dropped the notes onto the table as swiftly as though they were contaminated. If only she knew more. How long would she have to wait for that promised phone call?

She went into the kitchen and filled the kettle with water, having decided to make herself a cup of coffee before she spoke to Teresa, whom she knew would be anxiously waiting to hear from her.

He couldn't wait to get this whole wretched business sorted out, and the corrupt Zurani official unmasked, so that he could get on with his own life. A life that did not include in it a woman like Gwynneth Talbot, Tariq assured himself grimly, as he stepped out of the lift and slid the key card into the door of the apartment. He had such plans for the small desert kingdom he had inherited.

The discovery that an old legend attached to it, claiming that it had once been the site of some hanging gardens said to rival those of ancient Babylon, had actually been founded on fact had led to Tariq's decision to have the site of the original palace and its gardens excavated and if possible reconstructed. It was an ambitious and long-term plan, but one that would be richly rewarding, and Tariq was totally committed to its execution. The ongoing work on the project was already attracting the interest of both tourists and experts in the archaeological field.

Normally when Tariq was in Zuran he stayed either at the Palace or in his personal suite at one of the two hotels in which he had a financial interest. However, whenever he could he much preferred to spend his free time living simply in the desert, in one of the black tents of his mother's Bedouin ancestors. Bedouin tribesmen still travelled the old desert routes, although their numbers were dwindling now, and certain members of the Ruler's extended family had close connections with such tribes—as he did himself through his mother. Just thinking of the desert brought him a fierce longing for the feel of one of his fleet-footed Arabian horses beneath him as they raced together across the sands while dawn broke and the sun started to rise. Inside his head he could see the mental image his longing was creating. And he could see, too, the woman who rode at his side, her face turned towards his own, her green eyes brilliant with excitement for the desert and for him—

Tariq froze in furious rejection of the image that slipped so treacherously past his guard. The woman he would choose to share his life would *not* be that woman. Last night's woman. Gwynneth. He had seen her name in her passport when he had pushed the money into her bag this morning.

Gwynneth! The first thing Tariq heard when he walked into the apartment was the sound of her voice.

'There's a bit of a problem. But don't worry. I'll do whatever I have to do to make sure we get the money—just as I promised you I would, and no matter how long I have to stay here to get it or what I have to do.'

She was speaking grimly. As though she was trying to reassure someone. She was seated at the kitchen table with her back to him, the money he had left her this morning in an untidy pile beside her.

An uncomfortable mix of very powerful feelings was fighting for control of his emotions: righteous anger that she had dared to stay here when he had made it obvious that he wanted her to leave; and a deeper, darker feeling of savaged male pride at hearing her underline the fact that all he was to her was a source of income. The physical memories of last night were storming the defences he had put up against them like grains of sand chafing against his skin.

Gwynneth sighed as she ended her call to Teresa. She hadn't wanted to worry the younger girl by saying too much to her, even though she desperately wanted to have someone she could confide her own anxieties to. Her mind was still on Teresa and the problems of her father's apartment, but some sixth sense made her turn round, the colour momentarily leaving her face only to return in a hot wave of betraying soft pink awareness as she stood up shakily.

'*You!* You've come back!'

'Very dramatic—but somewhat ineffective, surely? Since you must have realised that I *would* come back.' Tariq responded curtly to her breathy gasp.

Had she? He had such a powerful air of authority about

him that for a moment she was almost in danger of believing him. Almost.

'Why would I do that?' she challenged him daringly.

'I should have thought that was obvious.'

Gwynneth couldn't help it. She could feel the colour burning up under her skin as her body reacted to what he had said. Her body couldn't actually be *pleased* that he had come back? That he wanted more of her? Could it? Surely that wasn't possible? She mustn't let it feel like that, she decided, panicking. What had happened last night was excusable—just—as an isolated, never to be repeated incident. So long as that was what it remained.

'After all,' Tariq continued, 'this does happen to be my apartment.'

His apartment? *His* apartment? She stared at him in shocked dismay. That couldn't possibly be true! Could it? A horrible cold feeling of uncertainty and dismay was creeping over her. What if it was true? If it was, then obviously he wasn't here because of her. He hadn't come back because he wanted a repeat performance of last night's sex, as she had so humiliatingly assumed.

If it was true— But it wasn't true. It couldn't possibly be true; she wasn't going to let it be true, she decided wildly, her normal facility for calm, rational, logical thinking disintegrating in the face of her emotional reaction to both him and his unwelcome information.

But worse was to come. As she struggled to assimilate his unwelcome news he added sharply, 'Since I've already added a generous bonus to what you were paid for last night—particularly generous under the circumstances—I fail to see why you are still here. Surely for a woman in your profession time is money? Or did you think I might be persuaded to keep you on for tonight as well?'

'Are you trying to suggest that I'm a prostitute?' Gwynneth demanded in disbelief.

'Are you trying to suggest that you aren't?' His voice was as derisive as the look in his eyes. 'Because if so you're wasting your time. I know what you are, why you were waiting in my bed for me, and who arranged for you to be there.'

'What? This is crazy!' Gwynneth protested shakily. 'Who—? Who—?'

'Stop right there. I don't want to hear another word. Pick up your money and go,' Tariq ordered, then frowned as his mobile—the one he used only for calls from the gang—started to ring.

'Wait,' he told Gwynneth contradictorily, striding out of the kitchen and closing the door behind him, leaving her inside.

'Get yourself down to the marina—pronto. Chad wants to see you—now.' The familiar voice of one of the gang members rasped in Tariq's ear.

The call was disconnected before he could make any response. He looked at the closed kitchen door. At this delicate stage in the proceedings he couldn't afford to antagonise the leader of the gang by refusing to obey him.

What on earth had she got herself into? Gwynneth worried anxiously. Suddenly she was seeing last night's uncharacteristic and admittedly very dangerous and foolish sexual adventure in a very different and sickeningly seedy and unpleasant light. She had been mistaken for a prostitute and she was about to be evicted from her own apartment. The situation she was in couldn't have been any worse. Could it? What about the fact that not so very long ago she had virtually caught herself wondering if last night's events might be repeated?

The kitchen door was opening.

Gwynneth took a deep breath.

'You've got this all wrong. I am *not* a prostitute.'

She certainly wasn't done up like one, Tariq acknowledged, unable to stop himself from looking not so much *at* her as *for* her, the moment he stepped into the kitchen. She wasn't wearing make-up, her clothes looked more suited to an office worker, and no man looking at her would feel that she was making any attempt to be alluring. And as for last night... He had been the one pleasuring her, not the other way around.

'I'd agree that you certainly aren't a good advertisement for your profession,' he agreed unkindly.

'Why won't you listen to me?' Gwynneth protested. 'I am not a prostitute! I'm—'

'An escort?' Tariq suggested silkily, and gave a condemnatory shrug. 'It doesn't matter what name you give what you do. It doesn't change the fact that you sell your body to men for their sexual pleasure. Do your family know what you do? Your father?' he demanded abruptly, without knowing why he should be asking her such a question—the kind of question that might almost suggest that he cared.

'My father is dead.'

So, like him, she was fatherless. That was no reason for him to feel the sudden surge of fellow feeling towards her, Tariq warned himself angrily.

'So is mine,' he told her coldly. 'That is no excuse. Surely there is some other way you could support yourself? Have you no pride? No self-respect? No—?'

'I don't need an excuse. And as for *me* not having any pride— what about you?' Gwynneth shot back, and took advantage of the sudden silence her attack had gained her to point out pithily, 'After all, you didn't exactly reject me, did you?'

What she was saying was perfectly true, but that didn't make it any easier to accept, Tariq admitted unwillingly.

He could almost feel her angry defiance burning through the air-conditioned chill of the small kitchen. No woman who lived as this one did had the right to look and behave as she was. She was positively exuding righteous indignation, forcing him to see and react to her as a human being and not a piece of human merchandise. He had to put an end to this dangerous emotional connection she had somehow brought to life between them. Apart from anything else, he was going to be late for his meeting on the yacht.

'You can stop right there,' he told Gwynneth, crossing the kitchen and taking hold of her arm before she could evade him.

Had he changed his mind? Was he, despite all he had said, going to drag her back to his bed right now and…? A shocking explicit thrill of female excitement shot through her, weakening her so much that she sagged slightly in his hold, leaning into him, her breasts pressing against the hardness of his arm. Without even having to think about it she leaned closer and harder, closing her eyes the better to relish her own pleasure at the sensual contact between her flesh and his. And in that hot darkness she was immediately transported back to the arousal-drenched hours of the previous night, complete with faithful audio as well as visual record.

Tariq looked down into the face turned up towards his own. Her eyes were closed and her lips were open; even her skin seemed to shimmer with sensual luminosity. He had been wrong, he realised savagely as he felt his own body react to her. She was not just good at her chosen profession. She was exceptional. He couldn't remember any woman arousing him either so immediately or so intensely—and certainly not both at the same time. His fingers bit into the softness of her arm as he made to shake her off, but still he couldn't drag his gaze from the temptation of her parted lips. Nor could he stop himself from wanting to reach out and fill his free hand with the weight of one of the soft warm breasts she had pressed so deliberately and enticingly against his arm. Was it because of last night that he was having so much trouble rejecting the images his mind was conjuring up? Because of how she had made him feel then that he wanted her so immediately and fiercely now?

Despite the coolness of the kitchen Tariq could feel sweat dampening his flesh whilst his mind raced with the turmoil of his emotions.

'Forget it,' he told her brutally, and pushed her away, keeping only a tight hold on one wrist.

Gwynneth's eyes snapped open, and she sucked in a distressed breath as reality crashed back down. 'Forget what?' she demanded, recouping. 'Forget that you've insulted me—verbally, physically and emotionally?' The numbing effect of her original shock and his sensual appeal had worn off now, leaving her sick with fury and disbelief.

'Forget those unsubtle plans you're hatching for tonight,' he corrected her. 'Because I'm telling you now, you won't be spending it my bed.'

No, she wouldn't. Because it wasn't *his* bed. It was hers, and she had the documents to prove it—or at least she hoped she did. She didn't have anywhere else to stay, and she certainly wasn't going to be bullied into moving out of the apartment by a man who had mistaken her for a prostitute!

'Let go of me!'

For a moment she thought he was going to ignore her, that instead he would pull her close to him again and…

The angry hiss of his breath as he exhaled told her she was wrong.

'I have to go out now,' he told her flatly. 'And you had better not be here when I get back.' The last thing he wanted was to be seen leaving the apartment with a woman of her type—otherwise he would have physically removed her himself.

And how will you do that? a small, cynical inner voice mocked him. *Via the bedroom?*

Silencing it, he continued, 'If you are, then I shall inform the police of your presence and your profession. And since, as I am sure you already know, prostitution is against the law in Zuran, you will be deported and refused future entry to the country.'

Now, abruptly, fear was crawling through her veins and locking onto her anger, feeding off its strength and smothering it.

'You can't do that,' she protested, adding emotionally, 'You're making a mistake!'

Tariq's mouth compressed. 'No. You are the one who is doing that.'

Gwynneth swung away from him to conceal her expression. Thinking that she was going to walk out on him, Tariq stepped in front of her. Immediately it was as though they were locked together inside an invisible bubble of sensual tension—or so it seemed to Gwynneth as she tried to make her lungs work properly and her heart slow to its normal rate. She couldn't seem to look anywhere but at the man standing in front of her, to do anything but remember last night—feel anything but the intense arousal that she was feeling.

What was it about her that had this effect on him? Tariq wondered savagely. At no time in the whole of his life had he wanted to take hold of any woman and kiss her until the only words her lips could frame were his name and a plea for more.

Hold me…touch me…make me yours. Gwynneth could feel the words pounding through her veins with every thud of her heartbeat, filling her mind and her senses. So much so that she felt as though they were written into her flesh. Her angry pride fought with the liquid heat of her desire and was overwhelmed by it as it flooded over the rigid barriers trickling through every tiny hole it could find to reunite in a fast-flowing surge that took her across the no man's land that was the space between them and into the heat zone of Tariq's body. She could sense the command going from his brain to his muscles to lift his arms so that they could enfold her. And once they had…

There was a ringing sound inside her head. No, not inside her head. The noise was coming from the mobile Tariq was lifting to his ear as he turned away from her. Who was calling him? A woman? Something previously unknown and darkly dangerous ripped at her emotions.

'Where are you? You were supposed to be at the marina ten minutes ago.'

'I've been delayed,' Tariq answered, looking briefly at Gwynneth and wondering how much she was being paid to spy on him as well as go to bed with him before he added coolly, 'Chad will understand why when I explain.'

'You'd better hope he does. Otherwise you're going to be in big trouble. Get yourself down here, double-quick.'

There was no time for him to argue with Gwynneth. Nor to do anything else with her either. Like what? There wasn't *anything* he wanted to do with her.

Liar, an inner voice goaded him as he opened the kitchen door. He ignored it as he paused to warn her, 'Remember what I told you. When I get back I don't want to find you here. If you are, you know what you can expect.'

CHAPTER FOUR

GWYNNETH tottered over to the table and sank down thankfully into one of the chairs. Her legs felt boneless, her heart was racing, her forehead was damp with sweat and her mouth was dry. Classic signs of fear—or sexual excitement.

What on earth was happening to her? A man—a stranger— a naked stranger—walked into her bedroom, and instead of screaming for help she went to bed with him. That same man accused her of being a prostitute and she still let herself be aroused by him. *Let* herself? Since when, in the whole of this nightmarish scenario, had what purported to be the thinking, reasoning part of her had any say in *anything*? Why hadn't she insisted on him listening to her? Why hadn't she made him understand just how wrong he was?

She would have to inform the young man who was trying to help her what had happened. Well, at least some of what had happened, she amended mentally. Why hadn't she insisted on *him*, her co-owner, giving her his name? That way at least she would have had something concrete to pass on to the authorities. Was he the rightful owner of the apartment or was she?

She looked for her handbag. It was on the worktop. She

found the card the young official had given her and tapped his phone number into her mobile.

He answered her call almost immediately. Introducing herself, she asked anxiously if he remembered their meeting, exhaling in relief when he assured her that he did. Quickly she told him what had happened.

'You say this man claims that he too is the owner of the apartment?' the young official questioned.

'That's what he said,' Gwynneth confirmed unhappily.

'We have no record as yet of anyone else lodging a claim against this apartment,' he assured her.

'So that means that I am in the clear to stay here, does it?' Gwynneth pressed him.

'Certainly,' he agreed promptly. 'We know that your apartment block is one of those involved in this unfortunate fraud, but as yet no one else has come forward to claim ownership of your particular apartment. However, as I explained to you, that does not mean another potential owner does not exist,' he cautioned.

'But until they actually present themselves to you and make a legal claim the apartment is notionally at least mine?'

'You are certainly free to make use of it until such time as we have ascertained who in fact *does* own it,' he corrected her gently.

Well, at least that meant that she didn't have to give in to *his* bullying, Gwynneth reassured herself later, in an attempt to quell the anxiety that was causing her to feel so on edge.

He might believe he had the upper hand, with his threats to tell the police about her and have her deported, but he was the one who was going to look foolish when he was forced to accept the truth. And she was going to make sure that he *did* accept it, Gwynneth decided vigorously. No matter what it took. No way was *any* man going to be allowed to make the kind of assumptions about her *he* had made, without her defending herself from them.

It felt bittersweet now to look back on her waking moments this morning and her dread that he might have realised how new she was to everything they had shared, and that from that he might have thought that he was something—someone—special. Ridiculously, she had even begun her defence against that. How naïve she had been, believing that all she had to protect herself from was a choice between two fears: one, that she had inherited her father's sexuality, the other that somehow or other in touching her flesh *he* had also touched her heart. She had thought then in her naïveté that nothing could be worse than being forced to defend herself with one of these two choices. But now she knew better.

How could he possibly believe that what had happened between them last night had been motivated on her part by money? Surely he had to have been able to see that she wasn't like that—that she couldn't cold-bloodedly sell her flesh for some man to use whilst she distracted herself from what he was doing by counting up the financial benefit she was going to gain. Behind her anger and her disbelief, and her fears about the apartment and the future of Teresa and Anthony, there was also a growing feeling of shocked misery and pain.

She wanted her self-respect back; she wanted back the person she had been before *him*. And as for her leaving the apartment—no way was she going anywhere. Not now.

'Ah, Tariq. Good. I'm glad you're here…finally.'

Chad Rheinvelt's smile and voice were as smooth as the satin skin of the half-naked girl he was caressing as he lounged in his chair in the main cabin of the luxurious yacht. Several other members of the gang were also in the cabin, standing with their arms folded across their chests or slouching against the cabin walls. Bully boys, heavies, enforcers— it didn't matter what label you put on them, their appearance made it obvious what they were, Tariq reflected grimly.

'I've got a job for you,' Chad told him. He had slipped his hand into the girl's skimpy top and she was now squirming in supposed delight as he played with her breast whilst his men looked on.

The girl he was fondling might easily have been Gwynneth.

Tariq's raw, savage emotional response to that knowledge caught him off guard. What the hell was he doing, allowing himself to react like this to a woman who sold her body to any man who could afford to buy it?

'You've told us all about your high status in Zuran. Here's your chance to prove it. I need official sanction for a few friends of mine to make a long-term stay in Zuran—no questions asked. And I need it quickly.'

'A few friends?' Tariq questioned.

Chad turned to the girl, who was now sliding one slim brown hand along his inner thigh, her tongue-tip pressed wetly against her bottom lip. Tariq could feel his belly curling with contempt and revulsion.

'Jeni here is one of them. Fancy her? Regretting that you turned down my offer to send her to you now, are you? Your loss. She's pretty good. The girls who work for me are all tried out first by one of us, and if they're especially good they might be lucky enough to have a few of us put them through their paces—eh, Jeni?' Chad was laughing as he tweaked her nipple, his erection straining openly against the cloth of his shorts.

Had he misunderstood what Chad had just said? Tariq re-played the words very carefully and slowly inside his head.

'Well, don't worry. There's plenty more where Jeni comes from if you change your mind. Or at least there will be once you do your stuff for us. How long will it take a man in your position to get this sorted, Tariq?'

Somehow Tariq managed to drag his thoughts away from the enormity of what he had just heard and focus them instead on the open challenge he was being given. As a test? Or as a trap?

'How long is a piece of string?' he responded, as carelessly as he could. 'I can make it possible for the girls to enter Zuran immediately.' That was certainly true. He gave a small shrug. 'But for me to do so without causing any questions to be asked or arousing any suspicions may take a little time.'

Chad was listening to him in silence. Had they somehow found out the truth about him? But, after a pause that Tariq felt was too long, Chad inclined his head and gave a small nod.

'Okay, you've got that time. But I want to be kept fully informed. Oh, and be warned. There isn't any room in this organisation for those who can't keep their promises.'

Was that merely a warning to him? Or an allusion to the Zurani official who was working on the fraudulent property scam with him? It would be impossible for anyone else to get permission for Chad's prostitutes to so much as enter the country, never mind work there as he plainly intended them to do. Even Tariq couldn't have done so other than as part of his current undercover operation.

He was strongly tempted to ask directly about the other Zurani national who was in Chad's pay. But that would, he knew, risk the whole operation. The urge only underlined how impatient he was to be free to walk away from the whole sordid affair. He needed to wait, to earn Chad's trust, before he could start digging for his criminal countryman's identity.

There was something he *could* ask, though.

'Are any of the girls actually working here yet?' he asked Chad as carelessly as he could.

'I'm not that much of a fool,' Chad told him. 'I've paid good money for them—they're clean, well taught, stunning to look at, not your out-of-the-gutter, everyone's-already-had-it tat. No way am I going to risk losing my investment by letting them work until I've got an official okay. Jeni and a few more are here on the yacht to show to certain special customers whom I can trust and who might want to prebook their services. No way do they go anywhere without my say-so, and one of my men is keeping a watch on them. The rest of them are in a safe house outside the country, and I've got a bunch of guys making sure they stay there. Do you want to have a look at the rest of them?'

Tariq nodded his head.

Five minutes later, six stunningly beautiful young women were lined up in front of him. Six totally unfamiliar young women. Not one of them was Gwynneth, and it was plain that if one of his expensive properties were missing Chad would know about it.

'If you like, you can have Jeni tonight. I'll get one of the guys to bring her over to your place for a couple of hours and then bring her back. Or you can have a couple of hours here with her now? Premium rates apply, though.' Chad laughed.

Tariq shook his head. 'Not right now. There are people I need to speak to with regard to what we've just been discussing,' he told him truthfully.

* * *

Gwynneth stiffened defensively as she heard Tariq come in, her mouth dry as she stared at the locked door of the study. The room had obviously been intended to be used as a bedroom but someone—him, no doubt—had furnished it as an office, with a desk and a computer, a small sofabed and a shelf of books. One of them in particular had caught her eye, because it was a history of Zuran. Under normal circumstances she would have felt tempted to pick it up and read it.

Her heart was pounding. She had discovered that this small room had a lock on it when she had explored the apartment after Tariq had gone, and she had decided to lock herself inside it to await his return. That way at least she could stop him from forcibly evicting her from the apartment—although the small study with its equally small *en suite* bathroom was now beginning to feel slightly claustrophobic.

Tariq looked around the apparently empty flat. Had she taken him at his word and left? He discovered that he wasn't as pleased by that thought as he ought to have been. His overdeveloped sense of duty was making him want to see a neat and tidy end to events, rather than having to worry about what a young woman as reckless as Ms Gwynneth Talbot might get herself involved with next.

He could still smell her scent on the air—prim, light and delicate. He strode into the kitchen and saw the handbag and mobile phone on the counter with some relief. She was clearly still here. He walked over to them and removed Gwynneth's passport from her bag.

He frowned as he heard a small rustle of sound. It was coming from his office.

'Gwynneth?'

Her tension increased when she heard him calling her

name, but not because she was alarmed this time. No, the tension tightening through her body had a very different cause. Images flashed through her head—a large bed, a satin-skinned naked male body, knowing hands whose touch she could still feel on her own flesh.

Tariq stalked over to the office, and cursed under his breath when he realised that she had locked herself in.

'Open this door!' he demanded.

'You have no right to tell me to do anything,' Gwynneth called back. 'You may think that you own this apartment, but I have the paperwork to prove that my father believed he owned it too. Now he's dead, and it's mine. And I'm not going to be bullied or threatened into walking out of it and leaving you in sole possession. This is a very valuable property, and until someone proves that it isn't mine I'm going to stay right here, where I can make sure no one can take it away from me.'

She was proud of the firmness in her voice, and proud too of the words she had been rehearsing so carefully.

So she wasn't a prostitute. But money was obviously important to her—very important, if she was prepared to stay here after the accusations he had made against her, Tariq thought scathingly. There had been no emotion whatsoever in her voice when she had spoken of her father's death.

'We need to talk properly about this,' he advised her.

'I've already tried to do that,' Gwynneth reminded him. 'But you wouldn't listen. For all I know everything you've said and done from the moment I walked into the apartment could be part of some plan you've hatched to try and get me to leave the country so that you can claim this place.'

'You're being ridiculous.'

'Am I? You obviously have a key for this place, just as I
do. You've got to know about this double-selling fraud that's
been going on, but you haven't registered your interest with
the authorities as I've done. I've checked up on that! Why
not?' she challenged him. 'If you genuinely believe the apartment to be yours then that is the first thing you would have
done. I think you are some kind of opportunist, and this place
isn't yours at all. You must have been over the moon when
you discovered your only rival for ownership was me.' It was
heaven being able to speak her mind to him like this, knowing
that she was safely out of his reach.

'So you're going to stay in there and starve, are you?' Tariq
demanded. 'The legal process here in Zuran is notoriously
long-winded.'

Food! She hadn't thought of that in her relief at discovering she could lock him out.

'A human being can live for weeks just on water.'

'Some can—certain members of the Bedouin tribe
amongst them—but I doubt you could. Besides, I have a spare
key to the study.'

Gwynneth looked at the door.

'I'm not a prostitute,' she warned him.

Tariq exhaled impatiently.

'No, I realise that now.'

'What? How? Why?' Why was she sounding as though she
was grateful to him for accepting what was, after all, the
truth? 'I could report you to the authorities for what you've
done—and said,' she said, attempting menace.

'Not from in there you can't,' Tariq told her succinctly. 'My
computer is locked and you left your mobile in the kitchen—
along with your handbag.' While he had been talking to her

he had also been punching into his own mobile the hotline number to Zuran's Chief of Police. He now had enough information on Gwynneth to get a full report on her. He walked away from the study and into the kitchen, putting her passport back into her bag as he passed it and shutting the door behind him, so that he could instruct the Chief to find out everything he could about her.

'Oh, and I think it could be worthwhile checking to see if anyone within the government has been making enquiries about the possibility of bringing fifty or so young women into the country. Chad Rheinvelt has asked me to make it possible for him to import a group of prostitutes to work in Zuran. I've had to pretend to agree to do what he's asked, but I've warned him it could take time.'

Gwynneth listened to the muffled sounds of speech and reflected on her situation. She had no food, no mobile, no means of contacting the outside world. He had at least accepted that she wasn't a prostitute. Didn't it therefore make sense for her to unlock the door and talk to him face-to-face?

Tariq heard the key turning in the lock as he opened the kitchen door. Impassively he stood and waited for Gwynneth to come out.

It was unfortunate that she was so determined to lay claim to the apartment. Not that he wanted it. However, whilst he was obliged to masquerade as a disaffected member of Zuran's ruling family, motivated by resentment and greed, he had no option but to stay here. Chad was a wily operator, a man who did not trust anyone easily. And to leave the apartment would inevitably arouse his suspicions.

Neither could he have his own interest in the apartment legally registered. That would lead to all manner of complications, and potentially increase the risk of him being unmasked. If anything, it was even more important now that Tariq should lull Chad into a false sense of security until they found out the identity of the Zurani in Chad's pay. He had to be unmasked before he and Chad found some way of perverting the law to enable Chad to bring his drug and prostitution rackets into Zuran. The international damage that would do to the credibility of the Ruler, and through him to Zuran itself, was incalculable. Zuran had a reputation to maintain, as a safe and law-abiding country, and it was on that reputation that its future success as an international tourist destination was based.

As Gwynneth stepped out and walked through to join him in the kitchen, Tariq's first thought was that somehow she looked smaller and more vulnerable than the image of her he had been carrying around in his mind.

It was difficult for her to lift her head and look him in the eye after not just what that happened but also what he had said and thought about her, but somehow Gwynneth managed to do so.

'So,' Tariq began, 'let me get this straight. You believe that your father owned this apartment?'

'No, I *know* that he owned it,' Gwynneth corrected him smartly. 'And I've got the papers to prove it.'

Ignoring that, Tariq asked, 'When did your father die?'

'Almost three weeks ago.'

'You mean you've waited as long as that to come here and claim your inheritance?' Tariq didn't bother to keep the contempt out of his voice.

Gwynneth's face started to burn, but before she could justify her behaviour by explaining about Teresa and Anthony his mobile started to ring. Tariq was looking at her in silence, waiting for her response. He continued to look at her, despite his ringing mobile, and the grim resoluteness of his concentration forced Gwynneth to look away as he finally answered it.

'Wait here,' he commanded, turning to walk out of the kitchen and closing the door behind him.

Tariq's caller was the Chief of Police, who was ringing to give him the information he had gathered on Gwynneth. He explained that she had taken leave from her job in the City of London to come to Zuran because she believed she had inherited an apartment purchased by her late father.

'Since this apartment is one of those involved in the recent double-selling fraud, she has been told that there could be a delay in establishing ownership. It seems she is anxious to register the property in her own name and then sell it as quickly as she can. She has been told, of course, about the Zurani compensation programme that is in force for victims of this fraud.'

'And she is legitimately the daughter and heir of this man?' Tariq demanded.

'The papers she produced were all in order,' the Chief of Police assured him.

'And this job in the City of London—what exactly is it?'

'She works as a financial analyst.'

'And that is her only source of income?' he persisted.

'Yes, as far as we know.'

Thanking the other man for the information he had obtained for him, Tariq ended the call and looked towards the closed door.

He had made a serious error of judgement. And that, for a man with his sense of pride and honour, was something he found very hard to bear. Even worse, he had allowed his emotions to conceal the truth from him in the same way that the silken veils of a dancing girl could obscure her body. A man watching her dance would be intoxicated and dazzled by the swirling colours and patterns of the silk, just as *he* had allowed himself to be deceived by the swirling mists of his anger. He had seen a naked woman and he had told himself that she was there to offer herself to him.

But that did not mean that he had to blame himself for what had happened. She had not attempted to stop him or to protest, had she? She had not behaved in any way that might have warned him he had made an error of judgement. She had not said or done anything to suggest that having sex with a stranger was not something she did regularly. But then, according to what he had heard, some modern young women were what he considered to be sexually promiscuous—although they did not see it that way. They boasted openly of one-night stands, and worse! And, that being the case, why should he berate himself for taking what she had given? He owed her nothing.

CHAPTER FIVE

TARIQ opened the door and strode back into the kitchen.

Gwynneth watched him with a small quiver of sensation gripping her stomach. It was ridiculous, she knew, but she was forced to admit that there was something about the sight of a tall, forbiddingly imposing man dressed in flowing white robes that triggered a dangerous and previously unknown reaction in her. Or was it just *this* man who caused that reaction? The question slipped under her guard before she could deflect it, leaving her feeling agitated and angrily defensive as she fought to deny that her reaction was based on anything personal.

'So, if you believe that your father owned this apartment, why didn't you say anything about it last night?'

It took Gwynneth several precious seconds to dismiss the effect he was having on her and to gather up the threads of their previous discussion.

'When?' she answered. 'You hardly gave me the chance. I thought I was alone in the apartment, and then I thought you had broken in, and…'

Tariq gave her a derisory look.

'Everything happened so quickly,' she defended herself. 'And you are a woman who has a hunger for money and no doubt thought that by going to bed with me you might be able to acquire a little more—perhaps in the form of a gift of some sort?'

'No!' Gwynneth denied sharply. But it wasn't true, was it? She *had* deep down inside, with that part of her she never normally allowed to surface, wanted a gift from him— the gift of her own sexual fulfilment via wild, passionate and abandoned sexual intimacy. 'I was just—taken by surprise.'

'So why, then, once you were over the shock of my presence, didn't you stop me?'

'I…I didn't know what to think.'

She hadn't stopped him because she hadn't been capable of doing so—hadn't wanted to do so. Because she had entered a state of physical delight that had totally overwhelmed any kind of rationality, where self-denial had been the last thing on her mind.

The look he was giving her made her face burn hotly.

'I was half asleep,' she defended herself. 'I hardly knew what was happening, never mind *why* it was happening.'

She couldn't tell him about her past, about her father. And she certainly couldn't tell him about the repression of her own sexuality, or the fact that in some unfathomable way he had been the key that had turned the lock to release that pent-up sensuality. How could she possibly explain that to him when she could not understand it herself? And besides, if she did he might take it as a sign that…

That what? That she was vulnerable to him? That she might want to repeat what had happened? That she might want *him*? Well, she didn't. And even if she had done she would not have allowed herself to go on doing so, Gwynneth assured herself fiercely.

Another man might have been fooled and flattered into succumbing to that note of emotional vulnerability in the soft shakiness of her voice, Tariq acknowledged. But he was not that other man. He was not so easily taken in.

Not mentally or emotionally, maybe, but what about physically? What about the way he had reacted to her last night, and then again earlier today? That had not been the reaction of a man who was fully in control of himself and his body, had it?

It irked him that he had to subject himself to such inner questioning and probing, and he gave Gwynneth a look of razor-sharp cynicism, his voice cutting and arrogant.

'But this morning, when you found the note I had left, the money, you must have realised—'

That flash of disdain in the cool grey eyes, accompanied by a dismissive downward curl of the mouth that only last night had so hungrily tasted her own, infuriated Gwynneth.

'I must have realised what? That you are the kind of man who regards women as a commodity, to be bought and used and then discarded?' she challenged him with angry heat. 'Yes, I did realise that. And I told myself that once I had put in hand all the necessary paperwork to transfer my father's apartment into my own name I would try to find out how you had managed to gain access to the apartment so that I could ensure you couldn't do so again.' She gave a very creditable imitation of his own earlier contemptuous shrug. 'Of course, one knows that men like you exist—men who are so inadequate emotionally and mentally that they are unable to have a normal relationship with a woman, and by "normal" I mean one based on real feelings and true respect—but I would never have willingly debased myself by having a relationship with such a man.'

'We did not have a relationship,' Tariq interrupted her icily. 'We had a night in bed.'

'*We?* What we?' Gwynneth countered wildly. 'There was no "we" involved. You used my body to gain sexual gratification, and then you—'

'Are you seriously trying to tell me that you found no pleasure in what we shared?' Tariq interrupted ominously. 'Because if you are—'

'So you get off on turning women on sexually,' Gwynneth flashed back. 'That doesn't alter the fact that you have to pay to do it!'

'*Have* to?'

No one, never mind a woman, had ever spoken to or looked at Tariq with contempt. He was a member of the ruling house of Zuran, and, more than that, he was the sole descendant of a noble house of great antiquity—the living, breathing reality of a royal name born out of mystery and legend. He possessed incalculable wealth; he was used to being treated with respect and deference; he considered himself to be a stringently moral man. Had anyone suggested to him even two nights ago that he would lose himself so completely in lust that he would take to his bed a woman of dubious morals he would have vehemently denied that he could ever do such a thing.

And now, to have this woman accusing him as she had just done, and with the contempt she had just shown, dug into his pride like the talons of a falcon tearing at its prey to leave its bloodied entrails spilling out onto the hot sand.

He wanted—no, *needed* to take hold of her and punish her for what she had said, for what she was making him feel.

'I do not *have* to pay any woman to give herself to me. As

I am more than happy to prove to you—right now,' he informed her grimly

Gwynneth fell back as Tariq strode purposefully towards her. But it wasn't fear that was turning her belly liquid as she wrenched her overheated gaze from his mouth and searched wildly for some way to disperse the sexual tension invading the small space.

He wanted her! How could that be? Furious with himself, Tariq stepped back from her, half turning away to conceal the evidence of his arousal as he demanded, 'Since you are now aware that I too consider this apartment to be my property, presumably you have informed the authorities accordingly?'

Gwynneth slid her tongue-tip over her suddenly dry lips. 'Not as such,' she said. Silence greeted her admission, and she filled it with defensive speech. 'It isn't up to *me* to register your interest—and anyway how could I? I don't even know your name. I did say that there was someone who believed they might own it, but the authorities said that no one else had registered any interest.'

'And of course that pleased you. Especially since you can expect to gain an additional bonus because of the rise in value of the apartment since your father purchased it.'

'And why not?' Gwynneth retorted angrily.

Tariq remained silent, leaning back against the doorframe and folding his arms. Where the sleeve of his robe had fallen back Gwynneth could see the tanned bare flesh of his forearm, sinewy and muscular and possessed of a strength she had seen last night, when he had lifted her and held her.

A treacherous physical memory of sensual pleasure gripped her achingly. Immediately she banished it.

'If you *really* believe this apartment is yours, then why haven't you registered your interest yourself?' she asked him, making it plain that she didn't believe his claim.

Tariq had had enough. 'Do you dare to accuse me of lying?' he demanded incredulously.

Gwynneth could see how much her deliberate insult had angered him. She could feel how that anger was filling the enclosed space in a wave of hostile tension. She flinched as Tariq unfolded his arms, half expecting him to take hold of her and demonstrate his anger physically, but to her relief he remained where he was. The look he was giving her, though, said that he had seen and relished her fear, and for Gwynneth that in itself was a form of punishment. But she wasn't going to give in—either to it or to him. Until she was officially told that her father had not owned the apartment, she was staying right where she was.

'Don't think I haven't worked out what all this is about,' she told him. 'You're trying to bully me into leaving. But I'm not going. We have a saying in England—possession is nine-tenths of the law—'

'We have a similar belief here,' he interrupted her.

'You mean you intend to stay here as well?' Gwynneth didn't even attempt to conceal her dismay.

'I have as much right to do so as you. Probably even more,' Tariq told her truthfully.

Now what had she done? She didn't want to back down, but the last thing she wanted to have to do was share the apartment with him and risk a repetition of last night. When she had thrown that challenge at him it simply hadn't occurred to her that he would retaliate in kind. But she couldn't back out now just because of the images crowding into her head,

Gwynneth warned herself. She had Teresa and baby Anthony to think about.

'I'm staying. It's what my father would have wanted me to do.'

'And he meant a lot to you, obviously. After all, his death left you so grief-stricken that you spent virtually three whole weeks grieving for him before coming out here to claim your inheritance.'

Tariq waited for her to deny his charge and to fake crocodile tears, but to his surprise she simply said quietly, 'No, we didn't have a particularly close relationship. My parents divorced when I was eight. I hardly saw my father after that until I was in my late teens. Neither he nor my mother really wanted me.'

Tariq started to frown. Was this the reason for her focus on material wealth? Or was she trying to gain his sympathy?

'So who brought you up?'

Gwynneth smiled mirthlessly.

'I was brought up in a very expensive boarding school, paid for by my stepfather. Neither he nor my mother wanted to be reminded that she had once been married to my father. My stepfather is a very wealthy man, so when he returned to Australia with my mother I was left behind in England. It was easy enough to pay someone else to take over the responsibility for me.'

Tariq looked away from her. He too had attended an English boarding school, and experienced the loneliness that brought.

'But my childhood was a long time ago and in the past,' Gwynneth said lightly. 'This is the present. My father had a peripatetic lifestyle. This apartment is virtually his only financial asset, and as his daughter—'

'You want your blood money?' Tariq suggested unkindly.

'I want what is right and just.' Gwynneth sidestepped the question neatly. She had already answered far too many questions, told him far too much about herself. Oddly, given their relationship, she didn't want to reveal her father's weaknesses—but, as she quickly discovered, Tariq had an even more uncomfortable question for her to answer.

'Is that why you have sex with men you don't know? Because you see it as a way of getting back at your parents for your childhood?'

'I don't—' *I don't have sex full-stop*, she had been about to say, but stopped herself in time, saying instead, 'I don't have to explain myself to you. All you need to know is that I am going to stay here in this apartment until ownership of it is resolved, and nothing is going to change my mind. So, like I've just said, if you are planning to browbeat and bully me into leaving, you are wasting your time.'

This was a wholly untenable situation, but he had no option other than to accept it. And with it her presence here in the apartment.

For only that reason? Was he sure about that? Was he sure that his decision, his determination to stay at the apartment, didn't have anything to do with last night and the fact that a part of him could still taste her, still hear her, still feel her in his arms, body-to-body with his own flesh?

He wasn't a boy, he was thirty-four years old, but though he had a man's needs he also had self-control. He'd had the occasional liaison with an understanding, experienced woman, but he felt nothing but contempt for the gold-digging females who went from one man to another.

He could, of course, marry. But his parents' marriage had

left him cynically wary of such a commitment. They might have claimed to be deeply in love with one another when they had married, but that love had not lasted. His father had walked out on both his wife and son when Tariq had been a mere four years old. Tariq could still remember how devastated he had been, and the tears he had wept. The experience had left him wary of ever being governed by his emotions. Emotional celibacy was something he had deliberately chosen. Physical celibacy was more of a state he had moved into by default rather than choice, but it was a state he preferred to any of the other options available to him.

'If you want to stay—'

'What I want is for you to leave,' Gwynneth burst out. 'And the sooner the better. We can't both stay here,' she added, when he made no response. 'For one thing, there's only one bedroom.'

'*My* bedroom,' Tariq agreed. 'Or were you hoping that I might invite you to share it with me?

'After last night?'

It was the wrong thing to have said.

'I don't recall hearing you complain. In fact—'

'I've had enough of this,' Gwynneth told him fiercely, almost running out of the kitchen.

Her heart was pumping and her whole body was protesting at the strain she was imposing on it. It was almost evening and she had no idea where the day had gone. Her head was throbbing almost as much as her heart was pounding. She needed some fresh air—and a breathing space, she acknowledged, but she dared not go out just in case he managed by some Machiavellian means to prevent her from getting back into the apartment. He wouldn't think twice about locking her out or changing the locks, she decided darkly as she pushed open the door to the apartment's main living room and realised that although she hadn't seen it last night there was actually a huge private terraced area beyond the floor-to-ceiling glass windows of the living room.

Fresh air. Eagerly she made her way towards them.

Tariq glanced at the plain gold watch strapped to his wrist, his mouth compressing. What motivated a woman like Gwynneth Talbot? Didn't she ever think about the danger she was risking when she gave herself to his sex? Or was danger part of the allure? Did she crave the hedonistic excitement her sexual encounters brought her? Didn't she care about the dark, seedy underbelly of the life she was living? Didn't it ever occur to her that she could end up physically harmed or even dead?

She was not his responsibility, he reminded himself angrily as he strode across the floor of the spacious living room after her. He owed her nothing. She meant nothing to him.

It was now dark outside, and unfamiliar scents filled the warm night air. The tantalising smell of food for one, making Gwynneth's stomach growl with hunger. What on earth had she got herself into? She, of all people, who normally lived her life so carefully and cautiously…

'So you're out here, are you?'

She turned round very carefully. The sensation prickling across her skin was arousing emotions that even she could recognise were dangerous. Apprehension, anger, hostility: they might be expected and acceptable, but that hot flare of excitement coupled with that searing mental flashback to last night was very definitely not! Caution urged her to ignore him, go straight to the study and lock herself back inside it. But, inexplicably, she was ignoring caution in favour of something far more confrontational and reckless.

'I needed some fresh air,' she told him pointedly. 'And I—'

Tariq interrupted her, demanding angrily, 'What is it that makes you take such risks? Have you any idea of the danger you could have been in?'

Of all the male moves she had ever experienced, this one had to take the prize. How dared he try to cloak his own behaviour in some kind of faked concern for her?

'Like you'd care!' she scoffed cynically. 'Or was that what you were doing last night—showing me your caring side?'

'My concern last night was directed towards the rather more personal issue of good sexual health,' he told her frankly. 'Something I should have thought would also be of primary importance to a woman of your obvious experience. Didn't last night teach you anything?' he added harshly. 'Or does the danger of what you're doing excite you in some perverted way?'

His anger ignited her own temper, pushing her over the limit of her own self-control. 'For your information, what happened last night isn't something— I'd never— Look, last night was a mistake, all right? It shouldn't have happened but it did. Not that it's any of your business. I don't have to explain myself to you, and I don't care what interpretation you choose to put on what I say or do.'

'No?' he challenged her.

'No,' Gwynneth asserted, and believed that she meant it.

'But you obviously *do* care that your behaviour last night led me to believe that you are a woman who is prepared to have sex with a stranger—and obviously not for the first time.'

Not for the first time? She was tired, she was hungry, and she was still in shock from everything she had experienced. In short, she had endured more than enough! 'Well, that's where you're wrong,' Gwynneth contradicted him angrily.

'And, what's more, last night wasn't only the first time, it was also the last time! I'd rather remain celibate for the rest of my life than—' Dammit, dammit, *dammit*. She was *not* going to cry in front of him! 'Than be subjected to the…the humiliation you forced on me last night!' It was as though his words had applied such unbearable pressure to the place inside her heart that hurt—very badly that she just wasn't able to stop herself from reacting to the pain.

How right she had been to repress her sexuality; how much she wished she had continued to do so. And how very, very much she wished she had never met *him*!

'*Celibate?* A woman like you?'

His contemptuous disbelief burned away what was left of her restraint.

'A woman like me? You mean that because I'm a virgin my sexual curiosity will drive me to sex? After last night?' She shook her head and laughed mirthlessly. 'I promise you, that was experience enough for me to know that celibacy is what I want.'

'*You*—a virgin?' Tariq shook his head incredulously. 'You're lying!' His rebuttal of her words was as emotionally charged as her own rejection of his accusation.

'No, I'm not lying,' Gwynneth said wearily. 'But I can see that you have a vested interest in refusing to believe me. Believe what you like. I don't care.' Her fierce inner emotional conflagration had burned itself out, leaving her feeling drained and vulnerably close to tears, unable to understand why she had made such an intimate disclosure to him.

She had to get away from him before he destabilised her emotional balance even more. Without waiting for him to say anything, she turned away from him and hurried back inside, automatically heading for the protection of the small study and its lock.

Her heart was pounding and she felt wretchedly over-wrought and upset as she leaned against the door and closed her eyes. How had he done this to her normal emotional stability and balance? The stability and balance she had dedicated her life to providing for herself?

Tariq was alone on the large balcony terrace.

A soft breeze whispered restlessly around him. The same breeze which would once surely have whispered against the wondrous hanging gardens of the Hidden Valley. It smelled of the desert and its purity, its freedom. Its sheer vastness and unrelenting harshness forced a man who chose to ignore the dangers inherent in making it his home to accept that he would always have to fight to master it. In the desert there was no mental energy to spare for the self-indulgence of personal feelings. There a man had to put the safety of those who depended on him first or risk extinction; there a man had to create beauty out of its harshness through dedication and vision and most of all by belief in himself, just as his ancestors had done in creating the gardens he was now seeking to restore to their original glory.

She had lied, of course, when she had said that she was a virgin.

But what if she hadn't? What if she was? The desert code was a strict code, a code that protected male honour and female virtue. A code that said an eye for an eye, like for like, and the only way a woman's stolen virtue could be restored to her was via marriage to her despoiler.

But she was *not* a virgin, and he had *not* despoiled her. The walls of the apartment and the building it was in enclosed him, just as marriage would enclose him—like a form of imprisonment. Marriage without love was like bread without salt, and he had no intention of allowing himself to fall in love. That was what his parents had done—or so they had believed.

Had she any idea how vulnerable she was? Didn't she realise how easy it would be for a man in his position, who lacked his scruples, to use her in the most primitive and abusive of ways before abandoning her? She could be kept here in an apartment like this one and not be allowed to leave. She could be forced to accept whatever intimacies a powerful man might choose to enforce on her, and no one would be the wiser until it was too late. She needed to be protected against herself as well as against those men who might abuse her. Didn't she realise the effect her claim to virginity could have on such men? How it would increase their lust for her rather than their respect?

Didn't he, though, have far more important things to worry about than a foolish woman?

CHAPTER SIX

SHE should have claimed the main bedroom and left him to have to sleep in here, Gwynneth thought as she looked at the small sofa pushed against the wall of the second-bedroom-cum-office. Obviously it was a sofabed, but there simply wasn't enough floor space to open it up.

She felt both emotionally and physically exhausted, and yet she still wasn't in the right frame of mind to sleep.

What was it about some people—people like her—that excluded them from the kind of childhood observation of adult love that would make it something to welcome rather than fear for themselves? If all human beings were hardwired to experience emotional love, then why had nature so cruelly decided that some would only ever experience it negatively? In a better world, surely every human being would live within the comfort of a loving relationship all of their lives. Perhaps adopting the 'love thyself' rationale of an egotist was the best way to experience love. But seeing all those other people at the airport in couples had made her painfully aware of the emotional emptiness of her own life. Was that why she had responded so hungrily to Tariq? Had some part of her wanted to play the alchemist and turn the base metal of sexual lust into emotional gold?

Now she was being ridiculous.

She went over to the bookshelves and removed the book on the history of Zuran she had noticed earlier, settling herself as comfortably as she could on the sofa and opening it. To her own surprise, within a very short space of time she had become deeply engrossed in it.

Tariq paused outside the door to the study. There was no sound from inside the room. It was almost midnight. He had eaten the meal he had had sent up, and the young waiter who had brought it from the restaurant had returned to remove his empty plate, along with the untouched meal he had felt morally obliged to order for Gwynneth. He might resent her presence in the apartment but he could hardly let her starve. However, if she wanted to deprive herself of food then that was her choice.

His fingers curled round the door handle. It turned easily in his grip.

A reading lamp illuminated the scene inside the room. Gwynneth was half lying, half sitting on the sofa, deeply asleep, the book she had obviously been reading on the floor. She looked cramped and uncomfortable. She hadn't even bothered to open up the small sofabed.

He turned back towards the door, and then stopped. If she continued to sleep like that she would wake up with a stiff neck, and surely with pins and needles in the foot she had tucked up beneath herself. In her sleep she looked young and oddly vulnerable, her dark lashes feathering shadows against the peach-soft flesh of her face.

Leaving the door open, he walked back over and stood

looking down at her. He was willing her to wake up, to save him the bother of a task he didn't want to perform, but she obviously wasn't going to oblige him. But then why had he expected that she might, in view of the acrimony that existed between them? Even in her sleep she was challenging him.

There was no real need for him to do this, Tariq told himself as he bent to lift her bodily into his arms. In fact, if he left her here the uncomfortable night she would undoubtedly endure might push her into leaving.

Her feet, he noticed, were small and slender, her instep delicately arched, her toenails painted a soft shade of pink.

Determinedly he focused on the open door instead of on her.

She made a small sound and nestled closer to him, her eyes still closed but her lips curling into a soft smile.

The king-sized bed in the main bedroom was large enough to sleep a whole family, never mind two adults, one of whom was fully dressed. And, that being the case, there was no reason why for tonight two adults should not share it, and be able to sleep in it as apart as though they were in separate beds—was there? Not from his point of view, Tariq assured himself. But as he pulled back the covers and placed Gwynneth on the bed his body's urgent response to losing the sensation of having her near made him curse inwardly as he tugged the covers up over her. He looked at the empty half of the bed and exhaled impatiently, before leaving the bedroom and heading back to his study.

There was work he needed to do, he told himself. That was why he had come in here Not because he couldn't trust himself to share the master bed with Gwynneth Talbot without giving in to his body's demand for her closeness.

* * *

Gwynneth studied the note in front of her on the kitchen worktop.

I have some business matters to attend to this morning,
but I shall be returning. Tariq.

Tariq. So that was his name. Tariq. She tested it, tasting it
and rolling it around her mouth until she was familiar with
the shape and feel of it, as though it were his flesh she was
sampling and allowing to pleasure her tastebuds.

What time exactly did later in the day mean? she wondered
as she smoothed the paper with her fingertip, unconsciously
lingering over the strong strokes with which he had written
his name. It was almost as though the potent strength of his
personality reached out to challenge her via his signature. Her
brain tried and failed to rationalise or analyse the complexity
of what she was feeling.

The facts—stick to the facts, she warned herself. Facts, unlike feelings and desires, could be firmly pinned down where
they belonged.

It had been a shock to wake up this morning and find that
she was lying fully dressed in bed, knowing that only one
person could have put her there. *The* bed, the one she had slept
in with *him* the night before that. Why had he done that? Why
had he come for her and, having found her, carried her off to
his own room? Had he done it because…? Because what?
Because he wanted her but hadn't wanted to wake her up? Get
real, she advised herself unsympathetically. She might be
fantasising about a repeat performance of last night but that
didn't mean that he was.

Fantasising…repeat performance? No way! Even though
she was on her own she shook her head in denial, as vigor-

ously as though the trenchant comment came from an alter ego that had a physical presence.

Desperate to distance herself from her unwanted thoughts, she opened the fridge and removed a yoghurt and some fresh fruit.

Outside the sky was a clear, hot blue, and the temptation to have breakfast on the balcony was too much for her to resist.

The warm air smelled faintly of incense and salt. Down below her she could see the hotels, and beyond them the marina and the beach.

Up here she had both the freedom to see what was happening and the privacy not to be seen herself. The warmth of the sun felt wonderful against her English-wintered skin, and had she been here on her own she might have been tempted to slip out of her clothes and bask in its delicious heat, safe in the knowledge that no one could see her. But she wasn't here on her own. And the last thing she wanted was for Tariq to come back and find her sunbathing in the nude.

Since she had come to Zuran on business, not expecting to stay for more than a couple of days, she hadn't brought any kind of resort wear with her—not that she saw herself as the kind of person who would ever want 'resort wear'. The words brought her a mental picture of a weirdly hybrid female—a cross between an aging fifties prom queen in diamonds and layers of chiffon, and a C-list celeb in pink sparkly matching everything, including cowboy boots, hat and tattoo. No, that wasn't her, she thought with a smile. Still, the reality was that if she stayed here much longer she was going to need a couple of clean T-shirts and some underwear.

She peeled back the top from her yoghurt and dipped her spoon into it, balancing the book on Zuran on the table in front of her so that she could continue to read it. She had retrieved it from Tariq's study earlier. She definitely hadn't wanted to go in there for any other reason than to get the book, she reminded herself. And anyway, it had been impossible to tell from its neatness if Tariq had spent the night in there, leaving her to sleep alone.

An hour later she was still reading, totally engrossed in the story of how Zuran had long ago been created out of empty desert by the family who still ruled here. The aim of the current Ruler was, it seemed, to turn Zuran into a good old-fashioned earthly paradise, open to visitors of every culture and colour. By the time Zuran's oil revenues had dwindled from their current gush to a mere trickle it was planned that the country would be *the* favoured and favourite destination of the world's holidaymakers and sports fans.

The book quoted an interview in which the Ruler acknowledged that he was taking a calculated gamble in investing so many billions in developing the small country in such a way. As a financial analyst, Gwynneth could easily imagine the damage that would be done to this plan if the double selling of property to overseas buyers became an open scandal.

A whole chapter of the book was devoted to explaining local customs, and some of the differences between Eastern and Western mindsets. Gwynneth frowned as she read that in the Middle East the giving and accepting of gifts to smooth the way for a variety of negotiations was considered the accepted norm, rather than being labelled detrimentally as bribery, as it would be in Western cultures. The author of the book advised would-be Western businessmen to employ the services of someone experienced in the way business was conducted in Zuran, so as not to cause any loss of face to themselves or others.

It would be far easier—and not merely financially—for Tariq to employ bribery to gain legal ownership of the apartment than it would for her. She had neither money nor contacts; he, she suspected, would have both.

She was about to close the book when she noticed a chapter entitled 'The Hidden Valley'. Her curiosity aroused, she turned to it.

The valley, Gwynneth learned, had originally been a place of great strategic importance, controlling and guarding a camel train route from Zuran into the lands that lay beyond it. According to legend, the valley had been gifted to the son of a favoured concubine by a long-ago Sultan. This son had fortified the valley and built within it a magnificent palace, funding the work with the money he charged travellers to pass through it and use the waters of its oasis. This was said to be replenished by a fast-flowing underground river that ran so far beneath the surface of the sand that no one had ever been able to find it.

It was the water from this river that had enabled the fabled and lost Hanging Gardens of Mjenat to flourish, until a terrible sandstorm—caused, so the story went, by the magic of a jealous rival—destroyed and obliterated the once beautiful gardens, reducing the tiered steps filled with luscious fruits and tropical plants to a series of sand-filled stone ledges where nothing could grow.

Current investigations taking place in the valley seemed to point to the fact that the gardens might actually have existed, the author continued, but they could proceed only very slowly, to minimise any risk to the existing environment. Additionally, the small oasis was definitely fed by an underground spring whose source had yet to be confirmed. Space satellites showed quite clearly where rivers might once have existed in the desert, and where indeed they might continue to exist deep down under the surface.

The current owner of this small, unique place was related to the Zurani royal family, and a prince in his own right. He was apparently dedicating his time and part of his wealth to researching the truth about the past history of his inheritance.

The whole project fascinated her—from its historical, almost fairy-tale past to its modern archaeological present—and she wanted to know more. And not just about the valley. There was something about the prince himself, and the paucity of information about him, that piqued her interest. A modern man who was part of past legend. How did he manage two such opposing parts of himself? Presumably far better than she managed the opposing parts of *herself*, although they were hardly the same. What she had read about him intrigued her. But it did not inflame her in the way that Tariq's dangerously charismatic personality did.

She put the book down, still open at the chapter on the Hidden Valley, and lay back in her chair with her eyes closed. And that was how Tariq found her several minutes later, when he walked sure-footedly and silently towards her.

He hadn't had a good morning. He had gone to the Palace to see the Ruler and the Chief of Police, who had advised them both that, thanks to Tariq's work, the police thought they had now discovered the identity of the Zurani official who was working for the gang. Unfortunately, he'd added, the situation was rather more complicated than they might have hoped.

'Why?' Tariq had asked baldly.

'The man we believe to be working for Chad Rheinvelt is Omar bin Saud al Javir. As you doubtless know, he is related to the traitor Prince Nazir, whose plot to murder the Ruler was thankfully thwarted.'

'This is a very serious accusation,' the Ruler intervened. 'When Prince Nazir and his family were exiled from Zuran, some members of his family disassociated themselves from him and begged for my clemency. Omar's father was one of them.'

'And this is how Omar repays your kindness,' Tariq said curtly.

'From the enquiries we have made we have discovered that the young man in question has given his family many causes to feel ashamed of him. He was dismissed from the University of Zuran for misbehaviour and poor grades. Without his family connections it is doubtful that he would have been given the responsible job he now holds. According to his superior he is a quarrelsome young man with a chip on his shoulder. However, this superior also told me that in recent months Omar had started to behave far more circumspectly, and has been showing a much greater interest in his work.'

'Presumably because Chad has been paying him to work for *him*!' Tariq put in grimly.

'Naturally it is impossible to do anything until we have positive concrete evidence of what is going on,' the Chief of Police continued. 'And for that reason I have now given instructions that Omar's every movement is to be closely watched. If all goes according to plan, we hope to have the evidence we need within the next twenty-four hours. Then we can take him into custody. However, until that happens, and until we have dealt with Chad Rheinvelt and his minions, I would ask, Highness—' the Chief of Police bowed in Tariq's direction '—that you would graciously consent to continuing to give us your assistance. It won't be for too much longer.'

'Keep me informed,' Tariq had instructed him just before he left. 'I want to know the moment anything changes.'

Then, the Chief of Police's request hadn't seemed too much to ask.

Right now, though, here in the apartment even a very few minutes felt dangerously like too much exposure to the growing problem of his reaction to his unwanted house guest.

Gwynneth wasn't just the cause of his lack of sleep last night, she was also the cause of the thoughts and needs that were currently tormenting him.

Gwynneth hadn't heard him come out onto the balcony. But when she opened her eyes the physical effect his presence had on her was so intimate and so disturbing that it shocked her. Her pulse was racing, and she could feel a warm flush rising from her breasts up over her throat. She realised how much she wanted to see him smile at her with warmth and delight.

Delight? Was she going completely mad? She had to put some distance between them, and fast.

He was blocking her path to the French doors, but she was too uncomfortably aware of her own unwanted reaction to him to let that stop her. She leapt up and, still holding the book tightly in her arms, made to push past him, gasping aloud when instead of moving he grabbed hold of her, his hands gripping the tender flesh of her upper arms so hard it felt as though he could break her bones if he chose to do so. It seemed as if he too realised that, and his grip slackened—not enough for her to be able to break free, but enough so that he could almost absently rhythmically rub her flesh with the pads of his thumbs, as though he was trying to smooth away any pain he might have caused.

'Let go of me,' she demanded, with more bravado than she was actually feeling. There was something very sensually disturbing and primitive about that rhythmic touch, and the answering surge it caused within her. As though something very dark and hidden deep inside her was responding to the rhythm he had set, just as it had done that first night when…

Her faced burned even more hotly as she realised where her thoughts were taking her and the trap that was waiting for her there. She wanted to close her eyes to blot him out, but she was afraid to do so in case that sensual pulse he was calling up took her over.

'Why?' The smile he gave her was knowing and unkind. As though to underline what he meant, he brushed the backs of his fingers down her bare arm.

Her body's reaction was immediate—and very physical. So much so that before she could stop herself she looked betrayingly down her at her breasts. Her nipples, clearly outlined and flauntingly erect, swelled eagerly against the fabric of her top.

Like someone in a trance she watched as he lifted his hand and brushed his knuckles very slowly over one nipple. Her breath jerked out of her body, visibly and audibly. She couldn't even use the retaliatory visual weapon of looking at his crotch. That all-encompassing immaculate white robe hid anything and everything there might have been to see. But her gaze had dropped to his body and his followed it, pinning it there whilst she tried to escape, as uselessly as a small bird trapped in honey.

'Wanton,' she heard him taunt her. 'You devour me with your eyes. Just as you—'

'No!' Gwynneth denied wildly, trying to pull away, forgetting that he was still holding her, shocked to discover that she was being yanked back into his possession, into his arms, his body, whilst his mouth covered hers, smothering its rebellion and stealing her will to fight.

What was this? Why was it happening? Her thoughts spilled dizzily into space, escaping her as fast as she tried to catch them, whilst inside her a whole new universe of sensation and need exploded in a shower of meteorites, blinding and dazzling her.

She could feel the engine of his heartbeat driving her own, as though it were pushing the blood through her veins, as though without it—without him—there could be no life for her. Behind the darkness of her closed eyes she felt the infinity of limitless aching need. His tongue prised apart her lips like a conqueror, and then dipped triumphantly into her mouth's sweetness. His hand enclosed her breast and her pulse seemed to stop beating before racing unsteadily in fierce excitement. The book slipped from her hold and onto the floor. The noise shocked through her.

Immediately Tariq released her.

'Why did you have to do that?'

The anguish he could hear in her voice hardened Tariq's mouth. She might not be the professional call girl he had first assumed, but neither was she the victim she was now trying to appear—and they both knew it.

'Why?' he answered mockingly. 'Because you let me.'

'I *let* you? That's what men like you always tell yourselves when you have to force yourself on a woman, when you make her give you something she doesn't want to, isn't it?' Gwynneth demanded bitterly. 'Well, if you're hoping to…to sexually harass me into leaving this apartment so that you can claim it, you're wasting your time.'

He was frowning at her, his mouth compressing with anger.

'Me? Sexually harass you? If that's true, then what was the

way you looked at my body all about? How exactly do you explain that?'

'I wasn't looking at your body,' Gwynneth insisted, but she knew the guilty colour darkening her face was giving her away.

'Liar. You looked at me to see if I was aroused.'

'And were you?'

Gwynneth blinked, as though she couldn't believe what she had just heard herself say—which she couldn't. She lifted her hand to her forehead, wondering grimly if some unseen and malevolently inclined genie had got out of his bottle and into her vocal cords.

Tariq looked at her sharply, thinking that she was being facetious. She must know that he had been aroused, otherwise he would never have done what he just had. But her expression told him quite plainly that she did not.

'I've got far more important things to do with my time than waste it on this kind of rubbish,' he told her flatly. That much at least was true. But it wasn't true that he wasn't thinking about her, despite the other calls on his time. He couldn't stop doing so. And not just thinking…

CHAPTER SEVEN

ANOTHER night spent sleeping in that huge bed, waking what felt like every few minutes just to check that she was still alone, her heart overdosing on adrenaline.

With fear, because she was afraid that Tariq might come to her, *for* her, sliding into the big bed beside her to take her in his arms and make her his?

Or with guilty excitement, because it was what she longed for him to do?

He drew her physically and emotionally as no other man had ever done, and fighting against the effect he was having on her had Gwynneth on a constant seesaw of thoughts and feelings.

Even when she closed her eyes and tried to sleep she couldn't get away from him, because her senses immediately assaulted her defences with sensually erotic images of their bodies entwined together, his hand resting possessively on her breast, playing with her eagerly erect nipple, then sliding teasingly down her body to push her legs open so that he could explore and enjoy her body and its response to him. And it wanted to respond to him so much.

How could she want him so badly? A man who…

A man who made her want to ask him a thousand questions

about himself. About what he was and how he had become that; how he had grown up; how he lived; how he thought and felt; what his dreams were, and his nightmares too.

And that wasn't just wanting him physically. That was… Not love, she denied in panic, thrusting the thought away from her. It couldn't be love. Or at least not love as she had always imagined it to be. Love came from knowing a person; it meant trusting them and feeling safe with them. She didn't know Tariq, she didn't trust him, and she certainly didn't feel safe with him.

And yet he had given her nothing to fear. As the bed evidenced, she had slept alone in it last night. Could it be truer to say that she did not *want* to feel safe with him, that she enjoyed that exciting frisson of fear the thought of him touching her gave her? Maybe she didn't really want to trust him either. It was a long time since she had fully trusted anyone and she had grown used to refusing to do so. Trusting someone meant allowing herself to be vulnerable to them, letting them into the inner sanctum of her most private emotional places—places she had kept guarded for so long…

It was time she got up, instead of allowing her thoughts to roam such dangerous byways.

'You are to be congratulated on such a speedy conclusion to what might have been a most unpleasant business.' The Ruler smiled approvingly at the Chief of Police, who had just announced to both his master and Tariq that Omar was now in prison, having admitted his involvement with the gang, and that all the members of the gang, including Chad Rheinvelt, had been apprehended and would be facing either trial or deportation.

'Unfortunately, we do still have one area of concern,' the Chief of Police admitted.

'Which is?' Tariq asked.

'We arrested Omar in the early hours of this morning, as he left a meeting with Rheinvelt. Later, when he was questioned, he told us that Rheinvelt had been asking him about Prince Tariq. It seems the gang leader was suspicious of His Highness's reasons for agreeing to assist him. Omar told Rheinvelt that in his opinion there was no way His Highness would ever do anything that might harm the Ruler or his family, and that far from needing money, as Rheinvelt apparently believed, His Highness is an extremely wealthy man. Omar further claimed that Rheinvelt swore to punish His Highness for deceiving him, and that he heard Rheinvelt giving instructions to this effect.'

'What exactly are you trying to say?' Tariq demanded. 'The gang is under lock and key.'

'Yes, but Rheinvelt has many contacts, not all of whom were visibly attached to this gang. He is a man who does not trust anyone. We have questioned him, of course, but he is an old hand at this sort of thing and has told us nothing. However, Omar remains adamant that Rheinvelt has put out a contract on His Highness—and on the somewhat softer targets, perhaps, of those close to him,' the Chief announced portentously. 'Naturally we are treating this threat very seriously, and if it does exist, then we shall discover the identity and whereabouts of his hitman. But until we do I have to warn His Highness to be on guard. We will provide bodyguards.'

Tariq shook his head in immediate refusal.

'That is not the way I have lived my life, nor is it the way I intend to live it,' he informed the Chief coolly.

'I would counsel you to think again, Highness,' the Chief of Police urged him, adding meaningfully, 'Please recall, your intimate friends could also be vulnerable to such an attack.'

Tariq frowned heavily at the policeman's words and told him curtly, 'They cannot possibly get close enough to the Ruler to harm him or his family.'

'It is not the Greatest amongst the Great of whom I am thinking,' was the Chief of Police's deliberately emphasised reply.

'Then to whom *are* you referring?' Tariq demanded impatiently. The Ruler was, after all, his closest relative.

The Chief of Police salaamed and informed him apologetically, 'Highness, because of the risks involved in this affair, I appointed men to keep a watch over the apartment block at Al Mirahmi. A young woman has been seen to leave and enter His Highness's apartment on a number of separate occasions. I beg forgiveness for this intrusion,' he added hastily, 'but His Highness will understand that his position within the family of our esteemed Ruler—may Allah protect him—has necessitated this.'

There were a good many more heavily embellished courtly effusions, but in the end it all boiled down to one thing. Gwynneth had been seen leaving and entering his apartment. In the eyes of the Chief of Police, and therefore very possibly in the eyes of anyone else who had seen her, she was his, and therefore potentially at risk should it turn out that Omar's information was correct.

This was how men of his country thought. Even if he attempted to explain the tangle of circumstances which had led to Gwynneth occupying the apartment at the same time as he was doing so, knowing what he did, the Chief of Police would still not be totally convinced. And neither, Tariq suspected, would Chad. Tariq had refused the offer of a prostitute; Tariq had a woman living with him; that woman must be important enough to him for any harm done there to serve as a warning to him. That was how men like Chad thought, and it was as pointless trying to change his thinking as it was trying to change that of his own countrymen.

'She, of course, is a more vulnerable target for them. It may even be that they will attempt to kill her as a warning to you,' the Chief of Police murmured almost apologetically, plainly sensing Tariq's anger.

This was exactly what he had just thought himself. And Tariq had to admit that the scenario the Chief of Police was outlining to him was all too feasible. Which meant...

Which meant that for her own safety Ms Gwynneth Talbot had to be packed off back to her own country and her own life just as quickly as possible. Quickly, discreetly, efficiently. Without any kind of fuss or delay. In a manner that would brook no opposition from Ms Gwynneth Talbot herself and that would not oblige him to tell her the truth. The thought of such a money-hungry young woman being free to approach a British journalist with her story, and the scale of potential damage to Zuran's future success as a safe tourist destination, was more than enough to convince him of that. Some plan would have to be made to get her to leave without arousing her suspicions, and Tariq decided he knew just the right one.

This time he made his way back to the apartment which thankfully he would soon be able to quit via his own chauffeur-driven limousine. But he still had his driver drop him off out of view of any of the windows of the apartment.

He found Gwynneth on the terrace, once again reading one of his books. This time one on local customs.

As always when he saw her afresh after any kind of absence from her, he had to struggle to control the sudden upsurge in his heartbeat and his desire to go to her and take hold of her.

The sooner she was back in her own country, the better, he decided grimly, as he glanced briefly at her and then looked away.

Gwynneth watched him in smouldering silence. The apartment had felt so empty without him, and she hated it that he could make her feel like that.

'I've been thinking about your situation with regard to this apartment,' Tariq announced without any preamble.

'*My* situation?' Gwynneth challenged him pointedly. Where the apartment was concerned, and with it Teresa and baby Anthony's future, she wasn't going to let him get away with anything—not one tiny little thing.

Tariq shrugged. 'As I understand it, if you are found to be the legal owner of this apartment it is your intention to return to your home and put it on the market—isn't that so?'

Cautiously Gwynneth nodded her head.

'In order to short-circuit what could very probably be a long-drawn-out and complex set of procedures, I am prepared to offer you the full market price of the apartment. By tomorrow night you can be home in Britain.'

He was *what*? Had she heard him correctly?

'*You* want to buy the apartment—from *me*?' she asked him, spacing out the words slowly and carefully, as though she wasn't sure of their validity.

'That's right.'

Gwynneth stared at him suspiciously. Why was he suggesting this? She didn't believe for one minute that it was out of any desire to help her—far from it.

'Why would you want to do that?' she challenged him.

'I don't have the time to waste on haggling and bartering over this.'

Gwynneth's eyebrows rose in patent disbelief. 'But I thought that haggling and bartering was the bedrock of Middle Eastern business methods,' she told him sweetly.

Tariq was looking at her as though he itched to put his hands round her neck and shake her into submission. 'I am simply trying to help you,' he told her unconvincingly.

Gwynneth put on a coolly disbelieving look. 'Yeah—as if,' she responded inelegantly, and shot him a feral smile. She was enjoying riling him and getting under his skin so much that she must possess a rogue love-of-danger gene she hadn't hitherto known about, she decided, as she waited to see what his next move would be. At least this was keeping a safe distance between them physically, and helping her to erect crash barriers against him inside her head.

Her head—but what about her heart?

What about it? It didn't come into this equation and she wasn't going to let it.

'You don't fool me. You're trying to sell me this deal like it's in my interests and to my benefit. But no way am I going to fall for that. You've got some kind of personal agenda going on here that makes ownership of this apartment in a hurry something you want,' she challenged him.

The look on his face told her there was something important she had neglected to factor in. Talk about thunder clouds rolling down from on high—never mind the lightning glittering in those mercury-grey eyes! One direct hit from that and her will-power could well be history.

'Maybe what I want "in a hurry" is you out of my life,' he retorted savagely.

Gwynneth winced. She should have been expecting that.

'The market price of the apartment is three-quarters of a million pounds sterling. I am prepared to write you a cheque for one million pounds right now—that will cover your costs as well.'

The real market value of the apartment was closer to £500,000, but Tariq didn't want to waste valuable time arguing. He wanted her gone—and not just for her own sake. She was beginning to affect him too much and too often, and that wasn't something he intended to allow to continue.

'A cheque?' Gwynneth questioned suspiciously. Was he somehow trying to cheat her out of the apartment? Did he really think she was that much of a fool to fall for something like that? And besides, she already knew, because the young official had told her, that the apartment was worth in the region of £500,000. So why was Tariq offering her so much more? Because he thought her greed would make her jump to accept his offer? Which meant that he had to have an ulterior motive. But what? It could be that his offer was quite simply a scam. Or perhaps, whatever his reason for wanting the apartment, it had nothing to do with money.

What should she do? Her first duty was to Teresa and Anthony, and she owed it to them to get the highest price she could for the apartment. Perhaps she could shock Tariq into telling her a bit more by letting him know that she wasn't as easily deceived as he seemed to think.

Taking a deep breath, she asked him derisively, 'Do you really think I'm that much of a fool?'

'What do you mean?' There was a very ominous and warning note in his voice, but Gwynneth chose to ignore it.

'Isn't it obvious?' she said mock-sweetly. 'You give me a

cheque, I sign over the apartment, and then I find that your cheque can't be honoured.'

'*What?* You're accusing me of dishonesty?' he demanded in disbelief.

Gwynneth lifted her chin determinedly.

'You obviously want the apartment very badly, and common sense tells me that you must have an ulterior motive. On the face of it, you've offered me far more than the apartment is actually worth. Why would you do that? As an act of charity?' She gave him a thin smile and shook her head. 'I don't think so. Perhaps you expected me to be so eager to accept your offer that I wouldn't stop to question why you were making it. Perhaps you hoped to defraud me via a dud cheque—or perhaps you know something about the apartment that I don't know which increases its value. There has to be a reason that benefits you.' She gave a small shrug. 'Why else would you want it?'

'Is that how you assess everything?' Tariq asked her with open contempt. 'In terms of financial value?'

He was treating *her* with contempt? Surely it should be the other way around? Somehow he had wrongfooted her, Gwynneth knew, but she was not sure how. With the sleight of hand of some souk *fakir* switching tumblers and dice, he had managed to transform her moral superiority into his own, and make her look cheap and avaricious.

'This is a financial deal, and the apartment is a financial asset and must be valued as such,' she answered as firmly as she could. 'I can't and won't agree to your proposition until I have had it independently valued.'

'You *dare* to question my word?'

Gwynneth stood her ground.

'Yes, I do.'

She heard him mutter something under his breath which she suspected was not complimentary, and then he was striding towards her, reaching for her wrists and manacling them within the hard grip of his strong fingers.

'Get your hands off me!' Gwynneth demanded sharply, trying to pull herself free.

Tariq had simply intended to vent his fury by shaking her, but the moment she fought to break free of his hold his reasons for imprisoning her and the warning he had given himself earlier were forgotten, swamped by a surge of primitive male desire. He pulled her against his body, pinning her wrists behind her back and keeping them there in one swift movement that left her almost speechless—and seething.

'Let go of me!' she demanded through gritted teeth. But then she made the mistake of looking up at his mouth, and found that she couldn't stop looking. Now the liquid heat pouring through her veins wasn't just anger. Maybe it wasn't *even* anger. Maybe it was…

She heard him mutter something, and then he bent his head. She heard herself moan as the force of his kiss tipped her head back and he lifted one hand from her pinioned wrists to support the back of her neck, his fingers splaying into her hair. This time she didn't need to question whether or not he was aroused. She knew he was. She could feel the hot, hard pulse of his erection pressing into the softness of her own flesh.

Behind her closed eyelids a thousand and one erotic images tormented her. A thousand and one sensual intimacies spread out over a lifetime of dark starlit nights in a land where heaven and earth touched, where the desert met the sky, and where a woman touched that heaven in the arms of her lover. In that place they would share together the transforming wonder that was human passion and human desire and human love…

Frantically Gwynneth pulled her mouth from beneath Tariq's. What was happening to her was beginning to scare her—and badly.

Tariq could feel her heart thudding into his with quick fast beats like that of a trapped bird. He put his hand over it, watching the way her expression changed and her breath caught in her throat as though on a ratchet whilst her heart-beat almost doubled.

What was it about this pale-skinned, turbulent, impossible woman that pushed him beyond the boundaries of the self-control he had thought unbreachable? Inside his head, thoughts he hadn't known he could have jostled against one another, their sharp edges raking his pride, leaving it raw with open wounds. He took a deep breath, his chest lifting power-fully, and then shook his head, as though trying to shake off the unwanted reality of his thoughts. A heat like that of the desert sand under the midday sun seared through his body. There was no escape from it, or from the place it was taking him. The only release for him, the only place he could slake the thirst of his desire, was within her. Like an oasis in the desert, she lured and drew him to her.

In another age he would have summoned a Wise One to remove the spell she had surely put on him—but it was a spell which his senses told him had possessed her as well.

The frantic beat of her heart beneath his hand told him how much she wanted him, and his own reaction to it betrayed how much he wanted her. His desire for her was an insistent driving force that filled his mind and his body and drove his heart-beat. It was his life force, and without it he would die.

He lifted his hand to her breast, soft and round, filling his palm. He drew his fingertips to her nipple, tugging sensually on it whilst she shuddered against him and cried out with pleasure. Inside his head he could almost see the pale globe of flesh, almost taste its sweetness. His erection stiffened and throbbed painfully.

How could she be letting Tariq do this? How could she *not*? an inner eager voice demanded hungrily. Somehow the simple act of his fingertips playing with her nipple was enforcing a rhythmic urgency on her that had her grinding her lower body into him whilst she pressed her lips to his throat, her tongue-tip tasting the salty sweat on the heat of his skin. She felt him pushing her clothes out of the way, to expose her breasts to the coolness of the air-conditioned room and to the heat of his touch, her own arousal. In the mirror hanging on the adjacent wall she could see the dark splay of his fingers against the pale outline of her breast as she pressed herself into his body. The sight was unbearably erotic, making her shudder tightly in response to its message.

In a far-off century there would have been nothing to stop him from taking this pale-skinned seductress and making her his willing slave, locking her away in the luxury of his harem, where no other male eyes could see her and no other male hands could touch her. Then she would have been his to enjoy, whenever and wherever he wished. But this was now, and he was…he was dangerously, recklessly, unacceptably out of control, Tariq admitted grimly. He forced himself to release her.

He had let her go. So why was she standing here looking at him as though she wanted…? Quickly Gwynneth straightened her clothes, her fingers made clumsy by reluctance and thwarted physical need.

And it was *only* physical need that she felt, she reassured herself fiercely as she stepped back from him and told him jerkily, 'Wrong move! If that was supposed to make me change my mind and agree to sell the apartment to you, it hasn't worked!'

Before he could retaliate, she turned round and almost ran to the main door, yanking it open and slipping through it as he called out to her to stop.

CHAPTER EIGHT

WHAT an idiot she was, coming out without her bag, and with no hat or sunglasses, Gwynneth derided herself as she stood in the hot sunshine and shielded her eyes to look uncertainly back at the apartment building.

She could go back. She *should* go back. But she wasn't going to.

Because she was afraid of what could happen if she did? She was afraid, yes, but not of Tariq. An inner female knowledge she hadn't known she possessed told her that there was no likelihood of Tariq forcing himself on her. Why should he, after all, when they both knew he did not need to? She was so sexually attuned to him and by him that her whole body positively vibrated every time he came anywhere near her. Vibrated? Now, why had that particular word popped into her mind?

If she hadn't felt morally obliged to do what she could financially for Teresa and Anthony, she would have been tempted to simply walk away and leave Tariq in possession of the flat. After all, there were more important things in life than money, and her peace of mind was one of them. Her peace of mind and her self-respect.

Now that she was away from him, and had broken free of

the powerful orbit of his sexuality, she could think more clear-headedly about what had happened to her. The discovery that she had after all inherited her father's sensual nature made her feel a lifetime's worth of conflicting emotions. Anger and fear, resentment and a desire to fight her own need—but once she was in Tariq's arms these had immediately morphed into not so much eager compliance as something far more proactive. It had been a battle of age-old female sexual shame versus a glorious, wild 'I can touch the sky' feeling of power and plea-sure. And those were just the emotions she could easily rec-ognise. There was a whole lot more going on underneath that was too scary for her to investigate.

What she felt was like… She stood in the street, screwing up her eyes and wrinkling her nose as she concentrated on finding the perfect metaphor to describe her current state of mind. The closest she could get was to say it was like standing on a bridge looking down into unmoving very deep water, knowing that she was too close to the edge and that for her own safety she needed to move away. But instead of doing so, or even just staying where she was, she was moving for-ward, daring herself to see how much of a risk she could take. Because secretly she *wanted* to throw herself off that bridge and into that water? Because she *wanted* to take that risk and to feel the exhilaration of that freefall into danger before the water closed over her, dragging her down into its unknown depths?

Up above her in the apartment Tariq watched her. If he went after her and she ran off it would draw the kind of attention he most certainly didn't want to a situation he wanted even less.

What was the matter with him? He was behaving with the kind of recklessness he had always despised in others. He moved back from the window, all too aware of the swollen ache of his erection—something else to despise himself for. To a man who had always considered himself to be more aesthetic than carnal, his body's stubborn refusal to control its lust for a woman his mind wanted to reject was as distasteful as it was infuriating.

He turned away. Her reaction to his offer to buy the apartment from her was still rubbing his pride raw, like tiny grains of sand against skin. What was she up to? Did she think that by holding out she could get him to raise his offer still higher? He could taste the bitterness of his own angry contempt. For her or for himself?

He would have to find some way to bring an end to this increasingly dangerous situation. And it *was* dangerous—and not just because of Chad Rheinvelt, he admitted unwillingly.

One option would be to arrange for her to be told that she did not own the apartment but that she would be fully compensated for its value. Then he could leave everything to be dealt with by the Zurani government department concerned. But that would mean involving others, which in turn would mean talk—or, more relevantly, gossip. About Gwynneth, about him, about their shared nights together under the same roof. All leading to the kind of speculation he abhorred.

A look of grim hardness tightened the bones in his face. That was something he was not prepared to countenance. No way. The Ruler, of course, knew exactly why he had not been able to move out of the apartment prior to the discovery of Omar's identity. But Tariq had his own reasons for not wanting what had been going on to be made public.

He had wasted enough time already on Ms Gwynneth Talbot and the problems she was causing him. It was time they were brought to an end. He had other and far more important calls on his time and his emotions—not least several pre-organised meetings, some here in Zuran, others in the valley itself, with certain specialists to discuss various aspects of his plans for the valley.

With the encouragement of the Ruler he was considering the advantages of making the whole valley a heritage site, endowing it for the benefit of their people, but this was not a project that could be rushed. It was one, though, that was very close to his heart. Other men might leave children behind them to mark their existence; *his* mark upon the face of time would be made in the restoration of the legendary hanging gardens and by turning them into a place of wonder and beauty that could be enjoyed by many rather than kept for the pleasure of a chosen few. That was his dream and his goal.

And a long-legged fair-skinned woman was not going to deflect him from it. He glanced at his watch. If he didn't leave now he was going to be late for today's meeting with the Ruler's own specialist horticulturist, who had already been out to the valley to take some samples of its flora.

Why on earth hadn't she come back? Or was he being naïve? Was this yet another ploy of some kind?

Thank goodness for modern air-conditioned shopping centres, Gwynneth thought with relief, as she hurried out of the sun and into the welcome shaded coolness of the large shopping mall a small distance away from the apartment block. Not that she could do anything other than window shop, since she hadn't brought her bag out with her.

But at least she was away from Tariq.

An hour later, when she or rather her overheated passions

had had time to cool down, she decided that she needed to do everything she could to expedite a speedy decision with regard to ownership of the apartment. Even if that meant camping out in Zuran's land registry offices until she got an answer. But first she would have to go back to the apartment, smarten herself up a bit and get her purse. And that meant...

Don't think about it, she warned herself as she left the shopping mall.

She blinked in the fierce glare of the bright sunlight and paused to shade her eyes before looking to check that the road leading to the hotel was clear and starting to walk across it.

She had only taken a few steps when out of nowhere a car screeched round a corner and came racing towards her, its driver too busy speaking into his mobile to be aware of her. She could see the danger and her own vulnerability, but was too shocked to be able to move. And then suddenly firm hands grabbed hold of her, half dragging and half pushing her out of the path of the car as it swerved violently close to her and then roared off.

The entire incident had taken only a few seconds, but those few seconds could have been her last, Gwynneth realised, and she turned to give her rescuer a grateful smile and stammer her thanks. He was a shortish man, close to middle age, and obviously an Arab although he was wearing European clothes.

'You are all right?' he asked her courteously.

Gwynneth nodded, feeling suddenly shaky. 'When I checked the road there was nothing there.' She didn't want him to think she had just walked out in front of the car. 'And then suddenly the car was there, and the driver didn't see me. He was on the phone...' Her disjointed sentences quavered into the late-afternoon heat. She turned to look in the direction the car had come from as her rescuer guided her across the road.

'Thank you so much—' she began a second time, but he shook his head, turning away from her to disappear into the crowd of people emerging from the shopping mall.

She was still feeling slightly shaky when she reached the apartment block. Despite the coolness of its foyer, her heart was thumping erratically, and a fine film of dewy nervous perspiration was dampening her hairline. But it was the thought of Tariq that was responsible for her anxiety, not her close call with the car.

All the way up in the lift her stomach was churning.

Five minutes later she was standing outside the main door to the apartment. Automatically she put her hand down for her bag and her key card, before remembering that she had left the flat without bothering to pick up her bag. The foyer door was unlocked during the day, so she hadn't remembered till now.

No bag, no key card, no way of getting into the flat. Her shoulders rounded slightly with defeat. There was only one thing she could do now. Taking a heroically deep breath, she pulled herself up to her full height and rang the bell.

The seconds ticked by as she strained to hear some sound of movement inside the apartment.

Perhaps Tariq was asleep. Cue distracting mental image of him in bed, sheet pushed down to his hips, the warm sherry-gold of his skin satin-sleek, not just inviting but compelling her to reach out and touch it…

No! She didn't want *those* kind of thoughts, thank you very much. What would she do if he assumed that her return was an invitation to him to continue where he had left off? Would she have the strength of will to resist him if he picked her up in his arms and carried her into the cool shadows of her bedroom and once there…?

Gwynneth breathed in, and then exhaled gustily. If she was really keen for it not to happen, why exactly was she lingering so lovingly over every small mental detail of a supposedly threatening seduction scenario? Anyone peeking into her mind right now would be forgiven for thinking she was actually building an image of something she *wanted* to happen, not stressing over something she didn't.

Far better instead to imagine him standing in silence in the hallway, enjoying her distress. In silence, naked, a towel wrapped round his lower body... Oh, stop it! she told herself irritably.

Perhaps she should ring the bell one last time. She put her finger on the buzzer and pressed it hard.

Nothing. Nothing and no one. She leaned against the wall, feeling defeated.

Now what was she going to do? She was locked out of the apartment and instead of suggesting solutions her rebellious mind was playing games with her.

'So what is to be done about this young woman who claims ownership of the apartment via her late father?' The Ruler pursed his lips, and then remarked blandly, 'She is of your father's race, I understand?

Tariq's eyes narrowed.

'You are well informed, Greatest amongst the Great.'

The Ruler's plump face creased into a wide smile. Tariq only used this mode of address when he wanted to be sardonic.

'Our excellent Chief of Police, Saulud bin Sharif, felt obliged to give me a full report on the young woman.' His expression became far more serious. 'She must not be exposed to danger, Tariq.'

'She will not be.'

The Ruler waited patiently, but Tariq was plainly not going to say any more about the young woman the Ruler had been told was as beautiful as the morning sunrise.

'Excellent.' He smiled again at his grim-looking young relative who, as a prince in his own right, was seated cross-legged on the divan opposite his own. Tariq's height meant that the Ruler had to crick his neck to look up into his eyes.

A manservant was hovering close by with a coffee pot. Tariq covered his cup with the fluid movement of one long-fingered hand in an automatic gesture of denial, his mouth twitching slightly in disapproval when the Ruler reached for yet another sweetmeat.

'My physician warns me of the dangers of too many sweet things, Tariq, but…' The Ruler gave a small dismissive shrug. *'In Sha' Allah,'* he said, fatalistically.

'Your people need you to lead them into the future, and so do your sons,' Tariq murmured quietly.

The Ruler looked at him, and then put down the sugar-dusted square of Turkish delight he had been about to put in his mouth.

'It is when you make pronouncements such as that that I see your father in you the most, Tariq,' he sighed.

'There is nothing of him in me other than where he has left the physical marks of his fathering on me,' Tariq answered grimly. Somewhere deep inside he still felt the pain turned to bitterness of his father's desertion.

The Ruler shook his head patiently. 'Your father was a highly intelligent and far-seeing man in many ways. He saw what my father had done, and showed me how I could build upon those things. I know he caused your mother and you great pain, and that I cannot condone, but many of the projects I have undertaken sprang from the seeds of his vision. In that

I have much cause to be grateful to him. And much cause as well to be grateful for his bestowal on my household of his son. We should perhaps not blame him too much for not being able to adapt to our ways. Your mother, after all, refused to adapt to his.'

Tariq stared at him. 'He *abandoned* her.'

'He left Zuran alone because your mother refused to leave with him—as she had agreed to do when they married,' the Ruler corrected him quietly. 'They agreed they would live in Zuran for some years, and then in Britain. But when the time came she went back on her word.'

'That is not what she told me.'

'Nevertheless, it is the truth.'

'So why did she not say this to me?'

'Maybe she thought you too young, or perhaps she feared that you might judge her. I know that he would have taken you with him had he not felt that it was best for you that you remain here. He was a man who had the heart of a nomad, a man whose work and nature made it impossible for him to settle long in one place. He left you with your mother out of love for you, Tariq.'

'Why has this not been said to me before—by you if not by my mother?'

'Sometimes awareness must wait upon events,' the Ruler told him sagely, and then he inclined his head and clapped his hands, indicating that their meeting was over.

Tariq got to his feet with fluid ease, salaaming before leaving the room.

CHAPTER NINE

THE RULER had given him much to think about. But a deeper consideration of the unexpected revelations about his father would have to wait until another time. Tariq glanced at his watch and immediately lengthened his stride and increased his speed.

He had assumed, when he had seen Gwynneth standing in the street below the apartment block and frowning, that she had realised that she had left without either a key or any money, and so he had waited for her immediate return.

When she hadn't come back he had toyed with the idea of going out and leaving her to a long, uncomfortable wait for his return, but an inbuilt sense of responsibility had stopped him from taking that kind of retaliatory action. Zuran's temperatures topped forty degrees Centigrade at this time of year; she was British, and fair skinned, and she had gone out without anything to cover her exposed head and delicate skin. He wasn't going to take the risk of her doing something foolish that might result in her suffering from heatstroke or worse because she couldn't get into the apartment.

However, his good intentions had been undermined when he had received a telephone call from one of the Ruler's secretaries, requesting his presence at the palace.

He had planned to keep the meeting as short as he possibly could, but his second cousin's revelations about his own father had hijacked his intentions. It was now over four hours since he had left the apartment.

By the time he reached the doors to the palace used by family members, his car and driver were already there waiting for him, the bodywork of the black Mercedes polished to a dust-free gleam.

A uniformed palace guard opened the door for him and the cool silence of the air-conditioned interior embraced him. The imposing palm-lined dual carriageway that ran from the palace to the city had been modelled after London's Mall, although here the wide grass verges had to be kept green with a complex under-soil watering system, and the colourful formal bedding provided by flowering annuals in London was provided here by a rich array of tropical shrubs and plants. Gilded lamp standards were decorated with mosaic-tiled framed images of the Ruler, and in the distance the gold-leaf dome of a mosque glittered in the sunlight.

His driver turned off the imposing Road of the Ruler into an equally wide but far busier thoroughfare. Beyond the dark-tinted car windows Tariq could see the glass exteriors of the many new office and apartment blocks lining the road. He was a member of the select private conglomerate that was responsible for financing a large proportion of them. Zuran City was booming, but the Ruler and his advisers were keeping its development under firm control.

Up ahead of him he could see the shimmer of the new resort complex, and beyond that the area out in the Gulf where men were working on the final stages of building new hotels and villas on land reclaimed from the sea to create the magnificent Palm Island, its trunk the road connecting it to the shore and each palm leaf a long narrow spur of land complete with water frontage.

Tariq had a financial interest in this venture as well, the profit from which was projected to run into billions of dollars.

But it wasn't his growing wealth that occupied his thoughts as the Mercedes sped along the private lane reserved for use by the Royal Family, and neither was it the unexpectedness of the Ruler's revelations about his late father.

He instructed his driver to drop him off within walking distance of the apartment, oblivious to the eager female interest he was attracting as he slid on a pair of aviator sunglasses and emerged from the Mercedes to stride past the exclusive designer shops either side of the palm-lined street, the robe he had donned for the formality of his meeting billowing slightly in the warm breeze.

Gwynneth had been loath to leave the apartment block a second time without any money, and, given that the Zuran land registry office was too far away for her to walk there, she had decided that she had no alternative other than to wait for Tariq to return and let her into the apartment.

Always providing he did return.

Of course he would.

But what if he didn't?

She had brought back from the shopping mall a free magazine, which she had now read from cover to cover several times. During the course of this inspection she had discovered that an apartment similar to her own was currently on sale for £500,000, confirming all her suspicions. *Why* had Tariq offered her a million pounds to give up her claim to this one?

The hum of the air-conditioning was making her feel drowsy. She sat down on the cool tiled floor and leaned back against the wall. Within minutes she was fast asleep.

Tariq frowned when he got out of the lift and saw her seated on the floor, leaning against the wall. She was asleep, her face pale and her hair tousled. There was a small smudge of shadow along her cheekbone, as though she had rubbed it in distress. There was a bottle of water on the floor beside her, along with a magazine, both bearing the logo of a mall complex. Such items were given free to visitors, and he guessed that she must have been there.

The sight of her disturbed him more than he wanted to admit—and not sexually this time. This time his feelings were far, far more dangerous than merely sexual, because this time they contained both concern for her and a strong desire to protect her—if necessary from herself.

He hunkered down beside her and spoke her name quietly. 'Gwynneth.'

Gwynneth smiled in her sleep in acknowledgement of the familiar voice.

Tariq exhaled and lifted one hand to her face, to steady her in case she slipped, using the other to give her a small shake.

Gwynneth sighed luxuriously and turned her face into his hand, rubbing her cheek against it and making a soft purring sound.

Tariq's fingers bit into her shoulder and abruptly Gwynneth woke up.

Tariq was crouching down on the floor next to her, his eyes on a level with hers. Her own widened, whilst colour burned up under her skin. She tried to look away from him, but her gaze was trapped as helplessly as though his had magnetised it.

'How long have you been here?' he asked curtly.

Gwynneth shook her head. Her muscles felt slightly stiff.

'I don't know. What time is it now?'

Her breath rattled in her lungs as he lifted his wrist and shot back the hem of his sleeve to reveal the tawny, sinewy strength of his wrist. How on earth could such a simple action, the mere sight of a plain watch encircling a man's wrist, have this kind of effect on her?

'Almost six p.m.'

'I came back about three.'

Just over an hour after he had left.

'I hadn't intended to be gone so long. I realised after you'd gone that you hadn't taken your key or any money.'

He was *apologising* to her?

'I had a meeting which I couldn't not attend. Can you stand up?'

'I'm twenty-six, not eighty-six,' Gwynneth half joked. But nevertheless her semi-numbed legs, suffering the pins-and-needles burn of returning life, were glad of his help to support her as she struggled to stand up. He, of course, managed to uncoil himself from his hunkered-down position with enviable grace.

'Have you had anything to eat today?'

She shook her head. She wasn't sure she could cope with Tariq in this knight errant mood. It made her feel vulnerable, as though she was some kind of victim, and she didn't like that.

'So you haven't eaten since breakfast?' he demanded.

Gwynneth glared balefully at him as he unlocked the apartment door.

'Actually, no, I haven't. But there wasn't any need because I wasn't hungry. I had a big breakfast.'

'A yoghurt?'

'No one wants to eat much when it's hot.'

'No one?' His mouth twisted sardonically. That was more like it, she decided gratefully. 'By "no one", presumably you mean the British?' He was holding her arm, swinging her round to face him as he half dragged her into the hallway, pushing the door shut with one easy movement.

'You don't like us, do you?' she demanded. 'Why?'

'Congratulations on your powers of analysis,' Tariq told her sarcastically. 'As to why—that is my own business. But I certainly do not like the morals the young women of your country—of your type—adopt.'

Gwynneth glared at him. 'Do you know what?' she told him acerbically. 'You aren't just a bigot, you're a hypocrite as well.'

'Be careful,' Tariq warned her.

She was standing on that bridge again, Gwynneth knew. But she didn't seem able to stop herself.

'Of what? You? Why? In case you're tempted to do some close-up research into *my* morals? I wouldn't, if I were you.'

'Funny how sometimes a warning can sound more like an invitation,' Tariq derided her, adding unforgivably, 'You want me to take you to bed. We both know that.'

'We both know no such thing!' Gwynneth stormed back at him.

'It's the truth,' Tariq insisted, with another dismissive shrug of those powerful shoulders.

'I've never known any man as good at self-delusion as you!'

'And you've known a lot of men, of course,' he agreed smoothly.

Not in the Biblical sense, I haven't, Gwynneth was tempted to tell him. But a small inner voice warned her that that was a step too far right now. He might have already refused to believe she was still a virgin, but the mood he was in at the moment he might be tempted to *prove* to her that she wasn't. She knew he wouldn't force her, of course—the problem was that he wouldn't need to.

Hastily, she pointed out, 'Less than six hours ago I walked out of here rather than go to bed with you. Remember?'

'It was my decision not to proceed,' Tariq countered coolly. 'Whereupon you flounced out in a temper—no doubt expecting me to come after you and make you an offer you wouldn't want to refuse.'

The offer she wouldn't want to refuse from him would involve not money but a full bank account of sensual intimacy— a promise to pay in caresses and kisses that she could draw on whenever she felt the need.

Red-faced, Gwynneth shook herself free of her own dangerous thoughts.

'I have to go away for a few days,' Tariq told her abruptly. 'I shall be leaving later tonight. I have some business matters to attend to.' It was a four-hour drive at least to the valley, and he would normally have set out at dawn, but right now he ached for the solitude of the desert, with its infinite capacity to remind a man that his most basic struggle was that of survival. The desert was not a forgiving mistress; she made no allowances for human weakness in those who chose to embrace her. There, surely he would be able to see what he was experiencing for what it was—and that was a mere nothing. His desire for this woman whom he did not want to want was a minor inconvenience—a fire which would quickly burn itself out. He would call for police protection to ensure Chad's threats weren't carried out, and forget all about her.

Tariq had turned away from her, leaving Gwynneth free to watch him with hugely agonised dark eyes. He was going. He couldn't. He mustn't. She wanted him to stay here with her—she wanted him to stay with her for ever.

Gwynneth hadn't even realised she had made any sound at all until Tariq turned back to her, frowning as he demanded, 'What's wrong? You sound as though you are in pain.'

Her? In pain for him?

'That wasn't pain, it was relief,' she fibbed recklessly.

He gave her a taunting smile.

'I suggest that while I am away you give very serious thought to my offer to buy the apartment.' He looked at his watch again. 'It is now almost seven o'clock. I need to eat before I leave. I'm going to order in some food—for both of us.'

'I need to shower and change first,' Gwynneth protested.

'How long will that take you?'

'Twenty minutes—maybe half an hour.'

'Fine. I'll order the food for seven-thirty.'

He was walking away from her, leaving her standing there in the hallway, not even asking her if she had any preference as to what she wanted to eat. Gwynneth fumed. She had a good mind to tell him that she was perfectly capable of ordering her own food and that she preferred to eat alone rather than have her appetite ruined by his unwanted presence. That would be the only sensible thing to do, wouldn't it?

She was still refusing to answer that question ten minutes later as she stood under the shower, savouring the sensation of the water sluicing the detritus of the day from her skin. If only her heart could be as easily comforted and soothed.

* * *

The warmth of the water against his skin was almost as sensual as a woman's touch—which no doubt was why his thoughts were turning in a direction he did not wish them to go, and why his body was responding to those thoughts.

If he were holding her between his hands now, caressing her water-slick skin… Angrily Tariq turned the shower to 'cold', staying beneath it and willing it to douse the fire inside him. Had his father felt like this for his mother?

He reached up and switched off the shower. This was the first time he had allowed himself to think of his father in terms of his own experience. Like father, like son… But he had always sworn that he would never *allow* himself to be the son of the man who had given him life because of the way he had abandoned his mother. What had he been like? What would he see if he allowed his father to step out of the shadows into which he had thrust him?

He reached for a towel, his forehead furrowing as he tried to capture vague images of himself with his father as a child. Inside his head he could hear a faint echo of male laughter, feel the hard, sure warmth of paternal hands lifting him.

What had provoked this? It had to be her! How dared she look into his soul and disturb his secrets…?

He strode naked from the bathroom into his office, relieved to know that he wouldn't have to spend yet another night on the hugely uncomfortable sofabed. Quickly he pulled on clean clothes. No need to resume his headdress, since he was eating in the privacy of the apartment. He heard the door's security buzzer ring and checked his watch.

Twenty-five past seven.

If she wanted her food hot then she was going to have to hurry.

* * *

Was that the door she had just heard? Well, she was showered and dressed, in a black linen kaftan she had bought on impulse from a chainstore when she had seen it hanging on the reduced rail. She had plaited her damp hair for extra coolness, and put a slick of soft pink gloss on her lips. More important by far, she was very hungry. She opened her bedroom door and walked purposefully towards the kitchen.

The smell of the food was so deliciously appetising her stomach actually gave a small growl, causing her to place her hand against it and give Tariq a defiant look that melted in the heat of the sensual shock that hit her insides. He wasn't wearing his headdress, and his hair, like hers, was still damp, the sight of it unexpectedly erotic. Thick and cut short, more dark brown than black, it had a soft curl that made her long to slide her fingers into it and feel it curling round them. Beneath the hem of his robe she could see the indigo darkness of what looked like linen trousers of some description, whilst his feet were bare. For some reason that made her curl her own toes into her slip-on mules.

'I hope you like Lebanese food,' he told her. 'I ordered it for the variety. We can carry it out to the terrace; it will be pleasantly cool out there now.'

He certainly wasn't shy about giving orders, Gwynneth thought rebelliously, admitting at the same time that she was too hungry to waste time protesting. Instead she went to the cupboards, removing cutlery, plates and water glasses to put on a tray to carry outside, leaving Tariq to deal with the food.

The terrace was large enough to throw a party on, and seemed to have been equipped with just that in mind. Gwynneth put the tray down on a glass-topped low-level bamboo table and flicked on the light switch, which she discovered not only brought on the lights but activated an anti-mosquito unit as well.

Three long bamboo sofas, comfortably padded with cushions upholstered in a striking black, grey and off-white fabric, formed a U-shape around the table, so that one could look out over the balcony towards the sea.

Tariq had started to remove the lids from the food cartons, explaining as he did so, 'It is an Arab tradition for people to sit round what you would probably call a shared buffet, eating and talking, rather than to sit formally at a dining table.'

His gaze flicked over her as she stood by the balcony. The kaftan was obviously a deliberate ploy—but to what purpose?

'Come and eat while the food is still hot,' he commanded.

Without waiting to see if she would do so, he settled himself on one of the sofas, sitting cross-legged with enviable ease, the soles of his feet turned inward. Gwynneth remembered reading that it was considered a great insult to confront another man with the sole of one's foot or shoe.

It was impossible for her to match his fluid dexterity, so instead she sat primly opposite him with her feet placed firmly on the floor.

He paused in busily scooping up small amounts of food from the variety of containers to raise one eyebrow and drawl, 'Very proper, and I suspect most uncomfortable, but it's your choice.'

He had, Gwynneth noticed, used his fingers to remove the food, and was now dipping them into one of two bowls of water he must have brought out but which she hadn't previously noticed.

Hesitantly she inspected the contents of the containers, most of which she could recognise, and all of which smelled delicious.

'Spare ribs, chicken in herbs, couscous, taramasalata,' he

told her, naming several of the items as Gwynneth heaped her plate. She watched as Tariq used the flat unleavened pieces of bread to scoop up his food.

'I should have thought to ask if you wanted me to order you a bottle of wine. Since I'm going to be driving, alcohol is out for me.'

He saw her small questioning frown and added carelessly, as though it was of no great importance, 'I don't have any religious allegiance. My mother was Muslim but my father was British—and agnostic.'

'They must have loved one another very much to bridge that kind of cultural divide,' Gwynneth commented.

Tariq frowned. He had grown up hearing his father condemned, living with his mother's unhappiness, and now, abruptly, he realised that because of all that it had simply never occurred to him to think about how very much they must have once loved one another. How much…but still not enough.

But according to his second cousin it had been his mother whose love had weakened, not his father.

'Initially perhaps,'

'Initially?' Gwynneth queried.

'My parents separated when I was quite young,' he told her sombrely. 'Apparently they had an agreement that my father would live in my mother's country for the first few years and then she would move with him to his. She reneged on that agreement, so he left.'

'Oh, how dreadfully sad for all of you—but for you most especially,' Gwynneth sympathised.

Tariq shrugged dismissively. 'Not particularly. My mother moved back to live with her family, and I grew up surrounded by cousins and cousins of cousins. I lived very happily.'

'But you must have missed your father.'

'Why? Because you missed yours?'

'I missed both my parents,' Gwynneth told him, and then added honestly, 'Or rather, I missed sharing in what I imagined a happy family life would be. There is such a taboo surrounding the fact that mothers are not always able to love their children that people find it easier not to speak of it at all. I didn't myself for a long time.'

'So what changed?'

'I did. When I was able to accept that my mother hadn't loved me and equally able to accept that it wasn't my fault. I had to teach myself to accept that no one was to blame, and not just to accept that but to believe it as well.'

'And now you do?'

'Yes.'

'So will you have children yourself, or…?' Why was he talking to her like this? Asking her so many intimate and probing questions? Questions that went way beyond mere small talk. Why did he feel this deep, driving need to know everything there was to know about her, whether that knowledge related to her past experiences or her future plans? Too late, Tariq recognised just how much the questions he was asking her might reveal to her the feelings he had when he listened to her.

'It hasn't made me either hunger for them to rewrite my own childhood, nor fear the idea of them in case I repeat it with them, if that's what you mean. Were I to be in the right relationship with the right man…' She gave a small shrug, not daring to risk looking at him just in case he might see in her eyes the message her body was sending her. Right now, the only relationship it wanted her to have was with him! 'I do think women have a basic instinct and drive to have a child with the man they love; that way they can subconsciously perhaps both possess a bit of him and leave a lasting memory of their love. But children are individuals and have to be respected as such. Perhaps that is where the danger can lie.'

Heavens, she was opening up to him more than she had ever done with anyone. Didn't her head know or care abut the danger her heart was facing? Tariq was watching her and listening to her with a fixed concentration that made her heart hammer into her ribs as though it was trying to burst its way out of her chest and hurl itself into his arms.

'This is pretty deep stuff to discuss with a stranger,' she told him slightly breathlessly.

Stranger? She was right, of course; they were strangers to one another. And yet at some profoundly disturbing and deep level he felt so strongly connected to her... He pushed the thought away, barricading himself against it.

'Perhaps it is because we are strangers. Maybe it is with strangers that we feel most able to disclose our deepest thoughts and fears.' How could he be feeling like this about her when her values were so opposed to his own? She was a woman accustomed to the non-emotional, one-night stand type of sex; she was motivated by financial greed, as witnessed by the fact that she had refused his offer for the apartment, no doubt hoping to push the price up even further.

How could he even *think* about wanting her?

'Perhaps,' Gwynneth agreed. Whatever had existed between them over dinner to enable them to talk had now gone. She could sense it in the return of his coldness towards her.

'It's getting late, and I have a longish drive ahead of me—

so if you'll excuse me?' He spoke peremptorily, avoiding looking at her, standing up as easily and sinuously as he had sat down, whilst Gwynneth had to struggle somewhat to get up out of her cushioned comfort.

Had she bored and irritated him by spilling out her most personal thoughts to him like that? She tensed as he came towards her, leaning down to help her to her feet. In the small enclosed space between the sofa and the table they had to stand virtually body-to-body. He smelled of something cool and pleasant, but her senses were reacting to the more dangerous male scent of him that lay under it. Instinctively she closed her eyes, the better to focus on it, swaying slightly towards him.

Tariq exhaled fiercely. He could see the stiffness of her nipples silhouetted against the fabric of her kaftan and he had to clench his free hand into a fist to stop himself from lifting it to touch her. Her plaited hair exposed the vulnerability of the nape of her neck, tempting him to trace the shape of her bones with his lips and follow them down the length of her back, whilst his hands plundered the female curves of her breast and belly before…

The minute she felt the heat of Tariq's breath on her neck Gwynneth snapped her eyes open and stepped back from him, her face on fire with guilt.

How long would he be gone? For her own sake she hoped it would be long enough for the Zurani officials to untangle the complex ownership issues relating to the apartment. She desperately wanted to draw a line under the entire proceedings.

But not so desperately that she was willing to accept Tariq's offer?

That was because she didn't feel she could trust him—because her gut instinct told her that he had some kind of other agenda she wasn't aware of. Did it matter if he had? she asked herself as he released her arm and bent to start collecting the empty food cartons, stacking them on the tray.

Yes, it *did* matter, if that agenda involved money. Not for herself, but for Teresa and Anthony.

CHAPTER TEN

GWYNNETH shook her hair back off her face as she stepped out of the lift and headed for the apartment. She had been awake so early that she had decided to go for an early-morning run while it was still cool enough to do so. But although the exercise might have strengthened her body, it certainly hadn't strengthened her defences against her feelings for Tariq.

Tariq. She was getting dangerously close to living, breathing, thinking Tariq one hundred per cent of her time, and it didn't take a mathematical wizard to work out that that added up to loving him one hundred per cent.

Panic started to grip her. She must not love him. Not when he so patently did not love her. But he wanted her; it filled the space between them, infusing it with a predatory male sexual urgency that left her breathless, her heart pounding, as though the air had been robbed of oxygen.

This was crazy. She reached for her mobile in order to ring the young land registry official to find out what was happening, sighing when, instead of a human voice, she got his mechanised answering service, requesting her to leave a message. Leave a message? Saying what, exactly? That she had been offered twice the value of the apartment to relinquish her claim on it, but she was concerned about the validity of the offer and even more concerned that the apartment wouldn't be the only thing Tariq might steal from her.

Tariq. Where was he? What was he doing? What was he thinking? Was he thinking about her at all? Had he missed her last night? She had certainly missed him. Her hand trembled as she filled the kettle.

Her thoughts still on Tariq, Gwynneth browsed the bookshelves in his office, looking for something to read. She hesitated, torn between the book she had already read on Zuran and its history and what looked like a rather heavy book on the geological formation of the desert. Perhaps it wouldn't be as dull as it looked. As she removed it from the shelf she realised that another much thinner paperback book had been wedged behind it. Automatically she picked it up, intending to replace it, stopping when she saw the title: *Mjenat: The Hidden Valley and its Ruler.*

A book about the Hidden Valley? Smiling happily, she abandoned her original choice and headed for the terrace with her find.

Less than five minutes later the smile had disappeared from her face and she was sitting bolt upright, a look of angry disbelief widening her eyes as she stared at the photograph inside the front cover of the book.

Tariq! Or, to give him correct title, she corrected herself bitterly, His Highness Prince Tariq bin Salud Al Fwaisa. Tariq wasn't just Tariq, but a prince. And not just any old prince, either: he was the ruler of his own small kingdom.

On the opposite page to the photograph was a glowing tribute to him, and a discreet mention of his billionaire status not quite hidden in the flowery language giving thanks for his generosity to others.

Gwynneth threw the book down and went to the edge of the terrace, blinking back angry tears as she stared over the balcony.

Why hadn't he said something—anything? Why had he let her think…?

Did she *really* need to ask herself that question? she derided herself scornfully. He hadn't told her because men like him did not tell women like her—women they slept with once and then discarded, women they thought of as merely objects—*anything*. They didn't have a need to do so, and they certainly didn't have the desire to do so. Such men were users, and to them women like her were merely there to be exploited and then forgotten—women to be bought, played with for a while and then thrown out with the rubbish.

Only Tariq had not been able to do that with her, because she had refused to be thrown out of the apartment. He, no doubt wary of attracting unwanted attention to his off-duty pursuits, had had to resort to other measures by which to be rid of her. Measures such as offering her twice the value of the apartment. In order to get rid of her. That was all he wanted—to get rid of her! The pain caught her off guard, smashing through her anger and driving a stake right through her heart.

'And we think we've located the source of the underground spring that fills the oasis,' one of the team of scientists Tariq was employing on his Hidden Valley project told him excitedly. 'It looks as though it's fed by an overspill from something else—either a lake or maybe even a river. We already know that there's some kind of a cave formation beneath that outcrop of rocks at the head of the valley, below the foundations of the original palace.'

'It would have made sense to build a fortification around such a spring, to ensure that water would still be available in a siege situation—especially since at the time the original palace was built the valley lay close to one of the main camel train routes. Taking possession of the valley and its oasis meant my ancestors would have had both a financial asset and a need to protect it.' As he spoke, Tariq couldn't help thinking about Gwynneth, and the way she had reacted to his offer to buy the apartment from her.

'It strikes me,' Hal Derwent, chief archaeologist for the group, put in, 'that we could be looking at a situation where, if there are underground caves and passages, these could have been utilised to provide an escape route from the fortress if necessary—maybe even via the environs of the oasis in some way. This land, the desert, has always fascinated me. It holds so many secrets and gives them up so reluctantly.'

'Perhaps that is why my people think of the desert as female,' Tariq told him dryly.

'The earth's inner space is equally as fascinating as outer space—more so as far as I'm concerned,' Hal remarked, adding ruefully, 'What I could do with a tithe of a space exploration budget!'

'Well, I can't promise you that,' Tariq told him. 'But it may be that with the help of neighbouring countries we could investigate further. However, as you know, preserving the environment of the area's flora and fauna is of prime importance to me.'

'And me,' chimed in Bob Holmes, the team's natural history professor. 'Because the oasis is on private land which is virtually cut off from the rest of the desert, and not on any of the old camel trading routes, from a natural history point of view it is totally unique. I'm particularly interested in some of the species of fish we've taken from the oasis. They look like the kind of tropical saltwater fish you would expect to find on a coral reef, but the oasis is *not* salt water—even though its rock formation does provide a form of reef environment for them.'

Tariq smiled. 'There is a story that a long-ago prince built a private courtyard garden for his favourite houri, complete with a large glass tank filled with small reef fish. When the concubine died, after being poisoned by a rival, the Prince had the tank removed because he was unable to bear the sight of something that reminded him so painfully of the woman he had loved and lost. He gave orders that the tank and the fish were to be destroyed, but the young daughter of one of the men doing the work loved the fish so much she persuaded her father to help her remove them from the tank and place them in the oasis, praying to Allah as she did so that they might live.' He gave a small shrug. 'Who knows? Just as the flesh of a peach holds the kernel that is its seed, maybe there is an element of truth in the story, and the fish in the oasis are the offspring of saltwater fish who managed to survive and adapt.'

'Possibly. Or perhaps some seabird, or even a trained falcon, caught fish out over the gulf and then accidentally dropped its prey here.'

Tariq raised one eyebrow.

'Yes, it does sound pretty far-fetched.' Bob laughed. 'But one never knows.'

With summer setting in and the temperature rising steeply, all work on the valley had ceased. Tariq had not wanted to risk disturbing its animal life by setting up arc lighting so that the men could work in the cool hours of the night. The contractors were now securing the sites, ready to leave later in the day. He still had to talk to the men working on the excavation of the site of the original palace, and on the restoration of its hanging gardens, but instead of his thoughts being totally focused on this project which meant so much to him he was finding that they kept escaping from his control, subtly drifting away so that they could embrace Gwynneth Talbot. As he himself also ached to do?

With a brief nod to the other men he strode towards the villa where he and his parents had lived until their separation, unlocking the door and tensing as he stopped inside into the welcome dark coolness.

The villa had been built by his grandfather following the time-honoured principles of Middle Eastern architecture—which were to ensure that as much cool air as possible was drawn into a home and as much hot sunshine as possible kept out.

The villa was a solidly structured four-square building, enclosing four inner courtyards, three of which were gardens. Each corner of the building possessed a traditional wind tower, looking out across the desert and inward to the gardens beyond. An image slid into his head—a mental picture of himself with his father. He would have been about three, or maybe even four, clinging tightly to his father's hand as they climbed the stairs to one of the wind towers. His father, he remembered now, had looked out across the desert as he explained to him the principles behind their construction. Longing for his freedom? Or simply yearning for a broader horizon he could share with his wife and son?

His mother had said nothing to him of the promise his second cousin had described. But she, unlike his father, had craved the inner seclusion of the garden courtyards. Even when they had gone to live in Zuran she had preferred the solitude of her own company. Because—as he had always believed—of her grief at his father's betrayal? Or because, quite simply, she'd been a solitary person who had preferred to stand apart from others, as he did himself sometimes?

It was here that his father had taught him to play football and to read English, and here too that the older man had stood and watched quietly whilst Tariq had received his first lessons in the art of falconry. So many memories he hadn't previously allowed himself to acknowledge. Doing so now in the light of what he had learned was hauntingly bittersweet.

The apartment was silent and empty. It was gone midnight, but Gwynneth felt too restless and on edge to go to bed. Instead she went out onto the terrace. Was it really only yesterday that she and Tariq had eaten here together? Or rather, she and His Highness Prince Tariq bin Salud Al Fwaisa, she corrected herself grimly. No wonder she had thought him arrogant.

Someone on another balcony had been burning incense, and its heavy sensual scent was conjuring up images of a wide low-lying divan and night air softly wafting shadowy, gauzy fabrics. The East was all about the senses, Gwynneth decided; it reached out to all of them in ways that one didn't experience in the West.

There was a small shop in the souk where one could buy a wide range of different scents and the burners, and she was tempted to make a purchase there herself. For what purpose? So that when she went home she could light the burner and remember this and Tariq? She wasn't going to need any sensory aids to prompt her memory.

Tariq, who was no doubt ready to pay her anything so that he could get her out of his life!

Was that why he was so determined to keep this apartment? Because he came here to have sex with women, and needed it for the anonymity it afforded him? It all added up—right down to the way he had behaved towards her that first night.

Tariq—she refused to mentally address him any other way, she decided belligerently—used this apartment to have sex with women chosen either by himself or, even more unpalatably, on his behalf. Its anonymity here in the heart of Zuran's hotel quarter meant it was ideally suited for his needs. Although no doubt he could afford to buy others, plainly he did not wish to waste time or energy doing so. It was easier simply to buy her out, even if that meant he had to pay over the market price. What was an extra £500,000 to a man she now knew to be one of Zuran's wealthier billionaires?

Gwynneth paced the terrace, her face burning and her thoughts in turmoil. It made her skin crawl with loathing to know what the apartment really was, and to know too that she was simply another piece of female flesh who had been processed through it for a cold-hearted too-rich man's pleasure. She had been idiotically naïve, thinking that just because she felt shocked at wanting a man she barely knew, was tormented by the intensity of that wanting, Tariq must in some way be experiencing the male equivalent of her feelings. That he, like her, must be questioning the inappropriateness of their mutual desire at the same time as he was compelled to acknowledge the sheer force of it. That was the trouble with being an ageing virgin who didn't have the physical or emotional experience to recognise the reality of how modern sexual mores translated into real life.

She deplored her foolish belief that they shared a mutual but inadmissible and unspoken itch for one another they had been equally driven to scratch and equally infuriated by. They were not and never had been equals of any kind. In Tariq's eyes she was simply a piece of human flesh he'd wanted to use, he had used, and no doubt he would use many more pieces.

She derided herself for actually thinking that Tariq's reaction had been the male emotional stereotype. There had no emotional input into his reaction to her at all other than that of arrogant disbelief and anger.

And she had left it too late to defend herself from the fall-out—the humiliation of recognising that whilst she had engaged with him emotionally, physically and mentally, he had simply thought of her in terms of his own sexual satisfaction. The truth was that he had put about as much emotional effort into her as he would have done eating a fast-food meal—probably less.

That was what you got from sexually locking yourself away from modern life. Another woman of her age, wiser to the reality of things than she was, would no doubt have known immediately what his agenda was.

Of course he wanted to get rid of her. She was cramping his style.

And he was breaking her heart.

She stiffened, recoiling from her thoughts, but they wouldn't be denied. Tariq breaking her heart? That just wasn't possible. He had made her feel desire, yes. But desire was only physical. What she *felt* for him was only physical. It had to be.

She had to get away from him, and she had to put this whole episode totally behind her.

When he came back she would tell him that she had

changed her mind and that she was willing to accept his offer.
Then she would move out of the apartment and into the most
inexpensive hotel she could find—if there was such a thing
as an inexpensive hotel in Zuran—and she would stay there
until the formalities had been completed and Tariq's money
was safely in the bank account she had already opened to hold
the money from her father's estate.

Tariq frowned as he studied his computer screen. He was supposed to be dealing with a backlog of correspondence and
updating his files with regard to the fact that work in the
valley had now ceased until the cooler weather. Instead of
which he was wasting time thinking about Gwynneth and
wondering how much thought his parents had given to the
problems their different outlooks on life, and the manner in
which they'd wanted to live it, could cause them before they
had decided to get married. Or hadn't they given any thought
to those problems at all? Had they simply assumed that their
love was strong enough to overcome them?

If he left here now he could be back in Zuran before dawn.
But to what purpose? To wake Gwynneth from her sleep with
the touch of his hands and his mouth? To take from her her
words of denial and change them into soft sounds of delight?

He was crazy for thinking like this. The discovery that his
father had not been the contemptible figure he had always believed was not a licence for him to start believing that…

That what? That he did not need to fight against what he
was feeling anymore? What he was *feeling*—was he crazy?
She had made it plain by her behaviour that she relished the
danger of sex with strangers, and with ever-changing partners.
The woman he committed to would have to be his exclu-

sively and for ever, no matter what her past sexual lifestyle had been. There would have to be honesty and openness between them, a desire to understand and to bridge any cultural and emotional differences. Perhaps most importantly of all, the woman sharing his life would have to understand and support the fact that he had a duty to his heritage—to its past, its present and its future.

He looked towards the narrow window which gave on to the main courtyard where his 4x4 was parked. He could be back at the apartment in four hours. Less if he pushed himself.

He got up and went to stand by the window, looking down into the courtyard. And what if he did go back and make love to her? What then? All he would be doing was taking another step towards an end that was inevitable—because ultimately any relationship they had *would* end. The leopard couldn't change its spots, nor the falcon cease to fly. He knew himself well enough to know that he would not be able to live with the fear that ultimately she would leave him. Better the sharp agony of self-denial now than the long, slow putrefying death of his self-respect and pride.

He turned away from the window and went back to the computer.

CHAPTER ELEVEN

IT MIGHT be early, but she was far from the only person up and about, Gwynneth realised as she paid for the carton of milk she had hurried out to buy. No way could she drink black coffee, and no way could she face Tariq's return without the mind-sharpening protection of her regular caffeine fix.

As she made her way back to the apartment she was vaguely aware of a car crawling along the side of the quiet side street virtually beside her, but she was too busy worrying about how she was going to cope with seeing Tariq to do more than glance idly at it.

She had almost reached the apartment block when, suddenly and terrifyingly, the two men who had been casually walking behind her abruptly closed the distance, trapping her between them, grabbing hold of her and dragging her over to the now stationary car. Zuran was famed for the safety of its holidaymakers, and Gwynneth hadn't given a thought to the danger of walking around on her own because it hadn't occurred to her that there was any.

She struggled frantically to break free of her captors as she saw the rear passenger door of the car being thrust open.

They were on the point of pushing her into the car, virtually head first, when out of nowhere—or so it seemed to Gwynneth—three police cars screeched up, blocking in her would-be kidnappers. Their doors were flung open to allow half a dozen or more armed policemen to come running to her aid, so that within seconds of being grabbed she was free and her assailants were being marched to the waiting police cars in handcuffs, along with the driver of the car.

'It is fortunate that we happened to be driving past and saw what was happening,' the most senior-looking of the police-men told Gwynneth, after he had assured himself that she was all right, if very shocked, and she had thanked him for their timely appearance. 'Where were you going?' he asked.

Gwynneth inclined her head in the direction of the apart-ment building.

'One of my men will escort you back to your apartment,' he informed her.

A brief nod of his head brought not one but two thick-set police officers to her side. To her bemusement, they not only escorted her all the way back to the apartment, they also insisted on coming inside with her and on checking every single room.

Who needed caffeine? Gwynneth thought shakily once they had gone and reaction had begun to set in. She was having to fight against a very strong desire to sit down and have a good cry. Shock, she told herself pragmatically. It was just the effects of delayed shock. Perhaps she should have that coffee after all.

Tariq had left the valley just before dawn, watching the sun bring colour and light to the desert, turning the sand from grey to an almost blinding silver gilt.

The mobile he used for business was switched off, but the phone for his private line to the Ruler was as always on. He was an hour out of Zuran when it shrilled sharply, and he frowned and pulled up to take the call.

The Chief of Police was brief and matter-of-fact. Thanks to the round-the-clock surveillance he had put in place at the apartment, his men had already circumvented two attacks on Ms Gwynneth Talbot.

'What kind of attacks?' Tariq demanded.

'The first was an attempt to run her down in the street. They may only have intended to scare her; who can say? The second, though, was definitely more serious. They were attempting to kidnap her. We are currently questioning the men involved, who have admitted working for Rheinvelt. We think we have all the plotters now, but to be on the safe side, Highness, I would respectfully request that Ms Talbot move into a safe house until we are sure.'

He only had a heartbeat in which to make his decision, but that was all he needed. It was as simple as that—and as easy. Between one heartbeat and the next he had made up his mind.

'That won't be necessary,' he said crisply. 'I am on my way back to the apartment now, and when I leave later today to return to Mjenat Ms Talbot will be accompanying me. She will be safe there.'

'I shall have my men post a guard on the road to the Valley, Highness. Although I admit that I cannot think of anywhere safer for her. If these men we are questioning now are telling the truth, then we have all those involved in custody now, and the fact that they have been apprehended and will be punished according to Zurani law should stand as a warning to anyone else your friend might try to hire in their place. Our Esteemed

Ruler has made it plain that he will not tolerate Zuran being corrupted by money-laundering or other illicit activities, and that a clear message must be sent out to anyone who doubts his determination on the matter, so he will not be inclined to deal lightly with them.'

After he had ended the call and restarted the 4x4, Tariq discovered that his hands were shaking. His heart thudded impatiently into his chest wall, urging him to get to Gwynneth as fast as he possibly could. He should never have left her on her own, exposed to such danger. Any thoughts he might have had of sending her back to her home country had gone. There was only one place he wanted her to be from now on, and that was with him. He was finally prepared to admit that to himself.

Gwynneth had packed her case, and was ready to leave just as soon as she had informed Tariq that she was now prepared to accept his offer. When would he be back?

This would be the last time she would see him. Good. That was what she wanted.

Liar, liar! she mocked herself.

All right then, she mentally amended, to appease that inner knowing voice, it was what she needed! Satisfied? she asked her inner critic.

It was Friday, and Zuran City was busy with worshippers coming from the city's mosques as Tariq nosed the big vehicle down the same side street where earlier Gwynneth had so nearly been abducted. He drove down into the underground car park, leaving the 4x4 parked next to the new baby Bentley he preferred if he was driving himself in town. Unlike the other male members of his extended family, Tariq lived his life free of any kind of personal retinue as much as he could.

The service lift took him up to the apartment, where he slid his key card into the lock and thrust open the door.

Gwynneth was pacing the terrace, mentally rehearsing the speech she had tailored to be as brief as she could make it. She hadn't heard Tariq arrive and so he had the leisure to watch her for several seconds without her knowing that he was doing so.

It was some sixth sense that alerted her to his presence— a sharp surge of awareness that drew her gaze into the shadows where he stood as speedily as a she-falcon returning to the lure.

Tariq strode over to the terrace and stepped onto it to join her.

'There is something I want to say to you.'

'Really? Like what? A repeat of that offer you made me for this apartment? One million pounds? Why not make it two—after all, you can afford can't you, Your Highness? And before you try to deny it, I've read all about you in *this*!' she informed him, throwing the book onto the seating.

She had promised herself she wouldn't do this—so why, oh, why was she doing it? Dignified silence, that was how she had intended to greet him—and leave him. And now look at her, ranting and raving like a jealous lover!

That book! He had forgotten it even existed, and he cursed even more now than he had done when he had first discovered it had been written. But his pain was greater than his anger.

'Two million? Why stop at that?' he demanded bitingly. He could overlook much, but not this kind of greed. Not and still call himself a man. His heart felt as though it was being wrenched apart. 'Why not ask for three million? Or four? But let me tell you, if you do, the answer will be the same—and it is no. Contrary to what you seem to think, the fact that I am who I am does not make me a soft touch for greedy amoral women. I've already offered you more than this place is worth.'

'Yes, I know that.' Gwynneth stopped him. 'And I know why.'

Tariq watched her. Had one of the men the Chief of Police had sent to guard her broken with security protocol and told her why she was being guarded?

'No wonder you want to pay me to guarantee your own exclusive secret ownership of this place. Having me here must have been cramping your style!' Gwynneth burst out. 'It wasn't very hard for me to work it all out once I knew who you are. You use this apartment as…as your own private brothel—that's why you mistook me for a prostitute! And you had the gall to question *my* morals!'

She mustn't let him see how upset she was.

'Not that any of that matters now,' she added, getting her voice under control. How could she lie to herself like this? It mattered more than anything else in the whole of her life, just as *he* mattered more than anything or anyone else. 'I've decided to accept your offer and to sell you the apartment, but… but only at the real market price.'

She had really had to battle with herself over that. There was no way she would want to be paid more if she only had herself to consider, but by accepting less than he was prepared to pay she was depriving Teresa and Anthony of a considerable sum of money. But morally she could not bring herself to accept more than the apartment was worth—not even for them. And besides, £500,000 was still a very respectable nest egg.

'So perhaps we can just get on with things and get all the paperwork sorted out as quickly as possible,' she continued briskly. 'I'm prepared to move out of here until everything's done.'

Tariq shrugged dismissively, as though her words—like her feelings, no doubt—meant nothing to him.

'I'm afraid that isn't going to be possible now,' he told her.

Gwynneth stared at him, and then stammered, 'What—what do you mean?' Had he changed his mind and decided to buy somewhere else?

Tariq gestured towards the cane sofas, saying authoritatively, 'We may as well sit down.'

Reluctantly Gwynneth perched on the corner of the nearest seat, tensing when Tariq came and sat next to her, his long legs splayed out in front of him, his thigh touching her own. She wanted desperately to move away from him, but she was trapped against the side of the sofa with nowhere to go.

'First, allow me to correct your misapprehensions. Contrary to what you seem to imagine, my way of life does not include semi-clandestine sexual liaisons. Nor do I have any desire for it to do so.'

'You expect me to believe that, after—?'

'After what?' Tariq pressed her smoothly. 'After I allowed you to tempt me?'

'I did not tempt you! You were the one who—' Gwynneth took a deep breath and shook her head. 'Look, all I want—all I came here for—is to sell the apartment and take the money home with me.'

'Money is obviously very important to you,' he agreed unkindly.

Anger flashed in Gwynneth's eyes.

'Actually, you're wrong. It isn't. But on this occasion—'

'On this occasion you thought you would allow it to matter?'

'No! If I only had myself to consider I'd walk out of here right now and let you keep the wretched thing.'

'If you only had yourself to consider? And what exactly does that mean?' Tariq queried.

Gwynneth closed her eyes and then opened them again. 'If you must know…'

'I must,' Tariq confirmed grimly.

Gwynneth took a deep breath and began quietly, 'My father had a…a girlfriend. Teresa. And a baby—Anthony. My half-brother.' She could sense that Tariq was looking at her, but she refused to return his look, determinedly focusing her gaze away from him as she continued. 'Prior to his death, Dad came to England on business and he brought Teresa and their baby back with him. He introduced them to me. Until then I hadn't even realised they existed, but that was Dad all over. There'd been so many women in and out of his life for so long that I never thought…' She gave a small shrug, not wanting to stray into the painful history of her relationship with her father. 'Originally Teresa was from the Philippines. From what she's told me, it's obvious that her family have very little in the way of material assets. She wants to go back there and bring Anthony up. Even a little money would make a huge difference to their lives, but since my father hadn't changed his will, and they weren't married, he hadn't made any provision for her. Everything was left to me. The apartment was his only major asset, and I decided to sell it and to put the money in trust for Teresa and Anthony. That's why I came here.'

She heard Tariq's sharp intake of breath but she still refused to look at him.

'You want the money for someone else?' he demanded.

'Yes,' Gwynneth confirmed simply. Pride strengthened her voice as she told him, 'I don't need or want my father's money. I've supported myself financially since I left university, and to be quite frank I prefer it that way. All I ever wanted from my father was his love.' What on earth had made her tell him that?

'It seems to me that you and I share an emotional burden,' he said quietly. 'Problems with our fathers left over from the pain of our childhoods.'

Now she did look at him, unable to stop herself from doing so. What she could see in his eyes made her heart tighten with pain—his pain this time, though, not her own. She didn't speak. Not wanting to in case she broke the fragile bond Tariq was so unexpectedly creating between them with his confidences.

'I had always believed—been told—that my father abandoned my mother when I was quite young,' he told her. 'I only recently learned about the extenuating circumstances of which I spoke to you. After so many years of seeing my father as a man to despise and dislike, wanting to deny my cultural heritage from him, it is an odd sensation to realise that I may not have known the truth—that I misjudged him.'

Gwynneth swallowed against her own bittersweet emotions. Bitter because of her memories, and sweet because Tariq was confiding in her. 'I wish I could say the same about my own father,' she admitted. 'Unfortunately I have always known the reality of what he was, because he always made a point of telling me.'

Tariq could hear the stark sadness in her voice.

'But you are still prepared to put your life on hold in order to help his girlfriend and child?'

'They are not my father. And besides, despite everything, somehow I feel I owe it to him as well as them to do everything that I can for them.' She gave a small sigh. 'He wasn't a bad man so much as a selfish, amoral one.'

'Amoral?'

'He was very highly sexed,' Gwynneth told him bluntly. 'And he liked to talk about his conquests and his prowess.' She saw the way Tariq was frowning, and, realising too late the interpretation he must be putting on her admission, corrected it hastily, assuring him, 'Oh, not in any kind of abusive way.'

'For an adult to impose his sexuality on a child in any kind of way, even verbally, is abusive,' Tariq said grimly.

With a father who had boasted to her about his sexuality, perhaps it was no wonder that she herself was sexually promiscuous, he reflected. Maybe she had even felt subconsciously that she had to compete with her father in order to win his approval.

'That is why the apartment is so important to me,' Gwynneth repeated, unaware of the way in which he had interpreted her words. 'Because of Teresa and Anthony.'

'You have been honest and open with me. Now it is my turn to be equally open and honest with you,' Tariq informed her gravely. 'Prior to your arrival here in Zuran I was involved in an undercover operation to discover the identity of the leader of a criminal gang who were targeting Zuran with a variety of criminal activities—including the double-selling scam, which enabled them to launder money. In that role I had to pretend that I was prepared to assist the gang with the necessary legalities in exchange for a financial interest in the racket. As a sweetener they gave me this apartment, so in the interests of realism I had to be seen to be using it. The night I found you here I had been offered the reward of a night with one of the prostitutes they hoped to establish here in Zuran. I had turned that offer down, but when I found you here, I thought….'

'That I was a prostitute,' Gwynneth supplied for him. 'It's okay. You don't need to apologise,' she added flippantly, in an attempt to conceal the surge of giddily relieved joy foaming up inside her. 'I'll take it as read.'

'As to that, I wasn't aware that I had anything to apologise for,' Tariq informed her coolly. 'I may have been in error with regard to your professional status, but you made it very clear that you were enjoying what was happening.'

She couldn't argue with that, Gwynneth realised, but she still struggled to defend herself, protesting, 'That was a mistake! I wasn't... I didn't...'

She could see from the way he was looking at her that she wasn't having the effect she wanted to have. She might as well give up, she acknowledged, because she certainly wasn't going to tell him that her reaction to him had trashed every single conviction she had had about her own sexuality.

Instead she gave him a bright, determined smile and said lightly, 'Well, now that we've cleared the air, and we both know what the real situation is, I'll find a hotel to book into. I'm already packed—'

'No.'

'No?' Ridiculously, her heart was beating far too fast, and with far, far too much pleasure—as though it had interpreted his refusal as a sign that he wanted her to stay with him. How on earth had that happened? She had thought she had endured enough to be protected from the danger of that kind of emotional responsiveness to him.

'We're leaving for Mjenat immediately. The Hidden Valley,' he explained. 'We shall be staying there for the foreseeable future.'

He was taking her to his home. He wanted her with him. He wanted her. A second rush of joyful exhilaration followed the first before she could control it, telling its own story—as if she needed to be told how she felt about him.

'But...'

'I'm afraid there is no alternative. You are in too much danger to remain here in Zuran.'

She blinked at him. 'Danger?'

'Yes. I regret to say that because you have been seen entering and leaving this apartment you have become vulnerable. The Zurani Chief of Police has received information that hitmen have been hired to…punish me for my part in ensuring that the gang are not able to set up their operations in Zuran. He has warned me that anyone closely connected with me is at risk. In fact he rang me this morning to tell me that his men have already foiled two attempts to harm you.'

Gwynneth suddenly felt quite sick with shock and disbelief.

'The car…and then those men…' she whispered.

'Yes,' Tariq agreed. 'Fortunately the Chief of Police has his men keeping a watchful eye on you. These people obviously think that you are my lover, and that is why they are targeting you. The Chief of Police believes that they now have all those involved under lock and key, but he has said that he wants some more time to be totally sure. It is for that reason that you and I are going to the Valley. You will be safe there.'

Safe? With him? What a fool she had been to have thought…what she had thought. And how revealing her reaction had been. How had it happened that she had allowed herself to become so emotionally vulnerable to him? All her life she had guarded herself against just that kind of danger, yet now, and with a man her common sense should have told her was not for her, she had somehow or other let him into her heart. And now it was too late to try to bar it to him. Much too late. And *that* meant…

The enormity of what it meant made her feel sick and shaky. She couldn't go anywhere with him. Not now that she could no longer hide from the fact that she had fallen in love with him. And especially not now when she knew that he did not return that love. 'There's no need for me to go anywhere with you,' she told him unsteadily. 'I can go home. I'll be safe there.'

'Maybe. Maybe not. And I am not prepared to take the risk of that "maybe not".'

'*You* are not prepared?' She was using her anger to drive away those other feelings she must not feel. 'I am an adult, and I am perfectly capable of making up my own mind and taking my own decisions.'

'Indeed. But you must understand that I have a moral duty to protect you, since it is because of me that you are in danger. Were I to allow you to leave Zuran, I would have to send men with you to guard you.'

He obviously wasn't joking about the potential danger, Gwynneth saw apprehensively.

'But your Chief of Police said he's got those responsible,' she pointed out doggedly.

'I said he believes that he has. Naturally he wants to be totally sure.'

'But surely it isn't really necessary for me to go to the Valley with you?'

'Unfortunately, I'm afraid that it is.'

So in actual fact he *didn't* want her with him. She assimilated that information in silence as she fought down the pain it brought her. The truth was that she wanted to go with him as little as he wanted her to be there—although for a very different reason. She had felt much safer when the barrier between them had been her assumption about his way of life and her aversion to it. Then she had believed that, no matter how physically tempted by him she might be, her emotional revulsion to what he represented would keep her safe.

Now she was having to accept that he was a man of principle and integrity. And the only barrier she had to protect her was his lack of any real emotional interest in her.

But that was all the barrier she needed, wasn't it? After all, she wasn't going to throw herself at him! What would she say? *Take me—oh, and by the way, I'm still a virgin, even if you've refused to believe me, and now I get to prove it to you.*

'I appreciate your concern,' she told him, trying to sound as cool and professional as she could. 'But I'm sure I will be perfectly safe once I get home.'

'I can't afford to take the chance that you won't be,' Tariq informed her bluntly. 'You may be aware that Zuran is investing its oil revenues in developing the country as a resort and sports destination. In order for us to succeed we need to be able to assure visitors of their safety. If you were to be followed home and attacked in some way it wouldn't be very long before it became linked to your visit here. That could have an adverse effect on our reputation.'

She couldn't argue against what he was saying, Gwynneth knew, and, although she hated admitting it, what he had told her had left her feeling vulnerable and uneasy. He was plainly not going to give in—which meant that she would have to.

'How long would I have to stay with you?' she asked him with resignation.

'Not long. A matter of a few days—a week at the most. The Chief of Police is virtually sure that they have all those involved in custody now. He simply wants to double check.'

Gwynneth lifted her shoulders in a small shrug of defeat.

'Very well. Mjenat has a fascinating history. In different

circumstances I would have enjoyed visiting it, especially in view of your project to recreate the hanging gardens.'

'Work in the valley has finished now, until the cooler weather returns. I do not want to disturb the wildlife by lighting the area at night, but I confess I am impatient to move things forward. It was my father's idea originally, and I am sorry that he will never see the end result.'

'It will be a wonderful testimony to him, though, won't it?' Gwynneth said quietly. 'To both your parents, in fact. To create something so beautiful and fragile in such a hostile environment calls for a tremendous act of faith.'

'The same could well be said of love within marriage,' Tariq told her softly.

Gwynneth looked at him. He was looking back at her. Suddenly she felt as though a subtle emotional change of gear had taken place. The silence they had been filling with their conversation had somehow deepened and almost wrapped itself around them, locking them together in a dangerous intimacy. If he came to her now…

But he didn't. Instead he stood up and said dismissively, as though he couldn't even feel it, 'We need to leave as soon as we can.'

CHAPTER TWELVE

'I'M AFRAID we're going to have to fend for ourselves whilst we're here. My housekeeper and her husband are away on holiday,' Tariq informed Gwynneth,

They were in Mjenat, standing in the main courtyard to a large villa, having arrived only a few minutes earlier.

'I'll just deactivate the alarm system and then we can go in.'

Gwynneth studied her surroundings covertly. A high perimeter wall protected both the villa's privacy and its security. She had seen the discreetly placed security cameras as they drove into the valley itself, and Tariq had informed her that the collection of buildings just inside the valley were normally used to house those working there but that half a dozen policemen were already in residence there, along with back-up personnel to make sure that they didn't get any unwanted visitors.

His words were a reminder to her of just who and what he was.

'I suppose that by rights I ought to be addressing you by your title,' she commented, as he pushed open the high arched wooden doors.

'I don't use it—other than on State occasions or when my second cousin insists,' he told her matter-of-factly, adding,

'I don't see the need. A man should surely be able to command the respect of others by virtue of his own acts, or not at all.'

The interior of the villa, cool and shadowy after the heat outside, smelled faintly of incense and roses.

'I will take you to the women's quarters. Please follow me.'

The women's quarters. The words conjured up images of sloe-eyed concubines waiting dutifully to please their master.

'The villa was built for my grandfather, and after my father's death my mother chose to live as a traditional Muslim woman, keeping to her own quarters.'

'But what about you? Were you allowed to live there with her?'

He stopped walking to turn round and look at her, frowning slightly. Her question, with its obviously genuine concern, had caught him off guard. Listening to it, hearing the almost maternal anxiety of a woman for a child, touched gently on the painful bruises of his childhood which now as a man he preferred to forget he had once felt. And yet there was something sweetly healing and tender about hearing the emotion in Gwynneth's voice legitimise his childhood pain.

'I went to live in the palace in Zuran, where I became part of a household in which there were many other children,' he answered her lightly. 'As was the custom then, we were cared for by others.'

In other words he had been abandoned by his parents in much the same way as she had been abandoned by hers. Without thinking, she reached out to touch his arm in an automatic gentle gesture of compassion. To her shock just the simple act of her fingertips brushing against his robe-covered forearm made her heart lurch against her ribs and her belly turn to liquid female heat. Her reasons for touching him were forgotten as she was overwhelmed by a need to slide her hand beneath the fabric of his sleeve so that she could stroke her fingertips through the soft furring of hair on his arm. She wanted to trace a line of hungry kisses from his throat all the way down to the flatness of his belly whilst she watched his helpless reaction to her touch; she wanted to lace her fingers through the darkness of his body hair where it grew soft and thick around the base of his manhood; she wanted to slowly and thoroughly explore every rigid inch of that male part of him until she knew the shape, texture, heat, scent and taste of 'the pleasure giver—the great scimitar of love', as she had smiled to see it described in a book on the Middle East. Presumably the words sounded far more impressive in Arabic.

But she didn't need words—the image she had conjured up inside her head was enough to melt her bones—and the walls she had thrown up inside herself against this kind of desire. She should not have agreed to come here with him. She was too vulnerable, both to him and to the way she felt about him.

The way she loved him. The way she would always and for ever love only him. Fear quickened inside her, making her want to push back from the reality she had just exposed.

As a child, confronted with her parents' divorce, she had carefully picked up all the bits of the person who had once been her and tidied them away—just as her mother had always insisted she should pick up her toys and put them away. It had been her coping strategy then, and it still was now.

Only this time it wasn't working, and she wasn't coping—because this time her sexuality, which she had always so tightly controlled, had rebelled and broken down the doors to its prison. And, what was more, it had freed the emotion which had been its cellmate as well. Between the two of them they were now intent on taking over the controls.

This was crazy. How could she have let herself fall in love with Tariq?

Tariq looked down to where Gwynneth's hand lay against his arm.

No one—not anyone at all, not even when he had been a child—had managed to break through his barriers and touch the heart of his pain so immediately or so accurately.

But then, she was not just anyone. She was...

She was a woman with a string of lovers in her past, who could walk out of his life even more easily than his father had done and hurt him far more badly.

He lifted his own hand to remove hers from his body, but instead found he had placed it over hers, as though he wanted to keep it there.

How could a mere silence be this intense and profound? This charged with emotional and sensual urgency and promise? They were even breathing together, their hearts pumping the blood through their bodies in perfect time with one another. They stepped closer to one another, as though they were engaged in the mutually known steps of some intimate private dance. From one synchronised breath to the wild, driving thrust of his body and the clamouring, seeking need of her own to be filled with it—it was the dance of life itself, Gwynneth recognised.

Panic filled her. She wasn't ready for this; she was too afraid of the emotional pain that would follow. She snatched her hand away from under Tariq's and reminded him huskily, 'The women's quarters?'

'They're this way,' Tariq answered tersely, turning away

from her to stride so quickly down the corridor that she almost
had to run to catch up with him.

When he eventually pushed open the fretted double doors
at the end of the corridor, Gwynneth waited until she was
sure she wasn't going to risk coming into any kind of contact with his body before she followed him into the room
beyond them.

Large and rectangular, the room was decorated in a very
Moorish style, with stylised arches and alcoves and fretwork.
It was furnished with low divans piled high with richly col-
oured silk cushions and beautiful Persian rugs.

'This is the main salon. When the shutters are opened you
will see that the room opens out onto a private courtyard.
There are several bedrooms, all of which are prepared for oc-
cupation, so you may choose whichever you wish.'

'Which was your mother's?' Gwynneth asked. 'Only I
wouldn't want to…'

'She had her own private suite within the women's quarters. It is closed up now. I suggest you use the room closest
to this salon. It too has direct access to the garden.' He paused,
the terseness leaving his voice as he added, 'I am afraid that
until my staff return we shall be eating from the freezer. For
myself I don't mind, but…'

'You can cook?' Gwynneth couldn't conceal her disbelief.

He gave a brief shrug. 'Of course—if I have to. I learned
around the campfires of our people. But since there are only
the two of us here it makes more sense to eat the meals my
chef has prepared and frozen. I'll leave you to settle in now.'

Settle in? How could she do that when she was going
to be living under the same roof with him? Get a grip,
Gwynneth advised herself unkindly. You've been sharing a

two-bedroomed apartment, now you're sharing a small palace. You probably won't even see him.

But somehow being here in what was the childhood home he had shared with his parents was far more intimate than sharing the apartment with him.

Although she had told herself she would not do so, in the end Gwynneth settled on the bedroom Tariq had suggested— because it had access to the courtyard garden with which she had fallen totally in love.

Tiled pathways led to rose-covered arbours, and beyond them to formal beds set out with plants and fruit trees. Fat goldfish swam lazily beneath the equally fat lily pads of the central pond. Beautifully detailed ornamental trellises divided the garden into separate rooms, each shaped like a pome-granate seed, which together, Gwynneth realized, formed a stylised pattern.

But surely best of all was what she thought must be an Arabian Nights version of the modern Western outdoor hot tub. Enclosed by gold-and-blue painted trelliswork and smothered in scented pink roses, the rich blue-tiled tub was semi-sunken into the ground. Opposite the tub was an alcove containing a low wide divan the size of a double bed, its rich blue cover heaped with crimson, gold and jade silk cushions, and on the table between the divan and the tub there were several glass perfume bottles.

The small area was a sybarite's paradise, and it was all too easy for Gwynneth to imagine some naked houri enjoying the scented warmth of the water whilst her robed lover reclined against the cushions, enjoying watching her. Perhaps he would go to her, feed her a piece of sugar-dusted Turkish delight from his own plate with one hand whilst with the other he slowly caressed the naked curves of her exposed breasts, tasted the damask darkness of her nipples...

Stop that, Gwynneth warned herself, as she wiggled her fingers experimentally in the crystal-clear water, savouring its warmth.

She really shouldn't be doing this, she told herself less than half an hour later, and she glanced round just to check that she was totally alone, before dropping the towel she had wrapped around herself and stepping into the tub. But she just hadn't been able to resist.

She reached for an overhanging rose that was already dropping its petals, harvesting them to scatter on the surface of the tub, breathing in their perfume.

The water closed round her body like warm silk. There was no real reason why she shouldn't indulge herself other than her own awareness of the sensuality of her private thoughts. But only she was privy to those, and, since Tariq had already said that he had work to do, she wasn't going to be disturbed.

Not by his presence, at least. But the thoughts she was having about him were certainly disturbing her, she admitted as she pushed through the water to the far side of the tub. A giveaway burn of colour heated her face as she felt the soft pressure of the water stroking between her legs as she moved. If she closed her eyes she could almost imagine that Tariq...

The unfamiliar sensuality of her thoughts might be making her face burn, but her self-consciousness wasn't strong enough to stop her hand from sliding down her body. Her breasts felt heavy, her nipples tight and aching. She was acutely physically aware of her own female flesh, of its pulse within the folds of her sex. She moved, not sure if her movement was designed to stop the quickening sensual beat or to savour it. She closed her eyes and let her body dictate to her mind the fantasy it wanted it to create. *Tariq*. His name filled the air around her, its vibration shimmering on the water and filling all her senses, even though she had only spoken it within herself.

Tariq pushed back his computer chair and stood up. He had just received an e-mail from the Chief of Police, informing him that he now believed they had all the potential danger and those responsible for it under control.

I would ask that you remain in Mjenat for the time being, though. Until I am able to formally confirm that it is safe for you to return to Zuran City.

The Chief of Police and his men had been praiseworthily efficient and speedy. He glanced at his watch. He would go and tell Gwynneth. She would, he knew, be delighted to learn that their stay here in the villa was going to be so short-lived. And so, of course, was he.

So why did the prospect fill his heart with something more akin to heaviness than relief? He was falling victim to his own imaginings, he derided himself as he made his way towards the women's quarters.

The sitting room was empty, and then Tariq saw that the doors were open to the garden. He headed for them, stepping through them and out onto the tiled terrace. The garden was silent, apart from the singing of the birds, and then he heard the small sound of the movement of gently lapping water. He stepped out into the garden and stood there bareheaded, his concentration that of a desert hunter, watchful and still, before he started to walk, as soft-footed as a sleek-pelted panther, following the sound of the water.

She was half reclining, half seated in the hot tub, lying back, her eyes closed, her hair tied up on top of her head, loose tendrils caressing the pale oval of her face. Rose petals floated on the surface of the water, dappling small shadows through the water onto her naked body, their perfume intensified by the enclosed space and the heat of the sun. Unaware of his presence, she moved lazily in the water, her movement disturbing the petals and revealing the neat almost heart shape of her body hair, sleekly dark against the pearl beauty of her skin.

From where he was standing he could look down and see the delicate shaping of the outer lips of her sex, now furled as neatly and tightly together as the shell of an oyster. But, unlike the hard sharpness of a shell, the warm flesh of her lips could be teased apart by the stroke of his fingertip moving over and over again against them, until they swelled and parted of their own accord to offer him the pearl that lay within them, small and perfect, its female rigidity waiting eagerly for the caress of his hand and mouth.

The ache in his body pounded out its unmistakable message.

As he watched her she sighed and smiled, and lifted her hand to her midriff, letting it lie there as her fingers played against her own flesh. What was she thinking behind those closed eyelids? His own drooped as he let himself soak up the erotic visual stimulation of looking at her. A drifting rose petal rocked against the hard point of one not quite submerged nipple. A small convulsion rippled through her, as though even such slight stimulation was more than her body could endure without reacting. If a rose petal could do that, how would she react when it was his mouth that was stimulating those tight rose damson studs?

Swiftly and silently, without taking his gaze from her, he shed his clothes, the movement of his body as he stepped forward and leaned over her casting a shadow that flickered across her closed eyes.

By the time she had opened them he was already reaching into the water.

CHAPTER THIRTEEN

'TARIQ.'

Gwynneth stared up at him wonderingly. She had been daydreaming about him being here with her, and now he was. She exhaled on a long, slow sigh of arousal-induced acceptance.

'Shh.'

He reached into the water, one long finger slowly and delicately probing the soft closed lips of her sex whilst he watched her reaction darken her eyes and bring a sound of liquid pleasure to her lips. Her legs opened with the same sensual readiness as her sex. She felt warm and wet, his fingertip sliding slickly over the hard nub it was seeking. Tiny ripples scorched the surface of the water as she moved against his caress.

'No…' she protested helplessly, but her hands had already locked round his arm and her spine was arching up, bringing her breasts out of the water.

Tariq virtually felt his self-control shatter under the intensity of his response to her arousal. He released her briefly, a fine tremor jerking visibly through his body as he stepped into the tub to join her, his hands shaping her flesh beneath and above the water with a need he couldn't contain as he kneeled between her splayed legs. He kissed the taut arch of her throat and then her mouth, losing himself in its hot sweetness as he kissed her over and over again. The weight of her breasts filled his hands, his thumbs savouring the texture of her nipples as he rubbed his thumb-pads against their hardness.

'This is heaven,' Gwynneth whispered dreamily against his mouth. Her eyes shimmered with pleasure as she slid her fingers into the thick darkness of his hair, exploring the shape of his head, holding him against her so that she could taste and shape his lips with her tongue-tip before she plundered his mouth.

'I was lying here thinking about you, and now here you are…' she marvelled softly, knowing that what was happening was merely a dream. How could it possibly be anything else? How could Tariq be here with her, doing these incredibly sensual things to her and for her, otherwise? Because it was only happening inside her head she was free to enjoy it, free to say and do whatever she wished.

'Your thoughts must have called me to you,' Tariq told her softly, cupping her face between his hands, stroking his fingers slowly along the sensitive curve behind her earlobes.

She lifted her hands to his shoulders. His flesh felt warm and supple as her fingertips trailed over the muscles beneath his skin. His hands moved down her back and then round to cup her breasts, whilst he laced kisses along her jaw and down her neck.

Gwynneth trembled, letting her pleasure take hold of her and fill her.

His thumb-pads slowly circled the dark arousal-flushed aureoles, ignoring the fierce demand of her erect nipples. Only the lower half of her body was still beneath the water now, and Tariq was slowly kissing his way down to the valley between her breasts. And then up the slope of one of them, his tongue-tip following the circle being traced by his thumb, and then moving closer and closer to her nipple.

She trembled and moaned softly, and as though she had given a specific instruction his hand slipped between her still open legs, his fingers quickly finding the pulsing pearl within the oyster of her sex and plucking rhythmically at it. She could feel his tongue stroking against her nipple in time to the caress of his fingers, drawing from her such an intense reaction that her whole body was seized with her convulsive response to it. It gripped her, not gently but fiercely, almost frighteningly, so that she tensed against its possession, fearing its power over her.

'Relax.' Tariq whispered the word against her breast before his lips closed over her nipple and his fingers slid the length of her sex and began oh so slowly and carefully to penetrate its wetness.

She couldn't bear the pleasure of what he was doing to her. It was taking her and possessing her and rendering her helpless as it gripped and savaged her.

This was no dream.

'I think,' she heard Tariq murmur, lifting his mouth from her breast to her lips and from there making a deliciously slow and thorough journey to her ear, 'that this is something I would prefer to accomplish at leisure and on dry land.'

Gwynneth nodded her head.

'Hold on, then,' he told her, scooping her up and starting to carry her to the edge of the tub.

Her arms wrapped tightly around his neck and her head resting on his chest, Gwynneth looked down the length of his body, her breath leaving her lungs on an unsteady exhalation. He was big, but then she already knew that from that first night. And he was very aroused. As he stepped down onto the tiles she removed one arm from his neck, unable to stop herself from reaching out to circle the engorged head of his sex with one uncertain speculative fingertip before stroking the full length of him and back again.

The awareness came to her out of nowhere that she was changed for ever now, and there was no going back. Her body, her senses, would remember this pleasure for ever, and her own helpless captivity by it. A fierce pang of need tightened her body and then released it into a series of small quivering shudders.

'You've caught the sun on your shoulders,' Tariq told her. 'Does it hurt?'

'All I can feel is how much I want you,' Gwynneth admitted boldly, as he carried her over to the daybed and placed her on it. 'I've fought against feeling like this all my life,' she whispered emotionally, 'and now I know why. It *is* every bit as dangerous as I was always afraid it would be. More so, in fact.' She gave a small shudder, her eyes dark and huge as she asked huskily, 'If I feel like this now, how will I feel when you're deep inside me?'

Exhaling jaggedly, she reached up to stroke her fingertips along his forearm as he leaned over her and brushed the hair off her face.

'Much the same as you felt with your other lovers, I imagine,' he told her lightly.

Watching the stillness invade her body was like watching the sunlight fade from the desert, leaving it cold and barren. He stared at her, waiting for her to explain her reaction.

'Actually, there haven't been any others,' Gwynneth told him carefully.

She could feel him looking at her, willing her to look back at him, but she felt too self-conscious to be able to do so. He was bound to be shocked to learn that she had never had full sex—what man would not be?

When the seconds ticking by without him saying anything became totally unbearable, she forced herself to whisper croakily, 'I suppose you're turned off, now aren't you?'

'Yes,' he said curtly. 'Totally turned off. Any man worthy of the name would be—just as no woman who values what she is would ever think that she was flattering a man by assuming that he wanted her to pretend to be a youthful innocent. I don't merely find it a turn-off to be classed as the type of adult male who is excited by the thought of having sex with a virgin, I also find it offensive,' he said pithily. 'I'm a fully adult man. I don't need or require a fully adult woman to pretend for my benefit that she's a virgin.'

Gwynneth could hear the savage distaste in his voice. 'But I'm not—' She began to defend herself, and then stopped.

'No, neither am I anymore,' Tariq agreed. He had placed her discarded towel across his body, so that it was impossible for her to see whether he was still aroused or not—not that she had any intention of challenging him. The very thought threatened to cripple her emotionally and sexually.

Instead she gave a small, proud shrug and told him defensively, 'You were the one who came on to me.'

He looked at her in silence for so long that her heart began to beat in uncoordinated jerky thuds of apprehension.

'Correction. I took what you were offering. A woman does not bathe naked, exhibiting herself as you were, in the proximity of a man if she does not want him to be aware of her.'

There was nothing she could say to that, no defence she could honestly make, and her face stung with the heat of her humiliation and anger.

Whilst he had been speaking she had resorted to tucking several cushions strategically around herself, to screen her body, and now, as he stood up, she deliberately looked away from him so that he couldn't accuse her of anything else.

'I came to see what time you wanted to eat. Here in Zuran we eat later in the evening than you might in Britain, to benefit from the coolness.'

'I'm not really hungry.' Her voice sounded as brittle as her pride felt. She could hear the rustle of fabric and guessed that he was dressing.

'We'll eat later, then,' he told her blandly.

Tariq stood facing into the light breeze that was coming off the oasis, enjoying its freshness. In the reeds a bird called warningly to its mate, and in the moonlight he could see a fish jumping to snap at a hovering gnat.

Beneath his robe his body ached with unsatisfied desire. It was a dull heavy pulse he couldn't ignore, threatening to flare into almost priapic fury with every breath he took. Not even the sharp, destructive thrust of disappointment followed by distaste he had felt for Gwynneth's unwholesome claim to innocence had the power to silence the sexual clamour of his body. Her play-acting had destroyed something that for him had been uniquely rare. He had thought from the conversations they had shared that she would be above that sort of thing, that they were beginning to share something very special and that she would be honest with him instead of lying to him.

He remembered that he hadn't told her that they would soon be free to leave. Why not? There was no purpose in them staying here—no purpose in him hoping that they could share more than merely a relationship based on the sexual hunger they felt for one another.

And he had wanted that? Now who was playing games? he taunted himself. Of course he'd wanted that, and he'd wanted much more. He'd wanted... He'd wanted *her*, in his bed and in his life. He'd wanted her to give herself to him fully and completely, heart and soul, with honesty and commitment and love, and instead she had offered him a puerile claim to fake virginity.

As soon as they had eaten he would tell her that they were going back to Zuran.

Her shoulders, her back and her upper arms all stung slightly with the pain of her sunburned skin, and Gwynneth winced as she saw the bright red glow of it in the mirror. It wasn't bad enough to warrant being described as true sunburn, but it still tingled uncomfortably. She had been a fool to give in to the temptation of using the hot tub—and not just because of her sunburn.

The last thing she felt like doing was having to face Tariq again, but she had a feeling that if she didn't turn up then he would come looking for her, and if he found her in bed, using the excuse of her sore skin so as not to have to eat with him, he was all too likely to imagine that she was trying to seduce him, she decided bitterly.

Tariq had said that they might as well eat in his private quarters, which were on the opposite side of the villa. It was nearly ten o'clock—the time at which he had suggested they should eat. It was a pity she hadn't brought something with her that she could drape round her shoulders, she acknowledged, as she pulled a small face at her own reflection. Bright pink skin and a matt black strappy top. What a combination. But she didn't have any other choice.

Tariq was waiting for her in the entrance hall, the cold reserve of his voice as he said, 'I was just about to come and find you,' making her feel glad that he hadn't needed to do so.

The room he escorted her to was surprisingly modern, given the traditional style of the villa, and somehow the combination of the traditional design of the room teamed with pared-down modern furniture was one that soothed and yet also tantalised the senses. The sleek lines of the ebony console and coffee tables paired with off-white leather sofas over which brilliantly coloured kilims had been carelessly but effectively thrown created a room that offered comfort and style, its starkness broken by the splashes of rich colour. Paintings and sculptures echoed the brilliant flashes of colour, making Gwynneth itch to reach out and touch a painting thick with crimson and orange paint, depicting the sun rising over the rawness of the desert.

Double doors opened into a smaller dining room with a wall of huge glass doors, beyond which lay an illuminated courtyard.

'I have my own small kitchen on the other side of the dining room,' Tariq explained. 'Sometimes it is simpler and easier to cater for myself, and when I had these rooms converted for my own use I included a small kitchen so that I didn't have to invade Arub's territory and provoke an outcry.'

'Is there anything I can do to help?' Gwynneth asked him, feeling awkward.

'No. Everything's ready.'

She could see that he was frowning as he looked at her.

'Your skin looks sore,' he commented.

'It looks worse than it is,' Gwynneth assured him lightly.

'And it's my own fault. I should have taken more care.' And
not just against the danger of the sun. She had no idea how it
was possible to love a man so much whilst knowing that
doing so was self-damaging. But she did know that she wasn't
the first woman to discover that it was. The best possible
thing for her would be to return to Britain and forget that she
had ever met Tariq. Even supposing he had made love to her,
it would not have meant anything. Having sex with a man you
loved but who did not love you must surely be one of the most
soul-destroying things a woman could experience. Unless she
managed to temporarily deceive herself that he *did* love her—
if she could do that she could always carry with her a very
special memory. But the memory would be a lie.

Only if she let it be, a dangerous inner voice whispered.

Determinedly squashing it into silence, she took a deep
breath and asked Tariq, 'How long do you think we will have
to stay here?'

He looked away from her, as though something else had
caught his attention, his voice slightly blurred as he told her
dismissively, 'It's impossible to say.'

He was deliberately lying to her, Tariq knew. He, a man
who prided himself on his honesty. Why lie to keep her here
after the angry revulsion he had felt earlier? Because that
angry revulsion had been caused by his feelings for her. He
had felt let down by her, disappointed in her after the emotional intensity created when they had talked. Then she had
somehow reached out to him, touched all the sore places within him and soothed them as no other person ever had, and
because of that he had let down his guard and allowed himself
to admit that his feelings for her went much deeper than
merely sexual desire.

Holding her in his arms as he'd carried her to the daybed earlier, he had not checked the words of love and adoration forming inside his head, waiting to spill from his lips and be whispered against her skin. He had, he had thought then, formed a bond, adult to adult—a bedrock on which they could build a love that would sustain them for ever.

His tutors had warned him as a young man that he was too idealistic and that his ideals would be a heavy burden for others to carry.

They ate in a silence broken only by Gwynneth's slightly stilted complimentary comments about their food.

'My chef knows that I prefer to eat naturally produced food simply prepared, so that its flavours aren't obscured,' Tariq informed her, before suggesting, 'If you've finished eating, I suggest a stroll through the gardens to aid the digestion.'

'It sounds a good idea.' Gwynneth agreed. 'But please don't let me disrupt your normal routine. There's no need for you to accompany me.'

Something about his narrow-eyed gaze made her skin prickle uncomfortably.

'As you wish,' he agreed. 'Do you have some lotion for your skin?'

'No, I haven't,' Gwynneth admitted. 'But, as I said, it looks worse than it feels.'

'Maybe so, but it would still be wise to soothe it,' Tariq told her, commanding brusquely, 'Come with me.'

His hand was on her arm and it was all she could do not to tense betrayingly—but the sensitivity of her flesh had nothing to do with the sun and everything to do with Tariq himself. It was his touch that was affecting her so intensely and so intimately that she could hardly bear even to stand close to him, never mind be touched by him as he guided her out of the room and down an unfamiliar corridor.

It was only when he had opened the door and almost thrust her inside that she realised the room he had taken her to was his own bedroom. Like the other rooms, this one was a skilful blend of traditional and modern, its walls painted a flat shade of off-white to heighten the richness of the fabrics that that been used. Deep jewel shades in heavy silk fabric covered the chairs and the low divan, as well as the huge bed, echoing the colours in the rugs scattered on the polished wooden floor and hanging on the walls, whilst plain, fine white muslin curtains hung at the windows, caught back in intricately designed metal clasps.

'Wait here,' Tariq instructed, going to open a door which she could see led into a very modern crisp matt white and chrome bathroom.

The room held a very faint but altogether disturbing tang of the cool, discreet cologne Tariq wore, and Gwynneth had to catch herself up to stop herself from closing her eyes, the better to breathe in and relish the intimacy of it.

Tariq reappeared from the bathroom holding a plastic bottle of soothing skin lotion.

'I like to keep a reasonably well-stocked medicine cabinet here. Sometimes the young volunteers who come out to work with the archaeologists forget how dangerous the sun can be, even in the winter.'

Gwynneth smiled her polite thanks as she reached out to take the lotion from him. But instead of giving it to her he walked over to the bed and threw back the heavy cover to reveal the immaculate white bedlinen underneath it.

Gwynneth stared at the bed as though she had never seen one

before. Her heart was pounding ridiculously heavily, all her senses so acutely alive that her awareness of him unnerved her.

'I imagine that your back has suffered the most damage,' he told her coolly. 'If you want to sit on the bed, I'll put some of this on for you.'

CHAPTER FOURTEEN

She could have given any number of responses to that. But what with her emotions screaming a panicky *No, no, no and no again*, and the effort it took to keep the words inside her head instead of allowing them to her lips, all she could manage was a red-faced stutter. 'I…I can do it myself.'

One dark eyebrow rose in a mixture of disbelief and impatience.

'I doubt it.'

'Truthfully, I think I can manage to do it myself—and it isn't really hurting.'

Her face was as pink as her bare arms and she looked as modestly apprehensive as though they were strangers, and she was the kind of woman who was reluctant to expose her body even to the gaze of a lover. And, what was more, she wasn't faking her self-consciousness, Tariq recognised.

He dismissed this somewhat contradictory realisation with a mental shrug. He had no idea what exactly it was that was causing her apprehension, but she was perfectly safe from any threat from him.

'Despite your denials, I refuse to believe that you aren't in some discomfort,' he informed her dryly.

Oh, she was. But it was not the kind of discomfort he meant! Hers sprang from her awareness of what was going to happen to her the minute he touched her, and it had nothing to do with a bit of sunburn.

It was panic that was making her body tremble slightly as she turned her back, wasn't it? Certainly not excitement.

'This would be easier without your top,' Tariq pointed out.

'What? No!' Before she could stop herself Gwynneth had turned round, her face burning far more hotly than her body as she tried to control her own thoughts. And desires. Because she did desire him, didn't she? Her breath came quickly, in soft short bursts, as she struggled against the knowledge of just how much she loved him.

'You were naked in the pool, and therefore the whole of your back will have caught the sun,' he was saying, almost prosaically.

Why was she dragging out this torment? He was obviously determined to administer the lotion, and very probably capable of removing her top himself if she didn't do so for him. She might as well let him go ahead and get it over with as quickly as possible, Gwynneth told herself miserably, exhaling as she turned her back on him and tugged off her top.

Still keeping her back to him, she perched on the corner of the bed. She could feel the warmth of Tariq's breath against the nape of her neck, and then the firmness of his lotion-cooled hands. She gasped as she felt the coldness of the lotion on her sun-warmed flesh, and then suppressed a far more betraying gasp as Tariq started to smooth it into her skin, stroking and massaging his way up her spine, smoothing it round her ribcage so that his fingertips brushed against her breasts. Then, whilst her nipples were still peaking in arousal, making her stiffen every muscle apprehensively as she tried to control her need, he moved up to her shoulders, where he paused to push her hair out of the way before massaging the lotion into the back of her neck.

'Thank you—' she began, desperate to escape before she totally disgraced herself and let him see how much she wanted him. But she couldn't pull away because his hands were still resting on her shoulders.

'It was my pleasure.'

Was something wrong with her hearing? And, if not, why did his voice sound so thick and filled with pain?

'My pleasure,' he repeated. 'And my torment.'

Now she couldn't stop herself from turning to look at him.

'Tariq—' she began, and then stopped when Tariq leaned towards her, covering her mouth with his and kissing her with the kind of passion she had been yearning for.

Eagerly she kissed him back, parting her lips to the possessive demand of his tongue, clinging to his shoulders as he picked her up bodily and placed her on the bed.

'No words,' he told her as he joined her there. 'Not anything but this, my Gwynneth. Just this and us…'

Just us! Gwynneth closed her eyes and gave herself up to the magical touch of his hands, sighing in wanton pleasure as she felt them sliding over her. She wriggled out of her skirt and watched his eyes darken as he studied her almost naked body.

'Lie down.'

Quivering with excitement, she did so, watching him as he reached for the bottle of lotion.

There was no sunburn where he was using the pads of his thumbs to massage deliberately sensual slow circles of delicious pleasure, on the flesh just above the curve of her buttocks. But she didn't care. All she cared about was that he kept on doing what he was doing and didn't stop. How was it possible with such a simple touch for him to make her body respond to him in the way it was doing right now? She wanted to stretch out beneath those massaging fingers. She wanted to sigh and moan, to arch her spine and open her legs, to…

She felt him removing the tiny fluted-leg briefs that hugged her hips, barely covering her bottom.

'Oh, yes…' Had she actually said that or, please heaven, merely thought it? she wondered hazily as Tariq stroked the lotion into the round globes of her buttocks and then down the backs of her thighs.

'Turn over.' The words were a command, but his hoarse tones made them sound almost like a plea.

Gwynneth gave a voluptuous sigh and turned over, looking up at him, her flesh and her senses flooded with the sensuality he had aroused. Her whole body felt boneless and soft, his to mould and caress as he wished. The same bonelessness seemed to have softened the resistance from her thoughts as well, turned her into a creature of willing compliance…

She held her breath she watched as him undress, her expression mirroring everything that she was feeling. Had he ever seen a woman look at him like this before? Tariq wondered. If he had he couldn't remember it. Gwynneth's gaze, so openly aroused and ardent as it looked and lingered where he was already erect and ready for her, and her tongue-tip moistening her lips was the most powerful aphrodisiac he had ever known. Without speaking to him, without touching him, without him touching her, she had told him how it was going to be. How she would hold him within the warm caress of her body whilst he plunged within it over and over again,

until he took them both over the edge of that cliff at the end
of the universe beyond which lay eternity itself.

The way Tariq was looking at her made words redundant,
Gwynneth knew. A thousand times a thousand words would
not be enough to convey all that he was conveying to her as
their gazes meshed, hers clinging desperately to his, knowing
he was telling her that he was taking her into a place so far
away from anything she knew that, once there, she would be
wholly dependent on him.

When he came down to her, the feel of his skin on hers was
like the cool brush of silk, and the weight of his body answered a need she had not previously known she had. When
he kissed her mouth it was slowly and lingeringly, savouring
the taste and texture of her as she lay supine and soft beneath
him, letting him take her where he wanted to go.

He kissed her again, more deeply, causing her body to arch
up off the bed to his. Gwynneth clung to him, too afraid of
what was happening to her to risk letting go and being left
alone in the maelstrom of her own desire.

He kissed her throat and behind her ear, and then the curve
of her shoulder, and her fingers curled into his flesh whilst her
nipples pushed up against him.

When he kissed the slope of her breast her fingers splayed
against his buttocks, holding him tight against her body. She
was on fire for him now, consumed by a throbbing, pounding
ache that beat through her in hot demand.

His tongue flicked against her nipple, making her shudder
in the spasm of erotic delight that gripped her. When he raked
her nipple gently with his teeth she cried out against the
pleasure, welcoming the weight of his hand cupping her sex
and momentarily soothing its need. She was open and ready

for his touch, the swollen lips flushed with desire and as juicily ripe as the sweetest peach.

Tariq could feel the ache in his own body to taste and enjoy her. He kissed his way down her belly, his heart pounding heavily with the weight of his need as he rubbed the tip of his tongue over the pulsing thrust of her clitoris, feeling it swell and harden within his caress. Her soft cries of shocked pleasure drove him on to take her further and deeper, until her arousal overwhelmed her.

Gwynneth tried to hold back what she was feeling, what she was being driven to feel by the caress of Tariq's tongue, but it was impossible It crashed down over her and through her in surge upon surge of molten liquid pleasure until it finally receded, leaving her behind, satisfied and yet somehow not satisfied, fulfilled and yet still craving some other deeper unknown pleasure—a craving she had to communicate to him.

'Tariq, I want you.' Had she said it or only felt it? Was Tariq responding to her words or his own need when he held her and kissed her, with the taste of her own self still on his lips? Over and over again, his tongue thrust deeper and deeper within the warm cavity of her mouth, whilst his hands slid to her hips to lift and ready her.

It didn't matter how many men there had been, just so long as from this moment forward there was only him, Tariq thought passionately, all his doubts and reservations washed away by the overpowering surge of his love for her. Clean and new and whole, it filled and humbled him. She was so incomparably precious to him. She made him feel a thousand and one things he had never known it was possible to feel, and in a thousand and one different and unique ways. She touched the deepest part of him and brought it and him to life. Who could understand love? A man could merely experience it, give himself up to it and to the woman for whom he was born.

I love you. The words filled his head and his heart as he took Gwynneth's mouth in a kiss of possession and commitment, releasing his body to sink deep into her sleekly muscled warmth, and then deeper still. Only he couldn't. And she was lying rigidly beneath him, her eyes open wide with shocked apprehension and pain.

Whilst his mind grappled with the true meaning of her body's tightly held muscles, his body gave in to its own driving need. One thrust, fierce and quick, made her cry out, and then she was clinging to him, her eyes shimmering with the same emotion he could feel glittering in his own.

Gwynneth could feel Tariq's shock, but already the brief sharp pain was fading, to be replaced by a pulsing ache to feel him deeper inside her.

'No,' she whispered possessively as he tried to pull back. 'No…' As though to demonstrate her determination she moved against him, holding his gaze with her own until he gave in, shuddering with the release of his own tension. Slowly and carefully he thrust into her again, deeper and then deeper still, as she clung demandingly to him, grinding her hips against his, until he moved faster and deeper and her own body picked up the rhythm of his and moved in counterpoint to it. Up and up he took her, until there was nowhere left to go, and then they were poised on the pinnacle of a pleasure so acute it made her cry out in sweet agony as it pierced her. She felt its fierce surge grip her in the same heartbeat as Tariq gave a guttural moan of release and she felt the heat of his completion pulsing inside her.

* * *

'I've brought you a cup of tea.'

No matter how hard she tried, Gwynneth could neither control the hot colour storming her face, nor bring herself to look directly at Tariq as he put the tea on the bedside table next to her and then sat down on the bed.

'Is there any news yet about when—when we can leave here?' she asked unevenly. The last thing she wanted was for him to fear she was going to use what had happened last night as a means to try to cling to him. She had more pride than that!

She wanted to leave? After what they had shared? Tariq felt his heart slalom inside his chest wall. Too late to stop the pain wrenching him apart. No way was he letting her leave. Not now and, if he had his way, not ever. And certainly not before he had an opportunity to find a way to convince her that she wanted to spend the rest of her life with him as passionately as he wanted to spend his with her.

'No, not as yet,' he lied.

'Oh.' Gwynneth tried discreetly to moisten her dry lips with the tip of her tongue. She couldn't believe she had actually slept so deeply that she hadn't even known that Tariq was sleeping next to her. But it was obvious from the dent in the pillow and the scent of him all around her that he had done. It was too late now for her to grieve for the memories she might have stored up.

'I owe you an apology,' Tariq announced tersely.

Gwynneth plucked nervously at the sheet.

'I can understand why you would think… I mean why you wouldn't have thought…' She wrinkled her nose and took a deep breath. 'It is unusual for a woman of my age to be… I mean, not to have…'

'So why?' Tariq asked her.

'My father,' Gwynneth answered him honestly. 'As I told you, he was something of a sexual predator—a man who believed that sex was an appetite to be enjoyed and who didn't see why it should have any connection with his emotions. After he left, my mother used to complain that I was like him. I think that was one of the reasons she didn't want to have me around.'

Tariq looked away from her. There wasn't even the vaguest hint of self-pity in her voice, but he knew if he looked at her he wouldn't be able to stop himself from taking her in his arms and telling her exactly what he thought of both her parents, and especially her mother.

'I suppose it started then in a way,' Gwynneth admitted. 'Although I was too young to connect what I was feeling with sex. I just knew that I didn't want to be like my father. It was only when I got older, hearing him talk openly and without shame about his sex life, that I began to worry that I might have inherited whatever traits he possessed that were responsible for his immoral behaviour. Sex was just a physical appetite to him—the pursuit of a woman for sex was a challenge he couldn't resist. He loved the thrill of a new sexual conquest, but he was incapable of making any kind of real emotional contact with a partner. I was afraid that I might end up the same, so I decided that I wasn't going to have sex—and, more importantly, that I wasn't going to *want* to have sex. And it worked. I didn't. Until that first night with you. And then I realised…'

Abruptly Gwynneth stopped speaking, her face burning as she realised how close she had come to telling him that the knowledge that she had fallen in love with him had shown her how very different she was from her father.

'You realised what?' Tariq probed.

'I realised that I was missing out on a lot of fun, and that I didn't after all want to spend the rest of my life as a virgin,' she made herself say, as lightly as she could.

'Fun?'

'Well, I certainly enjoyed last night,' she told him.

Tariq looked at her. This wasn't what he wanted to hear.

What he wanted to hear was that in his arms she had realised that she couldn't live without him, that she loved him and she wanted to spend the rest of her life with him. And he was pretty sure that was *exactly* what she felt, having listened to her talking about her father and seen the shadows of her past lying darkly in her eyes.

He'd never been a gambler, but some things were so important that a man had to risk something of great value in order to gamble with life for the prize he wanted. Right now he was gambling with his pride. And Tariq's wasn't just any old male pride: it was the kind of pride it took generations of alpha male history to create.

'Really?' he asked her smoothly. 'How much?'

'H-how much?' Gwynneth wondered wildly what on earth she could say. This wasn't the way she had expected the conversation to proceed.

'Yes, how much? Enough, for instance, to do it again tonight?'

Gwynneth's heart was pounding so loudly she could hardly think.

'Er…yes. I mean, if you want to.'

'So, tonight, then?' he repeated, ignoring her small rider. 'And what about right now?'

'Right now?' A betraying ache was spreading through her body. 'Well…'

'Or maybe right now, tonight and all the nights for the rest of our lives?' Tariq suggested softly. 'And not because it was *fun*, but because we can't bear to be apart—because we love each other so much that life apart would be like the desert without the warmth of the sun or the water of its oases, an endless sterile darkness in which nothing could exist or survive. Because together we want to create the new life that will be our child, conceived and born in love—our love. Because we feel all those things for one another, and so much more I can't put into words. You have become my morning sunrise, Gwynneth, and my evening sunset. And all the hours of my life in between.'

'You…you *love* me?' Gwynneth felt as though all the blood had suddenly drained from her veins, leaving her hollow and light-headed.

'Can you doubt it? If you do, then at least allow me to spend the rest of our lives proving it to you—as my wife.'

'You want to *marry* me?' Gwynneth whispered, sitting bolt upright in the bed, oblivious to her nudity, the colour beating up under her skin. 'This is crazy. You're a prince. Princes marry princesses…'

Tariq was shaking his head. 'Not this prince. He marries only where he loves, and he loves you, only you and always you.'

The look in her eyes betrayed her, making Tariq hold his breath against the sudden fierce rush of exultation that seized him.

'Please don't,' Gwynneth begged him. 'Please don't look at me like that!'

'All right,' Tariq agreed easily. 'How about if I do this instead?'

She was so unprepared for him to take hold of her and kiss

her that she had no defence against the slow sweetness of her own helpless pleasure.

'I love you,' Tariq whispered against her lips. 'I wanted to tell you so last night, before I made you mine, but somehow the words never got spoken.'

'You loved me then…when you still thought…?'

'I fell in love with the woman you are, Gwynneth. With you, not your virginity,' he told her firmly. 'Now, please, put me out of my misery and tell me. Will you give me your love? Will you share my life and my hopes and ideals? Will you allow me to love and cherish and—?'

'Yes!' Gwynneth stopped him, the joy of what she was hearing filling her heart to the brim with happiness. To know that he loved her when she had believed he did not, when she had believed that her own once-in-a-lifetime love for him could never be returned, was a once-in-for-ever kind of very special happiness, she decided. She put her hand in his and then leaned forward to whisper lovingly against his mouth, 'Yes, yes, yes, yes, *yes*…' Until he silenced her with his kiss.

EPILOGUE

'HAPPY?' Tariq asked, his voice holding both tenderness and passion. 'No regrets?'

Gwynneth smiled up at him and shook her head. They were sharing the same rose-shaded and scented bathing pool where, in what now seemed like another life, she had lain alone in the sun-warmed water and indulged in what had then seemed like an impossible fantasy.

But, as she had now discovered, reality could sometimes be infinitely better than fantasy.

'How could I when I have you—and this?' she whispered softly, reaching up to kiss him with her newfound knowledge of just how sweetly vulnerable he was to her kisses.

'You love me?'

His voice was rougher now. Gwynneth nodded her head.

'Say it,' Tariq begged her hungrily. 'Let me hear the words.'

'I love you, Tariq,' she told him, laughing softly when he scarcely allowed her to finish before taking her in his arms and kissing her with a passion that set the rose petals that floated on the water surging rhythmically on small waves created by the eager movement of her body against his.

It had been her choice that they should honeymoon here

in the Hidden Valley, and although Tariq had insisted that she was free to choose any destination she wished, she had seen in his eyes how much her choice had touched his emotions.

'I want to come back every year of our lives together to celebrate our anniversary here,' Gwynneth told him lovingly, and then leaned forward to whisper in his ear, 'Do you realise that it's lunchtime and over three hours since breakfast?'

'You're hungry?'

'Yes—but for you, not food,' she told him boldly.

The colour came and went in her face, and, watching her, he wondered if even now, after he had told her so a hundred thousand times and more, she really knew just how much he loved her—just how complete his world was with her in it and how empty it would be without her.

'Here?' he suggested.

'In the pool?' Longing and excitement darkened the gaze she turned on him.

They had had so few opportunities for shared intimacy these last few weeks, in the run-up to the wedding, but now at last she had Tariq to herself.

When they returned to Zuran it would be to live in a rented villa until their own new villa was ready. Tariq was insistent that they had their own home, rather than live as part of his extended family, but she had told him that she wanted their villa to be close enough to the palace for him to be able to visit as often as he wished.

She was far from the first British bride to be welcomed into the Zurani royal family, and it had brought happy tears to her eyes to discover that the extended family members were so willing to become her friends.

She stroked his arm, still thinking of family. 'It was so

thoughtful of you to arrange for Teresa and baby Anthony to be flown out to our wedding.'

'They are a part of our family, and it was only right and proper that they should be there.'

His reply might sound formal and distant, but there was nothing distant about his generosity towards her half-brother and his mother. Not only had he taken on the financial responsibility for Anthony's education, he was also making Teresa an allowance that had enabled her to return home and set up her own small business.

Thinking of baby Anthony, and the gorgeous children of Tariq's extended family, caused a small fluttering sensation to tighten in her own body.

'It still scares me to think how close I came to listening to my fears instead of to my heart. In refusing to accept that I loved you I would have lost so much…'

'No. I would not have allowed that to happen—and besides, the fault was mine for so stupidly misjudging you,' he told her lovingly. 'Somehow I would have found a way to open the doors of your heart to my love, Gwynneth. I would never have given up—just as I will never give you up now. You are my love and my life, my heart, and all of me that goes beyond that. It is my belief that we were destined to be together, that we were created for one another, and that we fit together as one perfect whole in every single way.'

Emotional tears stung her eyes. She loved him so much, and to hear him voice his love for her had the power to touch the deepest wellspring of her feelings.

'I want our first child to be conceived here, Tariq,' she told him huskily. 'Here in this valley that is so much a part of your

heritage and where we first loved one another. Here and…
and now.'

She trembled as he lifted her bodily from the water and bent
to take her mouth in a fiercely passionate kiss, ready to begin.

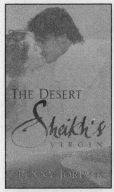

Queens of Romance

Bedding His Virgin Mistress
Ricardo Salvatore planned to take over Carly's company, so why not have her as well? But Ricardo was stunned when in the heat of passion he learned of Carly's innocence…

Expecting the Playboy's Heir
American billionaire and heir to an earldom, Silas Carter is one of the world's most eligible men. Beautiful Julia Fellowes is perfect wife material. And she's pregnant!

Blackmailing the Society Bride
When millionaire banker Marcus Canning decides it's time to get an heir, debt-ridden Lucy becomes a convenient wife. Their sexual chemistry is purely a bonus…

Available 5th September 2008

Collect all 10 superb books in the collection!

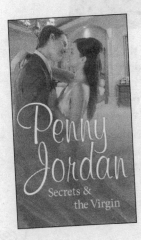
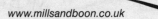

*What lurks beneath the surface
of the powerful and prestigious
Chrighton Dynasty?*

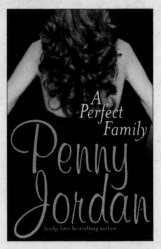

As three generations of the Chrighton family
gather for a special birthday celebration, no one
could possibly have anticipated that their secure
world was about to be rocked by the events of
one fateful weekend.

One dramatic revelation leads to another –
a secret war-time liaison, a carefully concealed
embezzlement scam, the illicit seduction
of somebody else's wife.

And the results are going to be explosive…

www.millsandboon.co.uk

MILLS & BOON
100 YEARS
of pure reading pleasure

100 Reasons to Celebrate

2008 is a very special year as we celebrate Mills and Boon's Centenary.

Each month throughout the year there will be something new and exciting to mark the centenary, so watch for your favourite authors, captivating new stories, special limited edition collections…and more!

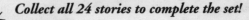